THE
CELTIC STALLION
RENDEZVOUS

AnnElise Makin

ISBN: 979-8-9902320-0-6

EDITOR: Edda Buchner
PROOFREADER: Renate Mousseux
COVER PHOTOS: 123rf.com
COVER DESIGN: AnnElise Makin
PRODUCTION: iMakinations BookProShop
DISTRIBUTION: Amazon.com
CONTACT: annelise@imakinations.com

iMakiNations

BookProShop

www.imakinations.com

St. George's Chapel Hill

Painting by Katharina Schlickenrieder, 1912

St. George's Hill is the source of many stories that Katrina wrote down. On this site of Celtic significance, solstice fires are still celebrated each year. The Hill is said to have several ghosts: a fiery dragon, a witch, a white stallion, and a hell hound. This sanctuary is alive with the spirits of the past. It has seen a lot of sorrows and fulfilled many miracles.

Candle offerings on top of the mystery boulder.

CONTENTS

In the Year Zero

Before the Metaverse, there was the Otherworld. It was a parallel universe. You could also say it was simultaneous. And all that ever happened and ever was said or thought or moved, was recorded in it. It's like with Google and the cloud: How many people talk simultaneously? Millions? And where does it all go? Onto the cloud. The cloud doesn't forget, and neither does the Otherworld.

As of old, we Celts had two universes. The physical here-and-now and the Otherworld. But the Otherworld was nowhere else but right here, all around. We used to travel across the boundaries of universes before this art was lost. Compare it to quarks. Quarks oscillate so fast that they return before they have left. You can never tell, where they really are. Do they ever leave their position? They could be in both places at the same time. Right, that is where time comes in. Time is actually not countable, that much we Celts knew. But objects, and wrinkles, and cycles were countable. Thus, we counted the seasons, the moons, the constellations, and the thunderstorms. That guided us through the turns of the years. However, astrology would lead us too far off here. Our story is very simple.

Back to the Otherworld. It harbors, as you might imagine, the memory and the spirits of the past. Those spirits may converse with the here-and-now for a purpose, regardless of whether they are being heard. I, Mara, am one of those spirits. And I had something to say. Katrina, the 17-year-old student, was the only one who listened, but she also misunderstood.

Why Katrina? She lived right next to me in my village, only 2000 years later. She dreamed up stories filled with spirits from the past, my white stallion ghost for one. Her mute grandfather might have been a ghost as well since that tragic day that snatched a life. The old man had lost all his words. So, Katrina listened to my whispers and wrote them down.

This is my story. It got released by an archaeological excavation in a small Bavarian village. A young Celtic maiden's burial site, mine, was discovered. The dig set many ancient spirits free. I, Mara, dictated this story to Katrina, so that the truth may finally see the light of day. Her stories happened almost exactly as she wrote them down. She traveled on her ancestors' thoughts. We spirits are still present in the Otherworld, just like the same air is still around, which I breathed back then.

We are only guests on earth, but our foregone loved ones are among us, next to us, and in us. Like water, our lives are first fluid, then frozen solid, and finally, in death, become like air and permeate everything. Our state changes continuously but the energy remains where the eternal bliss begins.

The air exists, even though unseen. It contains humidity, just as invisible. Imagine water, when the dewdrops from the air collect on blades of grass, the sun's rays lick them up again. Thus, every human life is merely a fragile dewdrop, touched by transience every second of its passing.

Life is but a dream, an astoundingly beautiful one. And nothing is as certain as the Otherworld. Many a soul whispers back from it. Just listen with your heart.

Katrina's heart had big ears. She heard my whispers. They had put me to rest in state, but I could not go to sleep for 2000 years, until I found my love again.

Now, follow Katrina through her story and you will get to know me too.

THE
CELTIC STALLION
RENDEZVOUS

CAUTION:

This book is infested with spirits from the past.

Read at your own risk. Handle with care. Enjoy the ride!

Essay Marathon

. . . and St. George's on the Hill, whose chapel still tops the waterline by 24 meters, protrudes like a forgotten island from the glacial inundation. Again, the floodwaters start to rise, to 640 meters. While of the lower-lying parish church only the spike of the cross remains visible, the cupola of St. George's on the Hill continues to keep a lookout over the newly risen sea. The floodwaters don't relent.

—Josef Dietrich, 1923 Village Almanach,
About the Geographical Names, 11

Wednesday, June 12

It was the year 1974. The terrorist attacks on the Munich Olympics had almost faded into history. The games had only lightly brushed the village, as the sports club relayed the Olympic fire four kilometers into the next town. Since then, the torches were mounted next to the trophies on the wall in the soccer clubhouse. Everyday life took its usual, quiet course. But something cracked in the village heavens, or somewhere far above it, barely audible, leaving a hairline fissure.

The sounds of silence almost shattered Katrina's ears. She was seventeen, bored out of her mind, and her writing was a strange pulp. Nevertheless, the Essay Marathon was on. There was no library nearby, and nobody to ask, but she had plenty ideas of her own. Out of nowhere, stories popped into her mind. With each of her fabrications, another hobgoblin bubbled up from the village underbelly.

Hello darkness, my old friend. Here she wrote again.

Back then, when the people still could fly, there was an island in the middle of the lake. The lake, about which we all learned in fourth grade, has since dried up, but it is the same hill, where St. George's chapel stands now. During the great flood, when people still could fly, that hill had a heavenly pillar, one of only two in the world, on it. God Atlas carried the other one on his shoulders far away in the Caucasus mountains. People had learned to fly because they were barefoot, like angels. They would have frozen their feet off on the glaciers during the ice age. So, the people, all of us, became air wights just in time. After the glacier melted, the earth was covered in floodwaters. We liked to linger and play, especially on the heaven's pillar island. We used the tall stalk as our turnaround pole. Whether it reached the heavens, nobody knew for sure, because nobody could fly that high. Yet this pillar was a great entertainment for us flyers. When a wight rushed in too fast, he would reach for the crystal pole and rotate down on it with a child's delight, until his feet safely touched the ground.

Back then, flying was our people's great passion. I remember it well. The wings were invisible, the wind, however, our supporting element, was very palpable. Trustily we drifted on the smooth layers of air, placidly sailing along. Some got so ecstatic over the thrill of speed that they drove deep, grooved spirals into our turnaround pole, or heaven's pillar. Those grooves were blue, a deep blue swiped from the sky. For us wights the pillar was pure joy and freedom! That's when we still lived in bliss."

"But then came the Celtic warrior tribe," the teacher read aloud. Words of her own making hailed down on Katrina like ice cubes. "Schiller," whose real name was Hildebrandt, continued to read, mercilessly.

"With their sharp arrows and fast boats, they shot us from the heavens. Most of the air wights fell into the glacier lake. Their wings soaked with water. The currents pulled them down into their wet grave. Many who crashed on land did not survive the fall. The wounded were locked up in cages until the druids unspelled their wings. I survived by luck, or fate? They made me a slave for their horse sacrifice rituals. The heaven's pillar became besmirched with blood. Yet still the Celts bragged about their torture skills. Their ferocious stake was visible from afar . . ."

Here the German teacher paused. It was deathly quiet in the classroom. You could have heard a pin drop. "Schiller" had his nickname from his passion for *Sturm und Drang* literature. However, as Katrina realized, her essay had come across as entirely too stormy for him.

Thunderclouds were brewing on Schiller's forehead. He looked strained.

"Where are you getting such ideas from, Frau Weber? Not one iota research in your writing. And let's see about the wording. Here we go, 'with their sharp arrows and fast boats, they shot us down'? Did you mean with 'bows and arrows'? I

3

haven't heard of anyone shooting a boat at someone, right?" Subdued snickers in the classroom.

Schiller paused. He scrutinized the pages. "By the way, the word 'unspelled' does not exist in the dictionary. Apparently, your druids must have been 'using spells' to wish away those imaginary wings of yours. And what in the world is a 'heaven's pillar'? You might have confused our Bavarian mythology with that of the old Greeks. And since when have the old Celts used a 'torture stake'? How did the Wild West get into this mess? Tell me, does any of this have anything to do with the tradition of our Bavarian May pole?"

The German teacher leafed through the remaining pages. He was looking for traditions, such as the selection procedure of the strongest pine tree, painting it with the blue-white pattern, and dances at the May pole raising party. No such thing in Katrina's essay. Only the Celts? If it were all that easy.

Hildebrandt blew a strain of unruly hairs from his forehead. He was lost in deep thought, scanning for some redemption in Katrina's essay. Finally, his tension relaxed.

"One thing is for sure, Frau Weber: you've got a wild imagination. D minus," he grumbled and slapped the papers on Katrina's desk.

Snicker and whisper.

"Schiller-the-Killer," aka Herr Hildebrandt, did not like fabrications, machinations, or spoilers, especially not what he called the collective "regurgitations," when students copied off too much from each other. He had been a teacher for too long as not to smell any old student trick against the wind. Except, he liked homemade things, one-of-a-kinds, which clearly showed in his love for hand-knitted sweaters. But Katrina's homebrewed concoctions were a trifle too spicy for him.

Fortunately, this was only the beginning of the Essay Marathon in Hildebrandt's class. Unfortunately, more chances were to come. Katrina had no explanation how the air wight people with their blue-spiraled heavens pillars had landed in her May pole story.

Schiller, with a wrinkled brow, distributed the remaining essays. In his long teaching career, he had encountered a few mad tales, but today he caught himself surprised again at such unrestrained bouts of a student's imagination. Writing that doesn't hold water, as he had explained year after year, leaves the reader thirsty. Unsubstantiated, or blah-blah writing, another quote of his, was like a brain fart. It leaves you stinky. He also liked crude, simple analogies.

Katrina ducked her head deeper, as the destroyed essay was slammed down in front of her. The ominous draft of air was a slap in her face. Now she was wide awake. She had had a hunch about this. Like a turtle, she retracted her neck deeper into the protective layers of her grandfather's chafed Sunday jacket. Only her nose and her thick red-brown mop of hair stuck out at the top. A worry line formed above her eyebrows.

And this was only the beginning of the catastrophe. This Essay Marathon chronologically started with the Celts. The later epochs, could only be more confusing because more facts were known about history. Consequently, more mistakes were to be made.

Each year, for the final quarter, Hildebrandt aka "Schiller" had become infamous for staging his Essay Marathon. He had found an effective tool to keep his sassy teenagers at bay through the end of the year. The Essay Marathon was Schiller's most serious business. This year's topic was "A day in the life of a historic person." Not only one person, but at least seven, all from different historic periods, were to be discussed. Three chances of extra credit were available to students who were willing to write ten instead of seven essays. Delivery of fine historic details was essential. For a good grade, a student had to "hit the nail on its head." Katrina liked to interview people, but unfortunately all the "historic characters" were dead already. What was left? Books. Katrina had not opened one of them. No wonder, her flight of fantasy had ended in a crash landing. She had made stuff up. Or had she?

"Well, he's got a point. You're for sure no historian." Luise whispered in Katrina's ear. She was her best friend and desk and bus neighbor.

"What's that supposed to mean? You didn't like my story either?" Katrina hissed.

"Come on! You should know me by now. I think your stuff is fantastic! Your heaven's pillar sounds awesome to me! But some square-head knucklebones teachers will never understand that."

Schiller heard "knucklebones." He turned around, red-faced.

"Frau Pfeiffer! Would you please stay out of this! Or do you have a contribution to make? Now, let's look at your story. If I am not mistaken, you have copied most of it off our city brochure, am I right? But I will give you another chance, and maybe you can delight us with a presentation next week? That would be great! You've just been volunteered."

And then Schiller turned to Katrina and said, "And my advice for you, Frau Weber! Nobody can suck an essay out of thin air. A little more effort, more research, please! Why don't you ask your grandmother at home about the good old days? Or, as you know, we have our city archives and library open for everyone. If you bus people could only commit to staying late one afternoon . . ."

Apparently, Schiller was having a really bad day today. The two young women sat in silence.

Grandmother? Katrina did not have a grandmother any more. Only a grandfather, but he hadn't spoken a word in years.

And the library, what was he thinking? That bus didn't run again in the afternoon. Only at 1:15 p.m., that was it. And they had to race to even catch that one after school.

"Never mind the old codger!" Luise whispered behind the teacher's back. "He keeps forgetting, we come from Upper-Lower-Backwater-Andershausen-in-the-Styx."

Katrina and Luise lived in the oldest Bachzeilendorf in the world. *Dorf* means village, *Bach* means creek, and *Zeile* means row or file. Put together it says "rows-of-houses-along-the-creek" village. If Katrina had paid more attention, she could have found many stories burbling down that creek. In the fourth grade, their class had built a scaled model of the village, each house and barn represented by Lorenz wood toy models. Katrina's village had one-and-a-half churches, three taverns, one guesthouse, a store for everything and about 800 residents, mostly farmers—a calmingly idyllic weekend destination for stressed Munich city people, but a boring play pad for growing teenagers. The bus only ran twice a day, to and from school. Luise, whose father had moved there from a larger town, had dubbed the village "Andershausen" and she repeated it often enough that it had stuck.

When her teacher in fourth grade persuaded Katrina—she had excellent grades—to transfer to the Gymnasium in the nearby city, her father gave her a stern warning: "I can't help you anymore, but if I should catch you with drugs, I will help you with a stick!" Drugs were the topic, as heroin had claimed deaths in the county. Katrina was the first in her family to attend high school, except for her uncle, who was bound for the priesthood seminary, but didn't complete because of the war. Gymnasium for a girl was still a novelty. Luise was the only other village girl attending the high school, but she hardly qualified as villager, since her mother, God rest her soul, had married this sculptor from the city.

For years, Katrina had drilled Latin vocabs and solved algebra equations, and gotten above average grades. Learning had always come easy to her. Lately, however, the lessons were no longer intuitive, school had become harder. At home, too, Katrina started bumping into sharp corners. Those bruises at times made her feel like a cuckoo's egg with lots of cracks in it, especially when her mother caught her with loopy ideas and rudely dragged her back to earth again. Her flights of fancy didn't stop short of church, although nobody noticed them there. To the contrary, the festive, almost hypnotic singing and the set-in-stone ritual of the service stimulated her fantasies even more. So, she dreamt away in church, with solemn devotions feeding her creative nature. She could tune out, completely. Unless she got sick from the holy smoke, the incense. Then she had to scramble to get out into fresh air. Light headed, cold hands, almost fainting.

"Sorry, Luise! Didn't mean to get you in trouble, too!"

Luise stabbed her with a glance. She wasn't too happy about the extra work. Some nauseating incense seemed to stifle the classroom now after the teacher's sermon. Katrina's stomach cramped. However, Schiller, instead of giving them a break and letting the "dumb-fuzzy-heads-air" escape out the window, continued teaching. Schiller drove his class to excellence.

"Come on, Lulu! Don't be cross with me! I will buy us a round at the disco tonight," Katrina whispered

Luise nodded with a grin.

By the shed, grandfather hammered away at the scythe. Regular, measured blows to thin out the blade to a sharp cutting edge. He wore his brown canvas apron, the green hat, and the grey knitted sweater with the elbow patches, because the evening air was quite crisp. Now he could have used his old Sunday jacket to keep the cold out of his bones, but his granddaughter Katrina had "borrowed" it. Why did this young girl want to wear his old ragged "Joppe," his favorite grey bad weather coat? That's how they dressed at the Gymnasium now? And why had she refused last year to don the magnificent "Tracht," the young women's folk costume made of royal black silk-and-lace gown with silver-chain-tied bodice and flowers stuck in the bosom? The gorgeous black silk dress, an inheritance from her grandmother, was worth a couple of thousand Marks and symbolized the pride of generations. How could Katrina refuse this tradition?

Gloomy thoughts brewed in grandfather's mind. With every dark thought, an angry puff of smoke rose from his pipe lodged between his teeth. He, resentfully, smoked the old-fashioned, s-shaped grandfather pipe, with a very long wooden chimney shaft and a porcelain smoke pot at the bottom. The pipe had a lid to extinguish the embers, but most of the time the fire died out on its own.

The old man concentrated on "dengling," or peening. The sharpening of the scythe blades was an almost forgotten skill. He had three scythes and one sickle to peen. Scythes were hardly used any more, since the tractors with their efficient mechanical blades so swiftly raced across the fields. However, for small-scale and uneven territory, like in an orchard, scythes were still in demand, although some farmers had gone as far as purchasing a lawn mower. Yet as long as he was able to mow and sharpen a scythe himself, there would not be a lawn mower on his—correction—on Girgl's farm. The sickle, which had seen so many barley harvests, was hardly used any more, only for the weeds under the berry bushes. For the rest of the year, it hung on the rafters in the barn.

He loved to peen his dark thoughts away, to hear the regular rhythm of the hammer on the blade. After each round he whetted the blade to achieve a cleaner cutting edge. One could have split hairs with his scythes. And he was proud of his skill. In regular intervals the hammer hit the metal and crawled forward on the blade, millimeter by millimeter, with careful precision. Peening proceeded with a regularity like the clock of eternity. Plink. Plink. Plink. 'Kathl, how are you doing up there? Are you looking down just now? If you could only tell me why everything has changed so much. Well, you are better off, you need not worry about a thing. Wish I could be with you, but I don't know whether they would to let me in up there.' Plink. Plink. Plink.

He kept on hammering, peening away at each thought of his wife. Thus, the scythe absorbed a piece of life with each blow, which it could not divulge. The old man with his steel-blue eyes had stopped talking because he knew too much.

'What on earth is she rattling about again,' the old man would have said if he hadn't unlearned how to speak. A cacophony of typewriter chatter escaped from the former hen house. Since she had started attending the Gymnasium, his granddaughter had obviously strayed from her family values. Or not totally. Like her gifted grandmother, Katrina could draw and paint with sublime talent, but she drew by far not such solemn and devotional pictures as Kathl had. To the contrary, Katrina's sketches and writings bordered on blasphemy. Once the old man had come across a sheet of paper with her writing on the kitchen table. Scowling, Katrina had torn the corpus delicti from his hands. No wonder. From the little he could make out, she had scribbled down a lot of crazy, socialist propaganda?

"When will the old guy out there finally end his clatter," Katrina sighed. "Where in the world can one find a fifteen-minutes peace around here!"

Despite the noisy competition from outside, she coaxed a few "brain farts" from the old Adler typewriter. Her first story had not taken. Well, so what! Again, something rattled her brain. She let it out. It was the Celts again.

Clank. Clank. Ding. Ding. Ding. Type, type, type.

When I lived with the Celts, we venerated the trees. They housed the souls of our ancestors, many of them. No wonder, considering how old some oaks can be. A thousand years, for the old souls. When a tree dies, a person dies with it. Seek the beech, avoid the oak. The oak bends to no one, not even lightning. The oak is the most masculine and weather-resistant tree. Compared to it, the white birch is a fairy, the cricket of springtime awakening. But woe to the one who encumbers the willow. Hex on him! He will not have a joy left in his life.

We followed the annual cycle like children their mothers, in full confidence that we could rely on nature. Death did not scare us because then we entered the Other World. Just a different state, like ice melts into water, and water turns into steam that invisibly fills the air. Daily we could hear our ancestors breathe. Dead or alive, it was all the same. The ancestors were always with us. The heavens, which I missed so much, had ceased to exist, but neither was there a hell or fear.

And how we loved the spectacles! Mummery fostered bonds in us and tied us to the spirits, took our fear away. Paint on our faces, the heavenly blue, protected us in battle. Muddy hair, cow horns, and sheep's pelts horrified our enemies and amused our children. And the fire told

11

us stories. When the logs crackled, the resin melted and the sparks danced, the smoke whirled or steeply ascended, when a fresh branch cracked and burst, the logs collapsed, and the glowing charcoal kept us warm, the fiery glow finally entered our eyes and deeply descended into our souls. There it burnt out all the black spots. If the fire was not strong enough to purify us, then a blood bath, a sacrifice was needed. Many times, I have led a stately horse, a valuable mount, preferably a white stallion, to the altar. The rock in the foundation of St. George's chapel was the butcher block. The torture stake stood right next to it. I remember it well.

Ding. Ding. Ding.

"If he does not stop this noise soon, I will freak out!"

Katrina hit her fist into the keys. Half a dozen letters jammed up in the middle. She fished out a cigarette from her jacket's internal pocket, lit up, and nestled into the old sofa chair. She stretched her strong, long legs. She could have been an athlete, but that was not part of her upbringing. "People who follow sports just don't have enough work to do," her father had said right after the new soccer field had been opened. In her brooding state, Katrina began to twist her brown curls until it hurt.

"Damn!" She took another smoke.

"Now she has stopped," her grandfather noted while trying to get his pipe going again. And then he returned to peening. Ding. Ding. Ding.

How could he ever understand this girl? Where was his little Katrina who had skipped alongside him on the way to the rosary, who had accompanied him when the church bells needed to be rung for the Angelus, and where was the impish doll who had helped him set up for the Easter Fire? Will she want to study at the university? Probably, but what? 'Can't become a pastor, that's for sure. Girls have no business going studying. She'll get married, then what? Children.'

"Is Katrina home?" a voice asked.

The old man didn't raise his eyes. He kept peening. He had not heard her coming. Luise. No surprise there. He could never suffer this girl with her red-dyed hair, patched up rag-doll jeans, and garishly polished fingernails. She was a year older than Katrina, a Lutheran on top, here in this Catholic country. Yet she would not even attend Protestant church services in the neighbor town. 'Lord have mercy on her late mother,' the old man prayed in his mind. Luise's mother had passed away from tuberculosis. 'Poor Marie! Why in the world had she married this artist from the city!' As soon as the cows were gone, the riffraff was in. 'A pity to see how the farm's run down.' He kept peening his row to the finish line.

Ping, ping, ping, he reached the tip of the scythe.

A nod was all he had for Luise. With that he nudged her toward the hen house. She promptly understood. Once upon a time she had tried to involve the old man in a conversation. It didn't go so well. All she had gotten out of him was an angry snarl, sounding somewhat like 'pack-of-ragamuffins.' Katrina, back then, had given Luise the full assurance that it had been a great success to coax any sound out of him at all.

"What are you writing there?" Luise had quietly entered the hen house and surprised Katrina, hunkering over her typewriter, from behind.

Katrina swiveled around. "Why do you always scare me so! And why are you asking? You know what Schiller said today. How far did you get with your presentation?"

"Didn't even start it yet. There is always time on the bus on Monday. Come on, let's go!"

2

Ghost Hunt

The St. George's Mound (Georgibichl) has been regarded as an especially suitable vantage point, despite its mediocre height, because it is situated amidst an extensive plain. It served many landlords as a defense lookout. Legend has it, the mound was an ancient cult site, where presumably horses were sacrificed to the god Wotan.

—*Gisela Schinzel-Penth, Sagen und Legenden, 103*

Late afternoon

Luise grabbed the steering wheel and stepped on the gas. She just had gotten her driver's license several months ago. On that occasion, her brother had handed his old, light-blue Opel Kadett down to her. The time-tested vehicle was dotted with spots of rust but had just passed inspection and would keep running for at least the next two years.

Soon they drove along a bumpy country road through pine-forested river meadows. Against the last rosy twilight of dusk, the sky increasingly became sprinkled with stars. The pine trees stuck out like ragged paper cuts. The air, which usually still carried a frosted tint this time of the year, was unseasonably mild.

Katrina stuck her head through the side window. Wild strands of hair whipped against her face. She deeply inhaled the resin-laced, intensely musty, earthy breeze.

"Katrina, are you nuts! Get your head back in!" Luise yelled.

"Mike might also come by later." Katrina settled back into her seat.

"Are you sure? I just saw him take off towards the lake."

"Oh, he and his stupid fish!" Katrina was miffed

"If he isn't a very slippery one himself."

"What?"

"A fish."

"Why do you say that?"

"Hard to catch." And then Luise mumbled into the steering wheel, "Or perhaps he's got all he needs."

"What do you mean by that?"

"Nothing. But you really should talk with him."

"Not so easy."

"Why?"

"Remember, he's a fish."

"Huh?"

"Fish don't talk."

Luise had had enough of this no-point conversation. She turned the music louder. She clearly evaded an answer. Sometimes she didn't make the least bit of sense.

The night was still young. Nothing much was happening at the disco. Serious dancing didn't start until after midnight. Only the regulars clung to the dimly lit bar. The disco ball sprinkled its fleeting confetti of light undisturbed on the empty dance floor and punctuated the incessant droning of the bass machine.

Katrina bought two Pilsners for her and Luise and they sat down in the dusky corner niche. By 10 p.m. the dance floor slowly started filling up. The music had taken on its own speed. An hour later, the crowd swayed and bumped against each other on the packed floor, with no room to fall over. Young people of all shapes, long-haired and short-skirted, tight-assed or lace-draped, bearded or bare-chested, stomped to the droning beat. It was a sweaty, rocking mess. Yet Katrina and Luise, in their corner, still clung to their first beers.

"Man, I just saw Daniel over there," Luise shouted in Katrina's ear and pointed to a lanky, bearded guy, beer glass in hand, on the opposite corner of the dance floor.

"I thought your brother is in Munich for his university studies?" Katrina shouted.

Luise waved her arms like crazy towards the opposite side of the dance floor. "I thought so, too. But he's here now, helping dad in the atelier at home. He always needs some dough."

The dark-haired guy now waved back. Katrina hadn't seen Daniel since he had moved to the city, only perhaps when he was driving by in his car. In elementary school—he was three years older than Katrina—she had been amused by his unusual haircut. Long bangs covered his eyebrows and he could have almost made a pony tail with the rest of it. Her little sister, Walli, had earlier admired his hair so much, that she had asked mother for the same cut. She had miscalculated. Mama didn't listen. Nice hair, don't cut, make some braids—done was the style. Apparently, Daniel was done with the bangs now, too. A tall, slender guy with long black hair, his hooves in cowboy boots, waved back at them.

"Wow, he looks really cool!" Katrina burst out. Luise looked at her, confused.

"Who? My brother?"

"I almost didn't recognize him."

"No worries, he is just as pesky as always."

"Must be the hair."

"Yeah, perhaps you need eyeglasses? Wait, Raffi is also there!" Luise flailed her arms again like a windmill in a storm. She got excited.

A man like a model from a beauty catalog—obviously not a country bumpkin—sashayed behind Daniel toward the girls. Katrina's heart raced. "Raffi" made a divine entry. Katrina could not help herself, but stare at this guy's faded 501 Levis jeans. He strode to the beat with endlessly long legs. His flowing, buttoned-down shirt gave him wide shoulders above some athletically narrow hips. With every seven-league stride, in what seemed to be slow motion, his angelic blond locks bounced off his shoulders. Blue eyes, he must have blue eyes, Katrina guessed. Right before him cantered the polar opposite with black hair, Daniel. Magically, like the Red Sea before the Israelites, the dancing crowd parted for the two strangers. Fittingly, *Smoke on the Water* roared from the speakers.

In the blink of an eye, the two men squeezed next to Luise onto the narrow bench. She squished Katrina over a few inches. There was hardly any room to breathe in this smoky dive. Katrina peeked across the beer glasses. Yes, these eyes were definitely blue. They glittered with humorous mischief. Was Luise flirting with the blond surprise cavalier? It was hard to talk over the noise, but he was easy to see.

"Little sister, dear, what are you doing in this joint so late?" Daniel teased Luise.

"Shouldn't I better ask you that? Nothing happening in the city that you've come out this far? I thought you hated farm discos?"

"You got me, us, wrong! We like variety, right, Raffi?" His companion agreed with a broad grin.

"Anyways," Daniel yelled across the table, "isn't it quite colorful in here?" And turning to Katrina, "By the way, this dude here is Raffi." The newcomer bent far across the table and reached out to shake Katrina's hand.

Katrina blushed, but the low light concealed that. She caught herself staring at the guys off and on, not only because of Raffi's angelic curls and handsome face, but also Daniel's exotic appearance. Was he wearing eyeliner? What for? She had never seen him this up close. The stubbly beard was apparently new, too. Secretly, she let her eyes wander over his face. Definitely, this was rhinestone—or a diamond—earring. Daniel moved like a pirate, it seemed.

"How are you holding up, girls?" Raffi asked, pointing at the last slug of warm beer in their Pilsner glasses. "So glad that you young ladies are brightening up this establishment here. Can I get you another beer?"

And before waiting for an answer, Raffi grabbed the hostess by the elbow, and with a charming grin scooped up four drinks from her tray. A fat tip left her no chance to protest this robbery. Emphatically, Raffi set the glasses in front of Katrina and Luise. "Cheers, to you!" All four took their big gulps.

"The evening is still young, people!" Raffi shouted across the table.

"You're right! It can only get better." Daniel started drumming the rhythm of the rock song with the heel of his boot. He had spoken too soon. Suddenly the music changed. Rock was gone, in came Abba. *Waterloo* blasted from the speakers now. It was the year's most popular hit.

"Man, are they still playing this shit! I can't stand it!" Luise grumbled and shifted from one butt cheek to the other.

"Right! You don't need no 'water loo.' You've already got a flushing toilet," Katrina recited one of Luise's favorite jokes. As on command, the girls broke into hysterical laughter.

"What's so funny about that?" Raffi asked.

The girls burst into a roar. Their giggles lasted until the next song came on. *Dancing Queen*. They spluttered more.

"So, no Dancing Queen, either one of you?" Raffi seemed even more confused and took another sip from his glass.

"Nah, only Queen. Because we are the champions." Louise snorted with laughter.

"Yes, Queen! Or Pink Floyd," Katrina flaunted her rock music repertoire before the assumed experts in front of her. She had gleaned many of the titles in the pop rock charts from Luise and her impressive collection of vinyl records.

"Wow, little Katie! Then let me take you to 'The Dark Side of the Moon'!" Daniel screamed behind Luise's back into Katrina's ear.

"Come on, Daniel, don't be mean!" Raffi yelled at his partner. "Obviously, she has an excellent taste in music, right?"

Daniel shrugged his shoulders. Then he pulled a small tin from his pant pocket and offered its contents under the table to Luise. "Want some?"

"No need to ask," Luise replied and popped a small pink pill in her mouth. "Love drops," she said and batted a suggestive smile at Katrina when she noticed the question mark in her eyes.

"How about you, Katrina?" Daniel asked.

"Leave her alone." Luise stopped him. Then she turned to Katrina and said, "Don't, Katrina. You are not used to these poppers. If you want to know, they just make life a tad happier, more positive. That's all."

"Then I don't know what your problem is, Lulu!" Quickly, Katrina snatched a pill for herself too.

Slowly but surely, Katrina started liking the disco better. From minute to minute, her lightness increased. Even the hard bench under her bottom now felt like an upholstered sofa. She never wanted to get up from her perfect spot again. Was she glued to it? Somehow the music no longer came from the speakers but emanated from her chest. With unbridled acumen she directed the perplexing drama in front of her.

The guys, who initially had intimidated her, seemed all of a sudden quite nice, like real brothers. Another hour later, Katrina had morphed into a prolific storyteller. She relayed her miserable experience with the school essays. Her inspiration seemed to flow faster and faster with each empty beer glass, the second, the third—and her table buddies, now kindred spirits, applauded her to tell more tales about any fictional or "historic" characters. Until then she had not realized, how entertaining she could be. Her voice had gotten hoarse. Fortunately, she had arrived at her crown jewel story, the white stallion ghost. There were many versions about this local specter, some claiming a Celtic source.

"When the raftsmen walked back along the Isar river, all the way from Munich to Wolfratshausen, and from there to their homes in the mountains, often at night, they had to pass by St. George's Hill in our valley. Some have seen a white horse cantering around the chapel, but could not get close to it. That white stallion is said to have starved to death in the chapel . . ."

"White horse, raftsmen, hah! Maybe they were just as tipsy as you and then . . ." Daniel teased.

"Daniel! Shut up!" Luise yelled across the noise. "A horse actually starved to death in the chapel. Katrina is not making this up. I did my research too. Of course, there isn't any proof for the ghost . . ."

". . . yet!" Katrina interrupted her with fiery passion. "The Celtic stallion has been riding on St. George's Hill since the beginning of human memory, even before it starved to death in the chapel." She was screaming at the top of her lungs to penetrate the droning noise.

"Katrina, stop that crazy nonsense! You've had too much beer. Don't talk such gibberish. How can this ghost horse ride around before there even was a chapel to be starved in?"

"Luise! Have you never heard of the Celtic stallion!" Katrina had no clue what had come over her. Some spark plug had gone off. This wouldn't be the first time that Luise had to reckon with her absurd fantasy.

"Nothing worth fighting over, girls," Raffi tried to placate the situation. "I don't mind either a white stallion nor a black charade, because ghosts always make for a good story."

"And, have you ever seen the white stallion?" Daniel teased Katrina. Obviously, he didn't want to put the ghost to rest.

"Do you think I am crazy? I am not going up this hill in the night. It's only one of those old stories that people talk about."

"If it's only a story, why are you sweating your pants? A minute ago, you wanted to convince us about the Celtic stallion and now you have changed your mind?" Daniel didn't let off.

"Maybe I'd rather spend my sleepless nights at the disco."

"How come? The horse ghost suddenly does not interest you anymore? I thought you were such a history buff." Raffi now baited her as well.

"I am currently having my problems with history."

"You don't say!" Daniel hit his flat hand on the table. "One more reason that we find out the truth right away. I had always wanted to hunt down a famous ghost."

"All right! Let's go, amigos!" Raffi said. "This lame place is getting too loud anyway. I need fresh country air."

"Are you all insane! Just you go ahead without me." Luise was in no mood for adventures.

"No, Luise! You must come along! Don't leave me now! I have never dumped you like that!"

Luise hesitated. "Fine, then!"

"You have my permission to slap me if the ghost happens to be on vacation, 'little sister'," Raffi teased Luise.

"If you say so, 'Long John'! But I am not your sister. One brother is enough already." Luise pinched Raffi in his side.

"Ouch!" Raffi made a pained face.

"That's what you get from your sister." Luise had an insidious grin on her face.

The four got up and wrestled their way through the throbbing bodies on the dance floor. They staggered out of the night club on wobbly legs.

Luise parked her blue Kadett at home in front of the atelier. Then the girls slunk into the back seat of Daniel's Turbo-Manta—or "mantra" as Luise liked to call it because it was embellished with racing stripes and a heck spoiler—and Daniel turned onto the country road.

Soon the bumpy dirt road got steeper. Daniel pulled off to the side, halted in a grassy meadow, and turned off his head lights. They had almost reached the chapel, but the last hundred meters led through a forest with gnarly roots in the path. Not a suitable racetrack for Daniel's souped-up car.

"There you go, all quiet here!" The men got out of the car. Raffi flashed his biggest smile at the backseat passengers.

"I don't see any ghosts. Can we turn around now?" Luise asked through the rolled down back window.

"Don't be a scaredy cat, sister!" Daniel pulled her outside into the fresh air.

It was so quiet after the roaring disco that they could hear each other's hearts pump, although it was only a soft incline. The chapel with its white walls glowed between the trees. The tall pines stuck out rigidly from the ground like oversized, jagged lightning rods. Against that backdrop, the trademark bulbous spire of the chapel commanded its attention. A faint fog undulated against the south side of the hill, whose terraces were said to have served the Romans as a vineyard 2000 years ago. Indeed, the scenery reminded Katrina of her dream reflected in her essay, in which the hill rose out of the lake like an island. The landscape beneath them was inundated by the wafting mist.

> When the logs crackled, the rosin melted and the sparks danced, the smoke whirled or steeply ascended, when a fresh branch cracked and burst, the logs collapsed, and the glowing charcoal kept us warm, . . .

"What now, can we go home?" Luise whimpered. "I am freezing." She was shivering. Her teeth clattered.

> If the fire was not strong enough to purify us, then a blood bath, a sacrifice was needed. Many times, I have led a stately horse, a valuable mount, preferably a white stallion, to the altar . . .

"Do you think the almighty stallion ghost whinnies on command? Or shows up only because of you?" Daniel scolded his sister. "True ghosts don't wait for you; you must wait for them."

"Don't smart aleck me, Daniel!" Luise was furious. She did not like to be patronized, especially not by her brother.

"Maybe the ghost still hunkers in the church," Raffi joked, but he had gotten notably quieter. "Let's peek inside the chapel!"

With a few long steps they had reached the cusp. The full moon lit their way. They walked around the little church and stopped at its entrance, a solid wood plank door.

"Wow, this looks old and impressive to me. But the people who built it must have been dwarfs." Raffi jolted the door handle with force. He was almost a head taller than the door itself. "No chance. It's locked. Do you know what's inside, Katrina?"

"Why do you want to know?"

"His crazy bug for art history just came out again," Daniel snarked.

"Crazy? And what about your folklore studies?" Raffi retorted.

"Just as crazy, I admit."

"Aren't you one bit interested?"

"Sorry, I know all that crap already. I have grown up here. No way around it."

"All right, then. But this little gem might hide great treasures right in front of our eyes." Raffi turned to Katrina.

"You can say that again!" Katrina confirmed. "This chapel has angels and saints, votive paintings, gilded candlesticks, and murals about the mar—hiccup—tyrdom of St. George. And a large cross from the black plague is in there too. It is terribly old . . ."

"Very interesting, but can we go now? I am freezing." Luise rubbed her arms and hands with dramatic gestures.

"Don't be such a dick, sister. Here, this will warm you up. Let's sit down and look at the starry sky." Daniel handed her a flat flask with amber liquid in it. Johnnie Walker. The day goes, Johnny Walker comes.

One by one they plopped into the dew-moistened grass in the flowery meadow, which would have resembled a Persian carpet by day.

"You're right, it's getting a little chilly around here." Raffi took a swig and handed the flask on. "Have a sip?" he said to Katrina. She drank from it and handed it back to Daniel. The flask made its round a couple of times.

Then Daniel rolled himself a smoke and gave the cigarette to Luise. She took a deep drag, held the air in for a while and then blew a long trail of smoke into the sky. Luise made a move to give the joint to Raffi, but Katrina grabbed it from her.

"May I?" Katrina surprised herself. She behaved more sassily than she had imagined herself capable of.

"I thought you didn't even like that stuff? You better slow down, girl!" Luise tried to grab the joint from Katrina.

Katrina, however, who was only smoking Camels in her chicken coop kingdom didn't heed her warning and took a deep drag. She held her breath down for as long as possible and then released the smoke with a snorting sound. Raffi took the next turn. Katrina laid down on her back.

Van Gogh must have been right. Stars move, they don't stand still. They pulsate and gyrate. How nice that was! Perhaps they are playing tag or hide-and-seek. Katrina believed to hear music in tune to the dancing stars. Locomotive breath. Hummh hummnh daah sheeh daah . . . Her companions' voices sounded from very far away, but she was happy by herself and her ballet of stars.

Happy or sad . . . Don McLean danced in her head.

Starry, starry night
Flaming flowers that brightly blaze
Swirling clouds in violet haze . . .

Daniel took another drag from the joint. He bent over Katrina. "You are so pretty, Katrina, I really like you." Holding his breath between his teeth and squinting his eyes, he blew the exhaust across Katrina's face.

Katrina was burning.

. . . dragons flying through the maze (not Don McLean)

The smoke vanished into thin air, but flames appeared behind it, wondrously beautiful to look at. This fire blazed from a dragon's mouth, a monstrous, finned, green-yellow-purple scaly, wormlike reptile. It had teeth as large as a backhoe's shovel.

Katrina froze, unable to scream or run. The awful monster hissed fiery cascades at her and cloaked her with smoke that it snorted from its bloated nostrils—which evaporated before they reached her. The dragon reared up and squirmed, thrashing its spiked tail left and right before her, lolloped, ascended into the air and raced at her in a free fall with its mouth full of teeth widely ajar, much like a burning locomotive tunnel.

Grandmother in heaven, please help!

Katrina instinctively popped an emergency prayer.

Suddenly the dragon deflated in front of her eyes like an empty balloon. A giant spout of steaming blood shot from the scaly monster, tinted the stars pink, while the dragon shape collapsed on the ground like the skin of a newly molted snake. Katrina looked up and saw a knight on a white horse. He had killed the dragon with his lance. The savior opened his visor, bent down to her, and reached for her arm to help her up.

His face looked so familiar.

3

Dragon Fog

In the olden times, several raftsmen, who had journeyed downstream the green Isar river and were passing by St. George's Hill on their way home after dark, reported independently from each other that they had spotted a dragon up there. The behemoth, they said, flew on wings through the air like the devil and scared them to their bones.

—*Gisela Schinzel Penth, Sagen und Geschichten, 104*

Thursday, June 13, morning

"Katrina! Get up! It's late!" Her mom's voice echoed in Katrina's ears like a death knell ringing from the Zugspitze. "It's high time. Don't you know it's Corpus Christi?" Katrina was unable to move. Her mother stomped out of the mansard room. "It stinks in here!" she said and banged the door shut.

Katrina forced her eyelids to open. She squinted. Her head felt like lead, and she wondered, a lot. What strange dreams she had. Just dreams! She blinked her eyes. Her head was heavy like a medicine ball. It might burst any second. She struggled to raise herself up. Like returning from another planet, she was still a captive in the murky yesterday. Someone had just screamed at her. Why?

"Say, have you gotten mad!" Her mother, Marianne, had returned after five minutes.

"Since when do you go to sleep with your clothes on! And, have you rolled around in garbage? Get going now, Avanti! If you can go gallivanting through the night, you might as well help me here. Bring me the tall candle sticks, quick! They are in the top drawer of the chest. And also bring me the altar cloths from the blue wardrobe, the one with the Christmas decorations in it."

"Fronleichnam," Corpus Christi, was the holiest of Catholic holidays in the village, holier than Christmas and Easter together. The whole village going on a glorious procession through the streets and fields with the sacred monstrance. The Weber altar, one of four, had to be set up by the old wayside cross at the bend in the road.

Like holy smoke, her mother evaporated into her downstairs business. Marianne was a Taurus. She went about her day in utter confidence that her orders would be obeyed. That much was clear to all family members.

Slowly, Katrina crawled out of bed. Her eyes flickered and would not focus. Her knees did not carry her weight yet. 'How the heck did I get back home?' she marveled. This uncertainty was many times worse than her nausea. How should she survive this miserable, holy day? Everybody was in the procession.

'Was it the blue drawer chest or the wardrobe in the corner?' The attic was a hodge-podge of remnants of the past. Katrina pulled out the lowest drawer of an ancient wardrobe. It smelled like mold and mothballs. She rummaged through old Sunday school lessons, letter stencils, and tattered leaf gold booklets. 'No candelabras anywhere.' Under a portfolio with a dozen saintly watercolor paintings, she came across a large, flat chocolate box. It contained a stack of memento pictures from funerals long ago, a couple of rosaries, a framed-up quote "In Memory of Your First Holy Communion," grandfather's soldier's ID with a leave pass from World War I, a bundle of several million Reichsmark bills from the inflation, an exquisitely decorated candle, and a small, chafed notebook. It had entries in the old German cursive. Katrina could barely decipher the letters, which her father had taught her so long ago. The jagged lines looked more like an embroidery pattern than words.

"Katrina, where are you? Hurry up!" The command echoed up two flights of stairs. Taurus people were known for their short fuse and temper. Her mother was a typical Taurus in that regard.

"Will be right there!" Katrina yelled down. She stuffed all the treasures back into the chocolate box, except for the notebook, grabbed the candelabras and altar cloth from the other chest, and prepared to descend. Quickly she stuck the slender notebook behind her well-organized series of Karl May novels in her room and padded down the stairs.

"That took a while!" Marianne abruptly grabbed the religious implements, and, with the candelabras under her arm, took course on the field altar in preparation.

"Shit! What happened to you! You look like puke!" A familiar voice slapped Katrina's ears. The insult came from the far end of the breakfast table.

Katrina's younger sister, Walli, sat cross-legged on the cushioned corner bench. She devoured her honey bread with a voracious appetite. She could destroy a wagonload of food and never gain a pound. A pot of hot cocoa sat in front of her. Her unruly hair was put up in a ponytail. She was still wearing her favorite "nightie," an Abba t-shirt and cut-off jeans. She chewed, swallowed, and got ready for another bite.

"I am sure glad that I'm not allowed into the Disco yet, if they mess you up this bad . . ."

"Shut up, Walli! Gnomes like you shouldn't even be allowed in a cloister."

"What makes you think I want to be in a cloister?" Walli was an abbreviation of St. Walburga.

"As sanctimonious as you are?"

"Sank-ta-Mo-nika-what!" Walli, not sure of the meaning of that word, was offended. "You are so mean! Now I won't tell you what I just read in the paper."

"No need to! Yesterday's news doesn't interest me. And if I want to, I'll read it myself."

Still, Walli had piqued Katrina's curiosity. Katrina grabbed the tattered pages. Calendar of events, local politics, small times ads, death announcements. Nothing interesting. "So, what's the deal here?" Katrina grumbled.

"Open your eyes, if you can, and you will see. Here!" Walli pointed her sticky index finger on a marginal column in the paper, under "Various."

"Call for entries: Stories from the Hearth," Walli read, emphasizing every single syllable as if talking to a feeble-minded person.

"So, what! Why should I care?"

"First prize, 300 Marks. Look here!"

"Get your sticky hands off!" Katrina tore the paper away from her.

Walli grimaced and prepared for a long sulk.

Katrina continued reading. "Deadline on Saturday before office closes . . . announcement of winners next week . . . chosen stories to be published . . ." she murmured. "For heaven's sake, why do they always want *local* stories? There is nothing going on around here at all."

"Then make something up. You are a good writer. You say so yourself. You should really give this a try!" Walli paused. "Or this will be the last fabulous hint from me."

"Will you stop it now! I have had enough of these silly local stories. Do you know how hard it is to come up with a story every week for the Essay Marathon in school? Schiller's crap is already coming out my ears. From the Neanderthals . . . to . . . whatever, . . . the first Bavarians on the moon!"

Walli snatched the paper from Katrina. "Stupid cow!"

They made more noise than a bunch of monkeys, as their father liked to say.

"What is going on here!" First the voice thundered through the door, then the man followed. Girgl, whose given name was Georg, their father, stood there, razor in hand, his shirt unbuttoned, shaving cream over half his face. He loomed over his unruly daughters at the breakfast table like the lightning of justice.

"Are you still not dressed?" Girgl roared. "Walli, will you get to it, put some clothes on! And you, Katrina, check on grandfather upstairs how he is doing with the flag, but pronto!"

Walli jumped off the bench and slinked around her father through the door. Katrina's complexion morphed from tomato red to snow white. Instantly she dashed after Walli up the stairs, just a level higher into the attic. She suddenly felt so dizzy. She slowed down her steps, panting.

Grandfather stood on the upper balcony. He had already attached the Bavarian flag with its blue-white diamond pattern to the pole, but he struggled with hoisting it. It was the same flag that he had hung during Corpus Christi in 1940. Back then a spy from the NS party had denounced him. He was supposed to fly the swastika or nothing at all. But he plainly stated that he just couldn't find it. Thus, the next day, block warden Wastl Schroll brought him the "correct" Nazi colors. Case closed. Not so fortunate, the poor pastor. He preached the wrong stuff from his Christian pulpit and was therefore incarcerated for three weeks in the county jail. Only divine intervention and the rage of the rosary women saved him from the concentration camp. One of the ladies later was to be awarded a "Mothers Merit Cross," for having born so many children for the Führer. "Why don't you hang this thing around your cat's neck! She certainly has produced more offspring than me!" And with that she slammed the great honor in the dirt before the block warden's feet. These were some of the stories that the village helper, Frau Bürkel, a Hungarian refugee, liked to tell the children on occasion, like yesterday as they were decorating figurines for the Corpus Christi procession with green garlands.

"Wait, Grandfather, let me help you!" Katrina grabbed the lower end of the pole, and together they hoisted the flag in its fixture. She looked up. Right above her, under the eaves, there was a dragonhead! That fire-spitting image was carved out of the end of the top beam. Last night's memory came to life again. As the fresh air rushed to her head, her vision blurred. She had to lean back against the wall so as not to topple off the balcony. Frantically, she wiped the imaginary cobwebs from her eyes.

"Grandfather, what's the dragon doing up there?"

She had forgotten that he was mute, but still he looked up to where she had pointed. His moustache seemed to quiver. He shook his head in indignation about such a stupid question. Yes, his wife's grandfather, a master carpenter, had carved that one, to make it like the one before, and like all the other ones, that had guarded the roof previously. The dragon head kept watch over a very, very, very old house, the newest, stone-built version of it merely a measly 200 years old. Before the fully masoned house, there stood a lowly wood cabin in its place, so low in fact, that the inhabitants conveniently hid the key in the eaves trough. Whatever job the dragon had—to avert fire, malady, or mishap—disaster had struck anyway. The old man was still terribly sore about it.

'Grandfather seems a little shaken. I will never get an answer from that old man.'

The procession already took order on the church square by the Botenwirt guest house. Katrina was late. She was in plain clothes, a skirt and a blouse. Many other young women of her age had gotten up at the crack of dawn to don their *Mieder Tracht*, a complicated, traditional costume. Anxious mothers and grandmothers had helped the girls into the silken costume fashioned after the Spanish royal court tradition of 1620. It was like a piece of armor. First attach the underskirt to the chemise, slip into the narrow, tailored blouse, then pin the fishbone bodice on the chemise, hook the heavy skirt to the bodice. Then tie the apron and pin the folded silk scarf around the neckline with long silver acorn needles. So many pins and buttons! Next, lace up the bodice with a long silver chain with medals dangling from it. Finally, stick roses or carnations into the maidens' bosom lines. Filigreed silver hairpins stuck in a neatly knotted bun completed the hairdo. The *Mieder* outfit looked absolutely royal. Had Katrina worn the *Mieder* too, she would have been much closer to her heartthrob Mike. Mike was the flag bearer for the *Mieder* girls. The red velvet banner with the Virgin Mary that he carried had by far the longest flagpole.

The procession followed its ancient ritual. Ahead the altar boys with the cross, then the little girls with their flower baskets, then the First Communion group with the Baby Jesus statue on a handbarrow, then the young women in their *Mieders* with the lovingly decorated Our Lady statue, then the escort with baldachin for the priest with the holy monstrance, then the firemen, Alpine marksmen association and other village clubs, and at the tail end the common people and elderly. That's where Katrina walked.

The flower girls had excitedly plucked wild flowers the night before, such as marguerites, red clover, sticky cockles, and poppy flowers. Some had even plundered the peonies in their mothers' gardens. That way they filled up their baskets much faster. Once a year, the mothers allowed the pilfering of their blooming paradises for the higher purpose of Corpus Christi—although some still raised a regretful brow.

> Rosen, Tulpen, Nelken—Roses, tulips and carnation
> alle Blumen welken—all flowers must wilt
> außer einer nicht—except for one,
> which is called Vergißmeinnicht—Forget-me-not . . .
> Jasmine? Didn't it smell like Jasmine here, or lilac?

A very strong fragrance wafted through the air.

With every misstep on one of the strewn flowers, a pungent aroma stung Katrina's nose. She was blessed—or cursed—with a very fine nose. There it was again, strong, sweet, nauseating. So, she skipped about from here to there to avoid stepping on the blooms, which eventually upset the rhythm of the dual file of marching women. Finally, Irmi, the salesgirl from the bakery, who walked right behind her, sternly tapped Katrina on the shoulder to bring her back in line. Katrina blushed and followed suit. She stopped marching to her very different tune. Each of the four times when the procession came to a halt for the Gospel reading and solemn blessing with cannon shots, the pungent smell was gone, as if the sweetly air stopped only to hover over each field altar. Inexplicable! When the brass band or prayers stopped, everything fell dead silent, except for the shrill ringing in Katrina's ears. Like silence on the airwaves.

Drei weiße Birken in meiner Heimat stehen—three white
birches standing at my home . . .

Katrina found herself humming an old pop song in her head.
She didn't know why. It was a very schmaltzy song.

Listen, Katrina, did you know? The birch is a fairy, the
cricket of springtime awakening.

Katrina flinched. She hadn't said that, she hadn't thought
that, she had heard it. She swiveled around, but Irmi was lost in
pious contemplation sinking on her knees to cross her chest for
the blessing. Apparently, it wasn't she who had spoken. But
who had? Was she going crazy? Katrina's thoughts went on a
wild goose chase. Maybe it was the decorative birches, which
the farmers had cut and stuck into the ground along the wayside.
Were they whispering to her? Young birches were a vigorous
symbol for the love of life. One time, on Corpus Christi day, it
rained so much that, after the birches were left stuck in the dirt
for several weeks, they had taken root. This was the origin of
Birch Street, people said. It was named so after the village had
grown large enough to receive street names.

It was a picture book day. The fresh air revived Katrina,
but her spirit was still conversing with the lilac, marguerites,
and poppies in an absurd way, while she automatically followed
the scripted ritual of prayer responses and reverent knee falls.

Hochgelobt und gebenedeit sei das allerheiligste
Sakrament des Altares . . . Ehre, Ehre sei Gott in der Höhe
. . . —Exalted and blessed be the most holy sacrament on
this altar . . . Glory, glory to God in the highest . . .

'Where the heck am I? Is this a movie?' The relentless
piety in front of her eyes seriously clashed with her nebulous
experience from last night. Without qualms, the procession

already moved on. If she could have only shaken those dreams. Or recalled them. She drew a blank.

'Wait a minute. Who is waving over there?' Luise, almost completely covered behind the bushes at her parents' house, flicked sign language at Katrina. Right, she signaled 'soccer' or 'ball,' Finally, it clicked. Soccer field, right!

Luise made a peace sign. It meant 2 o'clock.

Katrina signaled back. OK.

The procession ended as always inside the church. And as always, after the last blessing, the young men were the first ones out. They gathered in a large throng around the linden tree, including Mike. Each time after mass, Katrina tried to catch a glance from Mike. Sometimes she succeeded, but many times she didn't. The young men always had very important matters to discuss, it seemed. Inevitably, they huddled under the linden tree, the tree of divine wisdom and eternal decree. Sometimes they didn't make it into church at all. Although the young men talked their mouths fuzzy from the bell call to dismissal, they still blamed all the gossip on the "women folk," as if their mothers even had time to chat while cooking the Sunday roast with all its fixings.

'Why are they all staring at me?' Katrina wondered, as she passed by the throng of young men on her way out through the cemetery gate. All eyes turned on her.

"Hey, how did you sleep last night, Katrina?" the chunkiest of them, Beni, called out to her unexpected loudly.

The hulky "Moar-Bub[i]," mayor's boy, as Frau Bürkel and other old ladies liked to call Benedikt, or Beni, for short, at the tender age of 25 and almost 300 pounds, was the headman of the young men's club. He liked to brag about his chinchilla breeding business and his long-haired Scottish Highlands cattle, both novelty industries. Just the same, he often flaunted his love conquests, all happening on his frequent Mallorca vacations.

Beni was feared for his polemics, crude manners, and foul temper. When the rage got ahold of him, nobody was safe from his hammer-like fists. Thus, he continued to be reelected as the young men's chief officer. As long as one was on his side, regardless if in the wrong or right, everything was good. Somehow Beni's attitude had a way of rubbing off on his entourage. When Beni was absent, Katrina had noticed, the young men, each one by himself, could be quite jovial. But when Beni peacocked around, they all played up to him, and crudeness took over. Katrina once had denied Beni a dance at the carnival masquerade. He kept insulting her until she ran home like Cinderella, not losing a shoe but forgetting her purse at the dance. Fortunately, the innkeeper put it away safely.

"Katrina, Beni has asked you something!" An anonymous snicker escaped the huddle of men.

"So, did you have a good night, Katrina?" Beni asked again. Beni still stood there, both thumbs hooked in the suspenders of his *Lederhosen,* blocking Katrina's way. Giggles escaped from the men's group.

"None of your bees wax!" Katrina blurted out. She could not think of a better answer and dashed away before worse things could have been said. She didn't know the answer herself. Yesterday was only a deep blackout gash on her mind.

"In a rush today, aren't you!" Beni yelled after her.

"Crazy chick!" It was unclear who had said it.

The young men turned inward to their circle again. Katrina accelerated her walk and went straight to the chicken coop. Perhaps, Beni was right, she was a crazy chick. But why had he asked her about last night?

She sat down in front of the typewriter. She still had an hour before her mother would call everybody for the family lunch.

June 13, noon

The dragon belonged to the highest power of the heavens, Teutates, or Jupiter, or whatever you may call him. Many sacrificed themselves to him. The "Claws-Worm" had scales as big as the palm of a hand in all shades of colors. When he got angry, he blushed and puffs of smoke puckered around his widened nostrils. He had mighty hind legs and claws as sharp as a knife, big enough to scoop up a calf with ease. His ribbed underbelly resembled that of a lizard. Bone plates protruded from his spine like large thorns, and the end of his clubbed tail was spiked with razor-sharp hooks. In his fearsome skull, he rolled his bulbous eyes with targeted precision. Prey, as soon as sighted, would instantly be devoured.

The dragon was an excellent traveler of the air. He had fingered wings like a bat but with deadly daggers at the thumb claws. It seemed as if almost imperceptible fluffy downs covered his wing membranes. We Celtic people had the highest regard for him.

At that time, the druids could still read the winds, decipher the clouds, withstand the cold. But in order to wrest a harvest from the earth, we needed the collaboration of nature. Sometimes it cost us a good horse. After the fiery dragon had settled in the cave beneath the heavens pillar, the earth became increasingly dry. The dragon scorched everything with his fetid fire breath. Not that we were afraid of dying, but the behemoth threatened our way of life. We didn't know what had enraged him so much. Horses did not satisfy him for long. Only virgin girls put him to sleep for a year of hibernation. We sacrificed our daughters. They were happy to travel to the Otherworld. But then the Romans came and took the fairest women, before they could be sacrificed, as their brides. We continued to slaughter horses by the heavens pillar, which you call the torture stake. Luckily, the dragon held his breath.

"Oh, well! If you can believe it," Katrina sighed. "But nobody will." She had stopped typing. Definitely, Schiller will reject my first-person style,' she pondered. Her story was due tomorrow. She kicked back and stretched her legs under the old milk separator table. The chunky little table, splattered with countless grease stains after the separator drum had been removed, served as her writing table. She yawned. 'Too bad, it was a good try.'

She had released the dragon from her inexplicable nightmare of yesterday's disco adventure into the typewriter keys. A dull, disconcerting feeling remained. She couldn't shake that other dream. Dimly, very dimly, there was a fair maiden there. Why was that girl in such big trouble? She recalled the great fear, the heavy pressure on her chest, the paralysis, but not the story. Mara, who was Mara? That name had shot through her mind earlier. Dreams are none but shadows. She jumped up, darted out, and slammed the hen house door behind her. She had gotten hungry.

After a hearty lunch, schnitzel with potato salad, and the hand-in-hand dish washing ritual together with Walli, Katrina perked up. She threw the towel on the sink and headed towards the soccer field.

'This girl will plunge straight away into disaster.'

The old man simmered. He sat in his Sunday best on the front bench, smoking his pipe. He saw Katrina leave the house and easily guessed who she was running after. 'Gypsy and grifter pack! Bohemians, my ass,' his mind growled. 'Artists? All day they loiter around, I bet they are all hooked on drugs. For-Chrissakes-holy-mother-of-God-and-Saint-Joseph! And I must stand by and watch! Kathl, up there, help her, if you can!'

He knew his deceased wife was a saint, but why exactly should she put in a word for him? He hadn't treated her all too well in her lifetime. He was a man. That entitled him to pontificate from the house bench, while Kathl spread the manure; to frolic in the horse carriage, as the women folk sweated the hay harvest; to scold Kathl and her spinster sisters about the lousy grub, when he drank away the housekeeping money; and to chat away time in the village inn while the women tended to the cows at home.

Back then, women folk did not have a say. However, now times had changed. Perhaps, Girgl, a chip off the old block as well, had been too strict with Katrina and unwittingly nudged her out of the house? Or not strict enough, since she still conspired with riff raff the likes of Luise. But why should Katrina seek out such a rotten bunch? Those folks didn't know anything about the rules of the land, the forgotten souls, the deep roots down to purgatory and back? 'Kathl, help her, if you can!' the old man prayed again. 'Bring Katrina back to us.' Last time when he had sent a fervent emergency prayer to heaven, it had not helped one bit. The disaster happened anyway. Martl could not be saved. It was nobody's fault but his.

'Or at least keep an eye on her,' the old man begged.

Luise waited by the bench behind the soccer clubhouse. That was their secret meeting point for all occasions.

"Girlfriend, I am so glad you came!" Luise shouted.

"I still feel as sick as a dog. I can't remember anything."

"Man, my brother is on fire and you don't even notice it." Luise broke into laughter.

"What! How did that happen?"

"He lit up his hair with the joint! Can't believe you didn't notice the flash flame," Luise giggled behind her hand. "And then Raffi put it out with his jacket."

"What the eff! Did anyone get hurt?"

"No, but Daniel stank so bad that he had to borrow my hair spray." Luise still chuckled. Now Katrina also allowed herself to giggle. Her eyes wandered over Luise's outfit.

Luise's jeans had holes in both knees and every square centimeter was decorated with ballpoint pen. Flowers, cartoons, critters, and curlicues scurried across her pant legs. Around her wrist she wore one of her endless, hand-strung chain of micro beads. Such sense for detail and artistic expression had fascinated Katrina from the first day in Luise. And somehow also her brother, Daniel, seemed to have arrived from outer space in this village. Their house was quite remarkable since they added a planetarium to the attic. Sure, there was a telescope, but more importantly, the upper floor was filled with bookshelves to the ceiling. And that's where the 'riffraff,' aliens to the village, liked to land most often.

Out of nowhere David Bowie channeled in.

Ground Control to Major Tom
Your circuit's dead, there's something wrong

Katrina shook Bowie out of her ear. "And how did I get home?" She almost whispered.

"We somehow packed you into Daniel's car, and I already know where you keep the key hidden. When we got to the house, you had a light moment, and I dragged you up the stairs."

"These guys probably think I am a turd who can't have fun and only talks stupid." Katrina pulled her legs up on the bench, wrapped her arms around them, and laid her head on her knees.

"Don't you worry! These guys have had their own share of blunders. Have you noticed," she paused, "that my brother has eyes for you?"

"No, I thought it was the brandy talking." Obviously, Daniel had intimidated her yesterday with his plump advances. To change the topic, she asked, "Do you know if Raffi has a girl friend?"

"Why do you want to know? You will only get your fingers burned with that guy."

'What a rude reply.' Luise usually didn't snap like that.

For a while the girls sat quietly on the bench and did not speak a word. They watched the water passing by in the creek in front of them. Time after time, the small stream made a comforting chuckling sound. Luise pulled out a packet of tobacco and rolled a cigarette. She offered it to Katrina.

"No, thank you! I already feel sick."

"So, what is going on with Mike and you?" Luise lit up the cigarette and tossed the match into the creek. "How long have you been going out?"

"I don't know if you can call it that. But the whole thing started three years ago at a party."

During their first rendezvous, Mike had only danced with her. *San Francisco. Samba pa ti. Stairway to Heaven. Hotel California.* And much more from the Rolling Stones. Then they walked home together through the moonlit night until they came to the fork in the road, where it was good-bye. Mike pulled her close and kissed her. Actually, Katrina had thought that she would hear the angels sing for joy, but it was not quite like that. She could not sleep one wink that night. At first, she thought that she had been struck by the thunderclap of eternal love. But the explanation was quite simpler: she had drunk one too many colas.

"And now?"

"Oh, he kisses much better now."

Luise laughed out loud, but reduced her volume to a soft giggle, noticing Katrina's sour expression. "No, I mean, does he take you out dancing sometimes? Or to the movies?"

"Well, yes, I see him at village events."

"All right, like with the whole escort of buddies and hordes of chaperones?"

"You know what it's like."

"Who are you fooling here?" For some reason, Luise got highly agitated. "Take off your pink eye glasses and look at him up close. By the way, there are many other good fish to catch. Use your logic."

"You and your logic!" Katrina fell silent.

If Luise only knew that a single glance by Mike could make a thousand little ants crawl around inside of her. Or how a single word of his could make her heart freeze and then give it a really big jolt. Or how his slightest touch made her go ACDC, hot and cold, at lightning speed. Or how a lump rose in her throat when he asked her "How do you do?" so that she no longer could utter one word that made sense. But Luise never had had experienced such shivers, it seemed.

"And what do you want from Mike later on?" Luise asked Katrina straight on. "After you are done with school, I mean. Do you want to be a farmer's wife?"

"No, of course not. He is apprenticing with his uncle to be a carpenter."

"So, do you want to be a carpenter's wife?"

"Don't ask me such stupid questions. I haven't had time to think about it."

"Obviously not. Sorry that I asked. But be careful with types like him. Is he serious about you?"

"How would I know that?"

"Test his deeds, take off his pants. Find out the naked truth. Or something like that."

"You don't like him, do you?"

"I don't have to. He is not my crush."

Katrina was speechless. She watched Luise fan away a dragonfly that wanted to settle on her arm. They fell quiet and listened to the whisper of the wind, which played with the old reed grass from last year. The birds interjected an occasional tweet here or there.

"Do you never think about the right one, the great love, or getting married?" Katrina interrupted the silence.

"Absolutely, when I am stone old, dead-cold, and totally bored, perhaps." Luise flung the cigarette butt into the creek. Out of a smoke, she plucked a piece of grass to chew on. "Who says that you have to marry the first dumbo you sleep with?"

Katrina huffed. That sounded like love advice straight from the teen magazine *Bravo*, which they used to alternately buy copies of. They had devoured the picture novellas and advice columns. Each Thursday they waited with great suspense for the newest issue filled with pop gossip and pin up posters. Eventually, the stories started repeating themselves and the sex counseling became less satisfying. Good advice was hard to come by. Even Luise seemed out of whack today. She was also more than a little hung over.

Suddenly Luise perked up. "Hey! You are not wearing your charm today?"

"Of course . . ." Katrina touched around her neck. "Shit! It's gone! I think I might have lost it last night. I remember I still had it in the car, driving up there. It must have fallen off somewhere by the chapel . . . Will you help me look for it?"

"Are you nuts! How will you find a grass green clover in the green grass?"

"There is a chance . . ."

"As likely as a million in Lotto."

"Come on, Lulu, you know it's my luckiest charm! It's not far, just a short walk up the hill. Let's go!"

"What? Not another miserable expedition."

"Lulu! Get up now! Move!"

On the horizon, at the feet of the two girls, lay the scenic backdrop of the Alps. They had reached the top of St. George's Hill in no time. What flowers! Marguerites, devil's claws, blue bells, larkspur, sweet pea, quaking grass dotted the green carpet. Katrina's grandfather knew them all—even more so the healing-powered herbs. Sometimes the old man still hiked up here to pick chamomile, peppermint, rosehip for his tea mixture, or harvested the wild caraway for Marianne's kitchen. Her grandfather had also warned her about some poisonous plants, especially the true-lovers knot. Often there was a story behind the strangest blooms, like the Salomon's seal, which was said to bust prisoners' shackles. Mostly a realist, the old man did not believe in magical fern fairy dust. But he swore by the disinfecting potency of wolfs bane and fed the young heifers the carnivorous butterwort to increase their fertility.

Katrina scanned the area. In some places the grass was still flattened from their frolics the night before. No matter how frantically they turned each blade of grass, they found no trace of her pendant. Disappointed, Katrina sat down in the meadow.

"I give up!"

"Never mind, don't take this so hard. Here, have this instead!" Luise grabbed under her blouse, pulled out a thin necklace, and hung her own talisman around Katrina's neck.

"What is it?"

"A bear claw, from America. My brother gave it to me. It's supposed to have great protective strength."

Katrina critically looked at the pendant from all sides. "This is something special. Are you sure you don't want to keep it yourself?"

"Dead sure. If you don't need it any more, you can return it to me later."

The two friends sank down into the grass and stretched out. Laying in the flowery meadow on the hill, they watched the clouds drift by above them: a real classical, Bavarian, white-and-blue sky. It instantly brought up a song by balladeer Reinhard Mey:

> Above the clouds, freedom for sure must be limitless, one says, and all fears and sorrows remain hidden beneath, and what seems grand and important to us, becomes nothing and small . . .[ii]

Like in her dream the white cotton puffs drifted across the saturated blue. Yes, this must be where the May poles got their colors from, as she had written in her unfortunate essay. Schiller obviously had not bought into it. Above the clouds, that might also be where her brother was. She remembered him vaguely.

As if she had read her mind, Luise asked, "Do you still sometimes miss your brother?"

"Well, I hardly knew him, but once in a while I wish for an older brother. Then he would get the beatings instead of me."

"Or he would rough you up instead." She paused. "Everyone gets the beatings he deserves. As you know, I have sometimes fought with Daniel to the blood."

"So, I heard."

"But since he has gone off to the university, we get along much better."

"Looks like it . . ." Katrina drifted off into her head. "Wait a minute, I just remembered something. The noble knight yesterday . . ."

"What night? *Night in White Satin*?" She hummed. "What are you talking about?"

"Not in satin, in shining armor . . ."

Katrina told Luise her dream encounter with the terrible dragon and the rescue through the noble knight.

"I think I just recognized his face."

"Say! Who?"

"Guess!"

"I don't like guessing! Spit it out!"

"Mike!" Katrina almost shrieked.

Luise balled up in hysteric laughter and could not stop. At first, Katrina was surprised, but then she got more and more miffed. She turned her back on the roaring Luise.

"Come on, Katrina! I meant no harm! But that idea is just too comical," Luise spouted after she was able to speak again. "Still friends? Let's go. Perhaps I will start working on my presentation today after all."

As they walked by the church, they noticed something unusual.

"Wait a minute. Why is that door open?" Katrina cautiously pushed the door inside. It gave way with a creaking sound. They ducked into the dusky little chapel. Only faint beams of light permeated the small windows.

"How strange. Yesterday it was definitely locked." Luise looked around.

"Everything seems to be all right in here," Katrina said. "We have to report this to the custodian, Pauli. He must lock up the place." Katrina yanked the door shut and then they scampered down the forested hill past the cornfields to the village.

Pauli's house was the first one on the south side of the village and had a great view of St. George's Hill. He was the Messner, that is, custodian, of the churches. Pauli was a somewhat peculiar, aging bachelor who lived all alone. He was responsible for ringing the church bells, handing out invitations for special parish meetings, or trying his curative knowledge on dairy stock, before an expensive veterinarian was consulted. Pauli owned a dozen goats, which had given him his nickname, Goat Pauli. One of his goats had become infamous in the village. "Stasi" was her name. She had escaped many times and devastated numerous vegetable gardens. She even pulled on Pauli's old-fashioned doorbell string when she wanted to be fed. At any time of the day, numerous cats perched on Pauli's bench. Be it as it may, perhaps because he lived in close contact with so many animals on his little farm, or perhaps because he added raw garlic to his goat milk soup every morning, Pauli was permanently shrouded in a cloud of questionable odor. In church, people kept their distance from him and scooted over with no delay. Sometimes, however, he smoked a really pleasant tobacco, which luckily masked the other tangy scents. He also played the zither masterfully and sang old tunes from memory, which weren't written down anywhere.

Pauli stood in his garden, not far from his beehives, with a bunch of radishes in his fist. He saw the girls approaching and raised one eyebrow. A steep wrinkle appeared on his forehead and the tip of his nose started to itch with anticipation.

"Pauli!" Katrina shouted from afar. "Pauli, you must come to the chapel. The door is open!" By then she had reached the garden gate and flung it open.

"What do you say, Katrina?"

"The chapel, the door is unlocked. We thought you wanted to know."

"Don't tell me stories! I was up there just last Thursday for sweeping. I never forget to lock the door. I turned the key twice. I know that for sure. Somebody must have broken in!"

"But the lock was OK," Luise said.

"It will be best the two of you come along and we check it out together," Pauli grumbled. At least he would have witnesses in case of a criminal event. He tossed the radishes on the garden bench, grabbed a key from the hook inside his little hallway, and then hurried to kick-start his old motorbike in the shed. The odd vehicle had a sidecar, in which Pauli regularly transported his purchases home from the city. Katrina squeezed into the narrow, bumpy seat, and Luise jumped on the back of the bike behind Pauli. No sooner than the girls grabbed on for dear life, Pauli gave gas and the machine rumbled over the dirt road. By the forest all three jumped off and ran to the top.

"Dear-Heavens-and-Lord-of-the-Holy-Sack-of-Cement . . ." Pauli grated his teeth. "These bastards, they were here again!" The girls glanced into the direction of the curse. A flower wreath lay on one of the large boulders sticking out of the foundation of the church. The leftovers of two burnt down candles sullied the rocks with greasy blotches.

But today Pauli did not have time for a routine investigation. He would rather solve an emergency. He pressed down the door handle with full force.

"Damn! By the name of Holy Anthony! What is this!" He turned around and stared down the girls. "Are you playing tricks on me!" The door was locked.

"No, Pauli! You must believe us! The door was still open just half an hour ago," Luise assured him. "Maybe it locked on itself when Katrina slammed it."

"Girls, let me tell you! This old church is not a Sesame-lock-yourself. Nonsense. Someone pulled one over on us. Or did you? I am always good for a joke, but I am too old to be taken for a ride like this," Pauli sputtered. He was visibly agitated. He pulled the church key from his pocket and turned it in the lock, twice. All three walked inside the church.

"Thank God!" Pauli sighed, pulled off his hat, and crossed his brow. "At least in here everything is still in order." Although he still breathed hard, he instantly started a careful inspection.

The sun had already sunk to the lowest spot on the horizon so that only a single ray of light hit St. George over the altar: the proud knight in shining armor, riding a white stallion. There was the dragon slayer.

Katrina winced. The previous night instantly flashed before her eyes. A horrible claws worm recoiled through her murky memory, called the dragon of shame. Or was it another monster? And she remembered some more of the other dream too. A horrible scene.

She was burning up. She sank into the nearest pew.

"Girl, what's going on? You are as white as snow. Are you sick?" Pauli looked at Katrina, worried.

"Come on, you two! I will take you home. Pronto."

4

Dizzy Ditz

Compared with the Germanic marauding bands, the Roman legions could have been called widely traveled and worldly wise. That kind of Mediterranean civilization soon transcended the Alps and left its mark on this country and its inhabitants for all times and to this day.

—*Hans Nöhbauer, Die Bajuwaren, 106*

Friday, June 14

The Romans were neither proud nor smart. They were a bunch of debauched ragamuffins, and not one of them came from Rome. Many mercenaries were hired on from Egypt, Tunisia, Phoenicia, Mauretania, and other foreign corners of the Empire. Only the Centurio was truly Roman. What a wild bunch! Yet, all soldiers marched in unison obeying the smells of the field kitchen and the bangs of the drum beats. Remnants of these practices we can still witness today in form of brass bands and oxen rotisseries at the Bavarian carnivals. For us local people, however, the drums beat to a different tune. Incited by fife and bagpipe, their rhythms drove us to ecstasy. Thus, we conversed with the stars.

The Roman colonization didn't go smoothly. As commonly known, our brave Celtic ancestors thoroughly thrashed the clean-shaven sissies not only once. Unfortunately, when Brennus conquered the Capitol, the geese warned the Romans or else he would have torched their city. Hah, 'vae victis,' he made them pay their weight in gold. Soon, however, our brave warriors had seen enough of the Roman cesspool and marched into other battles, Delphi, Persia, and Egypt. Some of our men joined Alexander's Macedonian cohorts. They reached as far as Hindustan, their ancestral lands. There they took wives who likewise had red hair and blue eyes, later called the Afghan people. Our people were feared from Galatia to Iberia.

In the end, our brave men were no match for the Roman troops. In their conquest of our domain, they toppled our rock altar because they feared our magical subversion. What's one altar, when we had the whole forest as our sanctuary? The forest gave us cover. Soon the Romans built tall watch towers and barricades around their forts, they made streets and aqueducts as straight as a knife's edge. Little did they know that they were marching into their own demise. All those years, the dragon kept silent, and the Romans didn't give a damn about our conversion. They had their own Gods and mistook us for forest devils. We gave our virgins to the cohorts. But instead of offering them to the Gods, they took them home as wives.

Not everything that the Romans brought was bad. The

radish, for example, the pungent, white root from purgatory, received the druid's blessing as effective medicine. When the meat already reeked, a radish helped us digest the most terrible slop. The Roman wine, too, a heavenly revelation, was hard to come by. After their vineyard project on Lookout Mountain had floundered, the Romans sought better wine and wives elsewhere. But many drops of foreign blood now pulsated through our Celtic veins. Our world was not the same.

"Frau Weber, again, what were you thinking?" Hildebrandt aka "Schiller" furrowed his brow. Leaning against the wall next to the fire extinguisher, with one leg braced behind him, he studied Katrina's pages. The roaring noise in the hallway bounced off his knitted sweater. He ignored the unruly kids. Taking off his spectacles, he looked firmly at Katrina.

"Where are you going with this, Frau Weber? As we both know, dragons don't really exist, right? And," he cleared his throat, "have you ever read anything about the Romans?" Over the rim of his glasses, he stared Katrina down.

She looked at her shoe tips.

"And why are we still stuck on the Celts, here? You called them 'forest devils.' Aren't you afraid that one of them might come after you with a club in the dark?" He shook his head. "Here, your papers. Please bring me a real essay about the Germanic tribes next week. Don't forget the research!" He sighed. "We both know that you can do so much better!"

Katrina stuffed the foul pages into her bag. At least he hadn't lectured her in front of the whole class this time.

"Your friend, Frau Pfeiffer," Schiller said before Katrina could slink away, "has truly surprised me this time. She gathered many good subject points. Facts, facts, that is what you need in your essay!"

Defeated, Katrina cantered off to the bus station.

"Don't you worry about it one bit!" Luise comforted Katrina when she plopped into the seat next to her. "I can show you exactly what I did. We've got a book or two."

Katrina nodded with relief. Suddenly, she sensed a suspicious scratch in her throat. "Feel that," she said to Luise and made her touch her forehead.

"Ouch! You are really hot!"

"So glad, we're done for the day—and for the week."

"You must go to bed, right now! And that is a 'fact'." Luise wagged a threatening finger at her.

Katrina could not help but laugh.

It was a muggy, hot day with an overcast sky. In some places the haze let through a blue sheen. Katrina felt caged like a mouse under a cheese dome. She dozed off on the bus until Luise pulled her sleeve.

"Wake up, sleepy head!" They trundled off the bus with their bags in arm.

"Now look, who's here!" Luise had spotted Mike. She jabbed Katrina with her elbow.

Katrina's blood shot into her head. On the other side of the road, in front of the butcher shop, Mike was chatting with three of his friends in the shade of the chestnut trees. Leaning against his motorbike in his casual work outfit, he looked his part of a centerfold amidst a throng of sidekicks. He still seemed to be on lunch break. The girls made their heads turn.

"Well, then! Take care!" Luise had a suggestive grin on her face. "I've got to run!" She was off before Katrina could bat an eye. The throng around Mike had also dissipated.

"Lulu, wait!" Katrina shouted, in vain. "Dang!" She clenched her teeth.

"Hello, Katrina!" Mike shouted across the street. He waved to her.

Katrina waved back and slowly walked up to his bike. He looked dashing with his sleeves rolled up over his strong, tan arms. Any slightest move of his made the light playfully bounce off his toned muscles. A thin gold chain with a small cross on it glistened through the open collar on his chest. 'Blue looks darn good on him,' Katrina thought.

"Haven't seen you in ages!" Mike threw a brazen smile at her. His inviting grin unavoidably brought out the dimples on his cheeks and made his eyes sparkle with suggestive mischief. He paused, as if he was deliberating something.

"Where have you been all this time, Katrina?"

Katrina's heart fluttered. She blushed and stuttered. "Out, swimming, mostly."

"Swim, where?"

"In the lake, duh!"

"So, then it's you, who scares away my fish!"

"You won't catch anything anyway!"

"But maybe I'll catch you!" Mike's blue eyes turned a shade darker. There was an angry flicker in them. He grabbed her wrist. "Where were you on Wednesday?"

"At the Disco . . .,"

Katrina felt caught. She abruptly pulled away from Mike. Soon enough, because a pious church lady, Frau Bürkel, just walked by and winked at them.

"Only, you weren't there!" Katrina added a stab.

"Nonsense, of course I was! But it's not worth going there before 11 o'clock. Besides, we finished late with our home project. And . . . where did you all take off to so late?"

"What do you mean?"

"Well, I saw you all leave around midnight. Who were those fellas?"

"Luise's brother and his friend."

"Daniel?"

"Yes, you know him, too!" Katrina got increasingly irritated about the questioning.

"And where did you all go?"

"Oh, my God! To Luise's, of course!" And that was the half-truth anyway.

"Luise? So late at night?"

"Homework," Katrina heard herself lying. A cold shiver trickled down her back in remembrance of her nightly expedition cum memory gaps.

"Homework, alright? In the middle of the night?" He could not hide his sarcasm. "Do you have to work that hard at the chimpansium, ahem, Gymnasium?"

Katrina hated this mindless slander of high school, or as it was called, Gymnasium. Beni had invented this insult, after he had flunked the admissions exam the second time around, declaring that he didn't even want to attend a "chimpansium." Was Mike on to something?

"You don't believe it? We're doing an essay marathon."

"Essays? About what?"

"It's a long story and actually quite boring." To change the subject, she asked Mike, "Are you also going to the Volksfest[iii] tomorrow?"

"I'd rather not. Carnivals are not my thing, really. Besides, father needs my help again. We're not done tearing out the floor boards in the Stube."

"You will be missing out."

"I don't think so. I'd rather sit by the lake." He stroked Katrina with one of his sideways looks. "Want to come along some time?"

The church tower chimed twice for 1:30 pm. Katrina looked at Mike, speechless. She rejoiced internally but was not able to utter a word. She missed her opportunity.

"Good Lord, I have to go back to work," Mike sputtered, without waiting for Katrina's answer. "Hop on! I will give you a ride home."

Katrina mounted the backseat of his bike. The thought alone of snuggling up against Mike made her heart stop. Closeness was hard to come by with someone who rarely made appearances. One such memorable "date" occurred during the Krampus[iv] run a couple of years ago. Together with other fearsome horned (or horny) devils—masked and fur-clad village boys—Mike had invaded the Weber house. Already plenty loaded with schnapps, Mike had mustered the courage to make Katrina sit on his lap for ten minutes. Yet, he hadn't reckoned with Katrina's prankster father, Girgl, who liked to meddle with young people's business. When Mike didn't pay attention for a minute, Girgl dropped a dead chicken in Mikes plunder sack. This incident turned out to be a most treasured Christmas story in the family. Katrina also had the warmest memories of this crazy "Klöpfelnacht"[v] or knocking night. Now the same Krampus sat right in front of her. She grabbed on to Mike's shoulders.

"No, not like this. Here, put your arms around here."

Mike pulled her hand off his shoulder and placed it around his middle. Katrina understood. She wrapped her arms around his upper body. Katrina felt Mike's strong, warm muscles flex under his shirt. He got the bike rolling and increased speed after balancing his load. 'I will never ever let you go again,' Katrina prayed. She wished that the next 30 seconds stretched into eternity. But this eternity was, again, damn short.

As they approached the curve before the house, Katrina spotted her grandfather walking to the creek with a scythe.

Grandfather looked back at them. Did he even nod at them? Mike, the young Gabelsberger, had his approval. Yes, Mike came from a good Catholic family that knew the country way of life. Carpentry was a decent trade, unlike these useless studies and wicked writings that Katrina had fallen victim to. The young Gabelsberger obviously could put himself to work. And the Weber farm would eventually need a suitable man. There were only two girls to take this inheritance.

'In the end you simply can't write the manure away. You've got to load it with a fork and spread it with a tractor.'

Mike dropped Katrina off by the front door. "Have fun at the Volksfest!" He didn't mention any more fishing at the lake.

Katrina smoothed down her unruly hair. There was barely time to wave good-bye.

Grandfather set out to cut the creek-side grass, a job that he was definitely cut out for. Only a sharp scythe could do the mowing on the steep inclines. He often harvested the admiration of passersby for his expertise. His sinewy arms let the blade glide through the vegetation on the bank. Row by row, the blade whooshed bushels of grass to their demise. He kept an eye on flowers, such as the yellow sword lilies, and spared them, although this early in the year they still only looked like grass. His arms mechanically swung in front of him. He thought about the master cutter, the bony angel. 'One day we all will fall like blades of grass to the final cut.'

> Wir sind nur Gast auf Erden . . . we are only guests on earth . . . but we are not alone in this place . . . until we meet again in the other world our forgone loved ones are always amongst us, near us, beside us, in us

That's not quite how the song went, but he had seen so many people move on, his parents, several soldier comrades, his wife Kathl, and worst of all, his young grandson Martl. The grim reaper had snapped up all of them and left scars behind in the living.

Kathl? How could he explain to anyone that in the night of her departure she stood beside his bed and wished him good-bye. 'Jakob,' her spirit said, 'it is time for me to go. It will be all right, I hope. Take well care of Martl. Godspeed, pfiati!' And then the bright light around her figure faded and he realized she had fallen asleep forever in her bed. Unfortunately, he had failed miserably in fulfilling Kathl's request. Back then, when they were renovating the stables fifteen years ago, Martl perished in the most peculiar way. It had nothing to do with the dangers of a construction site or a working farm. Or did it? What did it matter in retrospect? The slightest negligence, a minuscule diversion, but the consequences were vast. A life beyond recall.

The old man took a deep breath.

Wir sind nur Gast auf Erden.

'Why am I so dizzy? The mowing never bothered me, but maybe it's too hot today.' And he wiped his brow and neck with his handkerchief. The straw hat was not much help either. In the old days they had to mow everything, hay, grommet, straw, by hand. Fortunately, mowing still came easy to him. With iron rhythm, the old man swung the scythe. Slowly his dark thoughts dissipated. He saw the flower carpet sink down before him and reminisced about the cornfields from the olden days. With each swing, his arms seemed to stretch out longer, and his beard had suddenly reached his waistband. His shirtsleeves dropped and expanded. 'Whoa there! What's happening now? Why are these sleeves so white, like scratchy old linen?' And the scythe morphed into a sickle in grandfather's hands. Or were they his?

He sank on his knees, to be closer to the grass. To bite it? Germans bite the grass instead the dust . . .

> Life is but a dream, just a small step from eternity. And many a one sends his regards from there. Just listen with your heart carefully . . .

"Weber dad!" The voice penetrated his eternal bliss. "Weber, what happened to you!" Someone conjured the old man back to reality from above.

"Wait! Let me help you!" Several suns blinded the old man's eyes. Then something wet and cold covered them. Mike had laid the wetted snuff kerchief on his forehead.

"Slow, slow, Weber! Just stay down a while!" Mike's motorbike lay on the embankment.

The old man wiped a dazed smile from his face. He tried to push himself up on his elbows, but did not quite succeed. The young helper was baffled by the old man's beaming smile. Apparently, the old farmer was not aware of the seriousness of the situation. He could have easily fallen into the blade of the scythe, or into the creek and he could have drowned. Mike grabbed the old man under the shoulders to prop him up. Slowly, the old man straightened up on wobbly legs. Mike grabbed the old man's hat and handed it to him.

"It's way too hot for this today," Mike said. "Leave the mowing alone, go home and rest for a while. Can you make it all right? I have to run back to work. I am already late."

'But I was just lying down so comfortably,' the old man protested in his mind.

"Did you say something?" But Mike didn't get an answer.

The old man put the scythe on his shoulder, nodded a good-bye to his savior, and slowly shuffled back to the house.

5

The Good Old Days

These were hard times. Day after day we threshed the corn with the wooden cudgel. At half of four we were up in the barn on most mornings. Our father was very strict: When he made the first stroke, we all had to be there. Then the threshing proceeded in its rhythm, four or five workers in unison, until the bells rang for morning mass, which we attended every day.

—*Elisabeth Melf (née Berger), Harte Adventwochen (Hard Advent Weeks), memoir*

Friday, June 14th, late afternoon

Katrina shivered to the bone. Her mother had made her cold compresses and hot tea, but her teeth still chattered. Half asleep, Katrina barely noticed that Walli repeatedly snuck into her room. She was too groggy to acknowledge her. Very late, when the sinking sun already stuck its rays through the small porthole windows in the attic room, the fever let off. Katrina stared at the ceiling. She felt weak but at the same time incredibly relieved.

She stretched. The last bit of tension abated. She wrapped the fluffy down comforter tighter around her body.

Marianne came to check on her. "Would you like more tea, or perhaps some zwieback?" A flu or cold hardly slowed her daughter down. Marianne was surprised that Katrina had stayed in bed all afternoon. 'Hopefully, it's nothing serious,' she thought. For some strange reason, her eldest followed mother's orders today.

"But can you bring me a fruit tea, please? Not this nettle and chamomile stuff?"

"That has the best medicine. It's an old home remedy. Revives even the dead."

"But it sure tastes like pee."

"What! Did you just call it piss-tea? You just don't know what's good for you!"

Marianne touched her daughter's forehead. She nodded and gave a satisfied smile. "Much better! The fever is gone. Didn't I tell you that this old medicine works miracles." She picked up the empty cup and headed downstairs.

Katrina started nibbling on the cookies that her mother had brought her. Despite her burning eyes she was too tired to sleep. The bookshelf was now bathed in golden sunlight. There it was, the notebook! A corner stuck out at the top row. How long ago yesterday seemed! Katrina picked it up and smelled it. 'How musty.' She lay down again and started leafing through the pages. Fascinated, she traced the edgy but orderly cursive letters of the old-German script. Letter by letter, line by line, she deciphered the diary entries ever faster. Katrina melted into the thoughts of a different world. Hardship, poverty, piety spoke out of every word of the carefully drafted curlicues. The life of a long-gone time revealed itself. She found out that the "good old days" weren't so good after all.

Nothing had been easy in that person's everyday life. There was little food—mostly schmalznoodles with potato soup or kraut, turnip salad, bread crusts, twice-cooked stew with tough chunks of a laying hen, or pig innards on butchering day—a feast. Work was plenty. The writer reported about hay harvests, manure spreading, and wood chopping. Four girls around Katrina's age were doing all kinds of heavy chores— until two of them, first Sophie, then Moni, entered a cloister. Marie started up a small grocery store. That's how the youngest, Kathl, got stuck with the farm. She confided her thoughts, sorrows, and all kinds of noteworthy events to these pages. For example, one entry reported the last and most infamous *Haberfeldtreiben,* a people's court or mock trial, also called "chivaree," which went terribly wrong. The people's court went after a poor farm wife, accusing her of having born an illegitimate child, a retard, fathered by the Monsignore. The mock court, all disguised with hoods or oven soot, made cat music, broke the windows, chased away the goats, and torched the shed, before the local police dispersed the mob. In the aftermath, the woman's husband died from shame. He cut off his head with the lumber saw. And who was to blame?

Katrina forgot to breathe. What? A certain Moar Gustl had led this chivaree? Were the Moars all shenanigans? Was that instigator perhaps Beni's great-grand-uncle? Not much seemed to have changed since then. Katrina was hooked. She could not put the notebook down.

September 8, 1910

Today, when I went to fetch a pint of beer from the inn for Pastor Magerl, the window to the kitchen was open. In passing by I heard the reverend talk to his housekeeper. "What a son-of-a-bitch," he said. I was so shocked about his words that I quickly ducked down below the window. I almost spilled all the beer. It got much worse. "Can you imagine, when I was about to give him his last rites, the old Waldleitner confessed to me that he actually hadn't donated the wayside cross in gratitude for his safe return from the 70ies war, but only for the gendarmes not catching him. Imagine, this bastard—Oh, Lord please forgive me my foul language—whacked a Jew! He had great debts with this shyster, this old scoundrel," so I heard the pastor say, but he still wished him a "Lord have mercy on his soul." But mercy doesn't come easy for murder, the pastor had taught us in Sunday school. "The blood guilt he will never be able to atone for," Pastor Magerl also said. But I could not believe that he took the Lord's name in vain. "May the Almighty absolve him from the eternal purgatory, the old whoremonger! He has a long list of sixth commandment sins too!" Such spoke the pastor! I didn't know what to do. I just left the beer mugs on the garden table and rushed home. I hope they found the beer. And a "may he rest in peace" was the last thing I heard.

Waldleitner. The name rang familiar in Katrina's ears, but she could not quite place it. As she continued reading, Katrina realized that bad ghosts and spirits were feared even more than sin. Apparently, a phantom white horse was to blame for the fact that old Aunt Nanni remained a spinster.

September 15, 1910

Nanni's Loisl saw a ghost and went crazy, mother told us today. On his way home to Mittenwald from a rafting tour, he saw the white horse up by St. George's Hill in the middle of the night. That scared him something awful. And when he heard the witch's scream, he fully lost his marbles. From then on, he had trouble steering his heavy float of timber. He feared the bad witch would catch him soon. And so she did. He told his story to Nanni on a Sunday. On Monday, the raft squished him against the pillar of a bridge. He was dead. And that's why Aunt Nanni never got to marry.

So many sad stories. One day, a certain maid of the house, known as Roserl, had to seek an "angel maker." Angels are something beautiful, Kathl thought until her sister Marie at the grocery store explained to her how these angels were made. That night Kathl could not get a wink of sleep and rattled off one "Our Ladies Length" after another. That was a prayer on a paper as long as the Holy Mother tall. Frau Bürkel had once shown them such an old-fashioned prayer roll. That Hungarian woman knew the strangest customs. The good old days, with all its piety, was not a place for children, much less for the illegitimate ones. Indentured servants could neither afford the disgrace of a child born out of wedlock nor the food to feed them. And marriage was out of the question for have-nots. Women had no choice but to submit to service, however questionable in nature. That's where old Frau Bürkel shut her mouth about the details of the story at the children's Communion preparation class. Unplanned pregnancies were unthinkable but they happened nonetheless. For many farm people, the "good old days" offered only anxiety filled dreams and existential turmoil. And, apparently, back then, people had strange dreams too.

November 11, 1910

One time I dreamed of grandmother. She was surrounded by angels and smiled down on me through a cloud-covered opening in the parlor ceiling. Then she turned very serious and ordered me to paint a memorial for a little boy. He was totally white and stiff. "A marterl for Marterl,"[vi] she said and smiled with great melancholy. At that point I jolted up from sleep. The painting just got finished. I painted St. George with his dragon and Our Mother of Sorrows on it, but I am not sure what it is supposed to mean . . .

"Finally, you are awake!" Walli had opened the door, unnoticed by Katrina. "What are you reading there?"

"Nothing." Katrina, busted from another world, quickly stuck the notebook under her bed cover.

"Since when do you hide secrets from me?" Walli sat down at the bedside. "But I know everything anyway. I saw you getting a ride home from Mike today. How was it?"

"Aren't you nosy!"

"Why? Believe me, I know what it's like to be in love."

That statement coming from her younger sister sounded so comical, Katrina had to laugh. In her baby-doll nightie, Walli looked pretty impish. Basically, she was too old for it and had outgrown that silly outfit a while ago. With her freckled face framed up by braids, she could have modeled for a Hummel figurine. Although she obviously wasn't as well behaved.

"Oh, grow out of it! A teacher crush! That doesn't even compare."

"You never take me seriously! Nobody around here does!" Walli moved to get up from the bedside. Katrina pulled her back.

"Hey, what are you doing?" Walli tried to free herself from the tight grip. "You are hurting me!"

"Come on, Walli! Don't be mad!"

"Let go! Stop making fun of me!"

"OK. Relax. I will tell you a secret, but only if you promise to keep your mouth shut."

"I swear! By St. Michael, St. Raphael and all fourteen archangels . . ." Walli was all ears.

"All right then!" Katrina paused for emphasis. She almost whispered. "Mike wants to take me fishing . . ."

"Can't he do better than that? Hasn't he ever heard of movie theaters?"

"Oh, come on, Walli! What do you know! At the lake it's much more romantic in the evening. He and I, hunker down, side by side, splashing our feet, and talk . . ."

". . . and kiss."

"Walli! Stupid! You have no idea!"

"I guess not. But your lake date sounds really boring to me! Whatever, I don't care. I hope he will he take the bait?"

"Bait? Who?"

"Mike."

"Walli, you are impossible!"

"Fine, then you just go fishing with him. Or fishing in the dark, what do I care. And when will that be?"

"Soon . . . "

"You don't even know it yet? Or you have to wait until his cows come home. Sounds like a real bore to me!"

"Walli! You are such a tadpole! And why do you grill me for hours?" She took a swipe at her sister with the pillow. "Get out!" Walli jumped out of harm's way and dashed off, giggling.

Katrina sank back into her pillows and closed her eyes. She pulled out the notebook again, switched on the night light, and slowly continued to read. She had gotten much better used to the old-fashioned handwriting.

Time and again there were stories about St. George's chapel, especially the horse part of it. The pastor once had condemned the Easter Monday horse parades around the small chapel as heathenish. Almost every year something bad happened, like a horse broke a leg, or the altar boy was hit in the head by a hoof, the bandwagon rolled backwards into the crowd, the speaker's podium collapsed, any calamity was to be expected. The notebook reported as well the most frightening adventures happening at St. George's on the Hill. Fascinated, Katrina turned each page.

June 16, 1911

Moni and I climbed out the living room window and walked up to the chapel yesterday. The night was quite bright because it was a full moon. We were a little scared, but very curious. We wanted to know if the white stallion would show himself up there. We brought with us a long stick and a rosary from the most holy black Madonna of Altötting, to be on the safe side. It was so wonderfully romantic up there on top of the hill that we must have sat there in the grass for about an hour. Suddenly a cloud covered up the moon and a cold wind swept by. There was a terrible bang. Terrified, we jumped up and ran off without the stick. Moni unfortunately forgot her shoes up there. So she had to run back again before milking time, and brought them back. If father had caught us, he would have whipped us. Sneaking out in the night, what were we thinking? And losing shoes? Even worse. I have learned my lesson. I won't ever go up on that hill again in the night, for as long as I live.

Katrina's heart fell into a racing gallop. The wild pumping in her chest took away her breath. She put the notebook down. Her nightmare stood fully before her eyes. Maybe something was bewitched on that hill? It took a while until she was able to focus on reading again. These notes were more thrilling than a *Tatort* krimi[vii]. Too bad that they contained nothing about the Germanic tribes, which she could have used for her essay.

The notebook author apparently was a good student. And if she had been a boy, she would have been sent to the seminary. She also loved to paint pious pictures and flowers, for which her mother apparently had no sense at all. Her sister Sophie, however, who had already received her eternal profess as religious sister in the Holy Spirit Cloister, always sent her the prettiest devotional images from their print shop. So, she would copy off these saints when all the work was done and mother wasn't watching. Along the way, this young woman also took an interest in witches and forest spirits. One time she reported about a spooky location, called the Witches Mound. Coals from a witch burning were said to be found there. And yet, on Our Lady's Ascension Day, August 15, the most vibrant flowers and herbs blossomed on that mound.

Another time, the budding pious artist experienced another curious incident at White Horse Chapel, as she had gone to paint a portrait of St. George above the altar.

September 15, 1911

How St. George pleases me so much! In the afternoon, as the sun went down, the noble knight on his white horse looked almost glorified. I had lost all my fear of the ghastly dragon. Bless St. George for delivering us from that monster. And what a stately man! If I had to marry, then I would look for a bridegroom like St. George. But then something really stupid happened. I left the key stuck in the door outside and the wind banged it shut. I could not get out, and it got slowly dark. The custodian obviously wondered and came looking for me, because I had not returned the key. He let me out and joked, "Did you want to starve to death in here like the poor white stallion did?"

"Do you want another cup of tea?"

Befuddled, Katrina raised her eyes. She had not heard her mother coming. Marianne usually had a firm step, at times a stomp, which carried a wave of brash energy ahead of her, but on rare occasions she seemed to be able to levitate. Or appear in multiple locations simultaneously. It must have been quite late because Marianne was already wearing her nightgown under the dress apron. Katrina inconspicuously put the notebook aside.

"You better get some sleep now!" Marianne dished out orders without waiting for an answer. "You read too much! No wonder that you can't look straight anymore."

Then something caught her attention in Katrina's wardrobe. She mechanically started organizing the blouses and hangers. 'These girls will never learn to keep order.' Marianne didn't give a farthing for bookish wisdom. She was the practical kind. Reading? 'If you read too much, that could be a problem, because nosy people die young,' she liked to remind her daughters when they were looking for an excuse for doing chores.

"No, I don't want any more tea."

"What did you say?" Marianne stopped fiddling with the hangers. "Oh, well then! Go to sleep now. Will you!" She turned on her heel and quietly closed the door behind her.

Katrina again grabbed the old diary. This life history jumped ahead by three years. The war had started, and reality became just another nightmare. "They mobilized, these idiots," the notebook author wrote. And apparently another Moar Gustl was part of the charade when the young men marched with their hunting rifles in hand to a pep rally at the village tavern, all to the defense of the murdered Hungaro-Austrian crown prince in Sarajevo. And, sure enough, there were fears galloping through many dreams.

November 30, 1914

I dreamt that now even women have to go to war. One of them put on a knight's armor and mounted a horse. A wild white stallion, but she controlled him well with her reins. She carried along a red waving banner with a dragon on it, approached me in full gallop, stopped short in front of me and said: "We women folk must correct history." I didn't understand that at all. First she pointed to the banner, then her lance at me. It looked like the tip of an ink pen. "Only you can help me," the warrior woman said. "You already know me, I am . . ."

Here a page had been torn out of the notebook.

The entries became sparse and fewer in between, as the booklet approached its end. The author apparently had too much work and no more time for writing. Only in times of great distress, the young writer either sought consolation in morning mass or confided her dreams and sorrows to the diary.

December 21, 1917

I had another strange dream. Up there on the hill by the chapel, a giant, garish claws worm came after me. I would have liked to run away, but my feet were like glued to the ground. Then suddenly a slew of burning wagon wheels rolled down the hill. I heard someone shout, "a whirlie for the girlie, a whirlie for the girlie." I quickly grabbed a burning wheel and flung it into the dragon's mouth, which was wide ajar. It got stuck in his throat, and he got devilishly mad. Instantly I took my sword and cut off the behemoth's ugly head, his stinking blood spilled everywhere. If I could only stuff the war dragon's mouth like that.

Katrina's mouth stood open. The fog-shrouded night before Corpus Christi came alive again in front of her eyes. Her vision of another dragon had been so similar. Now she felt even sicker. But this one was the last dream in the diary. Reality increasingly took over.

December 26, 1917

Today Weber Jakob asked father for my hand in marriage. Jakob was furloughed. He just had been assigned to the cavalry to go to Belgium, the trenches. Nonetheless he told father that our farm was almost too small for him. Since the war had started, we had no more horses, only two oxen. Jakob kept talking father's head off about the cavalry and his tough comrades there. I almost couldn't listen to him any longer. I told father that I was not in a great rush with this marriage arrangement. "But maybe I am," father only said.

One week later, Kathl's father passed away peacefully in an armchair with the pipe in his mouth. Without him, the farm work had become an insurmountable challenge. Plowing, manure spreading, and milking—the daily chores just got too much. Cynicism crept into the diary. "Horse expire, great quagmire, woman's demise, no one cries[viii]" the author had quoted a popular saying with great cynicism as she labored to spread the manure in the fields with her "stupid ass oxen." The horses had gone to war several years ago, never to be seen again. *Man*power was lacking all over the place. Many men had perished in the war, others were missing in action, and the returning soldiers had lost a limb or an eye and had become useless for hard farm work. Finally, the war was over.

December 5, 1919

Today Weber Jakob came home from captivity in France. He has spent much time in the field hospital and has stopped laughing and telling saucy jokes. But he still wants to marry me. I should be happy that anyone is left at all for me to marry. Well, then, one of us maidens has to pay the price. Or what should become of the farm?

December 21, 1919

If it's true that what you dream during St. Thomas' Night[ix] becomes reality, then I don't want to know anything else about this future that I saw. Another war had started. Mountains of corpses, gruesome to look at, all had a number on their arms. But they had not fallen in action, because none of them was wounded. Before long, flaming wheels rolled over these corpses and set them on fire. The brass band played a tune to it. The sky was yellow, the sun a foggy lilac, and the trees resembled dried up birch brooms. It simultaneously rained and hailed, until a reservoir dam broke. The gray water carried the mountains of corpses away. Only the tallest trees and some church steeples still poked out of the seawater. But a few hapless creatures still survived. They crawled along like maggots in striped suits on all fours, most dreadful to look at.

Something snapped inside Katrina. She ran over to the hen house and brought the typewriter up to her room. She started plucking away at it with a previously unknown madness. Her cacophonic typewriter clinking reverberated through the wood timbered ceiling.

Two floors down, at the kitchen table, her father, Girgl, tried to concentrate on his crossword puzzle in the paper. Without much success, because the clattering noise distracted him too much.

"Has that girl gone completely crazy!" Girgl fumed. Angrily, he turned another page in his newspaper. He had exhausted his knowledge of crossword puzzling.

"I am at a loss myself," Marianne said. "I have already knocked at her door three times, but she doesn't hear me. Why don't you go up there and get some sense into her!"

"The heck I will! That cackling will stop sooner or later."

"She's not cackling, she is writing," Walli corrected her father.

"Walli! Don't you sass your father!" One stern look of Marianne's shut Walli up. "Poor Katrina, with that much fever she should lie down and rest. But she never listens."

"Let her find out for herself, let her be miserable then tomorrow," Girgl muttered.

Having said that, he raised his eyes from the paper straight at Walli and stared at her over the rim of his reading glasses. "And you, young lady! Go to bed! Now!"

Walli instantly followed suit and wished her parents a good night.

"We never should have let her go to high school." Girgl returned to the crossword puzzle with a furrowed brow. He still had many gaps to fill in those little squares.

Grandfather already lay in bed. He always went to bed early because of the aches and pains. As always, he could not sleep this night either. He listened to the main reason for his wakefulness, the incessant clanking of Katrina's typewriter, her banging on the keys of the old Adler machine. Clank, clank, clank-edy-clank, ding, brrrh, stop, clank, clank, clang, and so on. It sounded as if a bunch of chickens were jabbing away at a metal lid, like one of those that came with their chicken feed. Or like the hammer hitting the scythe when he was peening. Or like the merciless dripping of drops of water on the forehead of a prisoner under torture. Or like the panic concert on the strings of grandfather's soul. The old man kept watch for the writer and hoped that she would not crash from the heights of her lofty ideas so that she might safely reach the terminal of her dreams.

And she wrote, "All similarities with persons still alive or already deceased are purely coincidental. Plot and characters are truly fictional. But somewhere, sometime, somehow in a small village in old Bavaria, some sixty, seventy years ago, stories such as these could have possibly happened."

Into the Rain

Blue and white were the national colors of the old Boiers, just like the Swabians had distinguished themselves with yellow, the Francs with red, the Saxons with black, and the old Cimbrians with white. The Celts, however, are said to have taken this game a step further: Their enthusiasm for the diamond pattern in their coat of arms was so imprinted upon their collective consciousness that they even plowed their fields crosswise in diagonal lines until they achieved a rhombus design.

—Hans Nöhbauer, *Die Kelten in Bayern,* 100

Saturday, June 15

One tribe of Teutonic origin, called the Boiers, raided the northern parts of our land. The Boiers were an irascible and gluttonous people, but hardly calculating. They loved pomp and splendor, followed a lavish lifestyle, and sought their wisdom in binges. They drowned out their inner voice, which should have served their great gods. The Boiers were individualists, each man a small ruler for himself. They cherished their elaborate celebrations, bred magnificent horses, and in drunken stupor smashed their beer mugs against each other's heads. They didn't give a damn about the rules and regulations of the Roman occupiers. At times, their knack for sentimental things deceived them into believing that they had mastered the art of courtship. They thought voracity counted as a form of seduction.

What great drinking binges they sometimes orchestrated! Many a woman was raped accidentally, in drunkenness. And the burly warrior dragged himself home to his wife after the act, like a beat-up dog. The overlord would have chopped off such a fella's head, but the wives always forgave. The Boiers' religious services were marvelous. One village outcompeted the other with splendor, because their gods were just as glamorous as the people on earth.

During that time, the dragon had become restless again. One sacrifice a year did not satisfy him anymore. He was lusting for blood like a mangy dog. On one rampage he killed a whole herd of sheep. All life was in danger, sheep, cattle, humans, what have you. One day, he poisoned the spring water for the whole township with his stinking breath. The Boiers had no other place to go, since they had taken up roots. So, they tried many ways to pacify the dragon. Horse sacrifice was useless, because who still believed in Celtic gods? Exorcism held no power over a legendary creature that had not heard about Christianity yet. In the end, the question remained, did the dragon even exist or had wolves done this bloody work?

At any rate, the beautiful virgin, who was chosen to be sacrificed on the druids' mound in the fall, resurfaced at the spring carnival. She was dancing naked to the drum beats on a tightrope, exposed to the lusting eyeballs of a hundred horny men. A Siegfried[x] was desperately needed . . .

". . . but unfortunately Siegfried is only a legend too." Luise's verdict about Katrina's most recent concoctions had come down fast yesterday. "How can your fables get any worse?"

Katrina couldn't help but grudgingly agree. On this dreary Saturday morning, she sat brooding over another historical misadventure. Luise could be so outspokenly cruel and direct, but she was almost always to the point. Instead of factually researching "A Day in the Life of an Old Teuton," Katrina had let her imagination fly again. She was totally drained, since she finished her story for the paper. She barely remembered what she had cobbled together in a flurry. Walli was going to drop off the pages just on deadline at the newspaper office this afternoon when their parents went shopping in 'Wolfstown.' That pressure had let off, but the marathon still loomed. For now, she was out of ideas.

Luise had promised help. Although Luise's writing talent was in no way exemplary, and even though she obviously took too many short cuts regarding her self-declared 'minimalistic expressionism,' she still scored enough points to pass. Katrina was a few notches smarter than Luise, more ambitious, studious, and conscientious, but her innate peasant rigidity could make her trip over her own smarts. Yet Luise had one keen edge on Katrina: with her unabashed sense for truth and unfettered criticism, she was able to set Katrina right.

Gray and very low the clouds hovered over the village rooftops. The spire of the church steeple faded into the dirt-colored tufts of dense cotton mass, which billowed and swathed, once thick, once thin, stewed up by a light breeze, letting themselves be torn into continuously transforming shreds. It was a rainy afternoon, not untypical for June.

"Oh shit," Katrina grumbled. She stuck her papers under her sweater and poked her head out the door. Her nose crinkled as if she had to sniff the wet air first.

"Get your anorak! It's raining," her mother yelled from the kitchen.

"No, it's not far at all," Katrina shouted back and took a large jump into the pouring rain. She skipped over the puddles, zigzagged until she reached the main street, where she fell into a fast trot to reach the third farmhouse behind the grocery store. Even though it looked its part, that house was not a farm any more. The former stables and hay barn had been converted into an atelier and foundry, and the strangest people walked in and out there.

Katrina had underestimated the rain. She got a good soaking. Her hair and shoulders were dripping wet, and her open sandals squeaked at every step. She slipped back and forth in her shoes. Her toes were getting cold. What a relief when Luise opened the door.

"You are as wet as a dog. Come, sit down here by the heater. Don't you have umbrellas at home?"

Luise was wearing black gym pants, an oversize glitter shirt, and her trademark Indian leather sandals, "Jesus-Slippers," which had a separate loop for the big toe. She pulled a box with rainbow-colored beads closer to her and, sitting on the bench, continued stringing a bead necklace. Katrina pulled her sweater off and hung it over the radiator. Then she removed her footwear, hopped on the windowsill, and put her feet against the toasty radiator below.

"So what! It's just a little rain," Katrina joked. Here in the Stube[xi] with its tiled stove, corner bench, and the deep window bays, everything looked like a living part of history, a backdrop to a movie, which made Katrina feel at home, an island of nostalgic reprise. Quite in contrast, her mother, for practical reasons, would not have been half as excited about the recycled antique objects, such as earthenware pitchers, coal-powered pressing irons, tin cups and plates, and those boxy old coffee grinders. Some of the coffee cans on the shelves had lost a spout or handle. Amongst other old cooking implements and tools, a spinning wheel stood by the corner of the ceramic tiled oven. Old junk. All the rooms downstairs came across as grandmotherly. And when Katrina sucked in the rustic scent through her nose, very slowly, she could discern the aromas of wood-burning smoke, schmalznoodles, and floor polish. 'My nose does not leave much to the imagination,' Katrina thought. Her acute sense of smell caused her pain at times but always delivered reliable information.

Maybe she could even smell words. There it was again, the whisper.

Eternity is not far away. In eternity we are all connected and all equal . . .

Katrina turned to Luise. "Did you just say something?"

"Yeah, are you hard of hearing? Where were you yesterday afternoon?"

. . . heaven on earth lies beside us only a hand's breadth apart . . .

Again. But Luise could not have said that.

"Hello, Katrina! I am talking to you! Anybody home up there?" And Luise tapped her on the forehead.

". . . what? Oh, well, that. Sorry, I thought I had heard something. What was yesterday, yes, right, I was sick, in bed,"

Katrina mumbled as if talking with herself. "Imagine, I also wrote something for the newspaper."

"How come? When you were sick? And what paper?"

"Our local paper . . ."

"What, don't tell me! You are doing the story competition? I thought you've had enough of local history?"

"So, I changed my mind."

"Why?"

"I had an idea."

"I thought you were out of ideas."

"Even a blind chick sometimes finds a corn."

"So? What's it about then?"

"Don't be so nosy!" Katrina hardly ever rebuffed Luise.

"But you always want me to read it first."

"Too late, Walli dropped it off at the newspaper already. But why don't you help me with my Teutons here." She stuck the wet and tattered pages under Luise's nose.

"Oh, my God! Haven't I already seen enough of these!" Luise sighed dramatically. She pinched a tiny corner of the wet pages in playful disgust.

Katrina laughed at her comical face. "True, I can barely decipher them myself. But listen!" She began to read in her best voice.

Like us Celts, the invading Teutons believed that for every man or woman a soul lives in a tree, and when this tree dies, then also the human's time is up. But they never knew which one was their soul tree. When a sapling didn't thrive, their headman blamed it for a person's death. Contrary to that, we Celtic people always knew which tree was ours. Every tree had its own healing powers.

The Teutons did not dare cut a tree, lest someone might

die, yet slaughtered many horses for their highest god, Wotan. As soon as the Romans had moved on, the Teutons built their own bloody altars. All small animals fled the hill and no more flowers grew on the sullied grounds. The Teutons could not bend the will of nature, so they tried to bend the will of man. The patriarch ruled over all things, even the marriage matches for their strictly celibate youth. As if! The curbed forces of nature sought a different outlet in wild honey beer orgies. The Boiers, a tribe of the Teutons, were fearless fighters, even the women . . ."

"Wait, stop right here!" Luise interrupted. "Where did you get this from?"

"Must have read it somewhere."

"Where?"

"Don't remember."

"No good. We both know, Schiller won't buy that! Do you have sources?"

"But you always liked my stories!"

"What does it matter if I like your stories? I don't give the grades. When will you understand, this has got nothing to do with either imagination or intelligence. Just give that pauker what he wants."

"Grrh, I guess you are right. But what's to write about people who have been dead for so long?"

"The thing with the trees and the souls in them came out quite nicely, good point. Where did you get that from?"

"Someone told me about it. But . . ."

". . . you don't know."

Katrina was at a loss. This wasn't working out. She still didn't have anything for Monday. She let her eyes wander across the endless water trails on the rain-blurred windowpanes.

It was like tears were streaming down the glass. It was such a terribly gray day. Katrina was tired and confused.

"The bear claw looks good on you," Luise suddenly complimented her.

"Hasn't helped much so far."

Luise put her beads project aside and rolled herself a cigarette. Katrina watched her pensively. Then a thought struck her. "Do you know why Pauli started cursing the other day when we were up by the chapel?"

"What do you mean?" Luise lit up.

"Well, remember, he said 'Were these bastards here again' or something like that. What was he talking about?"

Luise took a deep drag and blew out the smoke as she was apparently staring out the window. Raindrops still hammered against the glass panes, creating a landscape of ever-changing rivulets that merged or crossed or collided with each other. Long streaks of water darted down the slick surface.

"I don't have a clue." Luise puffed the smoke to the side as to avoid getting it into her eyes. She coughed a little. "Maybe poachers?"

"Are you kidding me? Those days are gone."

"Couples in love?

"That's nothing to get so upset about."

"Well then I don't know either, really." Luise seemed irritated. "And it does not interest me one bit. Come, let's go upstairs to the planetarium. We have tons of books. Maybe we can find you a quote or two."

The girls walked through the dusky hall and skipped up the stairway. As they were passing through the upper floor, Katrina noticed activity behind one door.

"Is Daniel home today?" Katrina asked. "How come?"

"He does not have classes right now, at least that is what he claims," Luise said. "Nothing's ever sure with him."

The door to Daniel's room was slightly ajar. Katrina could not believe her eyes. Daniel was gawking at himself in a floor-length mirror as he pulled a silk stocking over his knee, high up to the garter belt. And he was wearing a corsage dress like the damsels in a Western movie.

"Am I going crazy?"

"Why?"

"Was that Daniel?"

"The costume?"

Katrina nodded.

"Oh, that! Brother dear is auditioning for a stage play, the Rocky Horror Show. It's the newest hit in Munich."

"I see."

Katrina pretended to be relieved. 'Those artists,' she caught herself thinking, mocking her grandfather's genuine disdain. Every time that the old man spotted Luise from afar, his eyebrows started twitching. Her 'artist pack' clearly did not belong to the 'people.' Real people were country-bred and pursued honest work, such as cobbler, baker, carpenter, or farmer. Consequently, artists weren't people.

In the planetarium, the remodeled attic, a telescope stood right beneath the skylight. In the open-roof structure a swing was suspended from the highest beam. All around the walls, bookshelves served as smart tapestries. In the middle of the room two juxtaposed desks were buried under loads of papers, magazines, and drawing utensils. Especially inviting was the sofa corner, a cozy cuddling cove. Souvenirs from all over the world decorated the room. A light fragrance from incense sticks still hovered in the air. Luise's chafed old portfolio lay on the drawing table.

"What did you draw there? Let me see!" Katrina reached for the portfolio, but Luise snapped it up brusquely.

"What's wrong with you?" Katrina muttered.

"Maybe next time I will show you. I really don't have anything but scribbles yet. But sit down and grab a book. Hopefully your genius idea will fly by soon."

"And what will you be doing?"

"Waiting for the fair."

"You still want to go in this rain? What about your essay?"

"Already taken care of."

Sometimes Luise could be incredibly fast—if she wanted to.

Katrina reached for one of the fattest books and cooked up another story.

Late afternoon

Grandfather sat on the front bench, the cold pipe dangling from the corner of his mouth. The fire had gone out, but that didn't bother him much. Tomcat Maxi rubbed against his stiff legs. At least one creature dared to come close to him. Grandfather was actually not such a terrible person, but who would know? His silence instilled fear. Since his return from the forest cabin, he had started going to church again. As he sat there observing, blue flashes of lightning occasionally darted from his eyes.

On his sunny spot on the front bench, it was now comfortably warm. And from this perch he could watch the people's activities.

The neighbor woman goes to the store again because she forgets the yeast for baking, and chats away with the pastor's housekeeper for half an hour. What a gossip lady, running to the store three times, forgetting what she needs to buy. They probably have to eat the kraut without the schmalznoodles. The boys are still splashing in the water up to their midriffs, damming up the ice-cold creek with wooden boards, until the water breaks through and the boards wash away together with the howling gaggle. Farmer Huber drives by again on his brand-new tractor with a wet load of hay. Does that simpleton not know that his barn will ignite with this rotten stuff? Old Frau Bürkel, with her Hungarian headscarf, is weeding the rows of paprika in her vegetable garden by the creek. Has she still not understood that paprikas don't grow so well in our soil? Potatoes, beets, and cabbage have to be planted here, not tomatoes and paprika. 'Scratching around like an old chicken,' the old man pondered. 'Yes, they all run around like chickens with their heads cut off.'

The old man tried to puff a smoke, but only aspirated a piece of tobacco. He blew a raspberry to spit it out again. No, really! 'Father forgive them for they don't know what they do,' a Bible verse entered his mind. He heard it not from the church, but the newfangled American movie with the same title[xii] not too long ago. And even though he had shielded himself with an umbrella against the television intrusion—always shooting, always shooting, especially in Bonanza—he felt occasionally tempted to peek around the parasol. The movie with James Dean had pleased him nevertheless. At least it wasn't a shoot-them-up Western. And, yes, most people don't know what they are doing.

Look. The weather could not have been any more splendid after such a prolonged episode of rain. The low standing sun painted the houses along the village creek a glorious sheen. The colors were freshly renewed. Deepest blue ruled the all-clear sky. Only grandfather's head was still surrounded with thunderclouds.

'Has Katrina run off with that red-haired fox again?'

How can Girgl let his eldest daughter roam around like that? Does she not know anything? Asks me about the dragon under the roof. How could she not know? Kathl, I know you mean well for her. Watch out for her! Wherever she goes.

'I hope they didn't go to the Volksfest.'

Worried over many newfangled things, the old man decided to stay awake until Katrina came back home.

7

Volksfest

Mit 17 hat man noch Träume,
da wachsen noch alle Bäume
in den Himmel der Liebe

At 17 one still has dreams
and all trees still grow
into the sky of love

—Peggy March, Mit 17 hat man noch Träume,
top charts, 1965

Late afternoon

Volksfest was a roaring mess. Auto scooter, boat swing, shooting booth, fortune tellers, and all kinds of entertainment had set up shop on the gravel grounds. The stew of aromas from cotton candy, bratwurst, beer, and roasted almonds would soon be interlaced with the odors of perspiration, beer belches, urine, and vomit. But it was yet too early for the big stench. The very low standing sun now laid triple-length shadows on the terrain.

Some traditional Lederhosen lads were already rubbing against Hells Angels biker guys. One as well as the other puffed up their chests and sucked in their stomachs. Somebody was always itching for a fight.

It wasn't so much fun after all.

"Hello, there, pretty broads, want to hook up?" Three dudes with pimples and barely sprouting beards, yelled obscenities after Katrina and Luise.

"Stupid asses, still wet behind their ears," Luise hissed. "Is it just me, or are people nuts here?"

A wanna-be Lederhosen man with a garish knock-off pant stumbled, beer mug in hand, out of the "Bayernkurve" ride. His companion lady in heels and pop-color dirndl dress staggered hysterically laughing behind him, shrieking, "That thing turns like fuddle-duddle!" Next, the bald man folded like a pocketknife over the steel bannister of the roller coaster and barfed up the entire evening menu. Finally, he straightened himself up, boasting a popular saying, "The good ones will survive, but good riddance to the losers." Katrina had heard it plenty times before, when her father drove her to fork away the hay faster.

"That's right, honey," the dirndl on heels piped. "Let me give you a kiss." And she planted her lips smack dab on his pukey mouth.

"Careful, don't spill my beer. It would be a pity!" The man swayed a moment, found his balance, and took another large gulp.

So drunk. Katrina shuddered in memory of her own recent booze night. At least it had already been dark then, because such a disaster in broad daylight was embarrassing.

"Makes me feel sick. Let's go home now, Luise."

"What do you expect? At the Volksfest everyone gets to play the big cheese. Or do you think those dudes had real motorbikes?"

"Bike, no. Tractor, for sure."

They burst out laughing at this reference to a comical pop song, titled "Resi, I'll pick you up with my tractor."

"What is so funny here?" That voice from behind sounded curiously familiar. "Let us through, ladies! We're in a hurry!" Daniel and Raffi.

"That will cost you," Luise countered.

The two tall guys just laughed and tossed their manes. Their types even stood out at a crowded carnival.

"And what's your charge?" Raffi grinned.

"A dragon's ride," Luise retorted.

Raffi and Daniel looked at each other, puzzled. A bulb went off in Daniel. "Did you mean the ghost train, sister dear?" He grinned. "Sure, that will teach you the shivers."

"Let's do it!" Raffi joked. "Where did they hide that ugly thing?"

"You have no clue! Come on, I'll show you!"

Daniel and Raffi, both in black leather pants, stood out from the crowd like a sore thumb. Daniel was wearing a golden earring, and Raffi a frilled vest. They were showing off Lederhosen of the motorcycle kind. Despite the late hours, Daniel was wearing his sunshades and rainbow-colored butterfly shirt. Compared to him, Raffi with his long flowing hair and the dangling frills, almost looked normal. Alongside these guys, a draft of fresh, worldly-wise air had wafted on site. Or was it a faint scent of aftershave mixed with "the fragrance of the wide world" called Marlboro? No birds of paradise could have looked any more exotic. But they sure made for interesting company.

When the four finally stood in front of the noisy ghost train, Katrina felt uneasy. Why had Luise dragged them right away to this terrible rattlebox? Katrina had never liked roller coasters, ever since she took her first ride in one as a child. Right on top, on the steepest part, it had felt as if her head was being torn off. For that reason, she had never felt ready to ride the Claws Worm[xiii] so far, regardless how hard Luise had twisted her arm. Even now, she still hoped to get off the hook.

"You are nuts, Lulu!" Katrina whispered. "Fat chance that I will go on that!"

"Nonsense, it's not even half as bad as you think. And it's free. They are paying for it. Come on, this will be great fun!"

"No, I'd rather not. I get motion sick."

"Did you forget, you owe me one?"

"Don't even remind me!"

"Exactly!"

"All right, then." Katrina grudgingly gave in. She would have rather expunged the recent wild ghost chase from her memory.

Loud howling and rumbling streamed from the Claws Worm roller coaster. The sun had sunk behind the trees. Now the green and red bulbs in the plastic skeletons and papier maché monsters glowed even more eerily. Since the exit from the ride was in the back, the train cars always rolled out empty in front. Nobody could be asked what it was like. Since riders had to buckle down with iron bars, Katrina suspected the worst. In the narrow coaches there was hardly enough room for two slick herrings, much the less two average adults.

"I will sit with Raffi," Luise decided.

Katrina glared at her. "Luise, I changed my mind. I won't go."

"Don't be afraid of ghosts, dear!" Raffi whispered in Katrina's ear.

"Too late to chicken out now." Daniel gently pushed Katrina by her shoulders toward the ghost ride car. "With me you are safe. Just hold on to me tight."

The passengers in line ahead already jostled for the seats. Sit down. Close the bar. Snap the lock. With a jerk, the cogwheel engine tuckered off. The train moved forward and knocked open the swing doors into the giant jaws of a sea monster. Suddenly there was a monumental darkness, like before the big bang, in which only the vestibulocochlear nerve could make you guess that the train was clattering steeply upward. The bottom was out, vertigo crept up through the deafening ghost noise and screeching.

Katrina involuntarily clung to Daniel. Then all hell broke loose. Suddenly the train took a plunge into absolute darkness. They were freefalling, it seemed. In breakneck speed the train raced straight down, their heads being wrenched backwards, and with a tornado whirl they leaned into a right curve before knocking open a swing door. Against harsh, flashing strobe lights, several monsters reared up and gnashed their terrible fangs right at Katrina's face. Her fingernails burrowed deeper into Daniel's palm. She closed her eyes. Rattling, rocking, roaring, flashing, blasting air tore at her amidst being hurled about by centrifugal forces. If she only could have instantly flown away! No more monsters now, only specks of light, little jots, like a million miniature stars, a firework of lightning. A hot nausea rose from her stomach to her forehead bathed in cold sweat.

However, she survived and reached the light of day. And then everything was quiet. Except for a whisper.

Sacrifice the most beloved one. Good that father didn't know who her most beloved was. Mara, poor Mara . . .

"Katrina! What are you doing! Wake up! You scared us shitless." Whining did not sound good on Luise.

Katrina found herself sitting in the grass, leaning against the back exit of the horrible ghost coaster ride. Daniel knelt in front of her. He flashed an encouraging smile at her.

"Look, how you mangled me," he grinned and held his scratch marks under Katrina's nose. Then he helped her up. Still a little wobbly, she patted the dust from her pants.

"We really have to take better care of you in the future," Raffi joked.

"Yes, I can't believe she keels over twice in a row." Daniel sounded almost compassionate.

Luise shut him up with a furious glance. A black out was not a joke. She had never expected that Katrina, all ashen in the face, would collapse on the exit steps. Raffi and Daniel could barely catch her.

"So sorry. I really didn't want to spoil your fun."

"Nonsense," Raffi laughed. "The best part is, you have survived! Maybe these ghosts were worse than expected."

"Believe me, Katrina. We won't do that again so soon." Luise brushed more dirt off Katrina's pants.

"For sure not."

Luise guided Katrina to a bench and made her sit down. The men, visibly out of their comfort zone, tagged along.

"Good. The kid's already doing better," Daniel quipped. The color had returned to Katrina's face.

'Kid,' Katrina fumed. 'Does he think I am a child?'

"Are you coming with us to the beer tent?" Raffi asked Luise.

"Later perhaps," she began, but Katrina's mad glance shut her up quick. "You all go ahead. We still need a little fresh air."

"Don't wait too long. A small paycheck like mine is washed down in no time," Raffi joked. And off they took to the tent.

Katrina soon recovered, but her limbs were as heavy as lead. The sleeplessness of the last several days had taken its toll. Luise sat next to her for a while, her legs dangling off the bench. She was smoking a cigarette. She dropped the butt, stepped on it with her shoe, and said, "Come on, let's go!"

"Finally!" Katrina sighed. "Yes, let's go home!"

"Nah, who wants to go home? Look, how good you look, all bright-eyed and bushy-tailed. You got a second wind. Let's join the guys in the beer tent. We'll never get this chance again."

"Leave me out of it, Lulu! I don't feel well all," Katrina protested. 'Can't we go home?' But how? Luise was her ride. She had no choice but to pad after her.

Then she saw it. A Golden Eagle was parked in the second row behind the beer tent. Beni's Jeep! Obviously, her nemesis was sitting in the tent, too. She froze.

Luise noticed. "Don't be ridiculous, Katrina! You're not afraid of this mouse king, are you? Come on now!"

"No, I have had enough!"

"Don't be such a sissy! Daniel and Raffi won't be waiting on us forever. Free beer, and they are so much fun!"

'Fun? Again?'

Luise pulled Katrina by the sleeve forward. In tune with a brass band fanfare, the young women entered the stale, smoky, sweaty, malt-impregnated air of the beer tent.

"Looks like they had been expecting us," Luise joked.

The fanfare, however, was addressed to the strongest beer mug lifter in the stage competition. All heads in the front benches turned like on command to gawk at the new arrivals.

Luise, with her shrill red hair, and Katrina, in her old grandfather jacket, instantly drew dirty looks.

"Look, all that's missing is a nose ring," someone at the soccer table grunted after Luise. She ignored it. Not such a bad guess after all, since Luise wore Indian jewelry of all kind, even nose pins.

"There they are!" Luise had spotted Daniel and Raffi. They waved back at them all across the tent.

"Who is that, next to Raffi?" Luise shouted in Katrina's ear.

"I'll be darn! That's Resi, Beni's sister."

"What does Raffi want with that daisy? Come, let's find out!" Before they could reach their destination, a giant of a guy stepped up to the table. He grabbed Resi by the arm and pulled on her. She visibly resisted.

"Shucks, something's brewing," Katrina whispered.

"Big brother wants to cause a big stink, huh?" Luise pushed herself more vigorously through the crowd. Now they could hear the angry words.

"What are you thinking!" Beni thundered away at his sister. "Going around with such riff raff? Have you lost all decency?"

"Leave her alone, will you!" Raffi demanded.

"You, you shut up your mouth!"

"She can sit where she wants to!"

"No, definitely not next to you, you stray gypsy dog!" Beni puffed up. His face was flushed. "Rotten scoundrel!"

Raffi shot up from his seat, but Daniel pulled him back down on the bench.

"Who does this jackass think he is?" Raffi gasped. Daniel nudged Raffi's attention towards the table behind them. The men from the sports club were suspiciously staring at them. Resi got up to leave. Sparks could already be heard crackling.

"Well, then, if this seat is empty . . ." Luise plopped down on the bench and pulled Katrina after her.

"Lookee here," Beni spouted, "the artist floozie and the Weber tootsie! Aren't you wearing your slutty, ahem, studded pants again!"

"That's enough, you country mongrel!"

Faster than anyone expected, Raffi jumped up and pushed Beni on the chest. Beni, solid as a rock, shoved his sister Resi behind his back and swung at Raffi. Raffi quickly ducked. The blow coincidentally landed on a waiter who was passing by with a bundle of empty mugs on hand.

"You want trouble or what?" the beefy security-guard-turned-waiter growled at Beni. The well-trained man was struck but not shaken.

With a loud jangle the waiter-bouncer set down his beer mugs on the sportsmen's table, and grabbed Beni by his suspenders to move him out of the tent. But Beni's raging bull broke loose. He tore away from the grasp and tried a surprising karate move on the unprepared waiter. Beni lowered his shoulders, took aim, raced forward, picked the guy up, and threw him with a battle cry on top of the sports club table filled with roasted chickens and meatloaf rolls. Glasses spilling, plates tumbling, and gingerbread hearts flying.

The sportsmen jumped up in unison and knocked over the beers on the biker table next to them. Instantly, the bikers hit back at the sportsmen. All hell broke loose. Beer pitchers were flying. One man was hit badly in the head and took a somersault backwards under the bench behind him. His buddies sprang to the rescue. By now, the bouncers, thrilled about their business, raced towards the commotion from all corners of the tent.

Raffi and Daniel had ducked away under the tables soon enough. Katrina and Luise, amidst the turmoil, were looking for an escape.

Suddenly a motor roared up behind them. Somebody grabbed Katrina by the elbow.

"Come, quick! Hop on!" Katrina could not believe her eyes: a motorbike inside the beer tent, and Mike sitting on it. He appeared just in time.

"But what about Luise . . .?"

"Don't worry, she has got her brother. Jump on, quick!"

Katrina swung herself into the seat, clung to Mike tightly, and off they went. Mike revved up the machine to full throttle. The bike reared up on its hind wheel. Terrified by the deafening noise, the throng of people ahead of them magically parted. Some jumped up on benches or tables to be safe. Some wiped their eyes in amazement. Such a thing had indeed never happened before.

"I thought you didn't have time today," Katrina yelled into Mike's ear. Immediately she wanted to bite off her tongue over this stupid remark.

"But aren't you glad that I came anyway?" he shouted back.

Her hair whipped fiercely around her face. The harsh airstream drove tears into Katrina's eyes. Like distorted shadows the trees flew by. Solely the moon provided a stable orientation point on this night ride. Huddling against Mike's strong, warm back, Katrina felt safe.

They soon had reached the village, but Mike kept on driving until they had passed it. He turned into a familiar gravel road. After another ten minutes they were by the lake. Mike switched off the motor. The moon-bright silence seemed unreal after so much noise. Only a few crickets were chirping a sleepy song. The roaring of the motor receded in Katrina's head.

Mike pulled Katrina through the reeds towards the boat dock.

"Sit!" he ordered. She obeyed.

Mechanically, Katrina pulled off her shoes and let her feet hang into the water. Mike knelt down and pulled out a long rod from under the dock.

"What are we doing here?" Katrina asked.

"Fishing."

"So glum?"

"All your fault. You are due for a beating." Mike reached for the second part of the rod, assembled it and sat down next to Katrina on the gangplank. He took a swing and landed the fishing line in the lake. The moon cast a romantic light onto the scenery, but the mood was rotten. Like he said, he would take her fishing. Finally, he broke the silence.

"Why are you messing around with those guys? They don't belong to us."

"But Luise and Daniel are born here."

"Come on, their father is an artist from the city! Their mother probably died from the grief about all this riff raff he dragged in . . ."

"What nonsense. . ."

"They ruined the farm forever . . ."

"It wasn't profitable any more. The atelier and the planetarium turned out really nice . . ."

"But have you ever seen them at church, or at an event? They never join the people."

"Which people? Besides, they are Lutheran . . ."

"Do they go to a Lutheran church? I bet they don't."

"What's it to you? Seriously, they have morals, too . . ."

"How so? With incense sticks? What's wrong with you! You never bothered about gypsies before."

"Well, yeah. I didn't know any before. But now I sit next to Luise on the bus every day."

"I see, the chimpansium." Mike emphatically spat out the cuss word.

'Not again.' Katrina's skin tightened and her hair bristled with anger.

"Really, what business do you have with these people?" Mike continued his sermon in a more pacifying tone. "What do you even want in life?"

"Do I have to know that already?"

"Seriously? You just have to know." Mike rewound the fishing line and cast it again. "Ever since fifth grade, when I started helping my uncle, I had wanted to be a carpenter. And I will soon be a journeyman. What are you going to be?"

"How about a gypsy?" Katrina teased and mocked him with a suggestive wink.

"Whaaaat?" He flinched.

"Gypsy, or maybe fortune teller."

"See, what strange ideas you got from them!"

"Oh, give me a break!"

"You know what I mean." Before Katrina could object, Mike had grabbed the pendant on her neck.

"What kind of monkey tooth have we got here!"

"It's not a monkey tooth, it's a bear claw."

Katrina was still upset that she had lost her lucky clover charm. Mike's sister Angela had given it to her in the third grade. Mike had discovered it in a *Wundertüte* surprise bag long ago. For years the cloverleaf had rested in Katrina's jelly jar with many other childhood trinkets, until she retrieved it. She had worn it, without ever taking it off, since the big kiss happened. Mike didn't know anything about his fortune with that clover. But now there was the bear claw instead.

"And where did you get that from?"

"From Luise. It's from an American medicine man."

"Bullshit. Has Luise ever been to America?"

"No, but Daniel has, she says."

"I see. And what's up with that? Does she believe in witchcraft?" Mike put down the fishing rod, grabbed Katrina by her shoulders, and seriously pierced her eyes with a dark stare. "You better believe it. Some people just don't belong here."

"But some people are just more interesting."

"As interesting as the brawls they incite?"

Katrina scrambled to her feet.

"Not true!" she yelled. "And you know it! Beni started that mess, this tricky dickhead! I am sure glad he also got a whooping. Do you have any idea what awful things he accused me of! I've got nothing with nobody. So, there, I said it! I am going home!" She twirled around and stomped across the wooden planks towards the shore.

"Wait!" Mike jumped up as well. "On foot it will take you forever. Let me take you home."

With a few strides he caught up with her, grabbed her by the wrist, and pulled her close. Their nose tips almost touched. Katrina felt Mike's breath on her cheek. She closed her eyes. Then his fresh lips found their way to hers. He smelled bewitchingly appetizing, like a kitten that spent a night in the haystack and just snuck home in the morning dew. Mike tightened his clasp. The kiss was heavenly. The desirous lips melded the two individuals into one. Tongues cautiously explored and increasingly lusted for more. Nothing else existed, only the fusion of two into one. And yet there was a voice.

There we will meet again, in this heaven, which merely lies a hand's breadth beside us on earth . . .

Katrina could clearly see the heavens, too. Had true love just spoken? The kiss could have lasted all night long, for all she cared.

But Mike broke away, took her hands with brotherly love in his, and smiled at her. "Let's not be stupid."

'What stupid? Why not? Let's sit by the water a little longer and look at the stars,' Katrina begged in her mind.

"I'll bring you home now," Mike decided. Katrina's voice vanished. Maybe the cat ate it. She obeyed him mechanically. In silence.

Grandfather lay awake at home. From his room he heard a motorcycle slowly approaching the house. Then the fat key turned squeakily in the lock. The old man knew that sound very well. He had checked twice whether the key, the only one, was for sure placed correctly in the flowerpot hideaway. Katrina had reached home just before he was going to start the Sorrowful Mysteries of his rosary. Thus, he drove away the dark hours of many a night. As soon as he had reached one end of the mysteries, he would start churning the prayer mill from the beginning, until he virtually lost consciousness and emerged at another shore of the well-known river feeding the ocean of the night. 'Listen. Now the motorcycle is driving away.' Cautious footsteps climbed the two flights of stairs. Click, the door to the room one floor up closed with a soft click. He knew this sound all too well, like that of the clanking cows' chains in the attached stable.

'Thank you, Kathl,' he sighed and continued praying.

8

Earth Secrets

The church as well no longer wanted to sit back and went for the offensive. It appropriated the May pole as Easterly symbol for salvation and resurrection. (Hence some May poles have a rooster on top.) The brown villains (= Nazis) later abused the May pole for their insane "blood and turf" frenzy.

—*The May pole, Web page Gästehaus Winkler, Kreuth*

Monday, June 17

The Benedictines made holy order in the land. They separated ora from labora, divided prayer and work. But how could they? Isn't prayer work and work prayer? All the same, they cut the day in little slices. Yet time has neither a beginning nor an end. The people, however, believed the Benedictine artifice, because success proved them right.

Princely monasteries grew from ancient soils. And all pieces of the land were noted down and entered in registries. The drafting of precise boundaries caused many trees split through the middle. If anyone had only felt this pain like nature did! Perhaps for the same reason, many a fellow got whacked over a boundary stone.

We, the people, did not understand their Latin prayers. Rhymes and harmonies made them seductive and pierced our minds like siren song.

Thus, the Benedictines perfected the Romans' castle of dreams. They were smart. They coaxed the cycles of season from our druids, wrote them in their books, and called them natural laws. They experimented. They pilfered animals' and plants' mating secrets from nature to bastardize new crops and better output. But nature often foiled their breeding intentions. Big harvests rotted, because the fat wheat was not drought resistant, the heavy cattle barely made it through the winter, and the giant beans contracted worms and mildew.

Yet the Benedictines created glorious, hand-illustrated folios, and monumental abbeys. Their filigree structures, illustrated with dramatic Christian hero sagas, frescoes, and statues, were magnificently awash in light. They stole the music from the angels and wrote it down on paper. And they also reintroduced the human sacrifice, the suffering and death of Our Lord, Jesus. Nobody believed in dragons any longer. The monks banished them with their brushes on the walls and thus took away their power. New heroes, like Archangel Michael, Saint Margaret, and the holy knight St. George, vanquished the mystic beasts. And the beautiful custom of virgin sacrifice they now called witch-burning.

> But could they explain everything? How come the ghost
> lights still lured people into the deadly bog?

Another bad grade. What was she expecting? She hadn't followed Schiller's advice. The Essay Marathon was drastically picking up speed. This morning, before class, the students had submitted their works, and at noon they were already graded. And right away the next topic loomed.

All that was moot at the moment. Katrina was plucking potato bugs, her head flushed from bending down. This task was mere drudgery, but at least she could let her thoughts fly. Nobody watched. Mike. Why had he sent her home so abruptly from the lake? When would she see him again? Bending over the potato plants, many thoughts rushed to her head.

Now, in the middle of the afternoon, the sun burnt straight down. The potato field was located in the river plain. The air carried a mossy note, as if it had just rained. By the roadside, where the fertilizer and tractor mower never reached, marguerites, bellflowers, and red clover lined the road. Within the colorful mix, the fragile quaking grass shivered in the breeze. The shadows from the forested riverbank had almost reached the potato field. Here it was unusually quiet. Occasionally a cricket sang a few notes. A hawk emitted a piercing cry.

Appleseed-size rubies—droplets of mushy gummy bear consistency—dotted the leaves. No bird wanted to eat the temptingly red larvae; they must have tasted horribly. The adult bugs, which had laid the eggs that had hatched these larvae, were yellow with black stripes. The French were said to have dropped them as "biological weapons" from airplanes during World War II, just like so-called French weed, which proliferated so badly that it suffocated the wheat. These plagues had caused the German farmers several times more damage than the dud bombs, her father once said. Exactly in this potato field, an American warplane had some 30 years ago dumped its ordinance. Two of the shells could later be defused, but the third bomb was never found. It could have still exploded. Yet Girgl had no choice but to continue plowing. Strangely, this field always yielded the largest potatoes.

Blinged with miniature "strawberries," the underside of the potato leaves appeared to be ruby-studded. These larvae jeopardized the farmer's gold, the potato harvest. During the war, a farmer could have requested forced labor for a job like this. But that was just another kind of trouble, Girgl remembered.

Truth eventually arrived in May 1945. It snowed. The Death March was underway. Starving, miserable creatures from the concentration camps shuffled through the snow in wooden slippers on their evacuation order. Their shoes crunched as loud as rocks in a gravel mill. There were hundreds, if not thousands. Tattered rags marched right by the Webers' kitchen window. Girgl, a boy of twelve years then, hid for fear in the attic, but his good-hearted mother bravely threw her last few slices of bread to the death-bound wretches. Yet the SS guards drove the dreary procession on with a vengeance. Anyone who picked up a piece of bread received a thrashing or was shot. Fortunately, the Death March never reached its grisly goal, as the American planes flying above scattered the remnants of Nazi horror. In face of such drastic memories, no work had ever seemed too hard or grimy to Girgl ever again. And his children should learn the same value of hard work.

Ruby after ruby, Katrina picked the larvae with nimble fingers from the leaves in her row and plopped them strategically into the tin bucket. Her father was quite old-fashioned sometimes. He could have easily had the pests sprayed away with help of the farmers co-op chemicals, but he preferred to make his children do the work for free. And poisons of all kinds were suspect to him since he had seen the "hamster people," the forced labor POWs from the munitions factories across the Isar. Many a Saturday they would come to beg for scraps of food in the village. Sometimes they raided the pigs' slob. They looked so awful and jaundiced that Girgl had not touched a pesticide as of yet. Be this as it may, he also dearly cherished the unity of his family at work.

Not so Katrina. She moaned and wiped the sweat from her brow with the back of her hand. She wished it were time to quit. These awful, fake raspberries—yuck-shit, potato bugs—she plucked them with careful tenderness so as not to squish them. She'd rather have plucked the adult bugs. *"Colorado bugs" some people called them. 'Colorado, . . . there it must be so beautiful. Rockies, lakes, horses . . .'*

Three trenches west of her and much farther behind, Walli stood in the field, like a statue. Each time Katrina looked up, she caught her little sister dawdling or yawning or taking another gulp of lemonade. She never seemed to be bending down at all.

"Are you catching any bugs?" their father yelled across the field. Walli shuddered.

"Bucket's almost full!" Walli lied. She swiftly bent down to make herself look busy. She had only come along because her father had said so. To make time pass a little faster, she imagined herself hunting for treasures in the dirt.

Katrina as well turned her attention on the bugs again.

Girgl added a few logs to the fire pit. 'It's either the bugs or the potatoes,' he grumbled to himself. The fire was going strong by now. Marianne, who just finished her row, went to the tractor to get the picnic basket. She always made sure to bring enough food to cheer up her troops.

Grandfather viewed the activities on the potato field from a distance with almost a smile under his moustache. The whole family was at work like in the old days. That hardly happened any more. People working hand in hand. Although—reality bit him again—one was missing: Martl. He would have been old enough to drive the tractor by now.

Get back to work, you good for nothing!

The old man bent down to his tool box, pulled out a celery root, cut off a small sliver, dumped the root back into the crate, and stuck the slice on the pin in the trap. Then he carefully wiped his pocketknife on his cobbler's apron, clicked the blade shut against his thigh, and returned the knife to his pant pocket. Next, he cocked the neck-snapper trap, knelt down on stiff legs, and carefully inserted the mole catcher into one of those little beasties' tunnels, which he had partially excavated. Finally, he covered the small opening with the grass patch that he had taken out earlier and marked the future mole grave with a little stick. He pulled himself up and walked to the next molehill. Proudly he viewed the results of his work. A whole forest of little sticks, a mole cemetery, lay in front of his eyes.

'Damn little bastards!' He thought about his brave Tassilo. About fifty years ago, the moles had wreaked so much havoc with their diggings that his best workhorse broke a leg in one of their tunnels. Consequently, the beautiful, black coldblood met the butcher's fate. Moles had always been a problem, but since that tragic day they had become his sworn enemies. 'Just you wait, little snot-nosed grime balls. I will get each one of you!'

Katrina kept plucking speedily. 'He loves me, he loves me not,' she recited in her mind.

"Kerr-plonk, plink-plink, plonk," the bugs said when they landed in the bucket.

All the while, Katrina's bear claw around her neck swung in rhythm with her movements.

She clearly saw it in her mind's eye. The lifeless mane still fluttered proudly in the wind, spirited even after death ...

'Again? Am I cuckoo? Who is talking now?'

Bent over a large potato plant, she froze. Suddenly, the dangling bear claw startled her. She grabbed the pendant and stopped it in its tracks.

'Stop, hold tight! Or else I can't hear a thing.' Suspended like frozen in tabletop position, she released the bear claw. Slowly but surely the pendulum started circling again.

Again, Katrina stopped the pendant and stared at the amulet in her hands. How strange! Let's try again. With hands propped on her knees she observed the pendant activities. First it hung motionless, but then it started to swing almost imperceptibly. She stared in awe. The pendulum swung farther and farther in various directions. Eventually, it vibrated in place. Katrina took a deep breath and looked at the pendant again. There was nothing any more unusual about it today than yesterday. Luckily, the strange voice had now stopped, too.

'What's wrong with me? Am I going nuts?' She stepped forward to the next plant. Her bare foot banged against something hard. It was partially buried in a potato row, exactly in the spot over which the bear claw had vibrated.

It was a horseshoe.

Walli had observed Katrina from the corner of her eyes. For some things she had a sixth sense. She hurdled across the field in no time and tore the find from her sister's hands. "Wow, what is that?" She almost screamed with excitement.

"Give it back! I found it! That belongs to me, you dodo bird," Katrina tore the object away from Walli.

"But I just wanted to look at it!" Walli turned around. "Father, father," she yelled across the field. "Katrina found something."

"Don't scream like that!"

Girgl looked up from the fire. He dropped the fork, with which he had been stirring the embers, and hasted towards them. When he realized that it wasn't an emergency, he slowed down.

"What the hell is going on over here? What's all that noise?"

"Look, what Katrina found!"

Katrina handed her father the horseshoe.

"And because of that rusty old trash you are holding up our work? There are many horseshoes lying around. One of your grandfather's horses could have lost it."

"But this one looks a lot different, really peculiar," Katrina said. "Look how flat and broad it is, totally corroded. It almost crumbles apart."

"So, what! I have two of that sort on my barn door already." Girgl's two rusted horseshoes were mounted next to the inspection certificates for tuberculosis and hoof and mouth disease. Somewhat disappointed, Katrina walked over to her bicycle and dropped the trashy treasure into the carrying basket.

The father grabbed Walli's bucket. "There is hardly anything in here! Now, off you go, quickly! Work a little faster!" Girgl admonished both of them. "Unless you want to breathe some fresh air again tomorrow? These bugs certainly won't run away. And exercise is good for you!"

"My back hurts already," Walli moaned.

"No wonder, you're out of practice!" Girgl grinned and parodied some awkward squats for his daughters. "Up and down, and up and down, and repeat again. That keeps you trim and fit. That's how you grow muscles. How come that nothing ever hurts you when you do your sports? No pain, no gain. Hurry up now!"

Walli furrowed her brow, but resistance was pointless. Katrina also bent over her row again. A pesky fly kept buzzing around her ear. All dreams had flown away. Reality was much sweatier than any steaming romance. And their father could be quite a cheesecake.

"Want to see who fills up her bucket the fastest?" Walli challenged Katrina. She'd kill time rather sooner than later.

"It's on! You haven't got a fat chance against me, baby doll!" Katrina growled.

Grandfather had installed his last mole trap. He sat down on a boulder and lit up his pipe. 'Potato bugs,' he thought, 'never had them before. Everything in this world is changing.' Earlier the May bugs had eaten the fruit trees bare, and now people had their hands full with these devilish beetles. It seemed as if Satan had scratched over their yellow wings with his black claws and left ugly stripes on their backs. The old man would have plucked the bugs with a vengeance, but his crusty bones would not let him. For some time already, he had not minded doing "women's work," as long as he was good for anything at all. When he still ran the farm, he was only interested in horses, as he had been in the cavalry in World War I, and later he fancied tractors. He would have never stooped down so low as to pick up a potato himself, much less a bug. The women folk took care of that. He was in charge of plowing, mowing, and driving. He took care of the machines and the political discourse at the guesthouse. Back then there was still time for that. But the machines had always become stronger and life faster. After his return from exile, he had lost touch with everything. In solitude, he had aged faster than an ox under the yoke, although time had stood still since that fateful day.

Like water, life is fluid, then frozen solid in death, finally gaseous and permeating everything in eternity.

'Well, yes, if you say so.' The old man nodded his head in tune with the new whispers. He did not wonder any more when he heard voices like that in his head. As long as it wasn't the screams of desperation from the artillery trenches, or the saddening sobs for Martl, he was relieved. Of course, Kathl in heaven also occasionally entered his conscience. He contritely accepted that. If, however, all the voices talked over each other or started up heated arguments, he took to mowing or peening so that he could drown them out with work. Sometimes, it seemed to him, his granddaughter, Katrina, might have a similar problem. Often Marianne had to repeat her question three times, before the girl gave an incoherent reply. Hopefully, it wasn't the same evil spirits talking to that girl. He straightened up. It actually all made sense. Life was like water, passing by quickly, and yet you could swim against it, but, regardless, something of life always evaporates in the air.

The old man let life, or what was left of it, go by and did not resist it any longer. Time, once again, had acquired a tiny value. Perhaps for that reason he had set his longcase clock ahead by fifteen minutes, so that he might get ahead of his own old self and occasionally win the race against time. Nothing, however, had helped to sweep away the cobwebs from his mind. The voices kept on whispering.

A hawk let out a piercing cry. The old man looked into the blue. 'What is it this time, you old chicken robber? Forecasting another disaster?'

"Food is ready! Come and get it!" Marianne called out at the top of her voice. She had set the basket on a blanket and put the drink bottles next to it. Bread, cheese, boiled eggs, she unpacked one item after another and laid the table for a hearty picnic.

Katrina and Walli delivered their collection of potato beetle larvae to their father.

"You two, run over and tell your grandfather to come eat," Marianne ordered. She unwrapped the sandwich packet, making sure to divide up the portions. Then she arranged the bowls with boiled eggs, tomatoes, radishes, and gherkins in the middle. For the hunk of cheese and the bacon, she had brought a cutting knife and board. Extra bread rolls and a cheese spread were in the paper sack. Marianne approached all meal preparations, even a casual picnic, with a professional attitude. One reason being, she was clearly the boss of the food. And being in charge pleased her. Watching people enjoy her food, devouring it or relishing it, made her happy, too. Feeding people was important business. Finally, she had laid out the settings for the casual meal.

Meanwhile, her daughters raced each other down to the creek to wash their hands. From the embankment they called their grandfather. He slowly rose from his boulder throne, grabbed the crate with the mole traps, and slowly trudged towards the picnic spot. The girls dashed far ahead of him. With a clumsy leap, Walli parked herself on the picnic cloth. She scattered the food supplies. The boiled eggs rolled across the blanket.

"Careful, Walli! Look out!" Marianne exclaimed. She caught two eggs before they rolled off the blanket into the grass.

"You klutz! Put everything right back in place, but avanti!" Girgl growled. "This blanket is not a tumbling mat."

"Tumbleweed!" Katrina snickered.

Walli laughed out loud and quickly collected eggs, radishes, and tomatoes back into their bowls. She bit into a liverwurst sandwich with gusto.

"Fixed it already," she said, chewing with a full mouth. Girgl shook his head.

"Don't talk, eat," Marianne ordered her crew. "We still have a couple of hours ahead of us. No, Walli! Put that down! I brought this sausage specifically for your grandfather. Did he get lost?" She looked over her shoulder. "Oh, I see him now."

"Nothing will be left for him, if he doesn't walk a little faster," Walli quipped.

It felt nice to rest for a change. Katrina and Walli sat with their legs crossed, but Marianne had hers stretched out. She kept busy guarding her secret stash of cake in the basket and overseeing the equal rations for her workers. For that she had an innate sense of food justice.

Girgl was leaning against the tractor, absentmindedly chewing his bread. He stared down at his work boots. How many kilometers they had walked already! The tread worn off, the laces knotted in several places, hooks and eyelets broken, heels crooked, and the seam torn open, but they were a part of him. The shoes always stayed the same. Only the backdrop constantly kept changing. Today the rich lumps of dirt from the potato field, yesterday the fine dust from the gravel pit, tomorrow the needle-covered ground from the pine forest. These shoes had weathered so many locations and so many sceneries of mud, dust, puddles, or golden corn straw. In the near future perhaps snow again. And what about his feet? Through all the years, shoes and feet had become like one. True to measure, the leather had dutifully molded to the shape of his feet like a second skin, a callous without pain for all seasons.

A small, rattling cloud of dust approached on the dirt road. It grew larger until it finally halted right next to grandfather by the wayside. It turned out to be a motorbike with a sidecar. Katrina shivered. What did Pauli want from her grandfather? Hopefully he had not told him anything about their strange incident up by the chapel. Her grandfather climbed into the sidecar. The motorbike started rolling again and stopped right next to the tractor. All eyes were on the new arrival. Pauli jumped off the bike and marched with determination towards the Weber family. Before grandfather awkwardly extracted himself from the sidecar, Pauli had already reached Girgl standing by the tractor.

"Girgl," Pauli huffed without as much as a greeting, "the cops are at the Gabelsberger house."

"The police?"

"Yes, he called them himself."

"Why, on God's earth? What happened?"

"Bones . . ."

"Come again?"

"They found bones under the floor boards in their Stube."

"How can that be?"

Pauli always was the first one to know the village news. If he spotted a police car somewhere, nobody could slow down neither his curiosity nor his motorbike.

"Gabelsberger wants you to take a look as well, so that he has a witness," Pauli continued. "And he can't get the hay squared away all by himself before the cows come home. I might have helped him, but as you know, my sciatic . . ."

"All right then, Pauli, let's go," Girgl said and wiped his hands on his pants. He grabbed his hat from the tractor seat and turned around. "Marianne, you drive the tractor home. And, you two," he addressed his daughters, "don't forget to extinguish the fire, but all the way!" Then he hopped into Pauli's sidecar, as if he had done it a hundred times before, and off they puttered in a trail of dust.

"Isn't this exciting. Like in the movies!" Walli piped.

Katrina didn't say a word. She thought about Mike. What did all this mean? How had the skeleton gotten into their Stube? Under their floorboards? Lunch break was over.

The women went back to their potato bugs. Grandfather had received the strange news stone-faced, as usual. Leaning on the tractor like Girgl earlier, he slowly chewed down his bite-size cuts of liverwurst bread. Since he had been fitted with dentures, food hardly had a flavor. It all tasted the same, like Dentofix, the denture glue. After his meager meal, he slowly headed towards the forested riverbank to cut willow rods. If time allowed, he would weave a couple of brooms from birch twigs and willow bark in the evening. Realistically, there was always time, because the urgencies of life had no longer a hold on him. He gave a rat's ass about sensations. If it were something important, he would find out soon enough.

'Spare me your false excitement! Don't you know? Nothing melts as fast as yesterday's snow.'

Katrina rode her bicycle ahead of the tractor. The more her thoughts churned, the faster she hit the pedals. Soon she arrived at the stables-atelier. Luise seemed to be at home because the Kadett was parked in the drive. Katrina jumped off the still moving bike and almost shot over the handlebar. A worker dressed in dust-caked overalls and farmer's cap, with safety goggles and a long ponytail, came out of the studio. Daniel! Katrina had not recognized him in his workshop uniform. He carted the wheelbarrow past her without stopping.

"Luise is upstairs, in the planetarium," Daniel said with a side glance. "Just go up there. It's OK." The wheelbarrow was apparently quite heavy. He pushed the barrow with momentum back to the studio. A major project was in the works.

Slowly Katrina climbed the creaking stairs.

"Luise?" She peeked through the half-open door into the large salon. No answer. She went inside. Somebody seemed to have been up here just a little earlier, since the cigarette butt still glowed and numerous drawing utensils were scattered about.

Luise's portfolio stuck out from under a pile of magazines. She grabbed it and started leafing through it.

'Wow!' She had never seen any such drawings before, although Louise usually showed her everything. Gnomes, fairies, and toadstools populated Luise's pages—glimpses of chimeras, witches, and grisly specters. And there were so many renditions of dragons with sinister eyes, sharp teeth, long claws, gigantic hind legs, forked tongue, snorting nostrils . . . Katrina shivered. 'How could she have guessed my dream?' Stunned, she turned leaf after leaf. Now, these flowers were much nicer! Lady slippers, buttercups, gentians, forget-me-nots, a whole array of spring flowers populated the next sheet. She breathed a sigh of relief. Then, a punch to her stomach. 'But that's me!' The portrait had a striking likeness with her. Only, the girl in the drawing wore her hair open—not tied in a pony tail, like Katrina did—and had a wreath of flowers on her head. She wore a white chemise and had her arms crossed over her chest, her eyes cast down.

"Oh, here you are!"

"Luise! I hadn't heard you coming!" Katrina quickly slapped the portfolio shut.

"I hadn't expected you today either. What's up?" She was wrapped in a super skimpy Japanese bathrobe, wearing a towel turban on her head.

Calmly, she took the portfolio away from Katrina and stuck it high up on the bookshelf. "So, what's up? Why are you not out in the fields, like you said?"

"We were, but we all came home early. Something happened at Gabelsbergers'."

"Yeah?"

"They found a skeleton."

"Let me guess, in the closet!" Luise broke into hysterical laughter.

"Stop that, Lulu! Will you listen to me! No, they found bones when they dug up the floor inside the Stube. Even the police came to take a look at it. That's all I know. Father just drove over there to check it out."

"Maybe that's where Mr. G. put his ex away, that hound. Haven't I told you that something is foul with him?" Luise was still grinning from ear to ear.

"Oh, will you stop it, Luise! Imagine, if you had been living on top of a grave all this time and had no clue about it!"

"That would totally turn me on," Louise replied and started rolling a cigarette. "Aren't we all just living in a cemetery, on the dirt of the earth? As they always say, dust to dust, ashes to ashes! We humans are just in a transitional stage . . . What makes you so sure that these Gabelsbergers are as innocent as they say?" She paused and stared at Katrina.

"Stop your bullshit, Louise! You're not making the least bit of sense today."

Katrina fumed. She should have known better. Luise did not have a high opinion of Mike. After Katrina had shared her entirely confusing romantic encounter by the lake with her, Luise had quickly smothered the topic with another 'hadn't I told you so.' Why was she talking with Luise at all? But then, again, where did this unbridled sarcasm come from?

"Are you still mad at me?" Katrina asked.

"Think again!"

"What?"

"You left me to the wolves at the Volksfest!"

"Believe me, I had no choice, Lulu! Mike just grabbed me."

"Yep, and that's why I am still effing mad!" Luise glared at Katrina. "Hah! Just kidding." She broke into loud laughter. "Can you believe it? I had a ball later with Daniel and Raffi up here!"

"Lulu! You are so . . ."

"Oh, let's just forget about that stupid Volksfest." Luise pulled her legs up.

"You don't really like Mike!"

"He is your man, not mine. Except, that motorcycle stunt that he laid down was impressive, nevertheless."

"You're not taking anything I say seriously!"

"Sorry, amiga! Please, don't go ballistic on me! Here, have a smoke instead." Luise offered Katrina a cigarette.

"No, thanks!" Katrina ignored the cigarette. She furiously turned around and trampled down the stairs.

"Katrina! Wait, please!" Luise yelled after her, but in her curious bathrobe costume, she didn't dare run outside. She held off on the doorstep, frowning. Katrina had already mounted her bike and swished by the studio. She hadn't noticed Daniel. He was returning the wheelbarrow to its location by the wall.

"Wait, Katrina! You lost something!" Daniel called after Katrina. But she could not hear him anymore.

Daniel bent down and picked up the brittle horseshoe.

It was high time for the hen house. The faster Katrina's thoughts circled, the happier the keys danced. Her Adler machine was always ready to listen, never picked a fight, never contradicted. People, in return, were entirely annoying. Mike, Luise, anyone. Here she was finally alone.

Both parents tended the cows in the stable. Grandfather sat at the kitchen table, slowly leafing through the grease-stained newspaper, pretending to read. Intermittently he nodded off to sleep. And Walli was watching her favorite television show.

Still, down at the house there was hardly a quiet minute. A neighbor could stop by any time to relay some gossip or ask a favor. No peace and quiet anywhere. No place to think. Not even in her room. Last time she had tried to type her stories upstairs, her old Adler with its rusty wings had made such a clatter with each keystroke that it rattled all the windowpanes. The clanking shook up the whole house. Worried and sleepy-eyed her mother had come to check on her, and a little later Walli had banged on her door to stop her "darn rattletrap."

Clearly, there was no room for her activity in the house. Therefore, Katrina had set up shop in the former chicken coop. She had carted away chicken poop by the barrel loads, scrubbed the floor, until the concrete finally emerged under a gazillion layers of downtrodden manure. Her mother had long ago decided that chickens produced more poop than what they were worth in eggs. Eggs, anyway, were cheap at the store. Her coop was eventually furnished with an old shelf from the shed, which she freshly painted, an ancient lounge chair from the parish house, and the old milk separator table from the attic. All in all, it turned out a fairly cozy cave, especially when Katrina nested in the voluminous armchair. There was no electricity, only a petrol lamp. Eventually, Katrina had procured a strong flashlight, which was no fire hazard, and mounted it on an old floor lamp. It was a writer's paradise, a pretty cold one in the winter. All she wanted was to be left alone, alone with her strange thoughts.

Homework was yet to be done. How could she concentrate on her next essay amidst all the confusing dragon-motorcycle and lake-night-skeleton events? The cigarette smoldered in its final stages. Inadvertently, a book of saintly legends from her First Communion class caught Katrina's attention. She opened the pages. A stately knight slaying a dragon jumped out at her. She stared at the illustration. Her fantasy stampeded towards the edge with her. What if there really hadn't been any dragons? Then many a legend would have turned out differently.

Night from Monday to Tuesday, June 18

Georgius was a brave Roman knight from Cappadocia. He served emperor Diocletian in Asia Minor in the persecution of Christians. At that time, the fierce Galatians, far from being Christian, also continued to foment unrest in the Empire. The new slave religion, however, was even more disconcerting because it blasphemed the Roman deities. This new God from the Jewish province, whom not even his own people had wanted, was becoming too powerful. Therefore, Georgius brought all those to justice who did not renounce the miracle worker from Nazareth. His sword was forged from Damascus steel and his heavy lance was feared in all the land. Georgius rode a white stallion, visible from afar.

In the year 303, a dragon had poisoned the lake by the town Sila with its foul breath. To keep the monster appeased, the town sacrificed one sheep a day. But the dragon wanted more. Soon it became greedy for tender maidens. So the town complied, choosing virgins by drawing lots. Finally, it became the king's daughter's turn. The king was overcome by profound despair. His most lovely, graceful, precious flesh and blood, his child as fair and lovely as a flower, must not be cast to this monster. So, he proclaimed a challenge to all brave knights. Whoever was to kill the dragon should receive his daughter's hand in marriage and inherit the kingdom. But not even the bravest knights had vanquished the beast so far. Rather, every noble gentleman who tried his luck, was never to be seen or heard of again. Not one had accomplished to deliver that fearsome token, the dragon's claw. No more time was left. Should the lovely princess now be sacrificed? However, the untimely death of the heiress might have wrought fear and chaos of succession on the province.

Thus, Georgius took on the challenge, not an hour too soon. Warily, he approached the mist-enshrouded lake. On the path along the mountainside, his strong, white stallion cautiously set one foot before the other. It startled. The knight scanned the outcroppings in the rock above. The stallion moved on. Only the soft crunching of the horse's hooves on the gravel could be heard.

The princess, tied against a stake near the entrance to the dragon's cave, spotted the knight from afar. "Noble knight," she shouted, "in the name of Christ! I beg you, remove yourself! The dragon is near!"

Georgius froze. He had no fear of dragons, but why should he save a Christian? Even her father, the strict Celtic Lord, might have made short shrift of her, had he suspected such an insult. But she had warned him! How high-minded this young lady was! She cared not about herself but about a stranger!

That instant, a howling roar broke loose. White frocks bearing scythes, sickles, and axes plunged on the noble knight and his rearing steed. Brave Georgius, propelled by ire's elemental force, struck down the attackers with his lance and finished off the wailing wounded with his Damascus sword. Like a mirage the attackers vanished into thin air. The ground was strewn with bloodied bodies in white robes.

One frock barely stirred. Georgius grabbed him by the

neck. It was the high priest.

"Where is your goddamn dragon?" Georgius screamed at the shivering old man's fear-torn face.

"In the cave, noble knight!" the officiant whispered.

"You first!" Georgius commanded. With the sharp blade in his back the high priest slowly groped his way through the increasingly darkening cavern. In the other hand, Georgius dragged the resisting, fearful maiden with him.

They meandered through the dark galleries and passageways. Suddenly an atrium broke away the murkiness. Light fell through an opening in the ceiling. Right in front of them, shrouded by dramatically refracted rays of sunlight, stood a solid altar strewn with flower petals. In front of the platform, a thin wisp of smoke drifted towards the ceiling from an almost extinguished coal fire. A sulfurous odor, sickly sweet wafts of putrefaction, permeated the location. Around the cavern walls, an awesomely long, ferocious dragon fresco gnashed its terrible teeth at the intruders.

Stunned, Georgius brutally pushed the high priest to the ground. He grabbed a torch from a wall mount and shone the light into a grotto on the side. The princess emitted a piercing scream. In the sheen of the torchlight heads grinned back at them, each one in a different state of decay: the sacrificed virgins.

"By Jupiter! You hellhounds!" Georgius burst out like torn asunder by the Titans from Olympus. "You cannibals! You shall pay for this!"

Sooner than he could smash his sword down on the high priest, the druid had vanished into thin air. The sword stuck in the blood-tainted altar for good. A hyena's laughter sounded from the central opening in the cave. Then a trembling filled the air, grew louder to a grumble, roar, thunder. Right then the first boulders started falling. The awful terror converted the Roman knight to the true religion.

"You, Christian God up there! For crissakes, if you exist, so help us!" Georgius pleaded in the eye of certain death. "Not for my sake, but for truth's!"

He didn't know what had overcome him at that moment. But like guided by an invisible hand, the knight and princess rushed through the secret society's black-as-night tunnels toward the light of day. The faithful stallion already awaited them. No sooner had they escaped, as a dust cloud of thunder boulders buried the entrance to the cave.

Great rejoicing swept through the palace, as the knight and princess paraded through the town atop the noble steed. Georgius handed the lovely maiden to her teary-eyed lord and father.

And then?

The high priest came running into town, wheezing and panting like an undertaker's ox on his last leg, and screamed, "Murderer! He killed our priests!"

"Speak! Is it true?" the king thundered. "What about the dragon? Is it dead? Where is the token?"

"There is no token. The dragon is their fabrication!" Georgius pointed at the high priest.

Deathly silence.

"These hellhounds there, defiled your daughters! They are cannibals!"

But the evidence was buried with the virgins in the cave—and Georgius did not have a dragon's claw. As a matter of fact, a number of priests had been killed. And that was no fabrication.

The rest of the story is commonly known. Georgius' commander wished to redeem his best soldier. However, even the Roman Empire could no longer support Georgius, as he refused to take an oath on Minerva. Therefore, the Centurio discharged his man to the local court of justice.

The Galatians gave Georgius more than the due process. They put him in hot iron shoes, immersed him in boiling lime, bound him to the blade-spiked torture wheel to break his bones, and finally decapitated him.

Nothing more is known about the poor princess's fate. Also, the dragon was never heard of again. Truth or fiction, the brave knight had finished the dragon off for good.

Georgius, however, died a hero and sparked a Christian revolution in Asia Minor. Since then, nobody believes in dragons any more.

It had gotten so late in the hen house that it already was early again. Katrina woke up from a sharp pain against her forehead. She had fallen asleep over the Adler and her head banged on the typewriter shell. After that, the night had turned out to be very short. Be it as it may, exhausted and pale-faced, she submitted her marathon installment "A day in the life of a saint" to Schiller next morning. He had granted her an extension for helping her family with farm chores at home.

On Tuesday, Katrina dragged herself from one class to the next. She declined Luise's invitation to go window-shopping. And then something unexpected happened. Even her mother marveled. Unexpectedly, Marianne's eldest daughter went to bed early. No clanking disturbed the peace of the night. The scribe fell into a deep, well-earned coma.

She was totally drained.

Silent Exultation

No sooner has George, the brave yeoman,
Disavowed idol, flesh, devil, and this life
Diocletian, Christendom's tyrant, commands
"Away to torture, to death you bring this knight!"

—Inscription on fresco, Schimmelkirche

Wednesday, June 19, morning

Finally rested. The body had demanded its right of sleep. The strain of the last several days had been taxing. Dazed, Katrina staggered down the stairs. Walli sat by herself at the kitchen table and abruptly stared at her.

"Katrina! You're in the paper! You have won!"

"Huh, . . . what do you mean?"

"First prize! The essay contest!"

"But it's not Saturday . . .?" Katrina squinted. Her eyes didn't focus yet.

"No, Wednesday, you dummy! But they had to get the contest over with before the big soccer tournament this weekend."

"Why, what soccer . . .? Give me the paper, will you!" Katrina was suddenly widely awake. She reached for the paper.

"Hey, not fair! I had it first!" Walli quickly tugged at the paper. Katrina was left with just a small snippet between her fingers.

Walli began to read, emphatically. "'We congratulate the winners of our Hometown Essay Contest. Among numerous submissions, several young authors have excelled through their fresh perspectives and thorough research. Today we honor the work of our First-Place winner, Frau Katrina Weber. Her story is reprinted below . . .'" Walli stopped to catch her breath. "You must have hit the nail on its head, I'd say. Aren't you glad that I dropped it off . . ."

"Will you give me that paper now!" But Walli did not comply. She defiantly crouched in the farthest corner of the bench, scanning for more details.

Katrina was stupefied. After her rotten essays at school, she had not even expected to win a calendar or bandana, much less first place. Sure, she had poured her heart and soul into the typewriter, but that didn't mean anything. At least not to her German teacher Hildebrandt aka Schiller. And now—first place and 300 Marks on top? That was a lot of money. She could barely remember what she had written.

"Give me that stupid paper, will you!" Katrina growled at Walli. Her sister dodged her. Katrina wrestled the paper away from her. Walli shrieked.

"What is going on? Are you fighting again! Will you stop this, you dingbats! Right now!"

Marianne entered the kitchen with a bowl full of flour under the arm. She was preparing for schmalznoodles, her famous striezel, which by the nature of the dough—tiny yeast fungi are such slow workers—required a long start up time.

"Mama, Katrina has won!" Walli proclaimed.

"Win, what did she win?" Marianne absentmindedly poured the proof yeast into the flour bowl and began to mix the dough with expert kneading movements.

"300 Marks," Walli said. "And her story is in the paper, look!" Walli pushed the tattered pages under her mother's nose."

"Come on, Walli! Do you think I have time to read! This up close I can't see anything anyway."

Marianne refuted the newspaper with her batter-caked hand. Then she reconsidered, while batting the dough into obedience. "300 Marks you say? So much money just for writing something? Look at that! Not bad at all, Katrina! You can save that money up for your driving lessons."

Walli was still waving the newspaper at her mother.

"Get this paper out of my face, Walli!" Marianne could no longer ignore her wisecrack younger child. She stopped her kneading. "Can't you see? I have work to do!" Suddenly, she froze. She realized there was a real emergency.

"Katrina, quick, run to the store! I need a pound of curd cheese, or else we can forget about the striezel.[xiv]"

"Can't Walli do that? Luise will be here soon to take me to school." She had finally whisked the paper away from Walli, trying to conceal her panic about seeing her words actually printed. She nervously scanned over the passage.

But her mom, red-faced and relentlessly slamming the dough in the bowl, angrily blew a wayward strand of hair from her nose. "No, Walli is still in her nightgown and I can't wait any longer. Hurry up! The wallet is in the cupboard."

Katrina grabbed the wallet and darted out. She took long strides along Main Street, crossed the bridge over the creek, and only slowed down as she neared the store. On most mornings, such as this one, there always was a throng of people. Sometimes the queue of basket-armed homemakers and hungry handymen reached all the way down the stairs.

A motorbike overtook Katrina and slammed to a halt in her path. Mike pulled his helmet off. Katrina smiled at him.

"What a total mess!" Mike growled with unconcealed anger in his voice. He was on his way to the carpentry shop.

"Good morning!"

Mike barely gave a nod. He brushed an unruly shock of hair out of his face.

"I already heard what happened at your house. Any news? What have you found out so far?"

"Find out, what's there to find out?" Mike growled. "Perhaps I should leave that up to the writers. They know it all, don't they?"

Katrina noticed the bitterness in his voice. She gulped. "I don't understand."

"I am sure you don't!"

"What's wrong with you today?"

"Seriously? What a stupid question!" Mike was livid. "How can you even ask? Writing such a pile of turd!"

"What do you mean?" Katrina's anxiety erupted like Mount Vesuvius over Pompeii.

"Your home town stories, obviously," Mike fulminated. "Now everybody thinks my great-grandfather whacked a shyster."

Katrina gasped for air. Mike turned the motorbike around and took off like a rocket, spraying roadside gravel behind him.

"But I changed all the names in the story," Katrina whispered to herself. Mike could not have heard that any more.

The skeleton! Was that the connection with her stories? Shaken to her bones, Katrina stared after the diminishing motorbike.

Dazed, she continued on her path to the store. Suddenly, an ancient bulb went off in her head. Was Mike referring to this Peter Waldleitner? This man from the diary, whom the priest had cursed on his deathbed confession as someone "undeliverable from sin," must have obviously been a Gabelsberger ancestor, one of Mike's antecedents. Names had frequently changed on the farms, when there were no male heirs. Mike's father had married into the farm from "across" the Isar. Bingo. Even old Frau Bürkel liked to perform a few salty ballads of "old Peter" after a couple of mugs of Glühwein. Great lord! How in the world had she gotten stuck in this mud! At least she had changed all the names in her story.

Like in trance, Katrina climbed the last several steps to the store entrance. As soon as the doorbell chimed, the banter and laughter died out. All of the shoppers' eyes turned on her. Katrina closed the door behind her. The little bell above the door chimed again.

"Good morning!" she said quietly.

"Good morning!" Irmi, the store girl, replied. Irmi was generally in a sour mood, but today she definitely gave Katrina the evil eye. The other women didn't say a word. They checked their shopping list for the nth time or perused the merchandise displays in the windowsills. The only conversation was the transaction over the counter.

Five pounds of sugar, two packs of gelatin, a wedge of shmeerkas, what's the total? six mark eighty, three mark twenty back, is that right, aren't the strawberries so nicely ripe, then also a cucumber, if I may, and twenty rolls sliced for dumplings, these here are our last seasoned buns, how many do you need altogether? the light or the dark raisins? may it be a little more? please wrap that, no, it's not a bother, no problem at all, that would be everything, thank you, next please, is it your turn, Frau Wanninger?

"That's her, she is the one who wrote the story," somebody whispered behind Katrina. Sounded like Frau Huber. Katrina didn't dare to turn around.

"Hey, there!" Irmi addressed Katrina. "You still need to go to school today, right?"

Katrina nodded.

"Is it OK, if I serve her first?" Irmi asked the stone-faced ladies in waiting. Five heads nodded in unison.

"All right then, what do you need, Katrina?"

"A pound of quark, please." She had said "quark," the despicable high German equivalent word for curd cheese called "topfen" by the locals.

The whole store broke into hysterical laughter. "Now look at that! Listen to these studied people! They talk so smartly, as if it's printed," she heard Frau Huber giggle. "Some 'quark' she wants."

"If you ask me, it's always been topfen around here, not quark! What a bunch of baloney," the pastor's housekeeper chimed in.

"Quark, she wants quark," Frau Bürkel chuckled. "No need to wisecrack us common folk around here."

"Nothing sensible comes from studying anyways, I always say," Frau Pfister added with emphasis.

"And much the less from story writing," Frau Bürkel announced in her Hungarian accent.

'What does she know?' Katrina asked herself. Aside from cooking recipes and death announcements, this old woman had never read anything. Fair enough that Frau Gabelsberger,

Mike's mother, was not at the store now. That would have been a hundred times more painful.

"A pound of curds, there you go! Anything else? Maybe a pound of brain grease? It's on special today," Irmi declared with a vicious grin. Giggles and snickers flared up again in the store.

"No, thank you! You probably need that more than I do," Katrina retorted. "How much do I owe you?"

"One mark twenty," Irmi said starkly. She was irritated because her insult had backfired.

Katrina laid the money on the counter and elbowed her way towards the door, pushing through between the matrons and the candy display. She stumbled down the stairs and then ran back to the house as fast as she could.

Her mother sat on the bench by the kitchen table, one hand resting in the bowl with the batter. She stared at the newspaper headlines with high concentration. When Katrina entered, she looked up, perturbed.

"What took you so long? I need to get on with this," Marianne said. "I had almost started reading that paper."

"Sorry, there were just too many people at the store." Katrina set the packet of quark on the table. "Do you want me to open it for you?"

"Yes, if you would!"

Katrina dumped the quark into her mom's bowl and Marianne continued to knead the dough vigorously.

"I need to go now." Luise would be here any minute.

"Where are you running off to now with that paper?" her mom called after her.

"I'll bring it right back."

Katrina rushed upstairs to her room. She was bursting to read her newspaper story. With a pounding heart, she opened the page of the essay competition. Except for corrections of grammar and flow, everything was exactly printed as she had written it. Twisted stories from any old Bavarian village, a hundred years ago, all names changed, locations renamed, the deceased characters altered beyond recognition. Yet, maybe not camouflaged well enough? Mike apparently still had seen his family history reflected in her writing. Coincidentally, an actual skeleton surfaced in connection with her story. What were the odds for that? It fit her "invented" story so tragically well. Apparently, the old-timers around here knew more than they were willing to admit.

But where was the notebook?

The thin folio still stuck in the same spot on the bookshelf. Katrina picked it up and sank down on her bed. She stared at the booklet in her hands. It contained the most secret thoughts of a person, a girl perhaps her age. What had overcome her to intrude so rudely into somebody's inner sanctum? She felt as if she had just been caught cheating in a final exam. An F for you, Katrina! Two fat tears dripped on the butcher paper wrap. The letter H from the title, written in India ink, got smudged in the little flood, "My Heart's Corner." How affectionately exacting the wildflowers had been drawn on the cheap butcher paper. "Grandmother," she heard herself whisper. She had never really gotten to know her. As a four-year-old child she hadn't grasped the truth about people's passing yet.

"Katrina!" her mother yelled from below two flights. There was no more time to waste.

Katrina collected herself, wrapped the notebook inside the newspaper, and rushed down the stairs with her small packet under her arm.

At the bottom of the stairs, she ran, of all things, into her father. A disconcerting angry wrinkle showed above his nose. He grabbed her crudely by the shoulder.

"Where are you running off to with your pulp novel?" Girgl tore the newspaper from her. The notebook fell on the ground. Katrina quickly picked it up.

"What else have you got there?"

"Nothing. Just a notebook, for school."

"Hopefully not another bunch of crap. Where are you getting your crazy ideas from?" Girgl continued to grumble. When thunder rolled over him, it always took a long while for the air to clear afterwards. He had just returned from the milk collection station and all his neighbors had given him an ear full about his daughter's fantasy village. "All our neighbors are upset. How can I even show my face at the next council meeting? Huber actually accused us of libel."

"But I haven't written anything about Hubers."

"Fair enough," Girgl relented. "But how did you dig up all this half-baked criminal mischief around here?"

"None of it is real. I just made it all up." Katrina's voice quivered.

"And why are the people so upset then? Can you explain that to me? Where did you get all this trashy gossip from?"

"I cheated," Katrina stuttered. She surprised herself saying, "I copied it all off from an old chronicle from the Bavarian Forest."

Girgl's fiercest anger seemed to have subsided. Leafing through the newspaper, her father didn't seem to listen all the way. "And what you wrote about the Gabelsbergers . . ."

"Did not!"

"I don't want to hear another word," Girgl thundered. "Both Gabelsbergers, the old and the young, are stinking mad at you! How do you think it's ever going to work out with Mike and you after this?"

"Mike?" Katrina stuttered. "Why . . . what?"

"Do you think I am blind or deaf? It's as clear as glass to me where you sneak off to in the night. And your mother knows, too."

"Mother knows too?"

"Well, we also were young once," Girgl said in a more consolatory tone. "But you really got yourself into some hot soup. Now you just go and spoon it out yourself."

"Yes, father, I know." Katrina sounded contrite.

Girgl waved the tattered newspaper at her. "Now I even have to read this hogwash. Eventually I need to know why people got so upset."

A car honked.

"Katrina, where are you? Luise just pulled up!" Her mother's voice sounded irritated.

"Will be right there," Katrina shouted back.

"Where are you running off to now? There's the door! Hurry up and get yourself to school." Girgl flared up again.

"In a sec! I forgot my essay in the typewriter!"

"You won't get to school on time!" Marianne called from the kitchen.

"No worries!" Katrina yelled back, dashing in the wrong direction. She had left her father standing there like a garden statue. "School starts late today. Religion got canceled," she said under her breath.

That wasn't true, but one could easily get by without religion once in a while. Right now, she had to hide the notebook. It could not stay in her room. The hen house was the safest place. She wrapped the notebook in a plastic bag and stashed it away in the cabinet with garden tools, door locks, lumber nail packets, and a clutter-box with parts and pieces of all kinds such as mousetraps, door hinges, rusty files, and flowerpot shards. Luise meanwhile had pulled up to the hen house. It was an easy guess. If not the house, it must be the chicken coop.

This time grandfather didn't doze off over the newspaper. Girgl had only reluctantly handed him the section with Katrina's story in it. Absentmindedly, the old man stirred the crunching sugar around in his enamel coffee bowl[xv]. The churning, grating sound helped him sort his thoughts.

For the third time, he had arrived at the paragraph about the angel maker. For heaven's sake, how could something like that have happened? But it did. In those days there was no room for a bastard child in a servant's life. Luckily, he had sent Afra, that rotten whore immediately back to the Swabians. She had entirely twisted Wastl's head, his best farm hand. Once he had busted the two humping in the straw barn. Afra simply straightened her apron and pretended as if nothing had happened. Nose up in the air, she had marched straight past him, the master of this farmstead. Even Kathl, good soul, could only find her peace again after that slut had left. The maid had crazed Wastl so badly that he padded after her like a wide-eyed puppy. That idiot didn't even notice that she had a go at Huber's son and the cattle shyster as well. Not to imagine what could have resulted from such a mess! A brat out of wedlock was the last thing he needed on his farm. Or perhaps a false paternity suit fabricated against him?

Rotten women folk were a curse for every farmer, and he could for sure not do without Wastl, who was a wizard with the horses and the forestry work. Therefore, the bitch had to leave. She might have well been the one to seek an angel maker. Angel makers very well existed back then. He was old but not naïve. But luckily, this was one tragedy, he had been spared during his reign on the Weber farmstead. Or so he thought.

But hadn't his sister-in-law, shopkeeper Marie, made insinuations about such maleficent practice in the area? And how accurately Katrina had described the chivaree, as if she herself had observed it in person. As far as he could recall, the old aunt Nanni, had babbled about such a thing in her senile, incoherent ramblings, before she passed away. That was shortly after he, Jakob, had married into the farm.

The old man crinkled his nose and slowly twirled his moustache.

There it was, printed black on white, all of Katrina's stories were invented, fiction, made up. But why, on God's earth, did these stories tug so badly at the nerves of the village people? His subconscious stirred up another incident, a horrifying sawmill casualty. It happened in Kathl's village long before their marriage. But he would have heard about a possible suicide back then. Gossip traveled fast, even on an oxcart. Perhaps these stories were drivel after all.

Grandfather carefully folded the newspaper before Marianne, the house boss, would sweep him out with her broom. Marianne ran a tight ship and he had submitted to her rule. However, the good woman had also learned to starch his collars well enough so that they buttoned in tightly with his shirts. He would never want to wear a new-fangled, collar-sewn-on shirt. Hadn't it always been more practical to just wash the collar and save the soap on the big old shirt? Laundry back then was a lot of extra work without the modern conveniences. So, save your dime on that. He was most pleased with Marianne when she cooked his favorite dish for him, greasy boiled beef with potato salad. Only, she had never grasped why he set the clock fifteen minutes early. Any time she fixed the clock, he moved the minute hand fifteen minutes forward again. No discussion. Factually, this way he had fifteen minutes more time. That should not hurt anyone. Why did she mind?

After breakfast, grandfather settled for his third most favorite location after the peening bench and the saddler's corner, the old wicker chair by the straw shed. Depending on how well he did with the birch twigs and hazel rod bark, he would produce a couple of brooms until lunchtime.

"Finally!" Luise huffed, as Katrina plunged into the front seat next to her. "Did you oversleep, or what? By the way, congratulations!"

"What for?" Katrina nervously lit up a cigarette.

"Your story! First place! Everybody is talking about it . . . Hey, since when do you mooch my smokes without asking . . ."

"Talking? But what do they say?"

"Oh, a whole lot! You can be proud. I obviously never read the paper, but Daniel did. He thought your story was the rage. You hit the nail on the head with it."

"Yeah, the coffin-nail."

"How so?"

Katrina related all the rebuff she had received since the last few hours. Luise suppressed a giggle, but unavoidably snorted out loud with laughter at the episode with the Gabelsberger skeleton.

"Why are you laughing so dumb-assedly?"

"Told you so! Something's wrong with Gabelsbergers!"

"Well, I am not in the mood for jokes." Tears welled up in Katrina's eyes.

"Come on, girlfriend. Why cry over this little bit of spilled milk? Nothing that terrible has happened. But perhaps there was some truth to what you wrote. The truth makes people touchy. Your story must be really good then, if it shook up so many sleepyheads. And you made first place! Just be happy about the money, so much money. Or give it to me!"

"But what about the people?"

"What about them?"

"Everybody is mad at me."

"Oh, will you just forget about them! They always fret about one thing or another. By the way, how did you get all these wacky ideas?"

"How should that matter?"

"S'cuse me, for asking."

"From an old Bavarian Forest chronicle, if you must know." Katrina lied again.

"Well, then, you see how stupid people actually are. So, there was a can of worms without a label and you just opened it."

Katrina could not help but smile a crooked smile.

"By the way, Daniel says that your rusty horseshoe is actually ancient. It possibly dates back to the early Great Migration of Peoples."

"Really? When was that, do you know?"

"Don't ask me, I am no good at history. Guessing, maybe 500 A.D.? But why don't you ask Daniel himself? He is a real wisecrack with the old crap. Huh, that almost rhymes." Luise slowed down and pulled the Kadett in a parking spot.

"Well then, here we are." She turned off the motor. "What do you think? Let's celebrate at the disco tonight?"

"No, I better stay home, to keep the peace."

"Too bad! But hurry up now! If we are late, Schiller will bark at us again."

"Frau Weber! I can't believe that I would live to see this day," Schiller announced in his most unctuous voice. He placed the corrected essay with stolid grace on the table under Katrina's nose. She looked up.

Schiller said, "Very respectable, well done! You have bumped up your average by a notch. Keep it up!"

"Finally, he's got it. What took him so long? Dumbass," Luise whispered to Katrina.

Schiller glared at Luise. "Don't assume that I can't hear you, Frau Pfeifer."

Katrina gaped. She had gotten an A, perfect grade, for her portrait of a saint.

"There you go," Luise whispered to her. "Maybe you're a professional writer now." She shoved Katrina with her elbow.

Schiller, dishing out the grades left and right, suddenly turned around once again. "And, by the way, congratulations on your hometown essay as well, Frau Weber!"

"What did I tell you! You have a reason to celebrate!" Luise whispered. "Why don't you come by this afternoon."

"Maybe for a short while. But no disco, promise?" Factually, she had been grounded, but her parents had business in town this afternoon. There was a window of opportunity.

Wednesday Afternoon

Daniel stroked the horseshoe very carefully. It was trodden flat like a pancake. Layers of rust crumbled off it. The holes for the nails were barely recognizable.

"As I already told Luise, only our institute can date this horseshoe accurately. To the best of my knowledge, this rusty thing carries the dirt of some 1500 years on it." Daniel critically turned the horseshoe in his hands. As he bent into the window light for better vision, his long black hair covered his face.

Katrina had chanced on Daniel in the planetarium. Luise had left a note on the kitchen table that she might be running late from an errand. The window light sculpted Daniel's well-trained forearms as his hands caressed the historical treasure.

"Your horse might have traipsed around over a thousand years ago, all right? That's what it looks like to me. To be sure, I can have the horseshoe examined at the institute," Daniel said.

"No, I believe your judgment, totally."

"Why? What has faith got to do with it?"

"I am sure you know a thing or two."

"Thanks for your confidence. It's up to you. You have certainly made a most exceptional find with this." He handed Katrina the horseshoe. Their fingers briefly touched. One glance. Katrina quickly withdrew her hand.

"Probably the oldest thing in town," Katrina laughed one notch too shrill.

"No, not anymore. Gabelsbergers have a few much older things. By the way, that was a damn good story you wrote for the paper. Finally, something true among all the other garbage."

"But none of it is."

"Is what?"

"True."

"Hah! Good nevertheless!"

"Thank you," Katrina stuttered. She did not want to hear another word about that cursed newspaper article. Rather she was curious about something else. "What do you mean about the oldest things at Gabelsbergers?"

"Oh, I see! Is this about dashing Mike?"

"Huh? What . . .?"

"Your fancy knight in shining motorcycle helmet, right?"

"Bullshit! You have no idea, how much crap he gave me about my story!"

"How so?"

"The skeleton."

"Why?"

"He thought I insinuated murder, that his great-grandfather might have whacked a cattle dealer. . ."

Daniel laughed out loud, shaking his mane. Katrina silenced him with the evil eye. He soon collected himself. "Well, then, there must be something to it? People often get touchy about the truth." He was still giggling.

Katrina jumped up. "Stories, I only wrote a story. Made it all up. It had nothing to do with them! But will you tell me already what's up at Gabelsbergers?"

"Alright! Calm down, sit down, and hold on to your seat. The skeleton is possibly a Celtic princess."

"How do you know?"

"Our professor is working on this case. This morning at the institute, when he spoke on the phone with Gabelsberger, I overheard him. The jewelry seems to date back to the first century AD . . ."

It was an ancient skeleton! And not a Jewish cattle baron from a hundred years ago! Thus, Mike had no more reason to be mad at her.

"You just made my day!" Katrina didn't know what had suddenly overcome her. She spontaneously grabbed Daniel around his neck.

"What? A few old bones make you so happy? Wouldn't you rather prefer young juicy ones?" He pulled her towards him, tight, real tight, but Katrina was already done with the embrace. She squirmed in his iron grip.

"Let go, Daniel! I didn't mean it like that!"

"Katrina, I have a crush on you!"

It dawned on her. She had heard that once before. Katrina struggled, turned her head away from his forceful pass.

". . . I still have a bone to pick with you . . ." He murmured. Too sultry.

'Yeah, bone you've got, but I won't pick it. Let me go now, you maniac!' She turned her head left and right so that he could not kiss her.

". . . I could drink your fragrance . . ." He purred like a lusty tom cat and clasped her even tighter. She wriggled against his steely arms, no chance.

Then with force he searched for her mouth. He pressed his lips on her cheek and worked his way closer to her lips. Katrina coiled and contorted. Her assailant had not anticipated her vigorous legwork. They tumbled onto the sofa. Glasses crashed to the ground.

Never before had Katrina encountered such an eruption of passion. Daniel's full weight pressed her deeply into the sofa. He squished her in his vise, she wheezed and huffed. Her rib cage compressed and got stuck in an iron corset. She could only catch flat gasps of air, almost impossible to breathe any more. She stared at the ceiling beams in bewilderment. Daniel's body was hot and strong against hers, his rock-solid figure contorted like a backhoe trying to dredge into her. His hands went to places of opportunity, her pants zipper, under her shirt, to the clasp of the bra. The physical heat became contagious like a forest fire. She had no chance against the guy. Resistance was pointless. No more strength. Thus, she let the animal force wash over her. Her conqueror drove forward on his quest, interpreting no more resistance as collusion. The steaming bundle was writhing on the sofa. The bra clasp gave way.

"Oh, don't bother about me!"

Luise had bolted into the room. She was never at a loss of words and hard to throw off kilter. Daniel froze instantly and rolled off Katrina. He sat up, wiping strands of hair out of his face.

Katrina jumped lightning fast out of Daniel's reach. In utter embarrassment, she stuffed the T-shirt back into her pants and zipped up her jeans. Daniel brushed his hair out of his face. He was clearly mad.

"I hope I am not inconveniencing you!" Louise laughed. She had a very ambiguous grin on her face.

"Yes, typical you, sista!" Daniel gnashed between his teeth. Then he casually reached for a bag of tobacco on the table and started rolling a cigarette.

"I better go now," Katrina murmured. She gave her shirt a final tug.

"Katrina, don't do that to me!" Luise protested. "Are you forgetting we wanted to celebrate? Don't leave me now!" She held up a bottle of champaign.

"I am sorry," Katrina stuttered. "It is already late. My parents will be home any minute. See you!"

Katrina's feet knew the way home by heart. She cantered along the roadside like a startled horse. Better not look left or right, only straight ahead. Quick, Frau Bürkel is coming out of the grocery store. She waves at her. Katrina picked up speed.

"Katrina! Please wait up! I must speak with you." Whatever else spouted from her mouth petered out in the increasing distance. Just ignore it. Run, Katrina, run!

Now a motorcycle roared up. It overtook her and slid to a screeching halt in front of her. It was Mike. Again? Twice in one day? What now? It was the worst time. Her head was in complete shambles. Mike was on his way home from work. It was too late to run from him. On his motorcycle he was faster than limping old Frau Bürkel at any rate.

"Hey, Katinka!" Mike used this nickname only on very rare occasions, the first time at the party with that significant kiss. "You're not still mad at me, are you?" His voice had an affectionate satin tint to it, like radio announcers are trained to do. He pulled up the bike into its kickstand.

Katrina scrutinized him. She was not sure what to answer. In her state of confusion, a mild smile crinkled her eyes.

"Already forgotten," she said. Putting aside Mike's mad dog attack from this morning did not come easy to her. Then she burst out, "Are you happy about your princess?"

"Huh? How do you know about that already? I had wanted to be the first one to tell you . . ."

"You know how much the people talk . . ."

"But nobody but us and the Conservation Office knows about it yet . . .?"

"Gossip gets around."

"What gossip?"

"News about princesses always get out quick."

"Possible, but unlikely." Mike shook his suspicion off and lightened up. "If only she were still alive!" he joked.

"Yes, imagine that!" Katrina gave him a jovial shove on the shoulder.

"Look, here!" Mike said. "I haven't shown this to anyone." He pulled a little matchbox from his pant pocket. He carefully opened it. Inside was a golden ring with a lapis lazuli gemstone. Katrina made a move to touch the ring, but Mike pulled away the matchbox.

"Careful! This is very fragile."

"What a beautiful piece! Where did you get this?"

"Well, from the princess." He whispered in her ear.

"Shouldn't you rather have that thing examined?"

"The Conservation Office, you mean? I am not insane. They would just take it away, like the princess. Finders, keepers. This stays with the house. It's our heirloom." And looking at Katrina with a solemn glance, "And our secret."

"Right so!"

"Don't you tell anyone about this! Not anyone!"

Katrina nodded.

Then Mike quickly changed the topic. "Will you also be at the Midsummer Night?" Solstice celebration was a cut-in-stone annual event, which colloquially was known as St. John's fire.

"Yes, I think so." Katrina wasn't all too sure about it.

"Very well!" Mike replied. "Then you can help Irmi. We still need someone for bartending the liquor booth."

And off he pulled on the motorbike. He had almost taken the Bogelmüller corner. But then he swung around, as if he had forgotten something. He stopped short of Katrina. "Come, hop on! I'll give you a ride home." Katrina mounted the seat and held on tight to Mike. The bike cautiously pulled off, as not to lose its valuable freight.

That's when Frau Bürkel had approached within range. But too late.

"And about you, Gabelsberger, about you I have also dreamt something!" She raised her arms and wildly wagged them at the fast-disappearing motorbike.

"But it wasn't anything good!" Frau Bürkel huffed and lowered her arm in resignation.

They could not hear her anymore.

But the ring triggered a whole other story.

Wednesday Night

The ring shone like the golden moon, fragile lines of snake intertwined to the band of love, with a stone-like blue as deep as the clear village well.

A shiver slithered from Katrina's back of the neck to the back of her knees. 'Have you gone mad?' she asked herself. 'The band of love? As deep as the village well?' Which band are you talking about? Who is talking? What's the deal with Mike's ring? A perturbing vision pulled forward. Katrina grabbed the Adler before the inspiration would dissolve into nothing.

There was only one way out. From the cuts in her wrists, the blood pulsed in rhythmic small rivulets over her open palms, dripping off her fingertips.

'I mustn't stain the precious wedding gown, or mother will be mad.' Carefully, she folded herself into the chair by the wall and draped her arms over the backrest to keep the fabric out of harm's way. Her head leaned back on the wood-timbered wall of the granary. She looked up. The reed-covered timber above blurred in the flow of tears. Today was not a joyous day. But it should have been, because the elders had decreed it such.

'Amazing how fast blood congeals.' Stunned, she observed how dark crusts had formed along the ruby rivulets. She calmed down. Carefully, she let the mangled wrists slink out of sight again.

Her tears, in contrast, did not dry at all. They had wetted face and garment, yet did not leave a trace. They blended with the air, became invisible. Whereto did they fly? Into the Otherworld? How much I wish to go there too.

She had banged on the oaken door, but outside the drumming was much louder. The granary was an awesome fortress.

The village prepared for her day of honor. Nobody slept all night. The men gathered and butchered an ox. The women plucked the chickens, shoved breads into the oven, and filled the pitchers with barley brew. The young folk danced around the fire. They had it good. They cavorted as they pleased. She should have been out there dancing around the fire too. With Arno. Yet she was to be sacrificed against the will of nature. That mustn't happen.

Honor? Duty? Aren't you entitled to love at fourteen years of age?

Last Samhain, Arno had secretly sent her a precious token. A beautiful ring with a lapis lazuli stone inlaid. If her father had found out about their affair, he would have chased this 'sorry excuse of a nail smith' from the hamlet, and all his clan on top, or something worse.

The birch saplings had been cut, the horse sacrificed.

Her white stallion, the Falcon! That faithful companion was as strong-willed as herself, her father always said. According to time-honored custom, the spirits demanded the Most Beloved before sealing a marriage. However, the Falcon had escaped her father three times. Arno, of all, had led the faithful horse to do its duty.

Duty? No, just a lame excuse to cut her wings. So, her stallion had to pay the price. The stallion's head—she saw it in her mind's eye—now graced the sacrificial stake, his lifeless mane proudly fluttering in the wind, beyond death. This brave was her white Falcon.

Sacrifice the Most Beloved. Fortunately, her father didn't know who her other Most Beloved was. Or else the young lad's life would have ended too. Her father was a good man. He led by example and made sure that everybody honored the law as well. The law of old was stronger than any witch hazel, under which she and Arno had consummated their love. But the western cloud had obscured heaven's blessing.

Yesterday the Centurio, that greaseball of a pig, had sent her a precious necklace. It pulled on her like a millstone.

No escape. The Centurio had requested a virgin in return

for a load of victuals. The coming winter would be harsh, but the nearby Roman garrison always had plenty at any season. Raisins, figs, and wine sweetened up the soldiers' cold days, while her people survived on twice-cooked bone broth and bitter beechnut porridge.

Zum Sterben zu viel, zum Leben zu wenig. Too much to die, not enough to live. She wanted to save her people, yet she couldn't marry that fat pig.

A virgin. Only a virgin could save the clan. Her father had made a promise that his daughter could not keep. She already felt the new life inside.

What disgrace! She mustn't bring misery on her father and their clan. But there was no way out. In wise foresight, her mother had locked away all sharp pins in a chest. Apparently, there was nothing in this room, nothing at all.

No way out, no window, no door, no escape, not even from her own skin.

But there was the ring.

She wore the ring on a string under her dress. Arno had made it for her, a most exquisite design from bronze and lapis lazuli. Two snakes twirled together in a band of love, the lapis glistening in as many shades of blue as the light reflecting off it, a blue as clear as the midnight sky after a thunderstorm. What a miracle of artistry and truth her 'ordinary nail smith' was capable of!

The blue, sharp, precious stone was her way out.

'Eternity is not far. In eternity we are all the same. There the Centurio has no power. There we will meet again, in this heaven which only lies a hand's breadth between us.'

Only the druids could see the Otherworld, but the tears had cleared her eyes. Today she could see beyond.

What her brave horse was capable of, she could do as well. The lapis' edges were sharp. No mercy was to be expected from her father, regardless, dead or alive. But she would rectify him once she met him on the other side. The blood escaped much faster now.

Outside the drumming got much louder, the dancing faster, and the sparks a lot hotter. Mara's tears flowed like a river, her blood too. None of the young folks suspected that their bonfire would become the bride's pyre.

The marriage did not come to pass, but the family's honor was salvaged. The girl departed to the land of tears.

And her Most Beloved already awaited her.

10

June Snow

We are but guests on earth
And migrate without respite
Through many toils and burdens
To our eternal home's delight.

—*Gotteslob, Nr. 565, Georg Thurmair, 1935*

Wednesday, June 19, afternoon

'Migrate? That's not the right word. Not fast enough. Some can't help but hurtle towards their afterlife.'

Grandfather shivered. The popular ear worm tune from many a funeral ruminated through his head. It's June and I am cutting kindling wood, he thought. Bundled up in a knitted sweater and a heavy work apron, he had still gotten seriously cold in this corner by the straw shed. But there was no other work for him. No hay to rake, no ditch to mow, and for setting mole traps it was definitely too wet. It almost snowed, and that during solstice! The lumber for the St. John's fire was safely stashed away on a hay wagon under Huber's gigantic barn. The weather was supposed to brighten up in the next three days, but the weather reports could not be trusted anymore.

Weather reports, what a bunch of nonsense! 'For the time being, sunny and bright,' the announcer had declared. You say? Obviously, it would be raining cats and dogs soon. Gloomy, billowing clouds hovered over the roof tops. Something dark was brewing. And the radio had been just as misguided as the old wisdoms. 'When the elder blooms, the barometer booms.' Obviously not the correct prognosis for today. The old man scoffed. Some wisdoms were plain jokes, like this one. 'When the rooster crows on the dung pile, the weather might change or stay for a while.' Others contained smart-alecky, told-you-so advice: 'Before St. John's pray for rain, afterwards it's all disdain.' True enough, because after June 24 it was usually peak hay harvest season. But now it was still before St. John's, and the heavy clouds would not be able to hold the moisture much longer.

The old man grimaced under his moustache. Was he smiling? No, damn it, there was a branch knot in the pinewood. He threw the log back on the pile. This one was useless. Those darn weather rules! He could not remember when they used to be true. 'Before St. John's ask for rain,' he recalled. 'Right, rain we've had already enough. No more praying for that.' It was so cold it could have snowed. The old man shivered. Hopefully old spinster Nanni had been right when she said, 'June snow stays up high, does not come nigh!' He didn't give a damn about the snow up high, as long as it didn't come down here. So far, so good.

Who in the world had finagled those crappy weather rules?

The old man bobbed his head, nodded a couple of times, as if agreeing to himself, and blew out a puff of angry smoke. He was freezing and yet he was smoldering. He had long wanted to forget about all these rubbish sayings, but how? They had been burnished into his memory. If at all, he really only counted on the power of the moon. Depending on which phase the moon entered, one had to trim fruit trees, chop firewood, mow hay, or plant seeds. Too many of the moon rules had already been forgotten, yet he followed the moon's astrology as best he could. And if there were any weather rules to heed at all, he would have chosen the ones made by nature herself. Those came about when people still had the power of observation. 'If the ants build a big hill, a harsh winter is at the sill.' Truly the ants operated under that instinct, just as the bees did. 'If the bees stay close to the hive, rain is soon to arrive.' But he was done with the bees for good. He had handed the deadly critters over to farmer Huber right after the tragedy.

Anyways, the 'Three Icemen,' St. Mamertus, St. Pancras, and St. Servatius, as well as 'Cold Sophie' had already passed through, but it was still freezing. The old folks called these June chills the 'Sheep's Cold,' which perhaps had now put a spell on the land. Be it as it may, those darn weather rules never ran out of excuses for the cold temperatures. Unfortunately, the cold plagued his old bones a lot.

The old man stared at the burbling waterspout. Then he returned his attention to the pinewood log in his lap. He had selected this split log very carefully because it must not have any knots in it. The splitting knife sliced its way along the fiber, making a soft crackling sound. He had almost filled up the crate with kindling sticks. He would have much preferred to work on horse bridles. But those days were long gone. Marianne had made Girgl sell the last horses, Hektor and Wotan, his beloved half-bloods, to farmer Huber right after the old man had moved into the wood shack. There was no more use for horses on the farm. They were only extra work. Farmer Huber used the proud work horses for parading the summer guests through the village or pull timber out of the forest. For a while, his horses also earned a lot of admiration at the St. Leonhard's parades all around. St. Leonhard, the holy monk, was usually depicted with chains for his patronage of the wrongfully imprisoned or ailing livestock. Every July, except for one town that celebrated St. Leonhard on his proper date in November, the traditional organizations decorated their old iron-shoed wagons—some intricately painted with holy pictures—with fir, moss, boxwood wreaths, and flowers. Just as solemnly, the dressed-up men and women on it carried their prayers around the church. Devotion or not, some pilgrims could get plenty rowdy at the revelry afterwards. Not so he. He was the coachman. He had to keep his cool. And he was responsible for horses, passengers, and spectators back then. Responsible? Was he? At least with the horses, yes, always! *Der Mensch denkt und Gott lenkt. Man proposes, God disposes.* Thus, we're all at the mercy of God. Unfortunately.

Horse pageant aside, farmer Huber still got a respectable work performance out of Hektor and Wotan. Even though the old man had never seen his darlings again, how often had he held their bridles in his calloused hands? Farmer Huber frequently deposited the tattered leather straps on the bench in front of his wood shack, because nobody else could mend bridles as fast and cheap as he could. Saddlery had been the only positive thing he had learned in the cavalry on the Belgian frontlines. Luckily, he was spared the trenches, in which his comrades were blown up by grenades or poisoned with mustard gas. This saddlery business continued, until there was nothing to mend anymore, because even the best horses don't live forever. Saddlery skills had soon become obsolete. Except for one or the other calf halter, the old man had no more commissions. And even then, more and more calves were tied on a harsh chain. 'What a shame for the calves!'

Yes, he got lucky in the war. And he got lucky with Kathl. 'Fortune, what is that, Kathl, tell me? Yes, I got lucky with you. Was it the best of luck? Or did I bring misfortune to you? Yes, for Martl for sure.' If only calamity had struck me instead. Then I would have been done with this deplorable vale of tears. Spared the family some trouble. To be done with it, that he wished for every day. But no wishful thinking improved the ever after.

Grandfather laid the carving knife aside and poked at his pipe again. It wouldn't light up. He was on his next-to-last match, when the tobacco barely started to glow, very softly. Then he took a couple of deep drags and blew out a few heavy clouds of smoke. 'If only my thoughts would evaporate like this smoke.' He picked up the spruce log and the carving knife again. The waterspout only gurgled very softly now, like talking to itself. The rain had stopped.

Thirteen years ago, he had gone to his last St. John's fire on the hill. With little Martl by his side. What delight the young lad had displayed watching the cascades of sparks twirl into the night sky. He had to grab the boy lightning quick by his collar, as he merrily skipped towards the flames. Marianne, who was already expecting her third child, had stayed back home to watch little Katrina. The toddler was fussy and had a cold coming on, perhaps an ear infection. Girgl, as a member of the Veteran's Association, was in charge of refilling the beer supplies. Everybody was busy. Therefore, the old man was in charge of the boy. St. John's was a hoot with that little fella! Come St. Michael's Day—*that good-for-nothing archangel, most useless of the whole angelic empire, Lord have mercy on us*—Martl was gone. Vanished, as if he had never existed, that rascal. Many times, the old man asked himself if he had dreamt him up. But the little blond boy, that droll, wired madcap, had once-upon-a-time actually lived. It was his fault that he now wasn't here anymore. Why did this have to happen?

'Man proposes, God disposes?' Another angry puff of smoke soared from the old man's pipe. 'My ass, the devil alone disposes! And he also lures that girl into ruin! But what can I say, all talk is useless. The truth will finally come out when it's too late.' As he had feared, the memories of that fateful day, Michaelmas, returned like a thousand times before.

St. Michael's Day, September 29. As tradition would have it, in the old days, on that day the cows came home from the Alpine pastures and the servants rehire elsewhere on a farm. It was still a somewhat small holiday, but there were no more serfs. The farmers had now tractors and machines. Besides, Girgl didn't want to hear anything about the old ways. Anyway, on Michaeli, Huber came with his excavator to dig the hole for a new septic tank. After the machine was done, three workers, including Girgl, descended into the pit with shovels to clear away the extra debris. Marianne labored in the kitchen, cooking a roast and bread dumplings. There were many hungry mouths to feed. And Martl was with grandfather, playing with his toy bulldozer in the sand pile. Back then the senior farmer didn't feel his age yet and was not used to idling. As much as he loved the droll little boy, guarding a child didn't qualify as true work in his eyes. At first, he kept an eye on the boy from his position on the bench. Martl was munching on a piece of plum cake with abandon. All around the farmyard there was a hustle and bustle, machine noise, wheelbarrow carting, and what not, all without his participation. He could have still helped so much with pick and shovel.

Again, the events tumbled before the old man's eyes. Loud shouting and commotion sounded from the construction site in front of the house. Emergency, accident, or worse. The old man's heart jolted. His help was needed. Quick, what to do with the boy? Put him in a safe place. There, the empty pigsty! Give him another piece of plum cake. Grab the shovel and run!

They dug Girgl free in no time.

"Well then, now you all come inside after this. Let's eat!" Marianne ordered the crew. "But where is Martl?" A half dozen eyes stared at her.

Before anyone could say a word and break the paralysis, a shrill voice like a Saturday siren pierced the frozen air.

"Dear Lord, dear Lord! Quick! Help!" Quicker than a school boy on roller skates Frau Bürkel came pedaling around the house. "Your boy lies there and doesn't move! He is already turning blue!"

The whole group bolted in unison towards the farmyard. There Martl lay motionless in the driveway. His face was red and blue-speckled. Girgl picked him up, and carefully laid him on the bench. He frantically listened to his heartbeat.

"I am calling the ambulance," Huber shouted and ran over to the grocery store, which had a public phone.

"Watch out! Move away, I say!" Frau Bürkel shouted at the desperate father and pushed him aside. She was trained in first aid and went to work on the lifeless boy with resuscitation attempts. Marianne could not watch this torture and turned her face away. Soundlessly crying, she buried her face in the unrelenting cinder blocks of the stable wall.

Too late. The doctor, who arrived after only minutes, found that a bee had stung the child in the throat and the swelling would have asphyxiated him—if he hadn't gone into anaphylactic shock before. Until then, nobody knew that Martl was allergic.

But there hadn't been any bees around, right? Except for this one, on this day. And it had found its way inside Martl's mouth with the plum cake. And the plums themselves were a special import from Italy. But Marianne had bought them because they looked so appetizing and she wanted to keep her hungry workers in a good mood with her food. If she had not bought these plums, if she hadn't baked that cake, if the old man hadn't abandoned the child, if the boy hadn't been so mischievous, if there hadn't been a construction site, if old Bürkel had only come a little sooner—if, if, if—if only the word 'if' could be struck from the dictionary. It was the stupidest word of all, maybe even the deadliest.

> There we will meet again, in this heaven, which on earth exists only a hand's breadth next to us . . .

'Yeah, I hope you are right, stupid! Heaven on earth? Dead wrong! Sure, death looms by a hair's width, not a hand's breadth. So, how much longer, then, must I wait for this heaven?' Thus, the strangest thoughts, a little stranger than himself, rumbled through the old man's mind as he kept splicing one kindle stick after another. He was stewing in his old thoughts like the cows chewed their cud. Except he never swallowed any of it.

Damn heaven! It came all too soon.

Not a soul had suspected that he, the grandfather, had put the boy in the pigsty for safe keep in the first place. How could he have committed such a big stupidity? Now he had to live with that guilt. He much rather preferred to be dead.

The police as well could only record the cold facts.

Solely old Frau Bürkel had maintained composure in the fateful hours, that old undertaker wisenheimer. As a village helper, she was also in charge of funeral preparations. Sometimes her presence alone, the old man imagined, promised another calamity. But what would they have done without her?

"Go and lay down the boy in the Stube and bring me some water and towel for washing and Sunday clothes to dress him up, your little angel," Frau Bürkel ordered. She didn't even let the mother interfere with the mills of God almighty.

As pale as a porcelain doll, no more blue, just peaceful, little Martl's face glinted as the priest gave him the last blessing. Over the next two days filled with tears, whispering, and rosary praying, he seemed to increasingly become more angel-like. The mother stayed with him day and night. The neighbors visited, prayed, and took over chores in stable and kitchen.

All that was left for the old man was his lament.

'Kathl, what is going on up there? Why Martl?' He had sat in the darkest corner of the Stube for the two days of the wake, making himself invisible to the other mourners. 'What is going on up there? Was that bony Michael angel angry at me? About what? Why, then, did he not strike me down? I would have deserved it. Why the child? Now I know, Kathl, what you meant in your dying hour with to 'keep an eye on him.' And I failed. I would give my two eyes now . . . If only you had been here to watch out for him! I won't ever pray again! Is it not enough that we let this grisly worm take lodging under our roof? That we pour out the first blood from every butchered hog on the ground for bony Michael? Why, why did the archdevil number one take this child, that gravedigger? And not whack us useless suckers instead? I bet that bony Michael also drove poor Elsbeth to insanity. Why else would that poor, deranged woman whack her babies with an ax? It wasn't her fault that she saw ghosts when the doctor had prescribed her the wrong medicine. How heavy little Toni's coffin weighed on my shoulders! I was only ten years old myself. That same year the grim reaper also demanded your sister's untimely death. And what a pious nun she was! They called it "consumption" back then. Your mother lost her life on Michael's damn judging scales. Why, Kathl, why? Don't tell me, Kathl, that you are in the same creepy department with those rippers and body-strippers. Perhaps your old grandfather was right after all. One should not have converted St. Michael's into a St. Leonard's church. Are we now paying the price for it? Kathl, are you there? No offense, I renounce paradise. I don't care. Are you there? Kathl, say something!'

But there was no answer. Nobody talked with the old man any more. Not even his dear wife in heaven. That's why he shut himself up for good.

Gently, snowflakes settled on the leaves. First singular ones scattered about, then always more and bigger ones drifted around. Grandfather stared at the flurries of snow. He was not surprised. The larkspur accumulated white caps; the peonies bent under their heavy load; the marguerites became sugarcoated like cinnamon stars with meringue glaze. It snowed more and more. The fragile bell flowers kept jingling their little blue heads from under the white cover, because the June snow slid off of their steep caps like molasses from a warm house roof. A peaceful, relaxed sentiment overcame the old man. The whole world was uniformly beautiful and white. Then a red drop injured the white, harmonious blanket. Horrified the old man stared at the spot. There was another drop, and another, and a few more. Like a sheet of blotting paper, the snow greedily absorbed the red color. The red blotches grew in diameter. Then the red stains raised themselves up on thin stalks and sprouted the most formidable blossoms. A miracle! Slowly, the snow melted and the reds blossomed. Now grandfather was smiling.

'How nice, oriental poppies,' an internal voice whispered to the old man. 'White as snow, red as blood, dark as night . . .'

According to customs of old the spirits always demanded the most beloved.

The roaring of a motor jolted grandfather back to reality. Everything was a dripping-rainy, gray-green again. At his feet, red spots splattered on the concrete floor.

"G'day, Weber father!" Mike greeted him. The old man nodded. Katrina jumped from the backseat. 'How reckless,' the old man grumbled in thought. 'She should be wearing a helmet.' With a couple of steps, Katrina had reached the grouch's location.

"But Grandfather, you are bleeding! Did you cut yourself?" Katrina asked. "Wait a sec. I will get you a bandage."

The old man looked at his left hand and emphatically shook his head. Indeed, he must have skidded with the carving knife, but hadn't noticed anything. He awkwardly pulled out a crumpled handkerchief with his other hand. Mike stopped him short and took the tattered piece of cloth from the old man, straightened it out, folded it into a bandage, and expertly wrapped it around grandfather's hand.

"There you go. That's a little better. You still should show this to a doctor, you know! So that you don't get an infection."

The old man shook his head.

"Come, I'll help you up," Katrina offered. But her grandfather waved her off. He grabbed his walking cane and pushed himself up on his knuckles. Then he tottered off towards the tool shed.

Mike had already turned around his motorbike and pulled away full throttle. Katrina stared after him.

No time for good-bye?

Witch-Wenches

Witch Mound . . . . The people longed for an explanation of the name. The impression that narratives of witch trials and witch burnings had made on the people's consciousness, generated associations with the innocent location [Witch Mound] that were even more horrifying than the actual witch burnings.

—Josef Dietrich, About the Location Names, 34

Wednesday, June 19, evening, in the chicken coop

Katrina did not understand her grandfather any more. She sat in the hen house, pondering and smoking. Today the old man had nearly cut off his finger while splitting kindle wood. Luckily, Mike had bandaged him right away with the handkerchief. He stopped the bleeding. She herself could not stomach fresh blood. A few days earlier, Mike had rescued gramps from the creek embankment. It had not been the first time that grandfather had passed out. Herr Weber senior has a chronic heart condition, the doctor had concluded. What condition?

Hard to say without further diagnostics. Strange, did the old man even have a heart? Or was he carved from wood like Pinocchio? Material regardless, eventually his deficient pump was the reason why Marianne had been able to coax him out of his wood shack.

What to make of this old man? Did he perhaps spy on her? Coincidentally (or was it?), he showed up at the most inconvenient times. This old man, her grandfather, was impervious, stoic, and impossible to understand. But wasn't he a little like herself, a loner? Wasn't he many times out of his mind, lost in God-forsaken nether worlds, just like her?

Katrina fell into her familiar brooding state. Why had Daniel, in a swoop of passion, pushed himself so violently on her? The scent of his aftershave, a resiny-musky aroma, still lingered in her nostrils. As hard as she had tried to fend him off, she couldn't tell whether the contagious combustion had been more titillating than uncomfortable. Or were bouts of passion meant to happen this way?

Nested comfortably in the old armchair in her cave, her head was still flying through the timbered trusses of the planetarium. Every knothole and fiber seemed to be imprinted on her retina. Her heart pounded. And Luise had ignored the scene altogether and acted as cool as shit. What to make of that?

And then Mike comes darting along on his motorcycle, friendly and familiar like never before. What was he thinking to make her complicit in his secret? The lapis ring was beautiful, charming, but a little small. It might have only fit her pinky finger. Her imagination had gone wild about it and sparked a story of tragic proportions. Mara? How did that name even get into her head? Mike obviously should have declared his find, the precious ancient jewel, to the authorities. But in that case, he probably would have never caught sight of it again. And, anyway, why had he asked her, Katrina the village scribbler, to volunteer as a bartender in the schnapps booth? Did he still care about her? Of all people, she would be working side by side with snappy Irmi while serving schnapps to the locals. Or maybe this would not be so bad because strong schnapps makes for friendly people?

She knew the silly banter by heart. Stupid sayings were to be expected. Of course, many such slogans would get worse with each schnapps. An especially popular saying was, 'Better go boozing in the night than camping in the bog.' Some drinking maxims spelled out ultimate truths. 'Alcohol kills slowly, but we have so much time.' Yet alcohol killed so many young motorists pretty fast.

Katrina was prepared for slapstick word play and crude come-ons, but romantic advances always embarrassed her. She was not good at thwarting awkward serenades or accepting unwanted gifts. For Valentines, her cavalier Rupert from Wolfstown, had brought her an Avon perfume set with an amber pendant in it. She had never liked that scent and handed the perfume down to Walli. Ultimately, she was glad that this fling did not progress beyond a couple of movie nights.

Among the few gifts that Katrina had ever gotten from an admirer, the lucky clover was her most treasured. This hand-me-down, which hadn't cost anybody anything, was so insignificant that the giver hadn't even known he had made her so happy with it. Mike's clover leaf, given to her by his sister Angela, became Katrina's treasured charm. But now it was gone. Gone perhaps also her luck in love?

Forget the perfumes, at least there would be schnapps. Hopefully the cherry brandy or Williams Christ would bring her closer to her heartthrob. But she feared Irmi's sharp tongue. She was the queen of bawdy jokes. Katrina had no such talent and for that and many reasons, she felt glum towards her prospective task. However, the chance to spend the entire evening, the longest night of the year, in the vicinity of Mike, would be worth it. Between bouts of mixed feelings, sparks of joy brightened her mood.

Her heart jolted at an ominous thought. Could she have bewitched two guys at once? That was certainly not her intention. But how do you recognize your true love? Was it love, when your stomach felt nauseous to the point of puking and your head hummed like a beehive? Love, apparently, does make you sick. Or confused? And it can't be given to just anyone. It has to be the right one. But who is the right one? What had she done to cause Daniel to force himself on her with such a passion, and what was her standing with Mike? From him, she had gotten intermittent showers, hot this time, cold the next time.

In the end, if she was to believe Frau Bürkel, it was only the impure, promiscuous vixens who were a man's perdition, like the proverbial snake in paradise. According to rumors, Frau Bürkel once upon a time had been a real Valkyrie, long before she became a demented old hag, who predicted the future to anyone who didn't want to hear it. "About you I dreamt as well," she had shouted after Mike. Fortunately, he'd revved up the engine so hard that they could not hear the rest of her story.

What was it about the "impure broads"? Why were guys so helplessly at the mercy of them? Poor dudes?! Last year, after the St. Leonard's horse parade, old Bürkel had whispered something like "red-haired witch wench" behind Katrina's back. But she had heard it anyway. Obviously, Katrina's transparent Indian muslin blouse had shown the outlines of her bra. Such an indecency! Yet Katrina was not the only victim in the crosshairs of her gossip attacks. Bürkel, without doubt, was the self-proclaimed modesty police. Apparently, her bitchiness and snarky mouth were feared throughout. 'If someone is a witch, it's her and not me', Katrina thought. Witches are always to be blamed for everything. Like the one on the village mountain, who had driven Loisl to insanity, as her grandmother had recorded in her journal. Perhaps she herself, Katrina, was a men-warping witch.

Emanating from nowhere at all, or was it coming from the small sideboard with the mousetraps, ancient orbs billowed up. The more she listened, the more she felt compelled to type. Writing comforts. Thus, Katrina grabbed the Adler and started hacking away. Her grandfather, who sat on the front bench listened up. The clatter coming from the chicken coop reminded him of something. He laboriously raised himself up. Down in the straw shed he grabbed his favorite scythe from the hook, put it over his shoulder, and shuffled slowly to the peening bench under the roof of the garage.

"There he goes again!" Katrina muttered between her teeth and started hacking in competition with the old man. As a small child, without much of a will of her own, she had gotten along with him just perfectly. But by the time he returned from the wood shack, she was not a little kid anymore. Now the clanking of the peening hammer got on her nerves. He is doing this on purpose! Driving nails into the coffin of my fantasy world?

"Coffin nails," she murmured, contemplating the wad of smoke winding its way from the cigarette between her fingers. Her index finger had visibly yellowed from the tar and the cigarette packet was almost empty. Now she extinguished the butt and bent over the typewriter again.

'Witch-wench with indecent passion? Dangerous liaisons? Well, then, witches it is!'

And there had been a number of rumors about witches. Along the embankment of the windy upper creek that sprang from the village lake, a swampy field was abloom during spring with globeflowers, wild carnations, and indigo alpine gentian that had arrived there with the glaciers after the Ice Age. In the middle of that marsh meadow, a slight elevation was noticeable. When the farmer plowed over this field to plant potatoes, he broke through a layer of charcoal. Now the question was: had someone in ancient times fabricated charcoal there for sale or what else was burnt? That spot was called the Witch Mound. Ditto! What the people had been saying for ages might as well have been true. And the farmer was out of luck. The dirt there wasn't good. The potatoes never took and rotted.

This hook fitted the Middle Ages perfectly. She started typing and a long-gone world clattered from her typewriter keys. It was a story about forbidden love. Like in 99 percent of love affairs, things had gone terribly wrong in her story, too.

Who whispered this drama from the past? Katrina was all ears and typed it down.

She was a beautiful child. Brother Gottfried, one night, had discovered the newborn wrapped in a blanket on the doorstep to his hermitage. He had nursed many of God's creatures back to life, but not a human child so far.

He asked around all over town, looking for the mother or a nurse maid. But nobody wanted another mouth to feed. Therefore, he kept the girl and named her Benedikt. He raised her like a boy because a maiden would have had no place in a man's world like his. Gottfried taught Benedikt praying, reading, and writing, as well as the healing arts.

Over time, Brother Gottfried became increasingly sad. Benedikt, now at the age of twelve, had grown and matured splendidly. Soon the feminine charms would manifest themselves, then he/she could no longer stay in his hermitage. The monk struggled with his conscience, and after many long torturous nights he came to a decision. He took Benedikt on a journey many towns away to a well-known herbwife Roberta from the famous sanctuary of Our Dear Lady of the Fountain. Gottfried left Benedikt there and disappeared into the night.

Soon Benedikt got sick from loneliness and sorrow. Roberta feared the youth might die from his feverish delirium. She nursed him with bone broth and St. John's wort tea. Finally, one morning, Benedikt sat up in bed with clear eyes. Roberta brought him a bowl of tea and a bundle of clothes.

"What? You want me to wear these waif's garments? Don't you have anything else? Give me my habit!" Benedikt tossed the clothes into the farthest corner.

Roberta picked them up again.

"Now, just take them, will you!" Roberta was serious. "Women wear skirts. And what should people think? A mature woman such as I shacking up with a half-grown lad?"

"But I am not a woman!"

"Don't take offense with it . . ."

"But Brother Gottfried . . ."

". . . only protected you."

Roberta reached for her most valuable treasure from the sideboard. It was an illuminated and bound manuscript volume. With sure hands, she opened it up to a spread of anatomical illustrations.

"Here," she said. "This is what you will look like soon." She pointed to the anatomical image of the woman.

"Just like you?" Benedikt whispered.

Roberta nodded.

"I am a woman?"

Roberta flipped the book shut without comment. A squall of air hit Benedikta's face.

That was the naked truth. Like fundamental tremors that shook the man out of her, a crying spell washed her old self down the river Jordan. Benedikta was comforted by Roberta's strong arms.

Benedikta served the herbwife as an apprentice. Roberta lived remotely and alone and earned her living with herbs and health practices. She was very adept at her business. Because of that, jealous rumors had it that something strange was going on with her. That she had a pact with evil spirits. Educated women were suspicious. Nobody knew for sure where Roberta had come from. Speculations went as far as calling her an elf or a witch or a druid. But Roberta just laughed such undignified suspicions off.

Soon Benedikta morphed into an exceedingly pretty woman. She learned from Roberta not only vegetable farming but also the fabrication of tinctures, the processing of herbs, and many methods of wound care. The girl was intriguingly smart and dexterous. Even Roberta marveled at the girl's intelligence at times. One nagging worry, however, dug deep into Roberta's heart: that child was too kind, simply too kind. And she was oblivious of her abundant female graces. That was dangerous.

Benedikta always had two open ears for the afflictions of her customers. The sight alone of her radiant, picture-perfect face made the supplicants instantly better. And the remainder of the illness had to cede to her herb tinctures and prayers. Both herbwives knew that every person has only a limited amount of life light. But only Benedikta could see it exactly in her patients' eyes how much life light was still left. Roberta, however, had strictly forbidden her to share that knowledge with their clientele. "We mustn't intervene with destiny. The end of life is only up to God. The Lord gives, and the Lord taketh," Roberta always said. And thus, Benedikta, despite her better knowledge, had to muster the strength, case by case, to care for the next ill person's illness regardless of their light's brightness. If not a cure, improvement, through medicine or kindness, was for sure.

Benedikta was home alone when the vicar knocked on her door. Roberta had rushed off for midwifery to the Sattler family. This type of call was always unpredictable. Some babies took their dear time. The vicar, pale-faced with disheveled hair, stood frozen on the threshold. His hand, which rested on a cane, trembled.

"I am so cast about," he whispered almost inaudibly. "I don't know what plagues me. Help me, so God will."

Benedikta let him into the Stube and bade him sit down by the table. His condition was visibly morbid. His shoulders slumped, his back was bent, barely an ounce of flesh on his bones, and the pallid skin stretched tightly over his cheek bones. His life light barely flickered just a little bit.

"I am so plagued," the vicar repeated and started telling stories about spirit visitations, demons, and specters, as for example the naked broad, who was out to tempt him at the worst moments on the church pulpit. Praying, fasting, and flagellations had not helped him. He had become emaciated and weak and could not help himself anymore. It had been difficult for him, as a last resort, to make his pilgrimage to the healer women, fearing for his reputation. But now he was sure glad that at least one of the herb witches was available. Lucky for him, the friendlier one.

After the vicar was finished with his confession, Benedikta got up and brought two small flasks from the medicine cabinet.

"Five drops of this here in the morning," she said. "That will give you strength and appetite. He must eat and regain strength. Now is not the time for fasting. And seven drops of this blue juice for the nightly rest. This tincture shields from nightmares and calms the nerves."

The vicar looked at her, baffled. It seemed that he couldn't believe that this was the whole prescription.

Then he asked her, "What do I owe you?"

"Two farthings and an Our Father."

The vicar clumsily pulled a small wallet from his vest and laid two farthings on the table. When Benedikta reached out to pick up the coins, the vicar laid his hand on hers, and said, "I thank thee, dear maiden."

Benedikta froze. "Don't thank me, thank our dear Lord, the merciful God!"

The vicar let go of her hand. He put the wallet back into his vest and was about to go. He looked up once more at Benedikta.

"How is it that you women have such a hold on us?" He said it very pensively. And yet his life light flared up a little more. "I probably will never know," he mumbled and turned to leave.

Thus, she fulfilled his dying wish. Love was the only gift that multiplied when given away. And love she had in abundance. Therefore, she had mercy on that sick man.

Roberta returned home and smelled the mess. "Who disgraced you so?" she screamed. "Tell me!"

Benedikta didn't answer, but the hat on the bench gave away the culprit.

"He will pay for that! He will regret to have been born, that boar!" she screamed and threw the door shut with so much force that the cross fell from its hook on the wall. Benedikta could neither stop Roberta nor fate from taking its course.

On the same day, a horrible thunderstorm brewed up. It raged all night and made the little streams swell up, caused flash floods, and tore away the bridge across the Ice Creek. Roberta didn't come home. Nobody in the village had seen her.

Two days later, shepherd boy Dominik stumbled into Benedikta's garden. "Roberta," he gasped, "they found her in the Ice Creek. The floods swept her away. She is dead!"

"What do you say, dead?" Benedikta whispered. "We have to bring her home. Will you help me?"

"No! Run off! Now! Into the forest!" the boy begged her, pulling her in the other direction. "They will come any moment. They know everything! Roberta, . . . is a man!"

The Ice Creek had revealed Roberta's secret. But Benedikta didn't seem to have heard Dominik.

"I know a hiding place," the boy implored her. "Come!" He pulled her by the arm, but Benedikta remained standing on the spot like an iron statue. The people's court, armed with torches and pitchforks, noisily drew closer.

"There she is, the chimera!" someone screamed through the flood of noise.

"Grab her! These witches copulate with the wild animals and the devil." It was the vicar who screamed the loudest.

Benedikta didn't put up a fight. The village people tied her up, spit her in the face, and tore her clothes off her body. Then they gathered all the firewood that they could find in the courtyard and built a stack in the middle of the garden path. In the middle of the pyre, they placed a pole, on which they bound Benedikta.

In the meantime, it had gotten dusky. The women from the peoples' court tore the inside of the house apart and scavenged what they could carry. After nothing was left to take, the crowd got quiet and the mob collected around the pyre. A masked man read the indictment for witchcraft, sorcery, and conspiracy with the dark powers.

"How do you plead?" the ringleader asked the woman at the stake.

Benedikta didn't reply.

"Hear, hear! So, guilty she is! Guilty as charged," the accuser sneered. "Pray an Our Father for your sins!"

But Benedikta didn't pray.

"Light her up already!" a woman with a headscarf screamed. "Shameless witch! Because of her the lightning struck our house!"

And immediately a litany of accusations hailed down on the stake.

"This devil woman made our cows fall ill!"

"I am sure she conjured the tempest upon us!"

"They let my husband croak from smallpox, these witch broads!"

Several torches flew onto the pyre, which was primed with straw and pitch. A jet of flames shot up into the night sky, which abruptly quieted the mob. People retreated from the heat. The flames reduced again. Benedikta was standing upright in the fire.

"Save your soul before it is too late! Confess! You're guilty!" the mummed accuser shouted at her.

"Guilty?" she shouted through the crackling fire. "You're right about that. Guilty of love!"

"There! How blasphemous! This witch is sinning again!" the consumptive vicar shouted.

"No! You are the sinners!" Brother Gottfried parted the crowd with raging fury. He had learned about Roberta's disappearance and started looking for her, his former fellow brother in the monastery. He had not anticipated to encounter such a vicious spectacle.

The monk's habit impressed the mob and they let him pass. Benedikta had already collapsed on the stake.

Gottfried's intervention came too late. His heart split in his chest.

Before anyone could have moved, the monk hurled himself on the pyre and clasped the burning bundle. Both souls ascended to heaven in unison. And all who were standing by attested to it.

Katrina shivered. Witch burnings happened. Where had this strange story come from? So palpable, so real, so visual? Maybe she knew more about witches than she was willing to admit. She was tired. It was quite late, but she had felt compelled to ride her story out to the end. Outside everything was dead quiet. She had not even noticed that her grandfather had stopped peening. This ancient drama did not have much to do with her own love troubles, or did it? Talking about true love? Stop kidding yourself. It all burned up in the fire towards the end.

She leaned back, sober. What incredible things had poured out of her. True love could be quite cruel, but it passes the test of time and fire—was this "romantic"? Was this the right stuff for the essay marathon? Katrina laid the last page on the stack. So, this was the cleansing power of the fire. Let's see, if Schiller will buy it. She had no other choice. Love-fling desperation put aside, all she wanted was a decent grade. Not too much expected compared with trying to be truly happy.

She was looking forward to the St. Johns celebration, the fire of the heart.

12

St. John's Fire

The jumping over the fire was connected with many love and marriage oracles. [. . .] The fire was beholden as, and continues to be, a symbol of cleansing and rejuvenation in many religions. The smoke and light thereof are believed to ward off calamities and increase benediction

—*Günther Kapfhammer, Brauchtum in den Alpenländern (Customs in the Alpine Countries), 271*[xvi]

Saturday, June 22, evening

It was the longest day. At 7 o'clock in the evening the village mountain was still bathed in glowing sunlight. Towards the riverside forest, the golden disk appeared to have been nailed in place for the last three hours. It did not want to budge a bit. Rising from the flatland, cow bell sounds could be heard when the brass band took a break or the children's shrieks didn't drown out the fainter tunes. A cheerful mood had spread across the beer tables as the "liquid bread" flowed generously from the barrels and the fragrance of grilled sausages and pork chops overlaid the natural aroma of drying hay and other earthly scents. The dirt road up the hill was parked full with cars from out-of-towners. Most local family groups walked up the hill on foot, just as much for tradition as for caution. As nobody knew ahead of time, how much they would drink, walking was the safest transportation. As the golden sheen of the village chapel slowly turned from an egg yolk hue to ocher, hordes of kids played catch around the humongous wood stack built from forest clearing lumbers. All seats at the beer tables filled up quickly.

Katrina leaned her bike against the barbed wire, which ended where the steep part of the hill began. She looked at the shoulder-on-shoulder village community and became glum. Her parents and Walli were already seated among the revelers at Hubers' table. Luise had dumped her today because she didn't want to hang at the bar while Katrina was working. Besides, she had said, she had already made plans for a wild "rockin' dive." 'Probably the new Nirvana disco in Munich,' Katrina had guessed. And Angela, Mike's sister, couldn't be counted on either, since she had started her nurses training in another town. She was on duty this weekend.

Ever since Katrina had started the gymnasium, things had not been the same with Angela. How much fun had they had in the old days at the Gabelsberger house with dress up games from heirloom clothes, painting of old wooden chests, camp outs in the yard, jumping from hay stacks, table tennis matches, or cops-and-robber games in the nearby parish forest. Their summer creek adventures had been filled with thrills! Against all warnings, they frequently slithered down the canal sluice that used to power the blacksmith shop in the old days. It was the best waterslide on earth, what a rush! If they were lucky, and Frau Gabelsberger wasn't watching, they got to pluck a few raspberries unnoticed, because the bushes branched far into the creek. Even if she had noticed them, Frau Gabelsberger would have let it slide. However, when Katrina moved on to the gymnasium, and Angela two years later to the middle school, everything changed. Their closeness evaporated when they only rarely saw each other. Finally, Angela had completely disappeared from the monitor by moving away to the nursing school.

Just like the children who romped around the wood stack, Katrina and Angela had played there in the old days, in the most natural way. Children have a right to be happy. However, with increasing age, Katrina found herself entitled to ever less bliss. "You always think too much," her mother often criticized her when she was not able to make sense of the storm clouds forming on her daughter's forehead. With Angela by her side, Katrina would have felt a hundred times more comfortable at the solstice fire, especially since she was also Mike's sister.

Katrina marched quickly through the rows of tables and greeted only those heads who were coincidentally nodding at her. She realized her parents had squeezed onto one bench with the Hubers, with no room to fit another butt. Therefore, Katrina trudged over to the schnapps booth, where Irmi and Resi were busy shelving the spirits, liqueurs, and other potions. There were also two giant Emmentaler cheese wheels that had to be cut.

"We had not expected you this early," Irmi snapped at her without as much as a greeting. "This will only get going until after ten, when the fire's burning. We don't need you yet."

"But we will be busy soon, Katrina! Here, get yourself a pork chop," Resi said and handed her a food coupon. Since the fistfight in the beer tent, she was noticeably more friendly to Katrina, if only to get even with her ruffian brother, Beni.

Katrina got in line by the grill station. Mike was working there, shoulder on shoulder, with half a dozen friends to churn out enough cutlets and bratwursts from the smoking, sizzling grill. Many watering mouths had to be fed. He had noticed her instantly, kept her on the monitor, and when her turn came, he elbowed the other cooks away to serve her. He piled a double portion on her cardboard plate.

"How can I eat all that?" Katrina joked.

"Just you wait! You will need it. This will be a long night," he teased. And then he served the next customer.

Katrina, hands full, wiggled out backwards from the throng of hungry people. There did not seem any place left to sit down. She had reached the end of the set up and was about to resign herself to the children's table, at which wheely-jumpy gymnastics were performed.

Just then, someone called out to her. "Look, who's here! What a surprise, the fearsome princess!

She turned on her heel and found herself staring at two grinning faces. Not them again! Daniel and Raffi! Daniel was the last one she wanted to see, least of all up here, and much the less so quickly after what happened in the planetarium. But where should she go? Sink into the ground? She almost dropped her schnitzels. At least the boys looked more human today than back then at the Volksfest. They scooted over on their bench. Of all tables, there was room for her at theirs. The other strangers squeezed together as well.

"How did you all get here? I thought you didn't like beer parties," Katrina blurted out.

"Hey, come and sit down first. We can explain," Daniel joked. He pretended as if nothing had happened. Had he already forgotten everything?

"Not happy to see us?" Raffi teased. "But we are delighted! Now, sit down, dig in! What a large portion! You must be terribly hungry!"

"Not as hungry as you," Katrina replied and slammed one of her schnitzels on his empty plate, as she plummeted on the bench.

"Thanks! What a blessing! Just in time. I was starving," Raffi said. He cut the piece in half and gave Daniel his share. All three ate with relish. The grill staff knew what they were doing.

"Any idea where Luise is off to today?" Katrina asked her companions between two bites. "What rock dive is she going to? I thought you all were going together."

Daniel hesitated, chewed the cud down, and mumbled, "Can't say for sure what's her plan. I guess she is heading for the Nirvana." That was a place for the "in" crowd.

"Why, that's silly! Why hide in a cave when the weather is so nice outside." Raffi mustered a broad grin.

"And why didn't you all go along with her?"

"Don't ask me. I find snazzy discos just . . . pukey," Daniel said and raised his eyebrows in a comical, ambiguous way.

"I wish she were here."

"Luise? You better forget about her. She has the hots for our new journeyman at the foundry. He keeps her busy, ha!"

"Yep, that's why she ditched us today," Raffi joked.

"And me too," Katrina concluded.

"Then we fit together really well," Raffi said.

Katrina's embarrassment slowly melted away. Those two weren't so bad after all, especially not in daylight and while one kept the other in check.

They were not one bit boring. They could tell stories about worldwide adventures, the newest rock music hits, the best hairpin switchback loops in the Alps, exotic mixed drinks, and

Italian gourmet specialties. They told their stories so well that Katrina's mouth started watering when she heard about such specialties as tiramisu and zabaglione. And each description of a cappuccino here or there made for an enticing picture postcard. Gallantly, her table partners let her participate in this conversation, which was definitely out of her range. Moreover, they even seemed interested in her opinions, as worldly-wise and much traveled they were.

"Now, fess up! What really brings you here?" Katrina asked and pointed with her eyes towards the beer tables.

"The beautiful sights of course," Raffi snickered.

"Duh! Nicely put, my friend!" Daniel agreed. Then he turned to Katrina and asked, "And why are you here?"

"I have to sell schnapps, later."

"I see. And why are all these people here? Do they all want to buy a schnapps from you?" Daniel made a sweeping gesture.

"Why are you asking such stupid questions?" Katrina had seen such awkward banter coming. Yet she engaged, "Don't you all know anything? They are here because today is solstice. There are better celebrations elsewhere, but ours is authentic. So, now, tell me, why are you two here?"

"Because of you!" Raffi blindsided her, laughing out loud about her consternation.

"OK, so do you want to know the truth?" Daniel approached her with a mysterious tone in his voice. But Raffi interrupted him real fast.

"It's very simple. We just love such happenings!" Raffi said.

"Come again? Did you say 'happenings'? What do you mean by that?" Hopefully not another Volksfest? They noticed her confused look.

"Don't you know what is actually going on here?" Raffi stabbed at the bone on his plate with the plastic fork. Then he looked at her with an intense glow in his eyes. "Are you not aware of the spirits of nature that loiter around here under each rock and behind each tree? Look around you. For two thousand years, since time immemorial, people have guzzled beer here at this place. And, of course, they want to always blame their blackouts on a saint."

"Oh, I see," Katrina interrupted him. "Making fun of us plain country folks, huh? In that case, how far back do you want to go? The old Celts? Up there, in the foundation of the chapel, you can still see the blood rock. Every third-grader knows that."

"Exactly," Raffi said, "that bloody rock. Everything is still so refreshingly original here. In a village like this nothing changes in a thousand years. The haze of the past, especially around here"—he nodded towards the schnapps booth—"is almost palpable."

"Haze? The haze is all on you, man! How much beer have you had?" Katrina started getting annoyed. They had a more flowery imagination than she had expected.

"You're so enchanting!" Raffi chuckled. "Here's to you, Katrina! Prost!"

"Anyhow, just you watch!" Daniel winked at her. "I already feel the vibrations of the underworld. Especially on a day as beautiful as this . . ."

And the band began to play, "A Day as Beautiful as This."[xvii]

"All right. Back off now, Daniel!" Raffi had noticed Katrina's eyebrows furrowing. "It's so nice to sit together here. What a coincidence! Let's drink to that! Prost!"

They raised their glasses and clinked them together. *Coincidence?*

"Now it's my turn," Daniel insisted and grabbed Raffi's mug because his was already empty. "How about we drink to brotherhood?"

"What for? We're already saying du," Katrina said.

"Then let's toast to that!" Daniel hooked Katrina under the arm with his beer mug, and took a big gulp.

"Your turn how!" He had a brazen grin on his face.

Katrina followed suit, hooked under and drank a sip. And before she could react, Daniel had placed a wet smack on her mouth. His pirate tactics had proven successful once again. He had caught Katrina off guard.

Just at that moment, Mike stepped up to their table.

"You," he snorted at Katrina. "Resi needs you! Now!" And he swiveled around and stomped back to the grill station.

"Who was that?" Raffi giggled. "I hope not your big brother. Oh, no, your noble knight on the motorbike . . .?"

Katrina didn't answer. "I have to go," she said. Before her table companions could protest, she had escaped, rushing ten steps behind an obviously irate Mike. But she could not catch up with him. He had already resumed his chores behind the grill. She had to report to the schnapps booth now.

"Do you know what's wrong with Mike today?" Resi asked. "He's in such a foul mood. He knocked the tray from my hand and didn't even apologize, the klutz!"

"How would I know?" Katrina snapped and grabbed the bottle cherry brandy that farmer Huber had just ordered. Flustered, she was barely able to fill the shot glasses.

"Hey, what's gotten into *you*! Having a bad day already?" Resi muttered.

Some hard-boiled boozehounds had not wanted to wait for the lighting of the fire. They guzzled one "warm up" shot after another before the evening twilight faded. Then, finally, the red fireball of the sun melted into the forested horizon. It got noticeably cooler. The crickets chirped a little slower. Eventually, a velveteen dark blue with a gazillion sprinkles in it spread across the firmament. The evening star had settled immovably above the St. George's chapel spire. Loud chatter and laughter echoed across the village mountain.

"It's time now!" someone shouted across the brimming beer tables. The children raced towards the wood stack. The schnapps birds as well turned around and waddled blinded by the sudden dark towards the spectacle to come.

"All right! Now they are all running away. What are we going to do then?" Irmi could not conceal the irritation in her voice. She cleaned off the used glasses in the tub of water, let them drip off, and dried them with a dishcloth. She hated being bored.

"Just go ahead, you all! Take a look at the fire, too!" farmer Huber, who was the number one in charge of the whole event, called to them. So, Irmi locked up the booth and they joined the crowd.

Katrina found herself a spot in front of the woodpile in expectation of the ancient ritual. On the slopes of the Eastern Mountainside and straight south in the Alps one could already see other fires sparkle. Katrina hoped that Daniel and Raffi had cleared off just as fast as they had at the Volksfest. In the dark, she couldn't tell if they were still hanging around. Shadow silhouettes without faces gathered around the stack. With the help of a torch and some spirits, soon the brightest flames kicked up in the air. The pinewood poles crackled and rustled, and when one of them broke under the hard licks of the fire, then thousands of sparks whirled up into the air and the children shrieked with excitement. And like every year, the children were told the old story about how the sparks had burst into the sky this way, and that the diamonds of the firmament were nothing else but the high-flying sparks from the St. John's fire. It was just like last year, and the year before, and grandfather's time, and prehistoric times, just like she had written in her story:

When the logs crackled, the rosin melted and the sparks

danced, the smoke whirled or steeply ascended, when a fresh branch cracked and burst, the logs collapsed, and the glowing charcoal kept us warm, the fiery glow finally entered our eyes and deeply descended into our souls. There it burnt out all the black spots.

Katrina savored the warming glow of the fire and for the first time let down guard. Here she was unnoticed to a point that she could let her thoughts wander. Black spots. Yes, her innate worm of conscience had definitely burnt some dark holes in her psyche, all ahead the stupid hometown essay. And what about the haphazard Volksfest interlude, the Daniel episode, and what else was to come?

Suddenly she sensed that someone had stepped right behind her, a body energy or warmth. She felt the silent presence of a person without having to look, the aura touch. She knew this feeling all too well. At home she had enough opportunities to practice this talent, guessing whose aura had entered her radius. Without looking, she recognized a person by inhaling their scent through her very sensitive nose. Sometimes that precarious nose of hers gave her flashbacks when she smelled things that didn't exist anymore, like the unmistakable body odor of her long-deceased great-aunt Maria. Yes, frying schmalz, but also a hint of lavender and vanilla and congeniality. It might only have been a déjà vu experience, but she got a vibe that this terribly sweet person, who was her grandfather's sister-in-law and nemesis, silently and invisibly walked alongside her. Now she hoped that her sixth sense wasn't failing her at this moment and that the person who stood behind her in the light of the fire was the one who she wished he was.

Katrina didn't dare to move lest she drove away the magic. And she thought what she couldn't speak. 'Mike, stop being cross with me,' she begged in her mind. For a good while, she stared straight into the fire, not noticing the fading embers and the thinning crowd. There, a hand lightly touched her shoulder for a bit longer than necessary, but not very long, and Mike's businesslike voice behind her said, "Katinka, it's time! Irmi and Resi need you for sure now." As Katrina turned around, Mike rushed off at a brisk pace and disappeared into the night, returning to his duty at the grill. He had called her "Katinka." That was a good omen.

After the fire, the schnapps flowed even faster. It also made the blood rush madly. Judging by the volume of laughter and hooting, this party might as well have been a Spanish bullfight. Such frivolity rarely happened among the rather stoic village people, only perhaps during carnival masquerade balls. Yet in this uncommon scenario on the hill, it could well happen that farmer Huber coincidentally patted the rear end of Frau Kramer. Or that a tipsy girl toasted "brotherhood" with a boy three times just to score another kiss, regardless whether they used the informal du all their lives. This much schnapps and this many brothers and sisters only happened twice a year: on St. Stephen's Day (December 26), and at the bonfire on St. John's Day (June 24). Again, a few saints were blamed for the hangovers, but each solstice required some kind of sacrifice. While the sun turned its face slowly towards winter, time stood still for a couple of hours.

Katrina's worst fears had not come to pass. Tonight, nobody wasted stupid chatter on her. They used it on others. Luckily, her hands were busy serving cherry water, sticky apple liqueur, and wood-fire bread slices with sharp Emmental cheese. She had to fully watch out to collect the correct amounts of money for each fast-paced round of schnapps.

Suddenly two familiar faces pushed to the front row of the counter, parting the muscled elbows parked on it. Katrina's heart jolted. Daniel and Raffi! She had assumed they had already left.

"Well, then, what can you recommend for us, pretty maiden?" Daniel purred suggestively and made doggie eyes at her. The elbow to the right side of him, which belonged to Korbinian, suspiciously turned around, gave the longhaired strangers a dirty look, and then returned to the pretty girl on the better side of him.

"Stop it, Daniel! Don't embarrass Katrina!" Raffi surveyed with an experienced glance the lion's den. "Hurry up, Daniel! We have to leave soon anyway."

"There is always time for one more drink," Daniel said. "What could be nicer than a schnapps served by such a beautiful bar-maid!"

"You know what you want? Brandy, cherry liqueur, apple mixer, love with kiss . . ." Katrina counted down the menu. She had no time for small talk. Everybody knew that Love & Kiss was eggnog with cherry liqueur.

"Easy, I will have a kiss please," Daniel stopped her in mid-sentence.

"You wish! Kiss alone is not in *your* budget," Katrina retorted. *Not again, not with you.*

"OK, then let's add a little love to it," Daniel grinned.

"Gee, why do you want that sticky eggnog," Raffi scoffed. "Pour us two cherry brandies, Katrina." He turned to Daniel. "And then we will hit the road."

Katrina filled two shot glasses and placed them in front of her special clients.

"What have we got here? May I see your pendant?" Daniel spontaneously grabbed her necklace. She shrunk back.

"A bear claw? Interesting! These are only used by Comanche medicine men in Oklahoma." He seemed fixated.

Katrina pulled back more. Daniel didn't let go of the pendant. "Amazing, a real bear claw. Where did you get this?"

By now Raffi was rolling his eyes in helpless frustration.

Daniel pulled Katrina closer and closer to him across the counter by her necklace. So close that their noses almost touched. And he jokingly puckered his lips in expectation of a kiss.

"Will you leave Katrina alone!" Ernst yelled from across the corner. The stout mechanic was the only one who had not toasted to brotherhood yet. Because of his portly body mass, he could not land a girl easily. Besides, he was inherently shy. Regardless, he would not hesitate one second to defend the honor of a village maiden at any time. Ernst had been watching the scene around Katrina and drawn his own conclusions.

"What's going on over there!" Beni barked from the opposite corner. He had perked up from Ernst's shouting. He recognized the two bikers. All heads turned to Katrina and her two admirers.

"For Chrissakes, look at what the cat dragged in! Not you again, you street dogs!" Beni growled between his teeth. He pushed his broad shoulders through the sweaty mass of people. "When will you riff raff finally stop bothering our girls! Haven't you learned anything at the Volksfest, you gussied-up, deranged idiots! If you don't piss off at once, we will show you how!"

The crowd had fallen silent, gawking at bellwether Beni in anticipation of the confrontation to come. Last week at the Volksfest, he had called Katrina a schickse, or worse, a hooker, but now he had obviously found a hundred reasons to defend the honor of the local girls and start a fight. Half a dozen young men joined ranks with him. Daniel quickly downed his schnapps and braced himself in a boxing stance.

"Daniel, don't be a fool! Let's get the hell out of here," Raffi murmured. He was scanning the crammed booth for an escape hole. Katrina had retreated as far back into the board wall as she could. Being the fuse for a fight was the last of her intentions.

"Stop, Beni! Let it be! You don't want to dirty your hands with puny scoundrels like them!"

Mike had grabbed Beni tightly on his arm and pulled him away from the hotspot. "Come on, leave these wussies alone! The next round is on me! We definitely scored a record with the cutlets today. Let's celebrate!" And then he turned halfway around and snarled: "And you two strange buzzards, buzz off!"

Quickly, Raffi pulled Daniel out of the schnapps booth. Briskly, more shot glasses were filled. Katrina, however, no longer felt comfortable in her skin. All eyes had been on her. She wished she could turn invisible. Perhaps the incident didn't matter that much after all, because the mood got jollier by the minute. If only Luise had been around to pick her up with her Kadett.

After midnight, mostly the bachelors and their 98 percent proof playmates had remained. This hard core with a predilection for cherry, raspberry, apple, or other spirits held on to the raw timbered bar counter.

"Now we could jump over the fire," Korbinian announced. This crackpot idea was not all too dangerous, because only a few embers were left of the glow. Every young man as well as a few maidens darted across the glowing coals with momentum and loud hooting. Ernst thundered into the middle of the smoldering coals with all his weight, sending sparks flying all around. But he was quick enough to escape without burns. Beni vaulted with a pole across the pit and broke the distance record. The dare-devil fun always got wilder. Katrina watched with mixed feelings from the shadow of the bar hut. However, it was hard not to be infected with this enthusiasm. The respite in the cloak of darkness revived her. Suddenly, Mike materialized right next to her.

"Come, quick!" he whispered, grabbed her by the wrist and pulled her toward the forest on chapel hill. With a few steps, they were out of view and soon in the forest.

Mike had taken Katrina completely by surprise. Nothing better could have happened to her. For a while they silently walked through the forest, hand in hand. It was a dream. They had left the shrieking jamboree behind. Then Mike stopped Katrina by the mighty trunk of an ancient beech tree. He looked at her and brushed a strand of hair from her forehead. He bent down and kissed her softly.

> During the full moon she had betrothed herself to Arno under the Witch Hazel and desired eternal love for her.

Katrina wrapped her arms around Mike's trained, compact body. Again, this incredible dizziness of a hardly believable fairy tale enraptured her. A million little ants crawled in her stomach and made her knees tremble.

It was a rush of passion. Katrina pressed herself into his body like one creates snow angels after a winter storm. She recognized and savored Mike's fresh scent, a hint of after shave, overridden by a smoky grill flavor clinging to his shirt and hair. Firewater on his breath. Soft lips, exploring tongue. Strong hands finding their way to the buttons of the blouse. Blouse gliding off her shoulders, bra capitulating to impatient hands. Skin on skin, the heat wave rises, from the heaving chest to the spinning head. Endless moments passing in the realm of timeless, sensual bliss.

Something cracked in the underbrush. The rustling came closer.

"Fuck, someone is coming," Mike hissed. "Fucking pissers! Quick, duck down!" He pulled Katrina into the protective cover of the underbrush.

Now all was quiet again. They could hear nothing but the remote shouts and giggles rising from the festival location. Mike must have been mistaken, no pisser anywhere. Regardless, romance was out the window. Or Mike had decided that it was over. Was he that much afraid of being caught? What was the big deal about a little shmooze? Meanwhile, even married partners swapped playmates in plain sight. Why stop now?

"I will go ahead. Wait a little and then follow!" Mike stuffed his shirt quickly back into his pants and disappeared like a wood sprite between the trees.

Katrina straightened her blouse and combed her tousled hair with her fingers. She leaned against the massive beech trunk and took a deep breath. It all had happened too fast. Did Mike like her after all? If so, he had let her stew in her own juices for quite a long time. Or maybe he was just too shy to admit to love? Katrina glanced at the silent moon. When a cloud moved in front of it, she made her way back to the schnapps booth.

But the western cloud had darkened their fortune.

What was going on in there? She trudged closer. Barks of hysterical laughter rang from the schnapps counter. Mike seemed to be wrestling with Beni over something. A throng of shrieking drunkards wavered around the two wrestlers.

What was so hilarious?

"Mike, you scoundrel! Look, what we've got here!" Beni screeched in his highest falsetto. He wrestled free from the crazy mob and waved his trophy in the air. It was a bra, Katrina's bra. Mike had stuffed it into his pants in all the rush.

"Katrina, maybe this belongs to you?" Beni waved the bra at her, gloating all over his face.

She turned chalk white.

"No? Are you sure? Come a little closer. Let me size it up right now!" He reached out to grab at Katrina's chest. She ducked away with lightning speed.

What a shameless betrayal! Katrina's heart plunged to her knees. Fight or flight? For fighting she had already lost too much blood tonight. Deathly wounded, her horrified glance hit Mike like a well-targeted slap in his face. Not the slightest reaction was apparent in his demeanor. Not even a drop of support? She turned around on her heel and ran back into the black night up the hill and into the woods.

"Come on, Katrina! Sourpuss! Can't you take a little joke anymore?" Beni yelled after her. His voice cracked. "All right, then! At least you have something to write about again!" Exploding laughter.

Katrina ran and ran, nothing mattered any more, until she got her sleeve caught in a thorny bush. She tore loose and wandered aimlessly and crying through the forest. She drifted uphill. Then she leaned against a tree and slid her back down on it like the deflating bellows of an accordion. She hunkered down and buried her head between her knees.

Tears poured down. She had not noticed how exhausted she was. Everything calmed down. Except for a hooting owl. The wind gently fanned some sounds along. Was it music? It couldn't have been from the party, since she was far away from it. No, the sounds emitted from the chapel.

Katrina got up slowly and plodded closer to the music. What were those lights behind the church? Ghost lights? Couldn't be because they had been banished by the Pope a long time ago, as her grandfather had once explained to her. Halfway there, she discerned among the sound fragments of human voices. Was someone praying? She hesitated. Fear had arrived, but too late. She was magically attracted by these mysterious proceedings. Her curiosity got the upper hand.

She crept on all fours, like she had read it in her Karl May Western novels, without cracking a twig or bending a leaf, closer to the crime scene. Finally, she painfully inched forward on hands and knees. Indeed, those lights were burning candles.

Peeking between the branches of her cover, she counted about a dozen figures, dressed in white and cowering in a semicircle around the blood rock in the foundation of the chapel. On that protrusion, a few candles were lit. From her position in the hideout, she glimpsed the arm of a man with a dragon tattoo. That arm held something into the candle flame. The pungent smell of incense seasoned the air with a peculiar note.

Then the murmur started up again and increased to a chant. Katrina shoved the twigs apart for better vision. A young woman with long black hair and a flower garland around her head, also in a white robe like the other strange figures, sat amidst the circle with her head bowed down in meditation. Now she raised her arms and face towards the sky. Her face became visible. Luise!

Katrina froze. What in the world was she doing there? This was certainly not a hot "rock dive."

With a queasy stomach and aching knees and elbows, Katrina retreated as noiselessly as she had approached through the bushes. She cut across the chapel forest to the other side.

Run, Katrina, run!

She raced home across the moonlit pebbles, as if it were a shell plastered beach. Only after she arrived at the sports field, she reduced her pace. She sat down on the bench near the creek and listened to the comforting gurgling of the water. Her brain was dead, unable to process. Soon the sun would rise again.

Katrina tottered home, mechanically. She had all but forgotten about her bike.

Grandfather spotted her from his upper floor room window. He watched her unsteadily stalking towards the house. Then she clattered with the key in the lock. Finally, he heard her rumbling up the stairs. Thank God, thank you, Kathl!

He had never been able to sleep during St. John's eve.

The marriage did not come to pass, but the family's honor was salvaged. The girl departed to the land of tears.

13

Into the Woods

Each tree is one-of-a-kind—a unique specimen like every human being—and evolves just like that along the earlier described conditions in various ways, based on the given living environment. And the tree is, as is the human person, extremely dependent on light and sun. It sounds strange but is hardly deviant: If a tree is planted at the same time at the same location as a human is born, then you can clearly notice parallels during both their life-times.

—*Carla Ludwig, Das Horoskop der Druiden*
(The Horoscope of the Druids), 7

Monday, June 24, Jacob's story

Done with the fox-haired or black-haired or always-changeling vixen. The better for it! A while ago, grandfather had spied the painted fox streaking around the hen house, but Katrina had not let her in. By the looks of it, she was done with the young Gabelsberger too. Something must have happened Saturday, at the St. John's feast. Katrina had staggered home, alone. Too bad! She should have come home on Mike's motorbike. The old man had caught the guy making eyes at her not only once. Mike seemed to like her well enough. Why else would he have loitered around the farmhouse so often quite "coincidentally"?

Coincidentally, Mike had also crossed the old man's path when it hadn't suited him at all. Like when he had tumbled down the creek embankment with the scythe in hand, or when he cut his hand while splicing kindle wood. He could not count the times Katrina had arrived at the house on Mike's motorcycle. Yet recently something was askew. He had noticed how Katrina had slinked away after the Corpus Christi procession to avoid the throng of young men huddled by the churchyard linden. And why had they giggled after her? Yes, why? On the morning of Corpus Christi, Katrina had rumbled up the stairway during his Sorrowful Rosary, more exactly, during the First Mystery of "He who perspired blood for us." And he had heard several voices. Among them, he had picked out the chitter of the Bohemian schickse. Girgl apparently hadn't noticed anything, neither had Marianne. But, yes, he was sure! However, he no longer had anything to say. Therefore, he let all that rumbled take its course.

'Kathl, how will this end? What can I do?' he sighed in mental prayer. But Kathl never gave him an answer except for that one time when he had actually thought he had heard her speak to him posthumously, if not to his ears, to his mind. To this day, he wasn't sure whether it had really happened or he had just dreamt it. As a hundred times before, he mulled over a series of events that had catapulted him back from his shack in the woods to the farmhouse. A certain event had almost brought him back to the living, except that he became even more speechless than before. And this is, more or less, how the story went.

It was around that time in November, to be specific, the seventh year after the accident with Martl. He lived in the wood cabin since then, to see nobody, to talk with nobody, to be alone. 'Stupid talk does not bring the dead back,' he had concluded. In his cabin, he had arranged for everything he needed for a living. But what kind of life was it? He was done with it. Besides, what was he still good for? Just some easy, mostly obsolete farm chores.

To stay busy, and to generate some pocket cash, he clipped the branches off the felled trees for Girgl and bundled the pieces for sale at the store. Or he made kindle sticks by splitting pine logs, which was a popular item with the Hausfrauen. For this, he was soon nicknamed "Lumber Jack" based on his given name, Jakob. Occasionally, he mended tack, bridles, and halters for the farmers who could still afford the luxury of horses. It tore open a wound in him each time farmer Huber brought him gear to fix for Hektor and Wotan, his darlings that Girgl had sold. He hoped that his horses were in good hands and that they were treated to apples and carrots once in a while because he knew they were obedient, hard workers. When he wasn't home, the farmers simply stuck the pay behind the rough timbered shutters.

Jakob spent a lot of time in the forest. Over time he mapped out the best locations for porcini and chanterelle mushrooms and grazing grounds for the roebucks. He recognized them by the tips of their antlers, when he observed them, silently and motionless. Sometimes it seemed to him as if he could smell the deer, just like they obviously sensed his odor when they probingly flared their nostrils in the breeze. Yet the deer also had incredibly sharp eyes and acute hearing, their agile ears fanning for the slightest crackle. He didn't dare crimp a leaf or they would up and skip. Sometimes he got so close he could have touched them. Over time, he recognized their trails, habits, and family groups. He had morphed into a wood sprite after a while.

How quiet it is in the forest, and the twilight shines on it with abundance. In grade school Jakob had had to memorize reams of romantic poems, the forest with its moods and creatures being a major objective for the German soul. These poems still had a way of popping into his mind in the serenity at sundown. Mind you, there were also a few rather voluminous books. Not for entertainment, rather knowledge and spirituality. He didn't need much to read because the daily activities kept him quite busy and he went to sleep early. There were tattered herbal compendia, a Bible, and an old atlas with boundaries from before World War I. Forget about the books! What was most important to him, Jakob already carried in his head.

Colorful are now the forests, yellow the stubble fields, and autumn begins. Colored leaves descend, gray fogs waft—and, look around, there were so many hazelnuts and mushrooms too. Autumn with its extensive walks and mild, sun-drenched afternoons had a calming effect. Jakob's old school teacher had sometimes equaled October with "gold leaf month," or he had talked about the "cathedral of refracted light." That was a little eternity ago, but these strange images had stuck in his mind. When he was able to recall the stanzas, he indulged in the colorful impressions of his youth.

Winters were quite another story. They were mostly white. *All is brilliant in the woods, all is silent in the forest,* especially when the powder snow glistened in the sunlight and the pine branches curved under their white load, and *All roads are snowed in, and all ways are blown in.* For his friends, the birds, Jakob had collected sunflower heads in the summer. He hung their dried heads one after the other on the lower branches of the majestic pine tree in front of his cabin. They were picked empty of kernels in no time. *Hear you how the branches bend, see you how a bird takes flight?*

Wood winters could be extremely long. After the scant chores were done, Jakob often grabbed his pocket knife and carved figures of the creatures of the forest. He wasn't exactly a master carver, but his animal shapes turned out quite well. His little gallery of deer characters was each named after their real-life counterparts. There was Herkules, the prime roebuck, royal Apollonia, and right next to her on the ledge, Maxi, the capricious fawn from three years ago who had suddenly disappeared. Perhaps he got mowed down hiding in the tall hay, as it so often happened. Or the scrawny fox had gotten him. All his deer companions were immortalized on the book shelf.

When the weather was good, Jakob could not bear to be inside. Sunshine always drove him out to split the logs. He wanted to see wood chips fly and keep his continuously stiffening joints agile. It felt good to chop away like mad. The pain in his aching muscles cast out the murky thoughts. But every time he stopped chopping, the familiar anguish returned and took rest on his head like his old scratchy wool cap. The more he resisted the demons of the past, the more his scalp itched from the imaginary sheep's wool. For a long time now, he hadn't had any vermouth, his home remedy for sadness ever since Kathl had abandoned him on this earth. Somehow the bitter-sweet spirit didn't taste right any more. Instead, he had taken to herb tea with honey.

The cemetery. When desperation got the better of him, an invisible hand pulled him towards Kathl's grave. Martl was laid to rest in it too. Everybody in Kathl's lineage was buried there, and so would he be in due time. Jakob usually ventured towards the village under the protection of the dark. On his route, he had to pass by the farm, his former home. And if the curtains weren't pulled shut yet, then he peeked inside the window for a glance. How fast the kids are growing up, he wondered each time about Katrina or Walli. Only one was never there. What would Martl look like now? The old man sadly shook his head and continued his walk. At least once a month, his torment drove him to visit with Kathl. He talked with her. She never replied. It was a monolog. His pleads were useless. He might as well have talked to the roebucks, squirrels, or birds. The gravestone was just as speechless as the forest.

This could have gone on forever. But then, one day, suddenly, he was done with the silence in the woods. It happened on a gentian-blue day in the high noon heat. Jakob keeled over while splitting logs. The new huntsman, Norbert Pechtl, picked him up and put him back on his feet.

"Let me call a medic from the forester's house," Pechtl said. The old man, however, waved him off and staggered towards his cabin, uncertain on his legs like a newborn foal. He was still chalk white under his beard and breathed heavily.

"Or should I take you to the hospital?"

Jakob waved him off again, more forceful than before.

Pechtl didn't seem in a hurry to leave.

"A shot of brandy or an aspirin might serve you well just now. Do you have anything in the house?"

Pechtl worried there might have been a serious reason for the old man's collapse. They ended up in the wood shack together, with Jakob brewing tea for the hunter.

And they struck a deal.

Pechtl, new to this territory, hired the old man as a forest guide. At first, Jakob was nowhere close to comfortable with this task, because Pechtl talked too much. Naturally, the old man didn't want anyone shooting at "his" deer. But the hunter assured him that he would only take out the sick and weak animals. Talking wouldn't be necessary either, Pechtl blabbered enough for the both of them. Altogether, Jakob never quite understood what a certificated huntsman should want of him. With as difficult an exam as the huntsmen's boards under his belt, Pechtl should have known a hundred times more than an old horse handler like him. Yet soon enough the unequal pair went on their weekly morning expeditions. This went on all summer long until late fall.

Then, one day in November, Pechtl brought Jakob a commission from the village priest. He could not tell him exactly what it was, the forester said. The priest hadn't specified, but Jakob should stop by that day before evening mass. 'Maybe he has some wood to split,' the old man guessed. 'But he needn't make a secret out of that. Perhaps a cleanup is needed in the parish forest? Or did he want the old church benches cut down for fuel?' Obviously, many things were being renovated in the church at this time. He pondered his assignment for a while. This wasn't going to be easy for him. But even though life in the woods was cheap, it wasn't totally free of cost. Each additional income helped.

As always, he stopped by Kathl's grave. As there was light in the church, he ducked down behind the gravestones to avoid crossing paths with priest, custodian, or prayer mamsels, whoever it might be. The grave was always nicely decorated. Marianne did such a good job. And often a candle was lit on it.

'Kathl, I am not so well, perhaps we will see each other soon,' he grumbled in his mind. 'What's it like up there? Is it worth the trouble?'

No answer. Only a dog was barking in the distance.

'Or maybe I won't see you after all. Not sure they would let me in up there.'

As a farewell gesture, he stroked over the arch of the gravestone. Something fell to the ground with a dull thud. He picked it up. It was a fire-engine red matchbox car. Perplexed he stuck it in his pant pocket, where he carried his handkerchief, unsure what else to do with it.

He looked up to the tower clock. The steeple had been scaffolded since spring because several cracks in the wall had to be repaired. In the interior as well, from what one could tell from the outside, the plaster on the walls needed to be redone. He knew every little nook and cranny of the sacristy, since he had rung the bells there for many years, a custodian's job that had come with the family tradition. Soon an electrical mechanism should take on this task. Soon the altar boys wouldn't pull the ropes any more to ring the bells, only push a button. Well enough! Old St. Michael's bell was heavy.

It was time to go and meet the man of God before Mass would start.

Jakob halted on the doorstep of the sacristy, cautiously peeking inside. The door was half-way open. The priest stood by the refectory cabinet, putting on a stole, and the altar boy waited in the middle of the sacristy for the signal to pull the bell rope.

Jakob started sweating, beads of perspiration formed on his forehead. He pulled his handkerchief out of the pocket to wipe off his brow. The matchbox car clattered down the three steps and rolled across the stone floor into the sacristy.

Suddenly everything happened all at once.

The altar boy saw the red toy car rolling and dashed after it. Right at that moment, thunder rocked the steeple rafters, the sacristy quaked and trembled, like an air raid during the war.

'For heaven's sake, old Michael's coming down!' The bell had jumped its yoke.

The old man felt the tremors from the soles of his shoes to the roots of his hair. With the unhinged force of a renegade diesel locomotive and several tons of weight in its skirt, the main bell descended down the tower. Crashing through all rotted floor boards on its way. Mighty Michael went straight to hell! Tearing everything with him. Jakob knew all about the raw force of that bell because he once had helped hoist its five tons up there. Shucks, Jesus, Mary, and Joseph! Dear God in Heaven! Kathl! What to do? He blanked for a tenth of a second. Then he just jumped for the boy. He tore him away from the impact zone and whisked him over to the safe nave of the church.

With a roaring thunderclap the bell and its trail of debris slammed into the tile floor. The impact shrouded the sacristy in a thick cloud of dust. Michael's bell hit like an earthquake, as rocks and splinters and debris splattered to all sides.

The priest still stood, pale faced and dusty all over, in the same place by the wall cabinet as before. Miraculously, he had not been scraped one bit. Mechanically, he started patting off the dirt of ages to make sure all his bones were still there. The bell, after all its murderous journey, had remained intact as well.

Jakob set the shaken boy down on firm ground. He was a namesake of the bell that had almost crushed him. If the boy hadn't jumped after the matchbox car, the old man would have never been able to catch him by his collar and take him to safety. The evening mass was canceled that day, but Jakob did not stay long enough to find that out. He, also shaken to his bones, quickly escaped to the security of his wood cabin.

The next day, Jakob found a gift basket filled with fruit, cake, sausage, vermouth, and other goodies, on his front bench. The note said, "Please come home again, grandfather!" in Katrina's unskilled handwriting. And this was also what the priest had wanted to talk with him about. The commission was only a pretense. The huntsman, who had worried about him just as much as his family, had engaged the priest to reason with the old man. With his worsening heart problem, as far as Pechtl judged the symptoms, Jakob should no longer dwell all by himself in the forest but consult a doctor. With Marianne's permission, Pechtl had set the priest up to it. But the St. Michaels bell came through faster than the Reverend. And Jakob set a new speed record. Thus, the altar boy was saved and the old man returned to his family.

Now he sat there, like so often, with his pipe gone cold, on the peening spot. If all the scythes could have talked, this would have been a very long story. But they kept quiet, except when pounded with a hammer. Regardless, Jakob didn't surmise that anyone would have cared about his scythe songs. He just wanted to be useful. Sometimes he surprised himself. He was quite adept at so many tasks, needed or not.

'Nobody knows how to peen any more. It's a forgotten art.' He kept pounding the blade in front of him. It soothed his thoughts. The clatter in the chicken coop, by contrast, rather resembled the wild ride of a Wilhelm Tell overture.

'What an awful noise,' the old one grumbled in his mind. 'But at least she isn't consorting with the riff raff.'

14

Horseplay

Since its domestication, at about 2000 BC, the horse has played a special role as sacrificial animal in Celtic society ... skin and skull of the horse played a special role. The latter was mounted to the gables of houses or stuck on poles to avert disaster.

—Pferdeopfer, Reiterkrieger (Horse Sacrifice, Horse Warriors),
Webpage, Detlef Stender

Tuesday, June 25

'There she goes again,' grandfather sighed. He let go of his scythe, pushed his hat back for a better view, and lit up his pipe. He listened to the fast and angry clack-clack-clacks. Overture to Wilhelm Tell? A stampede? Right, it sounded just like a cavalry of horse hooves.

The white stallion took to full gallop onto the village mound, with flying mane and bobbing head, alive with the thirst for living.

The farmer let out a curse. His white stallion, Blizzard, a

rarified beauty with a dappled white coat, did not get along at all with his black rival. White Blizzard had failed in subjugating the black steed, although they had frequently scrimmaged on the moor meadow. Today, again, Blizzard showed off to his black rival what all he was capable of. The tall wooden fence was no obstacle. The farmer, barely spotted a small white dot taking flight towards Bog Forest. But then the stallion seemed to change direction and started racing up the village mound.

"Bloody devil! I will show you manners!" the farmer grumbled.

With a rope rolled across his chest and a halter in hand, the farmer and his churl headed after the horse. The men called for the animal, clicked their tongues, and kept dried bread and apple slices handy in their coat pockets. But nothing, not a tail in sight. At any rate, there were enough neighbors who would have recognized the animal and returned him. The white stallion, however, gloated. If the men had been a little smarter, they would have noticed that the horse kept ducking away behind the church. He kept circling the chapel for cover and the men could not see him.

Long story short, they didn't find the horse. Annoyed and bewildered, the farmer and his helper returned home with the empty halter. The very next day, the white stallion stood grazing on the pasture as usual next to his black companion.

"Holy terror!" the farmer cursed. This amount of disobedience was a bad omen. In three weeks, there would be a livestock market in Feldkirchen. There he would hopefully be able to sell the Blizzard off.

The white stallion did not wait that long. He was out to prove something. Soon he challenged his black rival called Raven again. They got at each other's necks. It turned into a heated battle for dominance. The Raven jumped the fence and the white one dashed right after. They cantered whinnying and biting each other, with flying manes, towards the moor meadows.

"For heaven's sake, good Lord have mercy . . .," the farmer cursed when he saw them run away. Again, the wild chase led them up the village mound, as the dirt from their hooves splattered in all directions.

"This time you won't get away from me!" the farmer swore. Aside from his churl, he also brought along farmer Huber and a couple of other helpers.

The white stallion knew the terrain as if it had been brandished in his brain. But the Raven countered his every move and also jumped creeks and bushes with ease. He did not miss an opportunity to kick his rival in his side or bite him in the neck. The white one paid him back one at a time.

Snorting and huffing the horses reached the top of the hill. Like boxing men in a ring fight, they danced about each other, always vying for an opportunity to strike. Pushed against the chapel and with no other escape in sight, Raven sought refuge inside the little church, barely fitting through the squat door opening. The white stallion squeezed through right after him. Raven, barely inside the small sanctuary, nervously spied for an exit. Blizzard set out to land a fierce kick on his opponent. But he misjudged. His hooves hit the rock-solid church door. The door fell shut with a loud bang, but Raven was already out again, bolting down the hill with a vengeance. Silence sank upon the chapel.

The farmer and his men caught the black steed trotting down the hill by the open field. Raven was amazingly tame. "Look, how he messed you up again," the farmer comforted the horse and stroked his head. "If you would only submit, if you would only submit," he murmured. At least he had one horse back.

There was, however, no trace of the white stallion. The churl put the halter over Raven's head, but he didn't want to come home. The horse pulled in the opposite direction towards the chapel on the hill.

"Whoa, you're not going to go crazy on me, too, are you!" The farmer soothingly stroked Raven's neck. The cows at home wanted to be milked badly. They pulled and pushed the resisting animal home with united force.

"By God's grace, Blizzard will show up again," the farmer thought.

But the white stallion did not come back. To the contrary, Raven seemed to have adopted his rival's escape act. Something kept steering the black one towards Chapel Hill. He knew more than the humans did, but nobody understood the animal. Soon enough, the farmer traded Raven in for a more docile horse at the next livestock auction.

Three weeks later, during the St. George's pilgrimage, the puzzle was solved. The white stallion lay dead in the chapel, starved to death. And ever since then, a white horse has occasionally been spotted cantering around Chapel Hill in the night.

Katrina had handed in her essay this morning before school. German class, the last subject of the day, was about to start. She settled into a front row seat next to nerd Beate, because Luise would never want to sit anywhere near the blackboard. Beate, a girl with large wire-rimmed glasses, who always knew the answers, seemed enchanted about her new companion. But she soon would notice that Katrina was glum and pouty. On the school bus, Katrina was the last one on and the first one off. Luise had no chance for an approach. Unfortunately, Katrina was now alone with her outlandish stories. No more encouragement to count on.

'That horse? A ghost? That's how your story goes? What have you made up this time? Research, local history needs research,' Katrina was mulling over her recent story. She could already hear Schiller condemn her essay. But by and large, the "local mythology" leads were always the same old stories all over again. Katrina shook her head in doubt. What, a white horse? A horse was not a historic person. Schiller wasn't likely to buy that. Yet the ghost horse on Chapel Hill was such a local fixture when one had been raised in "Andershausen." Besides, the ghost horse kept good company with a nefarious witch, who, according to the grandmother's diary, had scared the raftsman Loisl to death, literally. Katrina was apprehensive about German class.

Luise showed herself totally unconcerned, on the bus as well as at school. She greeted Katrina cheerfully and tried to strike up a chat with her, although that wasn't easy across so many benches on the bus. Katrina had curled up in the farthest corner seat and held her Latin vocabulary book in front of her nose.

'What's up with her! Can't she see that we are done?' Katrina grumbled inside. When Katrina sat down next to Beate in class, Luise got the message. She detoured to the far back corner of the classroom and took up the seat next to Ferdl, the only available spot. Nobody wanted to sit next to that beanstalk of a genius because he spread a penetrating body odor, not only after physical education class. "A sebaceous gland problem," he frankly explained to anyone who would listen or not. Ferdl was visibly enchanted by the unexpected grace of company.

Spiteful glee rose up in Katrina, but that "Schadenfreude" didn't last long. It was odd. Luise had been too friendly to her. Was that perhaps a guilty plea? Had she been innocent, Luise would have given Katrina something to cry about or "read her the riot act" about this cold shoulder treatment—but no such thing.

This wasn't like Luise. Her quirky friend had always been straightforward with her. Sometimes too frank even. "Your toilet smells like . . . shit," she had announced on that day that Katrina had feared the most. It was the day that Luise would use the Weber's latrine for the first time. The toilet was located in the stables right above the septic tank, wherein also the washing machine grey waters and the cow piss walloped. When the wooden lid was lifted from the thunder seat, the collective stench wafted forth. Compared to that the air quality of the cow stables seemed like a fresh mountain breeze. One could not dare stay in that retreat too long or else the stench would attach to the person until the next wash.

Although Katrina had gotten used to this outhouse expedition from an early age—traipsing down in a cold winter's night from her room in the attic, all the way to this remote corner of the stable, half asleep, while she could have easily slipped on a pile of cow poop—that toilet was a friendship spoiler. For that reason, Katrina never brought friends home from school. Everybody else had water closets. Only in Luise's case Katrina had finally overcome her inhibitions, because she was made from a sturdier material than other folks. Instantly after the cow barn toilet premier, she had cheerfully gloated, "This was the purest adventure! I must go again, right now!" And from there on the situation was clear and the friendship took its course.

There had never been any monkey business with Luise. She always told the truth from the tip of her tongue, regardless if it hurt sometimes. Why had she been messing around that night with that Celtic cult? And why had she lied to her, spinning together this stupid tale of a "badass rock dive"? Even if she knew that she would be so close by? That midnight scenario for sure hadn't been a disco, rather a bizarre circus.

Katrina thwarted all of Luise's approaches. Thus, the school routine morphed into a serious obstacle course of avoidance because their paths usually crossed a number of times. Things were off with Luise.

And so they were with Mike. Katrina ignored him with a vengeance. As on every morning, Mike had hung out with the other apprentices at the bus stop. They turned their heads, whispered and snickered. Katrina had rushed by, hopped on the bus at the last minute, and hid behind her Latin book. Had Mike waved at her? Too late.

Anyway, Mike seemed to be fully absorbed with getting famous. The "Gabelsberger Celtic princess" had made headlines statewide. Katrina pulled a newspaper article from her binder and read it inside her Latin book.

Section Bavaria, Saturday, June 22:

Regarding the recent archaeological find, the State Conservation Office confirmed that the skeletal remains belong to a young maiden from the early Roman empire of 2000 years ago. The young woman was laid to rest with her head in western direction. The expensive funeral gifts leave reason to assume that she was a well-to-do person of high social standing. The departed was

> endowed with expensive fibulas, two bronze rings, a
> perforated Roman coin . . .

Only the lapis ring obviously wasn't mentioned. Mike had just kept it. Compared to the other items in the smudged newspaper photo, the ring seemed like an extra precious piece of artistry with its delicate filigree work. Additionally, the article spoke about the fact that the burial coin was the first proof of the Roman presence in this region and that the anatomy of the maiden's bones gave indication as to her health status. Mike as well, was often enough cited about the course of his discovery. What a smart ass!

"Congratulations, Frau Weber! If you continue on this track, you might possibly earn a two as the final grade!"

Katrina winced. Schiller always had a sinister way of shaking her out of her fantasy world. His lessons didn't allow for idle dreams.

The papers swooshed down on Katrina's desk. One minus. Almost a perfect grade!

"Keep it up, Frau Weber, keep it up! Congratulations!" The only point deduction was about the natural territorial behavior of horses. Schiller didn't believe that a freedom-loving animal, such as a horse, would voluntarily seek refuge in a trap like a chapel. "I believe this contradicts all horse instinct."

Case closed.

Katrina couldn't help but flush at the bittersweet praise.

Meanwhile, the outrage over the "village scribbler," that is, Katrina and her homespun village stories, had given way to the insatiable curiosity about the archaeological finds on the Gabelsberger property. Since last Saturday, another local report had been published as the State Conservation Office evaluated the objects and catalogued each morsel in great detail. The noble maiden had apparently been laid to rest with such rich gifts because she was a "Celtic princess," this report concluded. The village, therefore, was much older than the 1200-year-old church records had noted. That was no news to its inhabitants. They had always suspected as much. Yet a newfound feeling of ancestral pride permeated the village.

A Celtic princess? Katrina could not stop obsessing about that precious ring. Although she had barely caught a glimpse of it, that image was engraved on her mind. Why? Was it out of her desperation about Mike? Or was it magic? What made this old jewelry so singular? Why had Mike even shared his secret treasure with her? Wasn't that closeness and trust? Nonsense! A couple of days ago, she would have died for such a show of confidence. Today it was a different story. Everything was different.

Katrina's world had gone upside down. As much as she cringed at Luise's deception and her diatribes by the chapel, she still greatly missed her friend on the other hand. Luise's cool attitude towards anything stuck-uppity had often bolstered her spirit. Now she realized how much she had fed on Luise, had almost eaten her up alive. Luise was a free spirit, and she wanted to feel like that, too.

With less room to escape, such as Luise's planetarium, Katrina became increasingly exposed to Walli's attacks of unbridled curiosity. Her sister even ventured to intrude on her solitude in the hen house.

"Mike drove to town to visit Angela today," Walli gloated in her typical snippy tone. She was in jeans and rubber boots, as she just had escaped a chore of weeding and thinning out radishes with their mother in the garden.

"What do I care? He can visit his sister, if he wants to."

"Aren't you even a little curious about his business there?" Walli had expected quite a different reaction.

"No, I would rather write something now."

"How come you don't know anything!"

"Stop bothering me, Walli!"

"He just scored a journeyman post in the city!"

"Who cares!"

"But then he won't be around here much anymore."

"I don't give a damn!"

"Stupid cow! And I tried so hard to find all of that out for you!"

"Walli! What did you do? I hope none of your stupid-ass tricks!"

"No, don't worry. But I still have ears in my head!"

"What! Did you spy at the telephone booth again!"

"If you snooze, you lose." Walli grinned broadly.

"You silly goose! Now he probably thinks that you are tracking him down for me!"

Katrina set out to knock Walli on her head, but Walli ducked away and Katrina's knuckles struck the wall behind her. She screamed, shaking her hand in pain. Then, she squished her fist firmly under her armpit and blew strands of hair off her nose. She huffed. Tears welled in her eyes.

"What were you thinking, Walli? I am done running after that dude. Get that into your brain!"

"Why, what happened?"

"Just you leave me alone!"

"Seriously?"

"Out!"

Walli understood. But she couldn't help rubbing it in. "For my sister I'll do anything, even espionage!"

And empty HB cigarette packet hit Walli on the forehead.

"You! You, get lost now!" Katrina meant it.

Walli slammed the door shut behind her. It was time to leave her big sister alone.

Fuming, Katrina grabbed her bike, clamped a towel onto the back porter, and hit the pedals across the dirt road to the lake.

It was a muggy hot day. The crickets sang an excited symphony. Purple thistles and yellow St. John's wort blossoms shone on the bog meadow in the evening glow. One could smell the scent of the heated moor, and in the cooler forest the aroma of fragrant mushrooms impregnated the blue haze nestled in its shade.

The lake basked in the golden light. Muffled screams of school kids filtered over from the swimming embankment. Katrina pushed her bike through the tall reeds. She headed for that old boardwalk, which was rarely used any more. Although the lake bottom was quite muddy there, the boardwalk provided the most scenic view across the lake and an ideal sunbathing platform.

She pulled her dress over her head, dropped it on the boards, and slowly glided into the water. The cool water felt good. With every swim stroke, she left a dark thought behind. Her head cleared up. She must have been in the lake for a while, because the shadow of the blue spruce forest had already touched the lakeshore. It was time to leave. She had swum herself tired. With a skilled move, she hoisted herself up on the boardwalk and started toweling herself dry.

"Hello, pretty mermaid," a voice said behind her.

Raffi. What was he doing here?

Katrina, quickly reached for her dress and slipped it on. The towel had dropped on the boards. Raffi picked it up for her. Katrina grabbed it from him and wanted to pass by him. But the tall guy with the blond curls stepped in front of her, blocked her escape. He had a broad grin on his face. Angrily Katrina glared at his bare chest. He was almost a head taller than her. Sleeves rolled up, shirt unbuttoned, his black vest fluttering around his elbows, he had spooked her like a blond version of Yanni, appearing out of thin air.

"Go away! Let me through . . .," she hissed at him.

"What's eating you? Why so sour?"

"Will you let me pass already!"

"All right, there you go, angry kitten! Just don't you use your sharp claws on me!"

He stepped aside. Katrina slithered by him and hastened towards the shore. Midway, she swiveled around.

"How did you even find this place?"

Raffi grinned. "Well, Daniel knows all the hideaways."

"Is he also here?" Nervously, she scanned the vegetation along the shore.

"No, he had other plans . . . but why are you so huffy? What's bugging you? Come, stay with me. Sit down here, just for fun!"

Katrina hesitated. He had said it so nicely. But what kind of "fun" was he talking about? Hair going up in flames, pukey situations at the Volksfest, and fists flying in the beer tent? Their encounters hadn't gone so well. At least he didn't know anything about her biggest calamity at the St. John's Fire, or only the schnapps part of the story.

"Fun? What kind of fun is that? I have had enough of your nightmare pills, rough ups, and drinking binges!"

"Well, thank your Lederhosen buddies for some or most of that." For the first time Raffi seemed a little irritated. Then his shoulders relaxed.

"What the heck, it's all yesterday's snow. I just wanted to enjoy the sunset here."

Katrina looked at him with a blank face.

Raffi, who had slowly moseyed closer to her, reached for her wrist and gently tugged her back to sit down with him. Yet

Katrina wrestled free from his grip and pulled away. "No, I must go home now!"

"What? You don't want to admire the sunset with me? Look, what I brought!" And he pulled out a bottle of red wine from his shoulder bag.

No sooner than he waved the bottle in the sunlight, Katrina skipped. She misjudged her step and plunged into the shallow, muddy waters near the shore. She gasped as she reemerged. The water reached up to her hips, the mud to her knees.

Raffi burst out laughing. "What's your rush? Are you always swimming with your clothes on? Couldn't you wait for me?"

Katrina sloshed towards the reeds. She glanced down on her dirtied summer dress. "Stupid wisecrack . . ." she grumbled and proceeded on her mud waddle.

"I always thought that Daniel and Luise were strange, but nothing beats your quirks! Priceless!" Raffi yelled after her, playfully shaking his mane.

Katrina stopped sloshing and turned around. "Strange? Who or what is strange?"

"Strange as the fresh air coming from a cow barn, I guess," Raffi mumbled

"What?"

"Or like the cobwebs . . ."

"You're not making any sense. What cobwebs?" Katrina's curiosity perked up, as her feet solidified in the mud sediment. She sank a little deeper.

"The cobwebs in you peoples' heads."

Raffi eased himself, cross-legged, onto the boardwalk. The bottle of wine stood in front of him. He slowly started to roll a cigarette. He paid her no longer any attention.

"Cobwebs? And who is 'you people'?" she shouted. She looked comical, standing mud splattered amidst the waterlily pad.

Raffi grinned and lit up. As he relished the first drag on his cigarette, he took a moment before answering.

"You don't know the half of it," he yelled back at her.

"Hey, don't you bait me!" Furious, she turned around and continued wading to the shore.

Raffi chuckled. "If you'd only come sit down with me, I could tell you more," he shouted.

How cheeky he was! Glancing down at her mud-splattered dress, she surprised herself with an unexpected conclusion: she better not show up at home in such a mess. Without saying a word, she turned around and took course towards the boardwalk.

"All right then," Raffi coaxed her with a big grin. He pulled her up on the platform. "We will get this cleaned up in a jiffy. It's not like we haven't got any water around here. What's your curfew today?"

They sat side by side on Raffi's towel, taking turns at the bottle. Their chitchat came easy. Raffi had stopped the teasing and seemed all ears. The wine was now halfway gone. Leaning against a post of the boardwalk, Raffi relished each puff from his self-rolled cigarette. Both listened to the faint whirring of dragonflies.

Katrina had just told Raffi the story of the white stallion ghost. "How sick, I never thought that horses could be almost humanly demented," he commented. Katrina didn't know what to make of that. She doubted that he had gotten the gist of her story.

The gnats laid down a wild dance on the calm waters between the waterlilies because they had not yet detected their human victims.

For a while they sat without speaking. Then Katrina broke the silence. She prodded after Raffi's earlier comment.

"So, will you tell me now why you think Luise and Daniel are so strange? Aren't they your friends, too?"

Raffi laughed. "Well, they for sure are more your friends than mine. I know Daniel from the university. We took a class in art history together."

"But I thought he was in ethnographic studies."

"Now he is, but he first started out in business management, I guess to prepare him for the foundry works he has at home. He's been all over the map, quite a character. But why ask me? Luise can fore sure tell you more details about her brother than I can."

"Well, just curious . . ."

"Do you have a crush on him?"

"Who?"

"Daniel!"

"How did you get that idea? No way!" None of his beeswax. She grabbed the wine bottle, took a gulp, and slightly scooted away from Raffi.

"Or did you have a spat with Luise?" Raffi hit the sore spot right on.

"Nonsense!" She had said it a little too loud.

"I knew it! Didn't I tell you that I can read thoughts?"

Katrina was sure glad that he could only partially read her thoughts. She decided to ignore his prying and tried another bait. "I just wanted to know what you meant by 'strange.' How strange are they?"

Raffi pinched the cigarette butt between his thumb and middle finger and splayed the others far out before he took a final puff. He squinted his eyes shut and let the exhaled wisps of smoke drift away. Then he puffed another plume toward Katrina's face. He grinned. Katrina waved away the fumes, although she smoked cigarettes herself.

"I actually thought you also belonged to them." He tossed the butt to the fishes. "But obviously not anymore."

"Them? Who or what are you talking about??"

"Well, that Celtic stuff, the lunar rituals, and the whole shebang."

Katrina was stunned. Raffi kept on talking. No, she hadn't had the faintest idea that Luise was one of those praying to the fertility goddess and making sacrifices on behalf of Mother Earth. Or that she joined in chants to pacify some mad swamp dragons. Or that she venerated the horse goddess Epona by the blood rock that was protruding from the chapel foundation, where she left flower offerings. According to legend, blood, perhaps human blood, had flowed over that boulder. All the locals believed as well that it had been part of a Celtic altar.

Nature worship? Pagans? Raffi didn't have a name for it. But they surely could have been the ones that custodian Pauli had discounted as "that riff raff." Those mystic cults, obviously, were heathenish humbug to the church caretaker. Did he perhaps feel threatened by it? Pauli had always had a strong hunch that alcohol or drugs were added to the game of religious shenanigans.

"For me, this whole Celtic mania is nothing but a fashion fad or ersatz religion. I just don't get it," Raffi said scanning the horizon for additional words. "That's why I left early from the solstice gathering. I am not sure what Luise and Daniel are after. It seemed contrived."

'Oh, he was there as well.' Katrina was flabbergasted about his revelation.

Finally, the red wine had done its full purpose. Raffi yawned. "Some people really seem to get off on such absurd nonsense."

Katrina kept her poker face. She was stunned. That explained the peculiar congregation by the chapel during St. John's Eve. And Luise was one of them! As was Daniel.

"Something wrong?" Raffi asked. "Come on, here, have another sip."

He handed her the bottle and then laid his arm around her shoulders. She kept staring out on the mirrored lake. Raffi noticed that she had fallen pensive.

"Don't worry, Katrina, there isn't all too much behind it. It's no different as if you were to turn Lutheran tomorrow. Just look at how many sins the Catholics have notched on their tallies. Mind you, who orchestrated the Holy Inquisition, and who knows how many witch burnings. See, all dragons are the same, the Chinese lucky dragon, St. George's dragon, St. Michael's dragon . . ."

"Wa . . .? Me? Lutheran?" Katrina stuttered. She was curled up like a ball hugging her knees with her chin resting on them. She squinted at Raffi. He didn't get her at all.

"You're so wrong! We're all born into religion. You don't just pick one for fun. But why has Luise never told me anything?"

"Perhaps because she knows you feel that way. Or perhaps, one fine day, she wants to sacrifice you pious, virgin maiden, on that bloody rock . . ."

He didn't get any farther. Katrina boxed Raffi hard on the ribs with her elbow. "Not funny at all," she said.

"Maybe she didn't want to spoil your friendship?"

"But friends don't lie."

Katrina again stared fixated at the gnats dancing across the lily pad. Once she got brooding, she didn't easily return to reality. In that case, her family usually let her stew in her own juices until she popped back again. Raffi had a different approach.

"Come on, girl! Let's swim one last time!" he joked and before she could catch herself, she tumbled into the lake. Raffi's push had come out of nowhere

Katrina splashed, yelped, and spouted. Raffi jumped right after her. With loud laughter and childish abandon, they started a water fight. Katrina had not laughed as much since Walli had toppled over with the Christmas tree. They challenged each other to swim across the lake, dive for the mussels on the bottom, and race each other with widely splashing backstrokes. Life seemed a blast and precisely in balance. Raffi even ventured into the lily pad to pick the only pink waterlily for her. 'Almost the same as with Luise,' Katrina pondered. 'She also likes that kind of horseplay.'

"Help! The water snakes! They are strangling me," Raffi shouted and dove under the lily pad until he remerged with the pink water lily between his teeth in front of Katrina. She didn't take his ruse lightly and as punishment dunked him right under again. The sun had now completely descended behind the trees.

"It's getting late, Katrina!" Raffi giggled, catching his breath. He took a few strokes towards the boardwalk. "Let's get you home before your people send the police out for you."

Raffi lifted himself on the bridge and reached for Katrina's hand to help her onto the boardwalk. She slipped into her dress. It was still a little damp from the lake laundering. She surprised herself being disappointed that this happy day should end so soon. Raffi was good to talk to after all. He seemed to listen to her with open ears.

Katrina grabbed her towel and plodded after Raffi towards the path through the reeds. Suddenly her heart skipped a beat. On the boardwalk, right in front of her, Mike had materialized out of nowhere, with his fishing gear in hand. He looked at her, bewildered.

"Oh, Dear! Here comes your motorcycle hero!" Raffi laughed. "Hi, there!"

Mike stared at "Yanni." He hadn't recognized the dude with the flying mane right away.

Katrina used the moment and jumped off the boardwalk for a shortcut through the reeds.

"Wait, Katinka!" Mike shouted after her. He dropped the fishing rod and set out to catch up with her. Raffi grabbed him by the shoulder.

"Yo, man! Can't you see she is in a hurry?"

Mike froze on the boardwalk. Raffi rushed after Katrina through the dense vegetation. He caught up with her before she could mount her bike.

"Can I take you home?"

"Duh, don't you see!" She patted the saddle of her bike.

"When can we get together again?"

"I don't know."

"Are you free tomorrow?"

"Why?"

"Will you show me the chapel?"

"What for?"

"Let's find your ghost horse."

"Again?"

"Seriously!"

"Good luck with that!"

And off she was.

15

Rays of Grace

The raftsmen from the headwaters region of the Isar over time earned themselves a reputation as trademark figures for their adventurous spirit. They had a dare devil radiance about them. Their skin was tanned dark by sun, wind, and water; their stature was tough and sinewy; and their arms resembled the branches of those trees that they ferried down the river. The Isar greeted them as a gushing, difficult, and often treacherous whitewater

—*Erika Groth-Schmachtenberger & Erica Schwarz, Die Isar, 9*

Wednesday, June 26, after school

Alois staggered out of the village tavern way past closing time. He had another 20 kilometers to walk to his home in the hamlet Gries, which means "Gravel." But for the steeled raftsman this last leg on his journey home from Budapest was a trifle, regardless of the heavy coils of rope he carried across his chest, the heavy boots, and the ax dangling over his knapsack.

Alois, nicknamed Loisl, had missed the last ride. All the carts and carriages had already passed on from the Green Hat tavern. At this late hour, the innkeeper had just gone to bed and only three beer guzzlers were left on the bench out front. The tunes from the bawdy ditties and the chords of the zither were still sounding in Loisl's ears, when he took the route through the pine forest towards the Alpine range, his home. First, he passed through the scant trails in the heathland, then sidled along the forest edge, until he found himself on the wide-open, fertile pastures . . .

Katrina halted right there. 'Dear Grandmother in heaven, please just forgive me one more time,' she mused hunched over her obstinate typewriter.

The Adler machine, her usual accomplice in crime, wouldn't cooperate so well today. Again, she was borrowing ideas from her grandmother's diary, but who else should she ask? Perhaps the old grumpy mute? Gramps was hopeless. She was now stuck with this essay about the preindustrial crafts in Upper Bavaria. Would this insane marathon ever end?

The rafting tradition was a good topic because Kathl had described these jacks-of-the-trade in great detail, not least because she must have had a good amount of admiration for those strong guys herself. Raftsmen, like her aunt Nanni's Loisl neither feared the snowmelt nor the white waters. These dare devils had been baptized with waters of all colors. They traveled on the Isar and Danube from Mittenwald to Budapest and walked it all back. Loisl, too, knew every trick in the book. His fellows called him a rapids hog. Inexplicably, he went crazy one day after he had seen a ghost. And a week later he perished, getting squished between the raft and a bridge pillar. What a story!

An ocean of lush, moon-bathed grasslands lay in front of Alois, and across from it was the road that would take him home. He stopped and inhaled the air deeply after his brisk march. The fresh air had purified his brain and sharpened his sight. The cows ruminated peacefully in the pasture, their bells occasionally chiming. All else was quiet.

"Oh my, how beautiful this is!" Alois glanced across the peaceful scenery and like under a pious spell pulled his hat off in adoration. There, right at the top of the small mountain over which the moon presided, the little chapel shone forth all white and quite heavenly. He inhaled the scent of flowers, the likes of roses, lilac, or jasmine, or some such. He wasn't exactly an expert in botanicals. For minutes he stared at the landscape spread out in front of him. Suddenly a white horse emerged from the small forest surrounding the chapel on the hill.

"Devil, devil, where did this horse get out?" Alois muttered. With determination, he headed to the forested dome of the hill. He figured it was his Christian duty to help whom he may. If he caught that horse, he could lock him up in the corral at the foot of the hill so that his owner could retrieve him the next day. Alois didn't let an eye off his target as he approached the chapel hill. The restless horse paced about in front of the tree line, anxiously shaking its mane.

By the time Alois had reached the first trees at the foot of the hill, the white horse had vanished. At the top, the courageous raftsman circulated the chapel several times, but he found no trace of a horse. He listened, but aside from his own footsteps there was no sound. "For Christ's sakes, am I going mad?" The horse was gone. Why should he care? It wasn't his anyway. He just had wanted to help, like any good Christian.

Alois stopped in front of the chapel. All in awe, he admired the serene Alpine range, visible better from up here in the moonshine than from the stoop of his own front door. He took his time. Before he continued on his journey home, he wanted to peek inside the church. He stretched up tall, but could not quite reach the latticed window. He stepped on a boulder sticking out of the foundation. Finally, he got a glimpse inside, where he barely could make out some shapes. One of the figures turned out to be a mounted soldier in full armor.

"Good old St. George, all right! A very nice one on top!" Alois admired the dragon slayer enshrined by the darkness. He gave that saint a lot of credit for answering his emergency prayers, especially when circumnavigating the treacherous rapids around the Georgen-Stein, the saint's namesake rock in the Isar.

Suddenly, the blood froze in Alois' veins. The white horse stared right at him from the reflection in the window pane. The raftsman spun around, too fast, and fell off his pedestal. He looked all over, but . . . nothing. No trace of a horse. Dumbfounded, Alois picked up his hat and dusted his pants off with it.

The moon drove behind a dense cloud. Black ink descended onto the forest. Slowly, and occasionally cursing in the dark, Alois tottered downhill through the forest, grasping for a hold in the bushes. Thorns tugged at his jacket sleeves. Suddenly an oak root tripped him and with an irate "Zefix Alleluia" he plunged fully on his belly, buried under his knapsack and all. As he fixed to

227

straighten himself out, a thunderous roar, whooshed over him like the stampede of a thousand hooves. Alois curled up in a ball on the ground. And no sooner than the white horse jumped right over him, it had disappeared. Out of nowhere into anywhere.

"Holy Jesus, Mary, and Joseph! Holy Nepomuk, protector of bridges, have mercy on us!" Shrill laughter rang in his tormented ears. And then—dead silence. All Alois could hear was the pounding of his own heart.

A lonely owl started to hoot. The dark cloud now released the bright moon again. The spooked man ran as fast as he could out of the bewitched forest and only started breathing again after he had reached the open road.

Wednesday, June 26, afternoon

Katrina turned the iron-forged key in the rusted lock, twice. It took all her strength. Rarely, the chapel saw visitors anymore. Custodian Pauli had given her a somewhat suspicious look, but finally handed her the key nonetheless.

"What exactly is your business up there, if I may ask?" Pauli was wary of her tall city slicker companion.

"Well, you know how all tourists want to admire the artistic gems around here." Thus, Katrina justified her recently awakened interest in cultural treasures.

But Pauli didn't buy it. Much the less did the "beautiful view" argument sit with him, because why would they need a key for that? Only after she explained to Pauli in detail that Raffi was researching the local folk art, especially votive paintings, for his final paper at the university, Pauli relented and handed over the key. He winked at Katrina with mischief in his eyes. "I get it, all right! You need a quiet spot for a flirt!"

Katrina was used to this typical village interrogation based on fear of strangers. But romance? Far from it, she protested.

Katrina herself would have never guessed that Raffi was that deep into folk art that he had chosen to write his thesis about it. At the lake, she had heard him breathlessly gushing about "piety" and "esotericism." Some of these terms, which he had attempted to explain to her at length, she still couldn't wrap her mind around, although they spurred her imagination. Curiosity had now gotten the better of her. It usually kicked in whenever she smelled rumors, secrets, and superstitions—or ghosts.

The cast-iron door handle resisted. Katrina jiggled it impatiently. Raffi pulled her aside and tested his luck as well. Finally, the timbered door gave way with a loud creak. A moldy odor wafted over the visitors. Their eyes took a while adjusting to the dusky interior.

Katrina's foot hit something soft. "Ooh, a dead bat!"

Raffi barely took note of her disgust and right away steered towards the small, old-fashioned amateur paintings covering the walls. He inspected each one with a critical eye. Many had collected a thick layer of patina so that it was hard to make out the shapes, figures, and letters. Almost all of the votive panels had a date and a miraculous story on them.

"Look at this!" Raffi pointed Katrina to a panel.

"Here this house was hit by lightning, but the estate could still be saved. And, look, the farmer lies obviously ill in bed and the husbandry and children are kneeling around him in prayer. Or, take a look at this one. The livestock was spared from an epidemic. And so many happy childbirth requests were granted. Check this out! This must be a newer one. The farmer's son has returned from the war, unharmed. Looks like a World War I uniform to me." Raffi kept on talking with glee and fascination.

Gradually, Katrina's childhood experiences, such as going on the pilgrimage to Our Dear Lady of the Sorrows and eating Weißwurst afterwards, took on another dimension. Her own village chapel, she realized, constituted another part of her inherited identity. Never before had she thought much about it. Perhaps that was about to change.

Katrina felt like an intruder in the shrine of the Holy Martyr St. George. With an unknown intensity, she stared at the frescoes high up on the walls. Quite a cruel torture that man went through. How had some of these fervent torture images seeped into her story? Subconsciously, perhaps. Have people always been this cruel? It seemed there was a lot of truth and compassion in these naively painted torture scenarios. However, the old-time painter also had clearly brought across great details. In one scenario, the pious hero was boiling in the lime pot. St. George's hands were folded in prayer, his eyes directed to heaven. The henchmen's tools lay nearby.

Raffi swiped her with a glance. "Why are you so quiet today?"

"Oh, nothing! All this misery! It just gets me down."

"Well, true, all right! On the upside, people had the saints to help them out in the old days." Raffi dug into his shoulder bag. "Any such martyrs who died for their faith, especially any of the Fourteen Auxiliary Saints, had a momentous influence in the heavens. And that is why people brought them offerings."

"Offerings? Are we talking about these old Celts again?"

"Huh? No, just these pictures here. See, they also have vows on them and they were costly at the time. In that sense, they were also offerings. It cost the farm folks a lot of money to have them painted. Usually, the carpenter or an itinerant painter produced these retablos. Each of the panels is a wish fulfilled. Let me show you. It's all in this description here."

Having said that, Raffi pulled a picture book from his bag. He thumbed to a marked page and began to read.

"What makes the votive paintings especially intriguing is the continuous coalescence of scenes from the terrestrial and heavenly worlds and the everlasting conjunction of reality and miracle." Then he repositioned the bookmark and snapped the book shut.

After that, he stopped talking altogether and began taking notes on his scratchpad. Obviously, he knew more about these pictures than she did. Katrina had grown up in these surroundings, but now she stepped across her own shadow for the first time and began to wonder. She soaked in more substance with every breath of moldy air. These dark-toned, naïve paintings, with their stiff, awkward human figures and the misspelled memorials, all documents of everyday farm life, were not so self-explanatory after all.

Most of the vows were dedicated to Our Holy Mother of the Sorrows, who sat on her throne in the heavens, her heart pierced with a sword. Sometimes the heavenly mother squashed the head of a dragon. The dragon slayer St. George played just as important a role. Next came St. Leonhard, the patron of the livestock, who was sought after for healthy blessings in the stables. St. Leonhard was usually depicted with a chain in hand, as he had according to legend liberated innocent prisoners. It was only a small step to associate those chains with the tethers for the cows in the stable.

Minding all these details, Raffi documented the contents of one votive panel after the other. When he got to the main altar figure, he looked up at St. George with awe.

"Well, aren't you a rare beauty!" he addressed the knight in shining armor on his white stallion. Below the hooves, the deadly wounded, cringing dragon. "What a story, much better than that of some motorcycle knights," Raffi mumbled.

Katrina ignored his snide remark. Undeniably, this dashing sculpture was a real eye catcher. Although at the same time she felt a little queasy about it.

Raffi took his dear time. Katrina had no choice but to also study the pictures. She was in many ways a good clue finder for Raffi. 'Those people should have had a lightning rod or a hospital,' she wished. There was so much illness, lightning and hail, war, desperation, child mortality, farming accidents, wagon crashes, and all kinds of tribulations. On a somewhat larger panel, a regiment of French troops, with pointed hats, baggage straps across their chests, bayonets ready to strike, marched past a little town. They missed that village for the fog, and people were spared from plunder and mayhem. That happened during the Napoleonic wars. And that village lay only a short distance from here.

Right next to the impressive historic scene hung a small, unassuming picture. Katrina stopped in her tracks. She stepped closer. The imagery drew her in.

A young boy lay lifeless on the driveway to a stately farmhouse. Around the boy were gathered the crying parents, and in the background an older man. Up in the heavens the Virgin Mary hovered on a cloud, stepping on the dragon's head. A ray of grace illuminated, like a spotlight, the lifeless boy on the ground. St. George came riding in on his white horse across the horizon. Two angels, one left, one right of the Heavenly Mother, peeked down on the terrestrial scene. One angel resembled the boy lying on the ground. The second angel's face was that of a youthful maiden, but older than the boy.

The year was 1912, "A marterl for Marterl" was written at the bottom, but it had no vows, blessing, or dedication, or thanks on it. Like all votive panels, this one wasn't signed either. Katrina shivered. She inadvertently turned around. Raffi was immersed in taking notes. Simultaneously, all color faded from her face and a chill climbed up from her stomach, gagging her dry throat. She swallowed fiercely. It dawned on her with a big bang that her grandmother must have painted this panel.

Just like it had been described in the diary, that's how it had been painted. And it so happened just the same.

November 11, 1910

"A marterl for Marterl," she said and smiled with great melancholy. At that point I woke up from sleep. The painting just got finished. I painted St. George with his dragon and Our Mother Full of Sorrows on it, but I am not sure what it is supposed to mean . . .

What Kathl had painted, Katrina had seen with her own eyes for real. The little boy, her brother, lying in the drive. She was a toddler then, but the image just flashed up, like freshly painted. Kathl had followed directions of the voice that spoke to her. But none of it had helped any. Two generations later, the boy perished nonetheless. Beads of cold sweat formed on Katrina's forehead. She had to get out.

"I need fresh air," she gasped and rushed off.

Raffi barely noticed.

Outside Katrina sat down on the visitor bench. Out here, with the unrestricted view on the familiar Alpine range, her heartbeat normalized. Votive panels are supposed to be an afterthought not a prediction.

What kind of a woman had her grandmother been? Katrina barely had any memory of her. The intimacy of the votive panel, however, had brought her grandmother alive again. Katrina's thoughts cruised like a swarm of panicked crows over the flooded Warm Valley. Just like the birds after the ice age, her thoughts couldn't find a landing spot either.

For how many generations had this chapel mound conjured up bursts of energy through fervent prayer? There was something to it, a natural magic. Kathl and Moni had experienced it as well some sixty years ago. The witch was after them, they fled. Not even the large stick and the Altötting rosary could avert those terrors during their nightly expedition. What good was a stick, a rosary, or the holy water nowadays? Could they protect us from drugs and dragons? Katrina envisioned their ghost hunt not too long ago, all of them inebriated after the disco. What a sobering experience! How stupid of her! She barely knew these fellows and had not had any experience with drugs.

Backtrack sixty years once more. After Kathl had locked herself by accident or providence in the chapel while painting St. George, she was, contrary to the reckless white stallion, freed by the custodian. This reminded Katrina of her strange episode with the key two weeks ago. Maybe there were portals that opened and locked themselves magically? Just like Sesame in the Ali Baba fairytale of *1000 and One Night*? Perhaps the chapel door had a spell on it?

Back up that time machine again. Her grandmother as well had had a nightmare about a dragon and described it so vividly in her diary that Katrina shivered at the thought of it. Kathl's saving grace from the nightmare had been the Bavarian mantra of the Three Holy Girls.[xviii] Each of them had their special insignia: St. Barbara had the tower, St. Margaret the dragon, and St. Kathl the wheel of torture.

The "three holy Bavarian Girls," however, could have easily been a Christian cover for their heathen forerunners, the triple Bethan goddesses Ainbeth, Borbeth, and Wilbeth. Who knew? Katrina didn't, but she recalled with a thundering heart the "wheel for the wench," the burning pagan wheel of solstice, which Kathl, in her dream, had slammed into the dragon's gullet. That's how Kathl finally overcame the nightly haunting.

Now it all made sense. Aside from documenting the ghost horse stories, piety, everyday dire straits, and other realities, her grandmother not only had acute powers of observation, but she could also see in between. She had been a visionary! Long before she knew if she would be married at all, she had forebodings about her descendants' fate. Unsure about how to deal with her vision, Kathl had painted a family tragedy as told in her dream.

Could this terrible accident have been prevented? Should it have been? It seemed that her grandfather thought so and took the blame for it. And why not? It was his brunt to bear. Katrina, however, had never quite gotten over the fact that her grandfather had vanished into thin air when she was a little child. At that young age, she would have needed his company and guiding hand the most.

For heaven on earth only lies a hand's breadth besides us.

Was she hearing things again? She turned around. Nobody. She snapped back into brooding. A "marterl for Marterl," what for? Not even her grandmother knew how to make sense of it. But she painted it anyway. And now this riddle still hung on the wall inside the chapel together with the other ninety-nine question marks. What good is prediction anyway when people still will die?

Time to go back. Katrina got up from the bench and almost stumbled. She stepped into the dusky church.

"What are you doing there?" Katrina asked Raffi in a strict tone. Raffi had put his camera up on a tripod.

"Taking pictures," he replied just as short.

"I don't think Pauli will like that. You should have asked him first."

"But how can I remember these million details here?"

Katrina let him continue because she was exhausted. And after a while she moaned, "Can we go now? I am a little tired."

Raffi frowned. "You really don't look so well. Come sit down here in the pew. Maybe I still have some aspirin," he said and started digging through his bag.

"No, don't worry. It's OK. I still need to get my homework done. How much longer?"

"Maybe an hour, or even less. I really want to finish. Because when do I get this opportunity again?"

"All right then! But hurry up!"

That's when a figure peeled itself from the stark sunlight streaming through the squat doorframe. As the haloed outline stepped deeper into the dusky interior, it shed its aura completely. Soon enough the shadow spoke to them.

"Good afternoon, you two!"

"Pauli? What are you doing here?" Katrina stammered.

"I just came to check. Are you lovebirds still not done here? You wanted to return the key already an hour ago."

"Give us just a little more time, Pauli. Then we will bring you the key right away."

"How much?"

"Perhaps an hour."

"I can't wait that long, Katrina! I still have business in town today."

"Sorry, Pauli, this took us longer than planned." Katrina nervously glanced at her watch. "He is almost done."

Raffi, in deep concentration, continued taking photos. Pauli nuzzled up to Katrina. She could definitely smell the garlic through the cloud of tobacco wafting around him. Katrina retreated. The church bench pushed against the back of her knees. She sank into the pew. Nonetheless, Pauli leaned over her and pulled together his best dramatic talent. He whispered to Katrina in confidence so that the student could not hear him.

"You know, Katrina, I don't want to keep the chapel open for so long. It makes me nervous. Do you remember when they stole our two Gothic saints just right after Leonhardi? Yes, you do? See, I was just fifteen minutes late for locking up. Just fifteen minutes!"

Then Pauli turned his head in Raffi's direction. "What the heck does he think he is doing there?"

"You mean the photos? He needs them for his Master Thesis in Art History. We thought it was all right with you if he takes pictures?"

Raffi nodded amicably in Pauli's directions. He had overheard the last part, but chose to ignore it. He instantly turned around to his work again. Pauli grabbed Katrina's elbow and nudged her outside. He had a serious objection on his face.

"Photographs? No, that's not so simple! Do you understand that what's in here are our priceless treasures, our heirlooms! We can't just let anyone take pictures in our sanctuary here. I don't even know that chap!"

"Calm down, Pauli! No need to be this distrustful," Katrina tried to pacify him. He sometimes took his office too seriously.

"I am just saying, you should have asked someone about the picture taking," Pauli insisted. He scanned the far-off Alpine scenery, thinking. Finally, he eased up. "Photographs are not my call anyway. You should have informed the parish council. Your father is in it, too. I can't be responsible for this!"

"But you are the most important caretaker, Pauli!" Katrina buttered him up. "The others don't mind, if you agree to the pictures. Perhaps we all will learn more about the history of our village and the chapel. I think that Raffi would be happy to give you copies of his pictures for the archives of the parish secretary. Aren't you interested at all in what the scientists have to say about our chapel here?"

"Wonder what that would be." Pauli scratched his head. "You and I know our history well enough. You even wrote in the paper about it. I believed you every word. We all did," Pauli snorted. "But he?" He nodded towards the church with Raffi in it, "What's *he* gonna teach us?"

Pauli pulled up his jacket sleeve to look at his watch. "All right, then," he said. "I will let it pass this time. But the responsibility is on you, Katrina! And, promise, he gives me two copies of his book plus all the pictures, right?"

"Yes, I will make sure of it. But why two copies?"

"Everything has its price," Pauli replied cryptically.

'I see, he wants to keep one copy for himself.' At least she was off the hook for now. And Pauli stood corrected about his false assumption about some hanky-panky.

Raffi hadn't bothered about their conversation because he was concentrating to get his job done. Finally, he noticed Katrina's absence and poked his head out the church portal.

"Is everything all right, Katrina?"

"Sure, sure, almost."

"I get it, sorry! Let's take you home," Raffi said and hurriedly stuffed his notebook and camera in his bag. "Too bad, I just only had a few more pictures . . ."

"No, you stay put!" Pauli ordered the scientist to be. "Katrina can ride home with me this instance. Right?"

Raffi glanced at Katrina. She nodded.

"That's quite all right, Raffi! Just finish up your work here," Katrina said. Then she turned to Pauli. "Where did you park your motorbike? We hadn't heard you coming."

"Huh, I got you there, didn't I? You won't believe me, but I have learned to levitate." He was all jokester again.

Katrina sighed with relief. Pauli the clown was much more pleasant than Pauli the detective.

"Make sure you turn the key twice in the lock and drop it in my mailbox. I count on you, young man!" Pauli said and turned around. "Let's go now, Katrina! I don't have all day!" Katrina rushed after him.

Pauli had given his ultimatum with emphasis. He didn't feel quite comfortable with the deal, because he would have to leave home before the key was returned. But so far, every mail carrier, even the vacation substitutes, had always found his large, homemade post box in front of his house. That was where the key needed to go.

Girgl had just brought his old man two of Huber's scythes to peen. A motorcycle roared up on the main road. Both men turned their heads toward the noise. Girgl in his youth had also ridden motorcycles and could still distinguish the sounds of various makes and guess their horse power by their drone. But this sputtering noise could only come from one motor vehicle, Pauli's old Quickly. Katrina climbed out of the side wagon. Then Pauli swung his vehicle around and drove off.

Girgl furrowed his brow. 'What business has she got with Pauli? Was she hitch-hiking again?'

The old one turned to his peening block without looking at Girgl. He already felt the storm clouds brewing on his son's forehead. He himself was itching for a smoke. Yes, he felt scratchy and restless. And he knew exactly why. The motley fox was on the prowl again. Yesterday he had seen the vixen sniff around the hen house. But the old man wasn't sure whether Katrina just wasn't in there or whether she hadn't opened up on purpose.

Anyway, better fox be gone.

16

Force of Nature

In addition, the French wars (1804–1806) often required the farmers to quarter soldiers. Although the French were allied with the Bavarians, they marauded the country population without mercy. Many times, the Upper Landers had to take the law into their own hands and quietly did away with some of the most hated bloodsuckers.

—Elisabeth Berger, Family Chronicles

Thursday, June 27

Luise had stuck to Katrina's heels all day in school. In vain. However, she didn't give up so easily.

"Come on, pout fish, what's wrong with you?" Luise confronted Katrina at the bus stop. "Why didn't you open up the door to your chicken coop? I know for sure that you were in there. Why are you so mean?"

Katrina hesitated, then looked Luise straight in the eye. "All right, if you want to, let's talk! Why don't you come over this afternoon?" That second the bus pulled up. Katrina hopped on and sat down in the front row next to an old lady with a headscarf. Luise squeezed through the aisle to snatch up the last seat on the backbench amidst an unruly bunch of middle school kids.

Quickly, Katrina got off at their station. Mike and his bunch were lounging at their usual spot. Yikes! She dashed around the front end of the bus, took cover, and escaped unnoticed on the path behind the guesthouse that led through several backyards towards her home.

"Katrina! Wait!"

Old Bürkel! Shit, that old witch, she hadn't seen her coming. However, Josefa Bürkel had already spotted her. She waggled her arms excitedly at Katrina. Too late! Running away? How rude! And it would have given that old gossip even more ammunition to spread her incoherent rumors. Katrina halted her step.

"Katrina! Don't run so fast! Wait up! I have something important to tell you!" Frau Bürkel was breathing heavily and seemed visibly dismayed.

"Sorry, I am in a hurry."

"Yes, so I see. But, Katrina, I had already wanted to talk with you the other day, but you couldn't hear me sitting on that noisy motorbike . . ."

"I must be going, really! I have two tests tomorrow . . ."

"Oh, well, you students, I understand," Frau Bürkel huffed. She pinned Katrina down with her serious, bulbous, grey-green eyes. She was pumping like a May bug before taking flight. Her chest under the dark, worn calico dress was heaving. A strand of her hair had escaped the meticulously braided knot on the back of her head. She wasn't wearing her flower-print headscarf today. Small beads of perspiration formed on her forehead wrinkles. Bürkel took another deep inhale.

"I see that you're in hurry, Katrina, but this is important for you. Will you just, please, hear me out!" She was still breathing laboriously, as if trying to catch a very slippery thought by its tail. It must have been an especially precarious one.

"Watch out for that Gabelsberger boy . . ."

"What?"

"I tell you, your thing with that Gabelsberger boy is a little jinxed . . ."

"What thing? What do you mean?" Katrina stopped cold. What did she know? Her dating game was none of that old woman's business.

"No need to blush! Don't you worry, I once was young myself." Judging by the number of her wrinkles, that was hard to believe. For the third time, Katrina had heard that statement flung at her from three different people. Enough of this! By now even the pastor's cat might have lost its patience and chased the devil down to bloody hell. But Katrina, trained to respect the elderly, kept silent. And that provided Frau Bürkel the chance to continue her crusade.

"See, I already know everything anyway. Everybody knows it. But I, for my part, I know even more. Or, should I say, too much. I see things coming. And that is what I wanted to tell you about." What incoherent nonsense!

Frau Bürkel took another deep breath to draw enough wind to catch some of the wildly churning words on her mind. Her revelation took careful consideration. Now it was to come out.

'Jesus! She really is as old and batty as people always say. Will she finally spit it out? This better be good.'

"I also dreamt about you yesterday, Katrina!" Josefa's creaking voice sounded concerned and foreboding at the same time. She glanced at Katrina, scanning for a reaction.

"I hope it wasn't a nightmare," Katrina joked.

"It sure was."

Silence, five breaths to count.

"It sure was, and you were in it. I am positive."

Katrina glared at her blankly. Josefa picked up speed.

"Remember the skeleton, you know, the excavation at the Gabelsberger house. Where they found the Celtic girl?" The old woman sideswiped her with an intense glance. She was again hunting for a reaction.

"The Celtic princess? That's yesterday's news. I don't really have time for this now! I better go. Bye now!" Katrina nervously turned around. But Frau Bürkel grabbed her arm.

"Yes, exactly, I dreamed about her," she snorted. "She was the most beautiful princess. And Gabelsberger did her in . . ."

"Have you gone full crazy, Josefa! That skeleton is already 2000 years old. How could Mike have killed such an old princess! Let me go now, I have had enough!" Katrina screamed at her. In her rage she had addressed the old woman by her first name. And called her crazy. Hard to say which was worse.

Before totally losing it, Katrina swiveled around and pelted away, leaving the old woman in mid-sentence.

"Just you wait . . ." Frau Bürkel shouted. But Katrina had already made too much of a head start.

"And the princess, that was you!" the old woman shouted after her. "And Gabelsberger threw her to the dragon . . ."

There was a pause for labored, heaving breaths. Then her shouts grew louder. "Just be careful with that guy! Don't forget I have warned you!"

When Katrina burst into her inner sanctum, Walli was already inside. 'How dare she! I need a new hiding place for the key.' Walli had nestled comfortably in the old armchair. She looked up from a handful of typed papers.

"That's so wrong," Walli commented without as much as greeting her older sister. "The white stallion did not starve for real. Did you forget that he started nibbling at the bell ropes and when the bell chimed they found him again . . ."

Katrina could have strangled Walli, but instead she tore the papers away from her with lightning speed.

"What I write is none of your business. And if you want to know the truth, at that time the bell tower did not even exist." Katrina said that in a frighteningly calm voice.

"Here, look! Wrong again. The bell tower has always been there. Just not the onion bulb cupola at the top. That was added later, father told me."

"All right, you know-it-all! Here is yet another story. Totally true. It's your turn to wash the dishes today. Mother already called for you. And she also wants to know how your homework is coming along."

Homework was a thorny subject for whirly Walli. She didn't like to take time out for that in her busy day. Katrina had only taken a blind guess there, but the sink was for sure overflowing with dirty dishes from lunch. What could be worse, doing homework or doing dishes? If you asked Walli, it was always that chore which came next.

"Oh, crap!" Walli moaned. She got out of the armchair and trotted off.

All means were justified for getting rid of the pesky sister. Only in an empty shack, Katrina could brew up a storm in her head. Just now her thoughts thundered like a thousand mustangs towards a bottomless abyss. Celtic princess? What had that old hag said? She was supposed to be that princess? And Mike had done the princess in? Incredible what this old spinster had concocted there. What if she spread this absurdity around?

Princess or no princess, she wished Mike a guilty conscience as bad as the fire-breathing dragon in her crazy dream.

It was no use. Neither smoking cigarettes nor indulging in her rage nor cursing her unfair lot in life helped her today. She still felt like a witch after a terrible crash on a broomstick. That wicked school writing marathon continued despite all that. She limped remarkably far behind. One epoch she had skipped completely. Thus, she had to turn back her time machine once more. Her boundless anger turned into excellent fuel.

She let off steam into the keys of her typewriter. 'A day in the life of a peasant'? What did that look like? Schiller had already chased them into the 19th century, but without water breaks unlike in a real marathon. The votive panels still drifted like freshly painted tableaus through Katrina's mind. There were hundreds of stories that she could have written. Finally, the soldiers with their pointed hats gained the upper hand.

Oh, Blessed Mother of God, willst thou protect us from the evil Frenchmen!

> The French troops marched through the land killing and plundering. Any resistance was instantly paid with a life. Sometimes the homestead went up in flames, after all the livestock and useful implements had been taken. Waldleitner stowed away his horses in the thicket of the riverbank, but they tied him up with a rope and dunked him into his own cesspool, until he handed over his precious animals. He barely survived that torture. The blacksmith's wife, an old lady with a goiter, not such a pretty appearance altogether, fared luckier than most. She sewed her jewelry, her children's dowry, onto the inside of her underskirts. French soldiers didn't want to touch old wives. Spared as well were the farmsteads at the hamlet Einöd. The Frenchmen had bypassed them because the houses were shrouded in dense fog. But,

aside from that, nothing was safe from the troops on their way to their ill-fated Russian disaster campaign. No cattle in the pasture, no horse in the stables, and no virgin in her chamber was spared by the Frenchmen.

The soldiers took over the farmhouses as their living quarters. So it happened that even landlord Suttner had to spend the night with his family in the feed shack next to the orphaned horse harnesses. The churl and maidservants had laid themselves to rest atop the fodder pile. The house was taken over by the officers and the barn stuffed full with their soldiers. It rained buckets. Only Annamirl and Resi, the farmer's school-age daughters, were kept in the house so that they could serve the officers at the table. They slept in their own chamber.

This was a most uncomfortable situation for Max Suttner, their father. He knew the nature of men. And wasn't he a man himself? Not the worst of them, mind you. But he knew as well as the next best man that it wasn't a woman's diabolical art of seduction that robbed men of their sanity. To the contrary, the devil was lurking in a much different location, in the crotches of men, which constantly itched. Female charms? They were only a phantasm of the menfolk, who had invented them as a silly excuse story for their own animalistic desires. Like the snake offering a forbidden fruit to man in paradise. That snake was the religious ticket for men to blame women for everything wrong, including their own lechery.

Such was the nature of man, Suttner realized. Therefore—should the Frenchmen take all his possessions, but NOT his daughters. And what hearsay had gone around about the Frenchmen. It stung Max immeasurably that his daughters had to stay in the house to serve at the table. He much rather would have wanted them with all others in the stables.

Suttner laid heavily breathing on the hard cot, obsessing about his daughters on the other side of the firewall in the house. His wife could feel his worry. She couldn't sleep either. Eventually, silence descended upon the farmstead. The French must have drunk all their beer.

Suttner raised himself quietly from his bed of hay.

"Where are you going?" the wife sleepily murmured to her husband.

"I must look after the cows. Alma is due for calving."

"Max, stay here! Alma will call us!"

"No, I better check."

Suttner had lied to his wife. He sneaked outside, bypassed the night guard, and climbed up the pear tree trellis with much more agility than anyone would have deigned possible given his husky build. The window was slightly ajar. He pushed it open.

"Annamirl, Resi," the father whispered into the room. He didn't want to scare the girls. As they had been awake as well, they quickly rushed to their father and pulled him inside the window.

"It will be best if the two of you run over to Zenzl's house tonight," Suttner urged his daughters. "Over there, in the herb witch's cabin, they will never find you."

The girls quickly slipped into their brothers' pants, tucked away their hair under their hats, and nimbly scaled down the old pear tree trellis. Their aunt Zenzl lived in a cottage up on the mountainside. Blessed with an unfaltering nature instinct and known for her curative talents, she would be an excellent guardian. In her remote forest cottage, the girls would be safe until the Frenchmen moved on.

Just as the father also wanted to climb down the trellis, he heard footsteps shuffling on the wooden boards of the upper hallway. Someone was snooping around.

"What the fuck!" Suttner cursed, grabbed the iron candlestick, and crawled under the downy bedspread. One of his home invaders, perhaps an officer from downstairs, approached the chamber. The door slowly creaked open and the dim light of a candle illuminated the rag rug. Suttner peeked out with one eye from under the bedcover.

"Mes ames," a smoky, bare-chested baritone purred.

The nightly visitor was only wearing riding britches and boots. When the Frenchman sat down on the edge of the bed, Suttner felt the mattress give way. Then slowly an inquisitive hand came crawling under the bedcover towards him. Now the volcano had to erupt. Suttner reared up from under the duvet with desperate force. He had the advantage of surprise. And with a sullen thud the candlestick crashed into the Frenchman's skull. The man sagged into the soft plumeau. It was a good blow.

Suttner could not remember how he had gotten down the trellis. He was visibly shaken. All he could tell his faithful wife was, "I have slain a Frenchman."

But the girls were safe.

The good wife acted with lightning speed, clothed her shocked man with a warm coat, and stuffed his pockets with bread and other edibles. Then she shoved him towards the moor meadows. Her husband ran as fast as he could into the reed thicket. He gained a good advantage because the slain corporal was only discovered after his companions wondered why his satisfaction took him so long.

Soon after, all hell broke loose on the farm. The whole company was awakened with whooping and yelling, the farmer's wife was interrogated about the whereabouts of her husband and daughters, the house was literally torn to shreds. But they couldn't find the culprit. He had crawled under the narrow bridge across the Moor Creek and made a vow to the Mother of All Sorrows to build her a nice, bulbous steeple top for her chapel, should he survive.

And St. Mary has helped. After a few days, the troops received orders to march on. The soldiers vacated the village. Shortly thereafter, Suttner resurfaced. And his girls as well returned unharmed. That's how the chapel got its fashionable bulbous turret.

There was a scrap on the door. Katrina peeked out and let Luise into her hen house. Louise carried her portfolio under her arm and without a comment sank into the old armchair. In school, Katrina had not noticed how tired she looked.

"You're as white as plaster. What happened?" Katrina asked her more brusquely than intended.

"What a night!" Luise yawned. She ignored Katrina's edgy tone.

"Oh, yes?" Katrina could not conceal her sarcasm. Would she finally come clean? With Luise it could be anything.

"I don't sleep so well these days."

"Did you have another pagan session?"

"Huh?" Luise snuggled deeper into the armchair and stared blankly ahead of herself. "That vernissage thing has been going on forever." Her eyelids drooped.

An uncomfortable pause crept up on them. Then Luise jolted back to life.

"Why are you avoiding me, Katrina?"

"Why do you lie to me?"

"What are you talking about? I don't lie." Luise crinkled her forehead.

"What about your 'super-rocking dive'!"

"I don't get it, what dive?"

"Are you kidding me? Don't tell me you have amnesia! Remember, Saturday? You said you couldn't go to the St. John's fire because of that super-cool rock dive, Nirvana . . ."

Luise sat up straight. She brushed some unruly strands of hair out of her face. "Wait, Katrina, let me tell you . . ."

"No, don't tell me anything. I know exactly where you went. I saw you!"

"Where did you see me?"

"Up by the chapel in the night! Don't lie to me again!" Katrina's eyes spew anger.

Luise's expression froze. She nervously poked for a cigarette in her jacket pockets. Then she lit it up a Camel with a match, trembling. She had finally lost composure. A drowsy swath of smoke crept from the tip of her cigarette. And the smoke made her face seem even paler.

"Oh, that! No big deal," Luise mumbled blowing out the smoke from a deep inhale. "Let me explain . . ."

"Yes, please do, if you can! What do I care if you loiter about in the forest in a nightgown doing mumbo jumbo. I don't give a crap about that! But lying is still lying!"

"See who is talking now! And who is making a move on Raffi? You knew exactly how I felt about him. Do you think I don't have eyes in my head?" Luise's eyes flashed daggers.

"All right, I see, there's the rub. Let me be clear, he is the one who ran after me . . ."

"You sure enough didn't mind! Daniel told me everything about your date by the lake."

"It was nothing. Only a coincidence."

"Man, I was hopping mad at you!"

"You were . . .? Not anymore . . .?"

"Well, he's a free man. I can't force him."

The two kept silent for a while and each one stared into her corner.

"But I still don't understand. You have never lied to me before, Lulu," Katrina picked up the conversation again. "You should really have told me about your 'happening'."

Luise sat up. "Yes, I probably should, but I didn't want to come across as too strange. So, you don't have any qualms about our 'heathen' rituals?"

"Whatever you are fooling around with on St. George's mound at midnight may be incomprehensible to me, but I could care less. Why didn't you trust me?"

"Well, since you are so catholic . . ."

"So, what! And what do you mean with 'catholic'? Do you think all the people who go to church are dim-wits?"

"Oh, no, sorry, I didn't mean it like that. But paganism is not everybody's cup of tea."

"Am I 'everybody'? I thought you knew me better than that! Your nature worship is no different from any other religion, just perhaps more primitive. And because of that you are playing these silly games with me?"

"Games? Who told you that? We pagans take earth matters seriously. We go along with the rhythm of nature. And solstices are our main celebrations. That has been going on for a few thousand years. Up by the chapel there is our portal to Epona, the horse goddess . . ."

"Horse goddess?"

"Sure, where do you think the ghost horse came from?"

"Easy, because a horse once starved to death in the chapel, that's why. But I personally don't know anyone who has ever seen that ghost."

"Just think a little harder, Katrina! Aren't horses also part of our spiritual world? Where do you think all the spooky stories and town names come from? I bet you ours isn't the only ghost horse around in these parts. And why call a town not too far from here 'Rosshaupten,' skull head of a horse? There is always some truth to these things. You want to know what we pagans do on the mountain top?"

Silence. Katrina stared at Luise without a twitch.

"I will explain it to you. We follow the cycle of nature and glance into the universe."

But Katrina still could not make much sense of what Luise had told her.

"Just like I suspected," Luise sighed. She grabbed her chafed portfolio next to the arm chair. That portfolio was for her what the typewriter was for Katrina.

"Come, let me show you some pictures. Then you will understand. Always when I attend a session, I have the most amazing ideas flying at me afterwards."

Luise opened her portfolio. Katrina again marveled at these drawings, which had propagated since she had stumbled across them the first time. There were so many fairytale creatures, like airy flower fairies, gnarled gnomes, flying lizards, jackalopey chimaeras, fire-breathing dragons, moor witches, trees with all kinds of facial expressions, curly-cued orchid flowers, dwarflike miniature munchkins living inside fly agaric, terrifying creatures of the sea, gigantic insect monsters, and hunchbacked witch-doctors aka druids—each page of her imagination abounded of things that crawled and flew. Katrina tried to sort out her impressions, but this much fantasy creeped her out.

"Here! Have this!" Luise beamed all over her face and handed the last drawing to Katrina. "I will just have to come up with another idea for your birthday then. What do you think? I worked on it some more."

"Great! Thanks!?" It was that spooky portrait of the girl with the flower wreath in her hair.

Shucks. What? Me a nature princess?

No, no, no. That's not me.

Down in the farmyard a motorcycle puttered closer. Luise perked up and looked at Katrina. She craned her neck through the window, trying to get a glimpse.

"Look, what is Pauli doing down there?"

"Well, he frequently drops in on us."

"He seems to be mighty excited about something, the way he is waving his arms at your dad. And now your dad is getting in his sidecar."

"Well, perhaps he had an emergency. Last time his water pipe broke. He always gets my dad to help him."

"You think so?" The moped sounds now puttered away again. "Then it has to be something really important, as fast as he is pulling off."

Luise turned towards Katrina again who still sat frozen staring at the drawing in her lap. "Can you tell me what the heck is going on with you and Mike?"

"What's going on? Nothing. What a jerk!"

"What now? Did you have a fight? Can it hopefully be fixed again?"

"No, there is nothing to fix." With that the whole darn story of the solstice fire burped up again. She let it flow. How liberating it felt to tell someone her experience, drop her baggage on Luise. Everything gushed forth, up to the spooky congregation of nature worshippers that Luise had been a part of. Luise listened with open ears, made an effort not to interrupt Katrina's narrative until she had finished, but gave her in between a few nods of compassion. Finally, Katrina had run out of words. Instead of a "Hadn't I told you so" Luise gave Katrina an honest hug.

Katrina's eyes welled with tears.

"Sorry, Katrina! I wasn't aware I had contributed so much to your terror. However, if you ask me, it does not seem like Mike to pull off such a nasty number on you. I can't imagine he is that vicious, can you? Wonder if you two had been set up, although"—she snorted a laugh—"he has a Celtic princess now. Anyway, he can't be that mean."

"Princess? Oh, he can keep those old bones all to himself. But why are you suddenly defending him?" Katrina snarled at Luise. "Aren't you on my side?"

"Katrina, how many times have I told you that Mike isn't my type, and probably not yours either? Excuse my stupid joke about the princess, but you know me, don't you? Such a dirty trick doesn't seem like him."

"But maybe it does fit him! Frau Bürkel warned me of him as well today."

"Oh, Katrina! Don't pay attention to that old hag!"

"Listen! She said that she had dreamt that Mike had done away with the Celtic princess, and that the princess was—me!"

"Huh?" Luise suppressed a giggle. "Someone bonked her on the head or what . . . what a bunch of nonsense! And when did he supposedly do that? Must have been a very, very long time ago? But if he buried her himself, why does he want to dig her up again? That doesn't make any sense. You aren't taking that old woman seriously, are you?"

"Lulu, will you stop it now? You don't get it! Save your black humor for someone else. Don't you see, that this creeps me out! I don't understand anything anymore!"

"Just let it go, Katrina! As everybody knows, that old woman has lost her marbles. Hasn't she always had lots of delusions, right? It obviously takes a little more brainpower than hers to process that archaeology."

"And what explanation do *you* have for all of this?"

"Sorry, none. You have to talk with Mike. Confront him. Let him justify his actions. And then perhaps you will also figure out the skeleton story."

"Absolutely not!"

"Then forget about him. Since you have Raffi now."

Katrina looked at her, stunned. She was speechless. "What gives you that idea? I barely know him."

"I think Raffi really likes you. He never bothered as much about me . . ."

"Why had you never told me that you liked him?"

"Because I never knew what was up with him. Just like with you and Mike. That's why I invited him to our solstice celebration. But he took off before we had even started. Well, then I knew. He is just not interested in me."

The motorbike puttered back into the farmyard. And suddenly a thunderstorm loomed in the henhouse. Girgl, Katrina's father, ducked through the squat door, his face flushed red, his blue eyes shooting sparks of lightning. A force of nature stomped in.

"Now you've done it!" Girgl thundered at Katrina. "Because you always drag such riff raff in! Now they plundered our chapel, those crooks!"

"What? That's impossible," Luise shouted, horrified.

"Impossible, what's impossible about that?" Girgl growled and stepped up threateningly close to Luise. "Last night it happened. Scruffy vagabonds, all of them! The most precious votive panels are gone, and two of our baroque saints on top." He stood there staring at Luise as if waiting for an answer.

"I don't get it, who does something like that?" Luise stammered.

"That g'damnit, good-for-nothing, Bohemian artists rat pack did it! Dared to snatch our most precious pieces for, what it looks like, the antique market! And you, you also belong to these new-fangled gypsies?"

The girls were blindsided, unable to speak.

Girgl couldn't stop his wrath of righteous justice any longer. Overcome with fury, he grabbed Luise's portfolio and slammed it into her hands.

"You, you get out of here! Get lost and take your garbage with you!" Girgl snorted. "Because I have to have a serious talk with that one there." Luise ducked around Girgl to slip through the door behind him.

Katrina was next.

"And you, you wacka-doo bird! Let me tell you something! First you write such a bunch of bogus that we all have to be ashamed of ourselves. And to top things off, you even give the robbers the key!"

Girgl couldn't help it. He smacked Katrina. A red blotch burned on her cheek.

"That's not how we have raised you!" Girgl thundered with unrelenting anger. "Just get lost! I don't want to see you around here any longer. Why don't you move in with your artist riff raff and that hodgepodge tart of yours!"

He turned on his heel and stomped out. Bang! That door was shut.

"What a disgrace! Never in my life have I seen such a foul up!" Katrina heard him still grumble on the outside.

And then Girgl rushed with giant steps down to the house, where the table was decked with the evening meal. Obviously, he would not enjoy the food, but the cows were already restlessly lowing to be fed and milked.

'Game over,' Katrina thought. 'Everything's over.'

And in the chamber there wasn't anything sharp or pointed or dangerous. No escape remained, not through window or door, not even out of her skin.

17

Knocking (K)nights[xix]

The scavenger woman had come almost 30 kilometers on her old bicycle, from the bombed-out city to our village. She begged for food for her family, if only an egg, which she collected in her basket hanging on the handlebars. As she mounted her bike by our house, her tire got caught in the gravel tracks and all the eggs fell out and cracked. She knelt down, sobbing and scraping the yolks from the dirt road. What a calamity!

—*Story told by my mother, Elisabeth Hanfstingl*

Thursday, June 27, early evening

Shattered to her bones, Katrina fled into the forest cabin that same afternoon. Like her grandfather had done once upon a time. She couldn't wait a second longer. That cabin on the mountainside wasn't all too far from the village, but was well hidden from sight on the forest margin. Only the trailing smoke from the wood stove would give away a sign of the life in it.

Conversely, the cabin window offered a panoramic view of the Alpine peaks looming over the village farmhouse gables.

Luise and Walli helped Katrina move. Luise had dropped off bed linens, blankets, dishes, as well as an old battery-operated radio, and several romance novels earlier. Now Walli delivered her typewriter, which she had fastened on her bicycle rack. Hanging in balance on the handlebars, she had lugged two shopping bags filled with edibles, such as sausage, cheese, bread and marmalade, biscuits, and all kinds of useful stuff.

"There, have your one-eagle-eye-search-system," Walli huffed and slammed the typewriter on the table. She was mad.

"Mother is all torn up," Walli scolded her sister.

With all the groceries, Walli also dropped a bad conscience on her older sister. She liked to rub it in. "Why don't you come home and make your peace with father. He doesn't talk anymore either. He is just like gramps now."

"No way, Walli! After all that happened? And if father thinks so badly of me . . ."

"He was just so mad at the first moment." Walli tried to comfort her and grabbed Katrina by the arm. "Now he growls only just a little. I think he calmed down again. Why don't you come home with us? It will be getting dark soon."

"No, that won't happen." Katrina shook off Walli's hand.

"Pighead! But don't you stay out here for too long!"

"Why?"

"Because without you it's all pretty boring at home."

"Sorry, I can't help you there. Now stop talking and start helping me!"

Grumbling, Walli set herself in motion. She was in jeans and her oldest t-shirt. Uncharacteristically, she had tied on a red headscarf, knotted at the back of her neck. She looked much like Widow Bolte out of the famous Wilhelm Busch cartoons, *Max und Moritz*. They cleared away old cans, boxes, and newspapers, wiped off cupboards, carried in fire wood, cleaned ash from the stove, and swept away a few pounds of cobwebs. Katrina pulled the old rags off the rods. The dust clouds made her cough so bad that she dumped them in the barrel by the water pump right away.

In the middle of the room, on the large rag rug, stood an old bucket. Katrina grabbed it to get water from the pump outside. She glanced inside the bucket and hesitated.

"What are you staring into that bucket for?" Walli chirped, both of her hands full with cups and cutlery. "Seen a jack-a-lope in there? I need water pronto, if you want a full clean up." Washing dishes, in Wallis opinion, was one of the most horrible jobs around. Her big sister better show a royal amount of appreciation for that sacrifice.

"Well, isn't that a little odd," Katrina mumbled without paying Walli much attention. "Do you think that grandfather drank colas out here?" She held up a cola bottle from the bucket.

"Jeez, what a rascal! Now we caught him! Now we know why he left for the forest back then," Walli chuckled.

Katrina kept staring at the bottle. She wasn't laughing. Her eyebrows were up.

"Sexy-mini-super-flower-pop-OPA-cola, everything is in Afri-Cola," Walli chirped away. She was reciting her favorite commercial slogan.

"Opa-Cola? Very funny, you wisecrack! I don't think so, Opa and cola don't mix," Katrina grumbled at the bottle. "I suspect that someone else has squatted in here."

"Who, do you think? Who comes around here?" Walli came closer. She peeked inside the bucket. "Oh, Bacardi! How Odd! But look, here is also a Cinzano bottle. That's for sure grandfather, we know that much, right? Hey, can I keep the bottles? They all have a deposit on them. I could get for sure one Mark or more for them at the store."

Instantly, she slammed her load of cups with a bang on the table and ran outside to stow away the empties in her bicycle basket.

Yikes. Katrina trudged to the water pump, filled up the bucket, and with disgust on her face washed the nasty curtain in the rain barrel. At no price did she want to sleep next to that revolting drapery. Finally, she tossed out the brown sludge on the rocks under the spot where the gutter ended. Walli had kept her promise, washed the dishes, and put them all back in the cupboard. This cleanup hadn't been quite as bad as scraping hardened chicken manure off the concrete floor in her hen house a couple of years ago. After they had beaten the holy dust out of the carpet, everything looked quite tidy. There was plenty of firewood, but the lamp oil was almost finished.

Despite the open windows, the cabin still smelled somewhat musty, but at least Katrina had a roof over her head. Although Walli had turned up her nose at the "cabin crap" initially, she still went to task. As a treat for helping with the cleanup, Katrina brewed up a cup of hot chocolate for Walli and opened a packet of her favorite cookies. But eventually Walli had to leave. The Angelus bells sounded loud and clear all the way up to the forest cabin. That was still her curfew. Far from believing their grandfather's old fairytale story about the bells releasing all the wild foxes, she didn't necessarily want to test that superstition either. So, she promptly went home. Katrina was now all by herself.

Forest-joy-hoy-hoy.[xx] That was an old German hit song bellowing from the radio. Now Katrina had a long evening ahead of herself. *Oh, how lonely throbs your chest.*

"It's your own fault, just get used to it," Katrina mumbled to herself.

Lovely birdies, yoi-yoi-yoi.

Despite her radio entertainment she was seriously lonely. She tuned the "yoi-yoi-yoi" away from her ears. Next, the Bohemian Forest song was blaring from the box. *It was in the Bohemian Forest? Where my cradle stood? Where I found my love? In the beautiful, green forest?* They can't be speaking about this forest here? Quite to the contrary, nobody goes looking for love in such a dark place. Perhaps they had meant squirrel love. First, they played the *Three White Birches* song and now this Bohemian Forest tune. Hopefully, this won't end with *In the Forest Dwell the Robbers,* because *Blue Spruces, Deep Forests* for sure surrounded her cabin, wherein, certainly, some robbers could hide away—some such who like to drink Bacardi colas?

Katrina turned the knob to the far right and chanced on the auto-motorist service radio. With full impact, the *Ghost Riders in the Sky* song galloped across the airwaves. Not quite her thing either. On the main station the Birthday Congratulations musical request program was still on, often dubbed the "legacy hunter" hour. An opera aria started yodeling through the speaker. 'All right, here we go with the Wald-küre,'[xxi] Katrina scoffed. The barrel had hit the bottom! Well, then, done with that! Switch off. Suddenly, however, it was awfully quiet in the cabin. But even the silence had sharp ears for the inner voices all around.

More than anything, Katrina wished to listen to the soothing clanking of the cow chains while falling asleep, but the sounds in the forest played a different tune. She lay awake eavesdropping on the lamenting song of an owl, the sonata of a mocking bird, or the whooshing of the pine trees. Finally, it started to rain. Although the splattering on the wooden tiles of the roof sounded very familiar and comforting, she worried at the same time about the leaks. Over by the wood stove the water started dripping through the roof.

"That's why the bucket was standing in the middle of the rug!"

No use trying to catch that elusive sleep. Katrina rolled from the cot, lit up the petrol lamp, and got busy making more order. She took an investigative tour of her cabin.

The forest cabin was very old, too old in fact, to be sure about the story of its origin. The foundation, it was said, was scrounged together from the remains of an old robber baron castle. Sort of like the Celtic boulders in the foundation of White Horse Chapel, but there was just as little proof for it. Perhaps this cabin, which now enveloped Katrina, had nevertheless been a witches' cottage. The Witches Mound, about which her grandmother had written in her diary, was only a stone's throw from this location. This would have been an ideal lair for one or two witches. Once there was a herbalist called "Zenz," from Creszentia, living here during the Napoleonic wars. Her grandfather used to tell that story, which old aunt Nanni had related to him. But none of these assumptions, be it robber baron fortress, monk's hermitage, or witch's cottage, had been tangibly cut in stone.

Katrina looked around. For the most part, the walls on the gable sides were constructed from rough field stones all the way up. They did seem reminiscent of old castle walls. Altogether that little cottage resembled an Alpine cowherd dwelling more than any of the typical barns down on the village pastures.

With the petrol lamp in hand, Katrina meticulously inspected every corner of her cabin and discovered heavy reams of books on the shelf. Herbalist compendiums, atlas, Bible, ancient elementary school primers, and a few tattered Karl May paperbacks had collected thick layers of dust. Her cleaning attempts clearly had not reached that high yet. A lot of desert dust seemed to have blown out of the famous "Llano Estacado" over the years. Had her grandfather read these novels as well?

She doubted it. They might have once migrated over from the old parish center library. Between the fat volumes a couple of carvings peeked forth. They were quite life-like. Especially a bambi caught Katrina's eyes. Had her grandfather only continued the carving trade instead of his pesky peening craft.

Katrina grabbed an herbalist book from the shelf. She leafed aimlessly through the pages and found an insert with perfect calligraphy, a romantic poem. How peculiarly beautiful . . .

> Oh, churchlike forest serenity
> You dream-forsaken silence
> You stream an air of peace
> So wonderful and unique.
>
> No foreign sound from far away
> Would disturbingly intrude on you
> Just quietly from the village far
> A little bell softly resounds.
>
> You gentle tranquility, mysterious
> You lovely countryside idyll
> How deeply longs my heart for you,
> Oh forest, for your silence.

Julius Gersdorff (1849-1907)

Poetry? Her grandfather? That just didn't seem like him, although who else would have used these old reams? The forest for sure would be a topic for him. Maybe he had to memorize that poem in school once upon a time. He was quite a character in many regards. Right after he returned from the forest cabin, Katrina had to regularly fetch him his vermouth from the grocery store. He didn't overdo it, but he drank it consistently.

He had a sweet tooth for biscuits as well. The first time that Katrina asked for 'vermouth' for her grandfather, she couldn't say it right. It came out like 'Wehmut,' the German word for melancholy. The store woman bent over laughing. "Luckily, that stuff isn't sold in bottles yet," she spluttered. But she knew exactly what her grandfather wanted and wrapped the Cinzano in a sheet of grey paper. Eventually, gramps broke his vermouth habit, but held on to his tick with the clock, setting it always ahead by 15 minutes. If he had passed away suddenly, he would only notice it after the fact. And perhaps, by then, he might have even gotten to like eternity.

Katrina rummaged through the bookshelf. Something small, a red thing, plopped on the wooden floor. She picked it up. It was a matchbox car. That was just so out of character for her grandfather, just like the cola bottles were. How did it even get here? She inspected the toy car from all sides. Something seemed familiar about it. The underbelly was scratched up and one front wheel was bent. The scratches could have been a W, or if you turned the car around, an M. The car did not want to stay put on the tilted shelf. It kept rolling off, no matter how one put it there.

You only have to listen with your heart.

Katrina cringed and dropped the car like a hot potato. She swiveled around. The door. Nobody there. Had the toy car whispered to her just now? 'I'm going nuts.' She picked the little red car up again. Possibly her brother, Martl, used to have one like that, but how did it get here? It didn't really matter. Brusquely, she stuffed the renitent miniature car into her carry bag.

There were a gazillion reasons in her primitive refuge that made Katrina worry. But she would rather investigate the smallest details there before facing the reason why she had been exiled into that cottage. Nobody to blame but herself, right? All she hoped for was to put some distance between her and the disaster.

How long would she be able to sustain herself in the forest? She had 300 Marks from the essay competition in her pocket. This amount wouldn't last forever. Luise and Walli had promised to help her out and get her the necessities. But how soon would she have to go looking for berries and mushrooms? Most likely her grandfather had done the same. At any rate, she would be eating a lot of noodles, potatoes, and rice.

Suddenly, Katrina had all the time in the world, not in little slices as usual, but as a whole salami all in one piece for reading and writing, as she pleased. Yet she didn't want to think too hard and slide into her dreaded brooding. When she felt a pencil in her hand or the keys of the typewriter under her fingers, she already felt better.

Katrina forgot about time during these late hours, like she wanted to forget about so many things. For sure she wouldn't be able to sleep. Writing always put her at ease. She just had to let it out. She stuck the torchlight into a knothole into the upper log. Then she dug in her school bag for paper to feed the Adler. The only sheets were the pages from her old school essays.

"Oh well," she grumbled. "I can still use the backside of these." As she was about to insert a sheet into her typewriter, she read, "When I was living with the Celts . . ."

. . . we venerated the trees. They housed the souls of our ancestors, many of them . . .

We followed the annual cycle like the children their mothers, in full confidence that we could rely on nature . . . And the fire told us stories. When the logs crackled, the rosin melted and the sparks danced . . .

"What a bunch of stinking nonsense," she snarled and crumpled the sheet. In retrospect, her essay sounded just as trite as Luise's blathering about her dubious pagan adventures. Schiller had condemned that essay most fervently as a pile of bogus, and she admittedly agreed with him by now. She had hit the keys without researching anything. This way she certainly could not progress in her craft. "Eagle nosedive" she called it when the talons of her typewriter entangled and twisted her thoughts. Already the first ball of paper had landed with precision in the wood basket next to the potbellied stove. Precisely there it was where all the "black blotches" belonged.

So much for St. John's Eve. Everything had burned down to ashes. She hadn't come very far with her vivid imagination, neither with her dragons nor her witches. Her boundless fantasy had gotten her into trouble in the first place.

Damned Celts, bloody tree philosophy! Schiller had been right, there was no rhyme or reason to her stories. Who was to blame for her misery but herself? Hadn't it all started with her darn stories? Even the falling out with her father? And she had caused her mother sorrow and missed the warmth of home and her nightcap with hot chocolate.

Arms crossed, hunched over the typewriter, Katrina let her tears flow. After the sluices had closed again, she inserted another paper disregarding the nonsense printed on its backside and typed: "Calculation of weekly expenses for an exiled witch at Chateau Tannenwald."

Miraculously, this planning task soothed her nerves in a sensible way. She concluded that her funds would last her at least eight weeks, if she stayed thrifty, perhaps even ten weeks. By that time, she hoped to have landed a part-time job in the town nearby. But eventually it would get cold. Shouldn't she procure a stack of firewood? The splitting block, which her grandfather had used, was still outside under the roof by the wall. For now, she had a small pile of logs for cooking, which would last her some time. But then? Let's cross that bridge when we get to it. Just now the June storms were still thundering above the forest.

Crushed, Katrina finally laid down on the musty cot. She had borrowed a pillow and blanket from Luise. Without them she would have been rather uncomfortable. In her head she allocated the food provisions back and forth over the coming weeks, and so her brain finally gave way to rest. She cuddled in her blanket. Slowly, she descended into a delirious slumber.

Cha-bang, cha-bang. Katrina forced her eyes open with great effort.

Cha-bang. She jolted up.

Cha-bang. Something was banging against the walls through the irregular aftershocks of a serious thunderstorm. She could have slept through thunder and lightning, but this persistent knocking clattered her awake. Furious, she jumped up from her bed, padded her way to the table, and grabbed the torchlight.

"Darn shutter," she grumbled. In the old toolbox she found hammer and nails. Then she stepped into the moonlit night. The wind had blown away the clouds for the most part. With a few well-targeted blows, she reattached the rickety slat on the shutter.

Whooosh-sszzt-hhouut. Her hair stood up. Not only the hair on her head but also the tiny soft bristles along her spine. A shapeless something yet to be felt like the huff of a whirlwind had just flitted by her, not to be seen but certainly noticed. The mind's eye was fully awake now. Katrina instinctively hollowed her back and swiveled around. Was somebody standing there? A man-like tree trunk? She flashed her torchlight on it. The light swept the figure away. She let her flashlight wander like a searchlight. Nothing. Cautiously, she approached the location where the phantom had vanished.

No, there was indeed nothing to see.

Something clicked behind her. Katrina turned around. Her flashlight struck a face. What a face! Bearded like Methuselah, a really tall guy. His clothes looked tattered, or was it fur? His shaggy hair lit up red. And bluish glowed his skin. She wanted to scream, but no sound escaped her. This apparition only lasted a second. Then the phantom blended into the trees.

Who or what was that?

Terrified, Katrina staggered backwards to her cabin shelter.

Done with sleeping for the night.

18

A New Western

Their appearance was terrifying . . . "They are mighty tall, with bulging muscles under white skin. Their hair is blond, but not only by nature, because they also bleach it artificially, they wash it in gypsum water and comb it back from the forehead to the top. This way they look like demons of the forest." *Didorus of Sicily.*

—*Hans F. Nöhbauer, Die Bajuwaren, 65*

Friday, June 28

As promised, Luise dropped in on her at the forest cabin the next day after school. She swooped in like a breath of fresh air. She was wearing her trademark purple, frilly-flowy hippie blouse.

"Hello, there! It's getting quite comfy in here!"

"Wisecrack!"

"Look, what I have brought for you!" Luise slapped the local paper and a bag of gummi bears on the table.

"What! Stop torturing me!" Terrified, Katrina jumped up from the table and almost tripped over the broom leaning against the wall.

"No, no, not at all, Katrina! Please, sit! Don't worry, there isn't a word about you in it this time. But I thought you wanted to know the official story about the break in . . ."

"Jeez! I'd rather not," Katrina groaned. "I just don't have the nerves for that right now. How could I have let myself be tricked like that . . ."

"What do you mean?"

"Well, Raffi, of course. He absolutely wanted to get into the chapel . . ."

"Now, gimme a break, sister!" Luise's eyebrows shot up in high arches. She had used her brother's phrase, when he was really flustered about her.

"But the key . . ."

"The key, the key! Is that all you know? Maybe there are some fucking duplicates then!" Luise boiled with anger. "Didn't we have this thing with Sesame-open-shut before? Remember? There was no key around either."

Katrina wrinkled her forehead and fell silent. Everything was possible, but that didn't explain anything yet. Perhaps Luise still clung to her old heartthrob and felt called to defend him? Luckily, Luise simmered down as quickly as she had puffed up.

"All right, Katrina! For how long have we known each other? You better believe me, the next best explanation need not always be the correct one."

"But why are there so many crazy things happening lately!" Katrina almost whined now. She sounded so deplorably sorry that Luise scooted closer to her and wrapped her arm around her shoulder.

"You'll see, everything will be all right. By the time you get married, this too will have passed."

An unintended giggle escaped Katrina. "You almost sound like my mother."

"And? Is it helping?"

"Well, just a little . . . Anyhow, I think I am slowly going crazy."

"Why so?"

Katrina reported to Luise her forest ghost encounter. Luise listened patiently. "That sounds just like one of those old Celtic dudes."

"You think? Just what I needed," Katrina moaned. And with somewhat more confidence and irony she added, "Can't a girl have her peace even in the forest anymore?"

"Of course not. Don't you know that there are ghosts roaming everywhere? Why don't you write it all down!"

"Well, as you know, I have lost my appetite for such stories."

"Perhaps there is an explanation for it after all."

"What do you mean?"

"Do you remember that hiking day?"

"Which one? We've had so many."

"Fifth grade?"

"Of course!" A cautious smile crinkled Katrina's lips. "The one where Klaus fell into the lake?"

"Right."

"But what does that have to do with my nightmare?"

"I will only tell you, if you promise me not to freak out." Katrina nodded. Luise took a deep breath. She continued.

"All right, didn't we march by the *Hügelgräber* (burial mounds) that day?"

Katrina nodded again.

"Listen, these Celtic burial mounds are just ten minutes from your cottage here."

"What? You are not saying . . . do you think it was a Celtic ghost?"

"Like I said, anybody can believe what they want. In my religion, however, this would have been entirely possible."

"Your religion? Sorry, I just don't get that . . ."

"And what, if I am right?"

Katrina's embarrassed smile froze on her lips. She didn't feel comfortable in her skin any more. 'If you want to get scared,' old Bürkel once had told them as children, 'then just you stay out in the forest one night.' All right, there must have been something to it then. Yes, ghoulish stories could happen to anyone, not only to poor raftsman Loisl, who encountered the village witch. *'From all bad spirits and evil wives deliver us, oh Lord, in all eternity, amen, yodel-di-yodeli-dio.'* That earworm again burrowed deep into Katrina's head. How could anybody request such an awful song for their radio birthday congratulations? It wasn't a happy song. But perhaps people didn't listen to the words, only the yodel tunes.

"And, what happens now? Do you think the old knotty Celtic hobgoblin will come back?" Katrina asked Luise.

"I sure don't."

Another thought suddenly struck Katrina. The Celtic princess. An ice-cold shiver poured over her back. 'Just be careful with that Mike,' old Bürkel had warned her. 'He has done in the princess. And the princess that was you!'

"No, for sure not," Luise comforted her.

Yodel-di-yodeli-dio-du-yeli-e, from all bad spirits and evil wives deliver us, oh Lord . . .

"What 'for sure not'?" Katrina asked her like in trance.

"Come back. We will make sure that he doesn't come back."

"How?"

"Have you ever heard of mistletoes?"

"What toes?"

"Hello, are you even listening to me?"

"Mike also has a Celtic princess like that . . ."

"Will you already forget about that guy! And don't you worry any longer about old Bürkel's horror stories. She definitely has a screw loose. First thing, we will make sure that you're safe out here. All right then, where have you seen any mistletoes around here?"

"Nowhere so far."

"Ooh, well, then let's make you a dara knot then."

"What's that?"

"You don't know? That's a Celtic symbol, a braided knot that catches all the bad ghosts. Nothing will get through, no ghost, no witch, no hobgoblin. Have you got a pencil for me? And some paper?"

Katrina sifted through her bag. All her papers were scribbled up, but the back of her spiral book was still clean. She tore it off and handed it to Luise. With a skilled hand, she drew the nicest curlicue pattern on the cardboard.

"What exactly will that be when it's done?"

"Can't you tell?"

"Looks like a bunch of twisted snakes to me. Or roots?"

"Yes, more or less. Can you also see the horns? Of course, that is my personal interpretation. But the old Celts, were some badass artists.—*Yes, for sure, the lapis lazuli ring!*—Now see, here, it's almost looking like a dragon face, right? Let me tell you, the old Celts were scared stiff of dragons."

Katrina nodded. She was ready to consider Luise's theory. The ornate hex pattern looked frighteningly pretty. Finally, Katrina nailed the drawing above the entrance. She let out a sigh of relief. "Now nothing bad can happen to me anymore," she joked.

"Obviously, you can always trust my witchcraft!"

"It looks so wonderful! You could probably sell copies of these."

"If you say so. So, how much is it worth to you?"

"Ha, ha, that's a good one! What old garbage do you want?" Katrina was only kidding, but Luise seemed serious.

"Can I have this?" She pointed to the old tea tin on the bookshelf, which her grandfather had left behind.

"Sure, whatever. I don't like to drink herb tea anyway. And who knows how old the stuff in there is."

Katrina grabbed the tin from the shelf. She handed it to Luise. Something clonked inside. Audibly.

"Thank you!" Luise snatched the tea tin from her.

"Hey, can I take a quick look inside?" Katrina had gotten curious.

"A gift is a gift. I have to go now."

Luise grabbed her stuff and headed for the door. Katrina followed her outside. Luise quickly shoved the pretty but faded tin with its chafed Chinese dragon on the lid onto the passenger seat of her car.

"Too bad you're leaving!" Katrina said. "Can't you stay a little longer? Brainstorm the World War II essay with me? This marathon is driving me crazy again. Schiller, the killer . . .?"

"I can't help you there. I myself haven't read anything about it. When is there even time? Sorry, I have to help pack up the pieces for our vernissage this evening. And you know me. I always do my homework on the bus."

"You aren't much help for me today!"

Luise stepped on the gas pedal. Cheerfully waving her arm out the window, she abandoned Katrina in the forest.

Dang it! Nobody to talk to and nobody to mooch filler paper off. Hung over from her latest night terror, she had altogether forgotten to buy more paper at the bus stop after school. The marathon, however, continued without mercy. She had to come up with an idea. The next essay could make or break her grade. She had plenty of time, except she knew squat about her dark war topic.

What should she write? Her head was a mess. She had too many shrapnel pieces in her head. One thing, however, was for sure: most of the war stories that she recalled had glossed over the brutality of what she had seen in pictures. The whole truth, and nothing but the truth, for as horrible as it was, could not be put in words. It was unspeakable, and therefore often unsaid. And if the truth was unspeakable, how could it ever be written? At best, she knew little bits and pieces of World War II episodes, as she had overheard them from the old folks.

Where in this darn cabin was any paper? Katrina went rummaging through the drawers and cabinets. Nothing. Was it rationed out here in the forest? Like the clothes and groceries were during the war? Luckily, the farmers always knew how to help themselves.

Should she write about the illegal butchering in the night? That carried the death penalty, but luckily her grandparents got away with it. Her mother often told her the story how the forced laborers from the Föhrenwald factory almost "smelled the rat" (sow, that is). The "canaries," so called because their skin was yellow from the gun powder, hastily gulped down the greasy broth from the cooked pork innards (*Schlachtschüssel*) in their canteens. Otherwise, they kept their mouths shut, hoping to scrounge another scrape or morsel on their next scavenging trip, after being so lucky to chance upon the aftermath of a butchering night.

Or should she write about the Volkssturm resistance of Thankirchen, when the deluded "wolf pack" under Nazi officer Esser fought the American troops and the village got shot to shreds and houses burned down? Or that episode, when her mother, a five-year-old child, swiped a box of cocoa powder from the American troops? Her father caught her eating it on the balcony, and thought it was poison. Instantly, he threw the cocoa over the banister.

Or should she write perhaps about her father? Girgl barely wasn't drafted to the Wehrmacht thanks to his young age and had to slog away on the farm instead. By contrast, his older brother, Uncle Hans, was drafted despite his tuberculosis-weakened lungs, then wounded on the western front and taken prisoner by the British. The war derailed his seminary studies, and instead of becoming a priest he ended up as a customs officer. Just another tale. Then there were the nights of fire bombs. When her father spoke of bunker digging, the nightly air raids on Munich, and the yet undiscovered duds (not spuds) in the potato field, he always got very serious. Each time he plowed, he feared that one of the yet unaccounted bombs could explode on him. Only when he digressed into his bartering deals with the Amis, eggs-for-cigarettes, for example, his eyes lit up with a mischievous glint. Grandmother apparently never found out who had stolen the eggs and blamed the martens for it.

Most dramatic were Oma Gabelsberger's stories because she was blessed with a prolific narrative talent. In one episode, she had to take up guns for the Volkssturm, but was trembling too much to use her old shooter. Or she would pull out some old handbills that had rained down on them from airplanes in the later part of the war, disseminating the Allieds' angle of demoralization. "Well," she would say, "some air planes dropped propaganda on us, the others dropped bombs." One British plane once crashed in the mountainside woods. They all ran to see it. The image of that charred body in the cockpit haunted her so badly that she would never in her life eat chocolate pudding again.

At the top of Oma Gabelsberger's list, however, was her harrowing adventure during the most horrible springtime of 1945, when the Death March crossed the land. At the collapse of the "total war," she pedaled with courageous desperation behind the garish, motley crew on her bike, on her father's orders. She was to keep an eye on their valuable tractor that had been confiscated for the prisoner transport by the Waffen-SS. Pedaling along the garish procession, she noticed that some of the ragged creatures had thrown themselves into the muddy ditches besides the road, feigning death. Soon the droning in the sky pulled closer, and suddenly the American machine guns riddled the dirt along the somber procession, which burst into total chaos. By a hair's breadth, Oma Gabelsberger escaped unscathed but without the tractor. None was more relieved than her father. "Oh, girl," he said, "what a terrible mistake I have made to send you out!" Oma Gabelsberger certainly could illustrate those events so lively that listeners thought they had been there themselves.

Or should she write about Frau Bürkel? Her flight on foot from the Russians in Silesia, stealing potatoes for survival, was something incredible. Although her adventures sounded truly harrowing, she might have made up some. After her gaga prophesy the other day, Katrina trusted her even less. Not only had she embellished her story about her first-time encounter with a real negro, she also fervently claimed that a real Indian, like Winnetou, had roamed about the forest back then.

Winnetou? Come on! Katrina glanced at the bookshelf. Maybe that was it! Nonsense! But here they were, all three volumes of Karl May's epic. The famous fictitious Apache chief and his German companion at arms, Old Shatterhand, had been tainted since the Third Reich. Some Nazi ideologists had used that widely popular fiction about American Indian tribes to claim that some races were better than others. But, in the end, even the most skewed theorists were thrown off by the nobility of the "wild" Apache chief because Winnetou was such a noble character. Anyway, one author in the *Völkischer Beobachter* at the time was not quite sure how to peg the "racial predicament." Tragically, the noble savage Winnetou with his silver rifle had been dragged into the totalitarian mess of world domination, weapons of mass destruction, and unspeakable human horror.

She dropped Winnetou back on the shelf. Paper, where was paper? On her frantic search, Katrina again dove into the old wardrobe, with little hope. What a bunch of garbage! Covered up by chafed old jackets, hats, shirts, and much other junk, she discovered a tattered cardboard box in the farthest corner. She pulled it out on the floor and carefully opened the flaps. The content was topped off with newspapers. She pulled them off. Underneath she found a crinkled paper bag. She carefully reached inside and pulled out some grey-black striped pants. A prisoner's suit? How in the world did that get in there? The dirty rag had a pungent body odor and also reeked from gasoline. Disgusted, she quickly bunched the garment up again, returned it inside the bag, and stuffed the whole strange collection of garments back into the box.

She kept some of the magazine clippings out and with suspense leafed through the yellowed handbills filled with garish war pictures of bombardments. Coventry! Horrific! If she read these flyers right, the "total" war was nearing its end. "The people of Germany neither had wanted this war nor believed it possible. Over and over again we perceive expressions of godless surprise, of how it can be possible for people to commit such atrocities."

There it was, her grandmother's diary was whispering to her . . . another war has started. *Mounds of bodies, horrible, all of them had a number on their arms . . .*

The impact was sudden, she had to let it out. Her spin on this topic was a little bold, but, what the heck, it matched her rubric well enough.

Katrina sat down at her typewriter and loaded a blotter paper, the only kind of paper left. The storm set in fast. She struggled to keep up speed with the downpour of thoughts.

Clickety-clack, clack, clack, clickety-click, type, type, shrooom-plink.

Nobody was bothered by her noise out here in the forest. Right? If she hadn't let it out, she might have exploded like a landmine when plowed over.

Since the fatal day of the landing of the 4th Infantry Division on Utah Beach in Normandy on June 6, 1944, Joe had cheated death three times. The first time, he stood face to face with a German Kraut when his gun magazine had just emptied. The young Wehrmacht soldier, with blond tufts for a moustache, just looked at him surprised, as if he had never seen the likes of him before, although many Amis were killed already. Joe took the German's hesitation to smack him over the head with the butt of his gun and wrest away his fully loaded weapon. Every inch of Utah beach was drenched in blood on D-Day.

The second time that Joe escaped he might have wished they killed him on the spot. Joe had taken cover with five of his comrades in the ruins of a French church, when they were captured by a German troop. In this battle for the ultimate victory, no prisoners were taken.

"Drop your guns, drop your pack, drop your helmet, hands against the wall!"

The Amis followed suit.

"Take aim, soldiers, . . . one, . . . and don't you dare miss, . . . two, . . ." The captain paused. One of his captives was out of line. That could not be, not on death row.

"Helmets off, I said!" the captain barked. You could see spit flying from his mouth. "Turn around!"

But Joe didn't move. A German soldier jumped forward and tore off the GI's helmet. Long braids fell over Joe's shoulders.

"What have we got here?" the captain mused. The guns stayed lifted. It seemed that the former Gestapo officer was thinking really hard. He didn't have much time because this here wasn't a practice run. It was do or die. He stared at his prisoner. A sarcastic smile crinkled the corners of his mouth.

"Lookee here, a red skin!" he snarled.

Joe stayed stone-faced. Cold contempt glinted in his eyes.

"Guns down!" The captain made a few strides toward the giant Ami to inspect him up close. He strutted slowly in a circle around him.

"Name? Neiiiim? What is your neiiim?" the captain screamed.

Joe didn't answer.

"Your name, tell him your name, Joe," the comrade next to him whispered in Joe's ear.

Joe didn't bat an eye. The German captain, however, excitedly turned towards the other American who had just whispered.

"Joe? Joe is his name? Indian? What tribe?" The officer screamed that captive in the face.

The American soldier, who realized his fatal mistake, shook his head. The captain pressed his gun barrel under the man's chin and cocked the trigger.

"Comanche," gasped the American. That was all he knew.

Joe froze like a salt pillar. He was tall enough to stare across everybody's heads at the smoldering ruins and the grey sky.

"Comanche? Very good warriors, ha, ha! Can you radio? Air weiiives?" the captain croaked.

No answer.

"What!!? Not talking, eh? Just you wait, our colleagues from the Schutzstaffel have made bigger birds than you sing. But we don't have time for this out here! Get them birds caged, pronto! You, there, why didn't you bring your feathers along, ha ha!"

The captain swiveled around to his men. "And you all! What are you staring at! Move it! Back to the frontline!"

Then he turned to the adjutant on his right. "Report to the Reichs Security Office. Request top security prisoner transport, political division south. Hurry, get on with it! I will make you personally liable for the safety of this freight."

And to himself, "Very well, our Standartenführer[xxii] will also be most interested in him." The Gestapo had long been waiting for a catch like this.

Joe Santiago was what his captors had been hoping for, a code talker. His tribal name was Standing Bear.

Indigenous languages were used by the Americans in the war as military code, especially because they had not been written down anywhere and were unknown in the Old World.

But Joe didn't sing. The Gestapo tormentors were slowly running out of ideas. Joe was near death after beatings, sleep deprivation, electro shocks, and burn injuries. Another round of interrogations might have killed him. But a dead Indian wasn't a good Indian for the Gestapo. Therefore, it was too soon to send him to the eternal hunting grounds. They started feeding him again and nursed him back to life. Next, his henchmen started lying to him, like Pinocchio to Father Gepetto. They told him that the war was already lost for the Allies. They tried to bribe him, with making a career as special scout for the "double flashes." If he were to spill the beans about the American strategy and help them listen to the cables, he would have a worthwhile post in the German military for sure.

But Joe kept silent.

Now the henchmen put Joe to a murderous choice. Every day, they would execute one of his American comrades in front of his eyes, until he sang. And that's just what happened. Bang. The first comrade toppled over lifeless like a sack of potatoes into a thin stream of his own blood. Shortly before his execution, the young "Ami" had pleaded with Joe for his life. He begged Joe to sell his language. But the Bear didn't rat out his country. Not with as much as a grunt. And so, the misery went on, until all Americans were done away with.

By then, Joe had fallen into a stupor, and the Gestapo

gave up on him, judging him deaf, and dumb, and crazy. Joe lost all the "privileges" of being a high priority political prisoner with the Gestapo and was sent, by default and lack of any better idea, and to keep him on hand, just in case, to the Penal Battalion of the Forced Labor Camp South. This kind of "treatment," cynically titled "God's judgment," hardly anyone was known to survive. Perhaps they would get him to talk out there.

On arrival, Joe was due, like all inmates, to have his hair cut. He stood in line, waiting his turn. At last, he faced a bald German in a grey coat. His torture instrument was a pair of scissors.

Joe stood up straight, glared down on the man. His coal-black eyes nailed the bald guy firmly to the messy, rough-hewn wooden floor. Joe almost imperceptibly shook his head. His eyes spelled n-o.

The barber pointed to the stool. No. The barber pointed to the stool again, more anger in his gesture. No. Again the grey coat stabbed at the chair. No.

It was a staring match, all right. It held up the line.

Without as much as a blink, Joe grabbed the stunned barber by the coat sleeve. He pressed something into the barber's hand. The hair cutter stared into his palm. A necklace, a token, something strange. Nobody back down the line dared to breathe.

Would he call the guards?

Suddenly, the barber broke into demonic laughter. "Now look at that! What a pretty maiden with long braids! We for sure could use some women folks around here. I hope you can dance for us later. Now, will someone get this girl her clothes, but quick!" He slipped the token into his coat pocket and yelled, "Keep it moving! Move it, you rotten scoundrels!"

That's how Joe got to keep his hair. They made him serve the officers dinner in the mess hall wearing women's garb. They always got a hoot out of it.

Finally, Joe cheated death a third time. He was unloading potato sacks from a farmer's truck, when a ruckus broke out over a slice of moldy bread in the kitchen barracks. Quickly he slipped into an empty sack on the delivery truck, passed the guards at the gate unnoticed, and then jumped off in a wooded area. He ran through the forest as fast as his legs would carry him. This was a foreign country, but the forest was his friend. Not that he could shape-shift but he knew how to melt into the natural environment. He made himself invisible.

Joe had a good head start before the internment camp authorities found him missing. Joe knew all the tricks of cover, but the Schutzstaffel had vicious dogs to sniff him out. He could hear them tearing closer. The black double-flash uniforms confronted him on the river bank. They sicked the dogs on him. Joe jumped into the rapids. He paddled for dear life. The guards sprayed bullets after him. Gone he was. Joe's cap with his number painted on it floated up. The rifle fire went silent.

GI Joe, heavily breathing, ducked way behind a heap of boulders in the water, hoping they believed him dead. Late in the afternoon, the German shepherd dogs, whining and tired, gave up on the Indian.

Joe stayed along the river shore. He found an overhang where he rested and fell into a coma-like sleep.

A cracking sound snapped the fugitive back to reality. Joe scrambled to his feet. A young shepherd stood before him. The boy stretched out his hand, in it a thick slice of bread and a piece of bacon. Joe hesitated. Then he grabbed the food, smelled it suspiciously, and wolfed it down. The farmer boy seemed to be pleased.

For a while both hunkered down wordlessly under the overhang. Cautiously, the farmer boy pulled on Joe's sleeve. "Not good," he said, meaning the miserable prison garb. He pointed at Joe. "You, wait here! I come back." Then he quickly disappeared in the underbrush.

Joe had better things to do than letting himself be caught. He stayed on the lookout in a safe distance. The shepherd indeed returned and sat down in the same spot where they had first met. Joe observed him quietly for a long while.

The shepherd boy had brought a bundle with him and laid it down by his side. He was alone. Nobody seemed to have followed him. Joe slipped out of his hiding place. An unimaginable hunger drove him to it. The boy had brought another loaf of bread. He also pulled an old shirt, some pants, and a typical farmer jacket out of his sack. A sloppy hat was part of the outfit too. The boy again pulled on Joe's prison rugs. Joe dumped his striped suit and slipped into the farmer tatters.

As the boy stuffed the prison rags into the sack, the Indian disappeared soundlessly, like a ghost. For a reason. The boy threw the sack with the rags behind the bush.

"Hey, rascal! There you are! What business have you got, roaming around down here?" a rough voice bellowed behind the boy's back.

"I was just looking for Stasi, father." Stasi was the mother of the herd, soon due for most likely twin lambs.

"You better be more careful next time, fellow!" The father strictly hissed at his son and knocked him with his knuckles on the head. "These are really bad times. Do you even know how many vagrants are on the loose? Just yesterday another guy skipped the camp."

"Don't worry, father! I am always careful."

"So, you think? Now, look here, if you don't want to believe me." The bald-headed father dug deep into his trouser pocket and pulled out a necklace with a pendant on it. It was a tooth or claw of some sort.

"Look! I got this from an American, a real Indian. He split and took off on the potato delivery truck yesterday. The camp command thinks that they got him, that he drowned, but his body was never found. He might still roam around here somewhere. And, mind you, there are so many forced laborers, gangsters, and other riff raff drifting about."

He paused. "Do you want this? Here!"

The boy briefly glanced at the necklace in his father's palm, then quickly pocketed it. He had had no choice but to lie. His father was still waiting for the Endsieg (final victory) and had volunteered for camp duty.

"Endsieg? The end will come regardless of a Sieg," the priest had mumbled once after mass. The young shepherd had heard it precisely, as he helped the priest disrobe. His pastor was a fair man who had gotten a taste of prison himself for preaching the truth. He couldn't help an occasional slip of the tongue. So, the altar boy came to trust the treasonous man of God more than his blinded-by-faith prison guard father.

The young shepherd was not afraid of Indians, since he had devoured all of Karl May's Winnetou books. And as an altar server he knew exactly where to find the key for the chapel on the hill. He figured that the priest, who earlier had been sent to camp for being a Catholic dissenter, with a purple triangle sewn on his sleeve, would be agreeable to his actions as long as he didn't know anything directly himself. A plan was made and executed.

Not much later, the Death March, a train of human misery in striped suits, poured from the concentration camp. The Nazi regime wanted to disappear and extinguish these inmates. In a seemingly endless sad, gray train of human bodies, the storm of a gazillion wooden clogs clattered through the snow covered landscape that late, frosty April. Some dropped by the wayside, others were made to ride in one of the scant rickety wagons. That strange human migration finally dispersed under the Allied airplanes flying overhead.

Soon the American tanks broke the grisly spell all together. The farmers hung white sheets in the windows. The total war was totally lost. One village didn't want to believe it and went up in flames under the Allied battery of gun fire.

The Indian, however, had escaped. Only the key still stuck in the chapel door.

Grandfather slowly walked to the henhouse. He would set some traps today. The peening bank felt lonely to him since Katrina didn't bang away on her typewriter any more. Sometimes they had generated a genuine, polyphonic clatter concert.

Now he understood that girl even less. How could she let herself get involved with the church robbers? What had really happened? Girgl should have not treated her this gruffly. Perhaps there would have been a better explanation? His worst fears had come to pass. The new rift in the family had opened up the old wounds again. Just too well, the old man could sympathize with the tempest that had driven Katrina into the forest. He remembered the cataclysm back then after the accident with Martl. Good Lord, the girl was much too young for such a shake up! She could not stay at the forest cabin for long, that much was certain. Too many ghosts were buzzing around out there. That old shack, for good reason, was not a suitable place for a young girl. It wasn't safe for many reasons.

Everything in the henhouse had stayed as Katrina had left it in a hurry. Even the ashtray was still half full. 'It stinks in here. Smoking, what a bad habit.'

He noticed that the typewriter was gone. Clumsily, he picked up a sheet of paper from the floor. It had a drawing on it. The image made him plummet into the old armchair. He looked at this portrait of a young maiden, stared at it for quite some time. No doubt, that face had a likeness with Katrina's— it could have also been Kathl, his dear, long-gone wife, when she was Katrina's age. There was an uncanny similarity of features. But what was the thing with the flower wreath in the hair? And why were the young maiden's eyes closed? 'That looks like a burial shroud . . . ,' He shivered and, horrified, threw the paper on the old milk separator table.

He shook off his disgust and got up to look for what he had come in for. He opened the doors to the old kitchen hutch and started rummaging through the old tools and spare parts. Finally, he got to the old box with his iron-clap mole traps. He had already used up all his usual traps in the morning, but farmer Huber had also asked him to set more traps. These extra traps had been buried deep under a lot of clutter.

'What's that now? How did this get in there?' He pulled out a bundle wrapped in a plastic shopping bag. It was stuck between the rusted mole traps. He opened the wrapping. It contained a somewhat tattered, yellowed school notebook. The old man put down the junk box with the mole traps and started leafing through the booklet. The script was very familiar to him. He sank into the old armchair again.

"Kathl!" His hands started to tremble. When he got them under control again, he began to read. This afternoon, many moles were lucky to get away

While the mole trapper read, the rusty sluices of his old heart opened up. Finally, Kathl was talking to him. He had been waiting for this so many years. That's how Katrina had gotten all those darn old stories! It wasn't right that she had pilfered such private thoughts for her homework, but she probably hadn't thought much of it. He surprised himself with a flush of clemency. If Katrina hadn't found the notes, then he probably would have never seen his long-time wife in a completely new and unknown light.

When he had reached the decisive passage, he solemnly whispered, "A marterl for Marterl," and he recalled how Kathl had instructed him on her deathbed to guard the future grandchild. He forgot all about his gout and rheumatism and studied every curlicue of the maiden's delicate script, that girl who should later become his faithful wife. The fact that he didn't get a very good review as a suitor at the time, didn't make a difference to him anymore. Voraciously, he ingested every single word, absorbed it like a blotter paper drinks ink, while his tears flowed heavily, as they had dammed up behind his bushy eyebrows for so many years. He kept reading until empty of thoughts.

Grandfather remained sitting in the chair, hands folded over the notebook, for quite some time. Then he reopened the place where the page had been torn out and inspected the spot more closely. He startled. He remembered something. Upstairs, in his room, in the commode with the mirror, in the drawer, under the box with his biscuits, there was one more such handwritten page. He had never paid much attention to those scribbles earlier. The script was identical. He tucked the notebook into his inner jacket pocket and laboriously wound himself out of the old armchair.

"I can't have this girl run into disaster too!"

He must have said it aloud because he cringed at his own voice. It sounded rough and unfamiliar.

But it still worked.

19

Crystal Clarity

The custom of dedicating votive tablets originated in a time where people were smitten by a thorough religious turmoil. They worried about the salvation of their souls, they fervently desired paradise and were searching for the grace of God by continuously purchasing indulgences from the Catholic church

—*Wilhelm Theopold, Votivmalerei und Medizin (Votive Tablets and Healing Arts), 16*

Friday, July 5, afternoon

Bumpy, the patched-up asphalt road was so bumpy. The tar surface was much rougher than one could have imagined sitting in the well-cushioned bus. Katrina strained in the saddle of her wire donkey[xxiii] and pedaled home. Home? Not home, her forest cabin. She stepped on the pedals with full force, just to get the last four kilometers behind her as quickly as possible.

In the past week, she had figured out new ways about her routines. The primitive cabin—no running water or electricity, only oil lamps and a wood-burning stove—had acquired a certain familiarity and comfort. For school, Katrina now used the less busy Feldkirchen bus stop, which also had a shortcut through the forest.

Meanwhile, the writing marathon raged on. Schiller had bought her Indian-at-the-Isar story at a surprisingly good grade. He had given her a one minus; therefore, an overall passing grade, a three, was secured. He had even indicated that her grade might jump up, if she did well in the next leg, "leaving the church in the village." What was that supposed to mean? Their church had *always* been standing at the helm of her village, for 2000 years, or longer, since the time it had been a Roman watchtower.

The next extra credit story could bump up Katrina's grade high enough for a two. Schiller had offered all his students with "wiggle grades," as he called them, the opportunity to shine with a Romeo and Juliet story. Schiller assumed that anyone of the ladies and gentlemen in his class would have had some sort of experience with love gone wrong. 'Thank you but no.' A romance essay was bound to flop. Her "experience" in terms of "romance" was hardly writeable. Or what could it be? Stolen lingerie on St. John's Eve, being pounced on by a lecherous dude, or dodging clumsy pickup lines such as 'after the fifth apple schnapps we will really start the smooching.' Her love experience could hardly be called romantic. And what was so romantic about Romeo and Juliet? That both lovers die due to a tragic misunderstanding? Perhaps love is always tragic.

To die in the name of love, what nonsense. She pedaled harder. Her breathing had improved in the last week. The foot action helped her vent the ruminating thoughts. Everything was one wrong mess. Mike hadn't shown his face since the miserable St. John's Eve disaster, neither had he offered an explanation for his betrayal. Hadn't he swung her bra through the air like a sultry trophy? Maybe he had bragged about his exploits to his work chums, too? Or was he still preoccupied with the Celtic princess? Perhaps old Bürkel was right. Mike had "done his princess in." No, love stories apparently never turned out well. Only movies had a happy end. Nevertheless, she had no choice but to face that dread, if she wanted a good grade. She had worked so hard. *Don't spoil it now, Katrina.*

Hopefully, Luise would have some ideas. She had promised her to spend the next weekend with her at the cabin and had just earlier waved her goodbye at the bus stop. She wanted to drop in after she had helped with a customer at the studio. Apparently, she had already packed her overnighter bag and promised to bring some wine from home and those Belgian chocolates that her father sometimes brought from a business trip. In return, Katrina would share her math results with Luise. But what about Romeo and Juliet? Hopeless!

Anger fueled Katrina's tired legs. She got her bottom off the saddle to lean all her weight into the pedals. That was the final incline. The roadway was tight for passing cars. At times, she had to move over to the embankment. Luckily, traffic was scant in this neck of the woods, because her tires easily got snagged in the gravel. Bike riding was a balancing act. She made good progress, although she was breathing heavily. She hardly noticed the roadside show. Bell flowers, marguerites, poppies, and corn flowers splashed colors on the narrow strip between the road and the golden wheat fields.

A jeep buzzed by Katrina, hardly leaving any room between her bike and the car. The vehicle slithered to a screeching halt right in front of her, blocking the throughway. Katrina almost hit the car. Startled she stepped fully on the brakes. She skidded on the gravel. Beni jumped out of the Jeep.

"Look, who's pedaling around! How is it going with the bike, huh? Where you're going? Have they kicked you out from home?" He stepped in front of her.

"You're in my way!" Katrina was prepared for any kind of attack from him.

"So why did they kick you out? Huh?" Hands on his hips.

"Let me pass!"

"I tell you why! Because you let the robbers into the chapel!" He threw his arms up, his face flushed.

"None of your business!"

But Beni's expression got darker. He wiped away his grin with his snuff-tainted sleeve and stomped closer. Katrina smelled the stale odor of sweat the sour scent of tobacco on him. His expensive after shave could not mask his musky odor. Beni grabbed Katrina's arm. He yanked her to his chest. His breath smelled of beer and cigarettes.

"None of my business? My great-grandfather was a tablet painter." Beni stared Katrina up and down. "Not my business that his paintings are gone now? Say, which of your gigolos has swiped them? Just talk to me, spill it! Or did you eventually hawk them away yourself?"

"Have you gone totally mad!" Katrina struggled in his iron hold. No chance.

"You people from the chimpansium always think that you are something better. You pretend to know everything but don't want to do anything, only smartassing everybody around." Beni cranked up his rage. "And what about the drugs, right? How many have you tried already?"

Katrina bit his arm.

"You bitch! Let's see how you like that." He didn't let go of her. The stinging pain just made him angrier. He gripped her so hard that she couldn't breathe.

"Fess up! You know precisely who the robbers are, you dragged them in in the first place," Beni huffed. His head was flushed dark red by now. "And your slutty follies are known all over. Have you also gone ape about the Celts, like Luise, that crazy chick?"

"I don't know what you're talking about." Katrina tried to kick his shin, but he clamped her leg between his massive thighs. "Luise is none of your beeswax. Let go of me now, or else . . ."

"What else?" Beni's devilish grin had returned. A lecherous feeling rose up in his crotch. The body-on-body scramble had awoken a primal instinct in him, which it didn't take much to raise.

"All right, what else? Will you tell me?" A malicious gloat rushed over his snarky grimace. "Or will you show me? How your types from the Gymnasium do it? I know exactly what you tarts want . . ." And he shoved Katrina down the steep incline towards the thicket by the creek side.

Suddenly a motorbike clattered up from behind them. "Let go of that girl, but pronto!" a voice cackled from above.

Faster than anyone could have expected, Messner Pauli skipped towards Beni. Without a moment's hesitation, he grabbed a piece of driftwood from the embankment along the way and slammed it with full force on Beni's back. It came down on him with a loud crash. The stick broke. Beni was stopped cold. He looked surprised, let go of Katrina, and turned around to knock Pauli in the face. Katrina skipped from his reach. Pauli, jumped back, out of Beni's range. Beni tumbled as he turned. Pauli scrambled up the incline towards his motorcycle.

"Pauli, you bloody bastard! Wait, you will pay for this!" With gargantuan steps, Beni scurried up the incline after Pauli.

Cut and run! Katrina grabbed her bike and pushed it up the steep mountainside away from the brawl towards the safe forest. She could not understand the battle cries, but she felt the raging vibrations through the tiny hairs on her back. For sure the heated battle continued. She never looked back.

Beni had meanwhile caught up to Pauli, who steadfastly clutched his driftwood stick. Unfortunately, Pauli stumbled over one of the many molehills in the meadow. Instantly, Beni pounced on Pauli, who lay on the ground helpless like a bug on his back. But the older one, limber like a circus artist, rolled away just in that moment. His knee hit Beni where it hurts men the most.

"Shit, awhh! You asshole! Fucking asshole!" Overcome with pain, Beni rolled around in the grass with his knees pulled up to his chin, back and forth, cursing like a broomsquire.[xxiv]

Pauli got up on all four and crawled away from him. From a safe distance, he peered around but could not make out a trace of Katrina. She had already taken cover in the forest. Pauli picked up his hat and leisurely strolled back to his motorbike with the sidecar, without paying Beni another glance. A little later, Beni dragged himself to his four-wheel drive and hit the gas so hard that it sprayed dirt far and wide.

Katrina sensed that Pauli waved after her, but she didn't have the guts to turn around.

When she reached her forest cabin, all out of breath, the door stood open. How could that be? She had made sure the door was locked behind her. Had Luise dropped in sooner than she said?' Katrina stalked to the entrance. She peeked in. Raffi! He sat by the table hunched over her typewriter. He looked up at her with his best Sunday smile. She had almost not recognized him. His mane was gone. He now had the same crewcut as all village men.

Katrina froze in the door frame. Another surprise out of nowhere. Rage kicked in. She threw her bag on the floor and rushed over to Raffi. With a lightning-quick move, she tore the pages from his hands. Blindsided, Raffi jumped up.

"Katrina . . .", he stammered. "You write really well. Sorry, I should have left your papers alone . . ."

Regardless of what he could have said, it would have bypassed her ears. She took a swing at him. It landed in the wrong spot because Raffi turned, trying to avoid the strike. Katrina's blow crashed down on the bridge of his nose.

"Katrina! Are you mad! What has gotten into you?" Raffi squeezed his painful nose between thumb and index finger. Tears welled up in his eyes. Slowly, blood started seeping from his nostrils. Katrina still stood there in karate stance with clenched fists, like a wildcat ready to pounce.

"I had no idea that your stories are this secret. The one with the Indian on the Isar banks is absolutely fascinating . . ." He was squeezing his bloody nose with one hand, barely able to mumble.

"Is this a joke or what? Who talks about stories?" She screamed at him. "You have nerves! You better buzz off! Right now!"

Hunched down and very carefully Raffi took a cautious step towards Katrina. "Katrina, what in the world have I done to you? What is going on?"

"You ask me? If I had a telephone, I would call the police on you right now!"

"Police? Why that?"

"Have you hawked off the 'folk art' yet? How do you even dare to come here!"

"I don't know what you are talking about." He lifted up both hands, one of them quite bloody, to underscore his innocence.

"Here!" She slammed the local section of the newspaper on the table. "Don't tell me you don't know anything about this either?"

Keeping one eye on Katrina, Raffi grabbed the newspaper. He read aloud with a muffled voice. "Nightly Break in at the Village Chapel. Robbers Make off with 25 Votive Tablets and Two Saints'—What! That's a major catastrophe!"

"That's all that you can say?"

"Katrina! You don't think . . .?"

"But you had the key!"

"Exactly! Why would I break in then? That would be quite stupid of me. And do you think, if it were so, I would have come to see you?"

"Mmmh . . . probably not," she murmured.

"Yep, go figure!"

"But how can I be sure about anything? The cops haven't found any signs of forced entry. How do you explain that?"

"Expert picks? Another key?" Raffi wheezed. He was still clamping the ridge of his nose to stop the bleeding.

"All right, then! You swear you have returned the key?"

"Just ask Pauli."

Pauli's name rang up a most unpleasant memory of their latest encounter. So, she kept on quizzing Raffi.

"And how come that you don't have the faintest idea of this robbery, if it's even been printed in the Bayern section?"

"Is this an interrogation? I've had a bunch of exams. I didn't have time to read newspapers."

"And how in the world did you figure out where to find me?" Katrina growled in a slightly more conciliatory tone.

"Luise told me."

"Luise? What was she thinking . . . and she hasn't told you anything about this"—she waved the newspaper in the air—"either?"

"No, I already told you! For heaven's sake! Will you pipe down already! Luise probably just meant well for you, I think. Although, I sure wondered why you had moved into the forest in the first place. By the way, anyone can easily get in here." He glanced around the cabin. "You are not safe here at all."

'Yes, not even from you!' Katrina's consternation showed in the fine crinkles on her nose.

As the conversation had turned more amicable, Raffi tried to smile despite his battered nose. Katrina reached for the dish towel from the sink. She awkwardly handed him the towel.

"Here!"

"Thank you!" Raffi snorted. It was clear that he had swallowed a lot of drainage from his broken capillaries. "So, how come you moved into this shack?"

She stared at him with a sullen gaze. Her shoulders slumped slightly, only the stubborn strand of hair still tickled her nose. She started twisting it around her index finger.

"Well, can you tell me, please, what's going on? Did this have something to do with your flight into the forest?" He waved the tattered newspaper in front of her nose.

"Father blamed me for it!" She burst into a sob.

"Blamed you for what . . .?"

"This damned stupid break in of course! What else?" she barked at him. Startled by so much anger, Raffi slowly retreated to the bench and plopped down on it.

"Because I had dragged the riff-raff in, he says, . . ." Another tortured howl.

"And the riff-raff is me, am I right?" Raffi asked her with a stern glance.

Katrina didn't quite know how to answer that. "Sorry, I didn't mean it like that." A tone of resignation swung in her voice. "But that's what the village thinks."

"The village? I don't care a fart about the village! I want to know what you think!"

"You don't have any clue what it's like in the country! You don't live here!"

"Will you just put the village aside for a minute! Who am I to you? A bozo? A rotten panhandler from the city who plunders churches just for fun?"

"No, of course not." Katrina had run out of steam. She sat down across from Raffi at the table. She propped her head with both hands and sighed, "To be honest, I hadn't really expected a church robbery from you. But you sure don't get this village drama."

"Oh, I have had more village drama than you could imagine! Gimme a sec. I'll show you."

With that he got up and turned his back on her. He opened the belt, pulled his shirt out and pushed the jeans down below his butt cheeks. Long, jagged scars stretched across his bottom.

"See the tracks of my village life?"

Katrina was stunned. 'Testing his action, seeing him without his pants.' Instantly, she was overcome with satirical thoughts. Luise sometimes brought wisdoms to light, which inevitably stuck. To cry or to laugh, was the question here. Katrina struggled for control of herself because to laugh would have been so wrong. Instead, she bashfully contemplated Raffi's hind side.

"Gosh! This looks terrible. What did you do there?"

"Better ask, who did that to me."

"All right, who scraped you so badly there?"

"The blacksmith son of Riedering." Raffi peered over his shoulder towards Katrina.

"But what on earth happened? How in the world . . .?"

"Child's play, stupid prank."

"Looks really serious to me."

He hesitated. "A farm accident, so to say."

He stuffed his shirt quickly back into his pants, while Katrina averted her eyes feigning interest in the bookshelf above Raffi's head.

"Accident? When? What happened?"

"I was in the first grade. Schmiedl, the most feared third-grader of Feldkirchen, took a jab at me with the hay gripper. Probably on purpose. The gripper fork cut open my back, but as you can see, I am still alive."

He stuffed the rest of his shirt under the belt and tugged the buckle to the middle above the zipper. Katrina watched his every movement, hypnotized. Raffi was done with the buttoning up. He looked at Katrina as if choosing every word very carefully.

"By then, my mother just had it with the country life and we moved to the city soon after that. And, for that, I am still grateful to the ruffian to this day."

Katrina furrowed her eyebrows. Thankful? Instead, she asked, "And your father? Did he not get involved?"

"Oh, he had passed away already. I hardly remember him. We think it was the picric acid. But that we found that out much later."

"The *what* acid?"

"The poison from the ammunitions factory."

"That's awful! Why was your father working there?"

"He had to. Forced labor. He was a Polack."

"And your mom?"

"My mother was the only daughter, a soon-to-be farm estate owner. She married her 'Polack' soon after the war because. . ."

"I get it. That didn't match."

"Not at all. Do you want to hear the whole story?"

Katrina nodded. Raffi settled into a more comfortable position at the table.

"This is how it goes: During the war, my mom was all by herself on the farm. Her best farm worker was killed in action in France and her father was missing without a trace on the Russian frontlines. But by herself she could not keep the fields, stables, and estate going. The block warden sent her a Polish worker from the Föhrenwald camp, the ammunitions factory. My father was still a handsome, youngish man despite his years of slave labor. So many German men had not come back from the war. Perhaps you can imagine the rest . . ."

He paused. "By the way, your story about the Indian roaming your riverside forest during the war is top notch, especially the part where the Gestapo chases after GI Joe. Very well written! It's almost believable."

"Almost?"

"The Gestapo would have sent such an important catch like him, a code talker, straight to the Reichs headquarters in Berlin. But most people won't notice these details. It's just that I have a knack for forced labor camps, Death March, and such."

A well-known, glum sulk rose up in Katrina. She swallowed it instantly back down again. Another wisecrack picking her stories apart? Was he just like any better-shitter bloke? A chip off the same block that all men were cut out of? She let him continue.

Raffi combed with his hands over his crew cut. He was searching for the reentry point to his story.

"Anyways, having an affair with a Polish worker was naturally unthinkable in the village. My father worked his heart and soul out for this farm, until the whacky old man against all expectations returned from the war. Imagine, my grandfather walked home from Russia on foot. He was a knotty old bloke. Under no circumstances did he want a Polack for a son-in-law.

But my mother and father stuck together. So grandpa just threw them out. Later, the old man cut my mother out of his will and continued working the farm all by himself until he rented out the property.

"And where did you all go?"

"We lived in the parish house for many years, my mother and I, the 'Polack bastard' and favorite scapegoat. If someone had busted a window, or torn someone's anorak, or been infected with lice, I always got the blame. I can't even remember how often a schoolmate ratted on me. My mother usually stuck by me. Good lady. Can't imagine how she learned to bear all that."

Katrina sat there like a marble statue hit by lightning. "Good that you told me. So, we both have a village defect. Yours is even bigger. And you've got real scars to show."

"I don't see it quite as tragic. Life goes on."

"You've got nerves!"

"You better believe it! Don't wreck your head over useless problems. Talking helps, too. You can always tell me anything that bothers you. We don't want you to start chasing nasty ghosts through the forest, right?"

She didn't answer. If he only knew how close he had gotten to her truth.

"My mother always says, time heals all wounds," Raffi joked. "Look!" He lifted his chin up for Katrina to inspect his nostrils. "My nose is already as good as new."

"Looks like it!" She was sorry for him but did not apologize.

"Right!"

Raffi cocked his ears, he waited, but Katrina kept silent, although he could sense the churning in her head. She was done talking. She didn't tell him about her newest encounter with Beni, nothing about the clipped wings and run ins, nothing about the peculiar nightly forest apparition, nothing about the famous Celtic maiden's skeleton in Mike's living room, zilch about Frau Bürkel's mysterious prophesies, zero about her own hopeless ambitions in the writing marathon, even less about her half-cooked stories like Pfanni Knödel (dumplings)—half cooked, half raw, half true, half invented, wait a minute, that's four halves already—and nothing at all for sure about her absurd escapades with men. All that counted was that Raffi didn't do the crime.

Finally, she asked, "Why in the world did you get a haircut? What a shame!"

"Shame? Why?" Raffi eyed her at a curious angle. "I thought perhaps you would feel less conspicuous with me this way. Unless you don't want to be seen with me at all?"

He dug into his shoulder bag and pulled out a fat, large envelope. "And regarding the votive paintings, here we have at least the photos for the police. Are you ready? Let's go!"

20

Glacier Snuff

At the time, the chapel still possessed a set of valuable votive tablets, some of which dated back to the 16th century. One tablet dated 1801 showed under the depiction of the saint a farmer couple standing next to their house and watching the French troops' exit. The inscription below says: "Jakob Bachmair and his housewife from Dättenkofen pledged themselves to St. George, the great miracle worker, because on his intercession the French were expelled. Anno 1801."

—*Heidnische Rituale und ein weißes Geisterroß (Heathen Rituals and a White Ghost Horse), Süddeutsche Zeitung, 8 Nov. 1995*

Katrina didn't get a chance to reply. Outside a motorbike stopped. She ran to the window. More unexpected visitors. Her grandfather extricated himself from the low-seated sidecar. Pauli bounced off the driver saddle.

Square and tall, her grandfather entered the cabin. He was wearing his best hunter's jacket. He looked around. The stranger irritated him. Visibly, the old man's moustache started vibrating. "Another one of those? What's that fellow got to snoop around here?"

"Grandfather . . .," Katrina stammered. She had heard her grandfather say those words loud and clear.

"Oh, who have we got here! If that isn't our archangel student." Pauli interrupted from behind old man Weber's back, raising himself on his toes to peek over his companion's shoulder. "But where have his goldilocks gone? What a pity! I can't even recognize him anymore!"

"Don't' tell me, is he the one who robbed our chapel?" Grandfather snubbed Katrina sternly while he pinned her down with his ice-blue eyes.

Unsure of how to deal with this new turn of events, Raffi sank back on the bench and continued to nurse his still slightly bleeding nose with the dish towel.

"Grandfather! You talk again!" Katrina stuttered.

"Yep, that guy only opens his mouth when it's really important," Pauli interjected. "And today it is."

"Katrina, has this fellow been messing with our chapel? Or does he know anything about it?" Old Weber repeated his interrogation, this time even louder. Glumly, he stalked inside the room and let more light through.

"Well, nothing is for sure at this point." Pauli's tone was as ambiguous as the circumstances were murky. "But he did return the key to me, all right."

"What? That fellow had a key?" Grandfather Weber got flustered with disgust. "Who gave him that?"

Pauli sucked his head between his shoulders, churning the crimp of his hat sheepishly around in his hands.

"Pauli, how reckless! You know better than that . . ."

"Actually, Katrina had let him in," Pauli defended himself not very gallantly. He turned slyly to Weber. "And see who's talking here! What about your key, then? You can't find it anywhere, is that right?"

Then Pauli addressed Katrina to divert the conversation. "Say, does your chum here like snuff? This round is on me."

Before she could answer, Pauli had pulled out his snuff box, knocked a little acrid dung hill on his rounded fist, and deployed the charge in either nostril with a skilled move.

"Want some? Glacier snuff, the best!" With a satisfied smile and brown dust around his nostrils, Pauli stretched his snuff box towards Raffi.

"No, thanks! Not today." Raffi lifted demonstratively the bloodied dish towel from his nose.

"Oh, dear, what happened there?" Pauli asked with true curiosity. He kept staring at Raffi while he handed off the snuff box to grandfather.

"Just a little accident," Raffi replied with a wink at Katrina. She glared back at him.

"Grandfather, this is Raffi," Katrina introduced the two. "He is innocent. He studies art history, and . . ."

"Art history, I see."

Raffi collected enough courage to stretch out his hand to the commanding presence.

"Jaworski, Raphael Jaworski! Grüß Gott!"

Jakob Weber emphatically hesitated before the reached out and grabbed the young man's hand for a firm shake.

"Jaworksi, aha, Grüß Gott! You're not from around here, I gather, but you're just talking like one of us." Old man Weber had said it with a question mark in his voice.

"Yes, of course, he didn't grow up all too far from here," Katrina threw in, but nobody seemed to notice her commentary. Yet Pauli turned to her.

"Katrina, your grandfather wanted to talk with you . . .," Pauli paused. "But what are we going to do with that bloke there?" He threw a nod in Raffi's direction.

"No worries, he can stay. He already knows everything anyway," Katrina assured them.

Pauli and grandfather Weber looked at each other for consent. "But he better stay out of this," old Weber demanded. Three heads nodded and three pairs of eyes were glued on the speaker. Grandfather Weber's natural authority granted him time to gather himself on Katrina

"You know, Katrina, Girgl couldn't help himself, he just boiled over. But he shouldn't have been so gruff with you. You never made it easy for him either with all your new-fangled antics, but," and he glanced from Raffi to Katrina, "I don't think that you or this Graffi there," he meant Raffi, "have anything to do with the robbery. Or that you are to blame for it."

"But does father still believe that I lured the robbers in?" Katrina's voice wavered. At that point she lost composure. She was close to sobbing. This made the men uncomfortable. Quickly, with the back of her hand, Katrina wiped the snot from her nose. She had barely caught herself.

"I am certain that this will clear up somehow. No more crying around here! Pauli also told me that Beni, that bastard, got after you . . ."

"What? Not him again! Katrina, what happened? Why didn't you tell me . . .?" Raffi got up from the bench and started pacing back and forth in the cabin.

Katrina kept quiet. Her grandfather didn't want to discuss those particulars with a stranger. At any rate, he didn't want to be interrupted in his speech, which cost him a remarkable effort after so many years of silence.

"No worries, that guy will get what he deserves, sooner or later. I will see to it." Weber spoke directly to Raffi.

"Pauli, I was so glad you showed up! Just in time," Katrina laid her hand on his shoulder.

"This piece of shit! Someone should stick his dirty dick in the grinder . . ." Raffi puffed up. But Pauli interrupted him instantly.

"Nothing happened, man! I kicked him in the right place, I believe." And to Katrina, "You took off so quickly that I could not tell you anymore that we are coming."

"Cut through the chase, Pauli! Tell them already what we know and why we're here!" Old Weber was losing his patience.

"Right!" Pauli turned to Katrina. He took a deep breath.

"See, Katrina, I know a couple of hawkers in the city because my auntie, God bless her, had also been in the antique business. That helped me a lot just two years ago. That's when one of them scoundrels, . . . dang it, son of a . . . panhandler, I could strangle him . . ."

Pauli made a gesture as if he were wringing out a cleaning rag. He pressed his eyes shut. His breathing labored with the suppression of an overwhelming bout of anger. He caught himself and looked at his audience. He took a deep breath.

"Good Lordy, it just makes me so mad. Like I said, one of them darn hippies or loiterers broke in through my window. What for, I don't have the slightest idea. I only have old junk. Of course, he swiped my best possession, the nice royal Prussian coffee set, which Aunt Amalie the antiques trifler, had bequeathed to me. So, the next days, with Aunt Amalie's guidance from heaven, I knocked on all the dealers' doors in the city. And, wouldn't you know it, I found my heirloom again."

"For real?" Katrina's face brightened up. "So, let's go and get our two saints back. Where, did you say, are these antique stores exactly . . .?"

"Done already, Katrina!" Pauli interrupted her. "Look, we already got the paintings back. Well, at least some of them."

Having said that, he swung a hefty hunting backpack on the table, pulled open the strings and laboriously started digging for his booty. He produced three painted tablets. He laid them out on the table surface.

"We chased down fifteen pictures at the Auer Dult market, but no trace yet of our two saints, St. Sebastian and St. Nepomuk." Pauli's face glowed with pride.

"Yes, but I see only three! Where are the others?"

"The police station has the other twelve because our parish council still needs to identify them. There was a lot more contraband than ours. The police want to make absolutely sure that this is all correct."

"We can help with that! Raffi, where are your photos?" Katrina was suddenly overcome with excitement.

Raffi pulled out the large prints and spread them out on the table around the actual three votive tablets. The surface was completely covered with photos.

"Yes, that's them, exactly, I recognize all of them," Pauli chattered. "This one with the young lad under the log sledge, and here the soldiers in uniform, they were all up there on the wall. I can still see them clearly in front of me." Duh, they *were* lying in front of him.

"Aren't you lucky that I snapped these, Pauli? How come you know these images so well?"

Pauli was visibly moved. "Photographic memory. Yes, they are all in my head. I wouldn't even need a camera."

"But who can look into your head, Pauli!"

Pauli shook a smirk off his face. "Yeah, that would for sure confuse the heck out of anyone, Katrina! And your pictures are a much better proof for the police. Hi, hi!"

"How did you pull off this big heist?"

"Oh, don't you think that was easy!" Pauli's eyes became as large as marbles. He stuck his nose really high up.

"You can't even imagine what scoundrels these antiques hawkers are. Of course, these crooks don't put their hot stuff into the shop window. We filched at least fifteen antique shops, before we got lucky at the rummage sale near the Auer Dult market. Naturally, this Aschenbrenner Luki didn't want to fork over our treasures voluntarily, but my fists convinced him of the better . . ."

"Right, you could have landed in the slammer yourself." Grandfather Weber had an ambiguous smirk under his moustache.

"But they didn't book me, they booked him! Serves him right!" Pauli cackled with sly satisfaction. "That hoodlum, he just made me so mad. . ." Pauli punched his left hand with the right fist, relishing the memory of his perfect uppercut. "Anyway, the police confiscated a whole bunch of loot. There must have been even more seasoned church robbers in the game than ours."

"That's criminal!" Katrina said.

"You can say that again. Now crooked Luki has to sit it out for peddling stolen artifacts! All right, then! Now let's see, which pictures we are still missing."

They went to task. Pauli, with the images burnished in his memory, picked out the photos of the votive tablets yet to be retrieved. None of them had ever looked at the votives this closely, not even art historian Raffi. He had mostly focused on getting the exposure right while he was taking shots in the dusky chapel.

Briefly Katrina's eyes brushed on the photo with the "marterl," which her grandmother had painted. That picture again gave her the shivers. No, Pauli remarked, this one had not been stolen. He had seen it hanging in its customary place. It was not of interest for the art market, too young and too primitive.

Katrina's face turned white. She was shivering. Nobody noticed her discomfort, preferably so. Of all the pictures spread out on the table, her grandmother's tablet, her prophesy, the predictive votive for her brother, again struck her core. What was she to make of it?

"There," Pauli declared, "there we have our selection. These twelve paintings are still at the police, but the other ten here are still missing, am I right? First, I will double-check up at the chapel that our proofs match up. Everything must be solid."

Pauli thumbed through the photos once more. "Katrina, did you know that your grandmother, God may rest her soul, was a votive painter as well? Maybe one of hers got stolen as well? Let's see, I thought I just saw one in here . . ." He was about to fan the photos out again.

"Yes, I know, that's all right, Pauli! You better get going!" No, she didn't want to talk about her brother's Marterl.

Pauli took the hint, stuffed the pictures carefully inside the envelope, and buried the packet in his backpack.

"If we hurry up, we could get the pictures back today." Pauli beamed all over his face. "That officer who we know works the late shift today. He will settle this for us. And then we can hang the pictures right up again." He shouldered his backpack.

"Yes, but not without me," Katrina insisted. "I want to be part of this too!"

"Me too," Raffi said.

"Agreed!" Pauli laughed and stretched his paw out to him. "But only because you have taken all these damned fine photos. And who knows, perhaps we will get our saints back again this way as well."

Grandfather stood ready to leave. Pauli as well grabbed his hat from the bench. He suddenly hesitated and turned to Katrina.

"What kind of pendant have you got there, Katrina?" he asked her casually on his way out.

"A bear claw."

"Interesting. Where did you get that?"

"From Luise."

"I see." Pauli said with a cryptical tone.

"Why do you ask, Pauli?"

"Pardon me, Katrina. May I take a look?" Pauli grabbed the bear claw turned and twisted it every which way under one squinty eye. "Who, did you say, gave you it?"

"Luise. She had it from her brother. From an America trip." Pauli seemed a little dim-witted today.

"Interesting," Pauli repeated himself. He moved to go outside but then turned around again on the doorstep. "Could I borrow it from you for a little while?"

"How long do you need it for?" Katrina could not make any sense of Pauli's request, but she gave him her talisman anyway. She trusted him enough by now. Pauli carefully stuffed the amulet and chain into his pants pockets.

"No worries, you will get this back in time," Pauli assured her.

With a thud, a bike was slammed against the wall outside.

"Katrina, mother also wanted you to have some of her schmalznoodles . . .," Walli stormed across the doorstep. She halted abruptly, stopped in the middle of her sentence.

"What the heck is going on here?" Walli looked around. In her typical panic haste, she had noticed neither the car nor the motorbike behind the cabin.

"Walli, you won't believe this! Grandfather and Pauli have found the pictures!"

"Where?"

"In the city, at an antique market. But just about half of them. The rest is still missing."

"No way! And the saints?"

"We don't have them yet, but we've got a lead, all right!" Pauli assured her.

"What lead?" Katrina listened up. Just a second ago he hadn't had the slightest idea. How had the situation turned so fast?

Grandfather too stared at Pauli with scrutinizing eyes.

"Official police secret," Pauli blurted out. He awkwardly fumbled with the crimp of his hat. "Yes, a strict police secret. But now, let's hurry! Quick, if we want to get our pictures back today!" And he turned on the heel and headed outside to his motorbike.

"Goodbye, pfüad euch!" grandfather Weber said. And he marched right after Pauli.

Walli cringed as if in time lapse. She shook her head so fiercely that her braids slapped her cheeks like a rattle drum. "Grandfather talks again? How can that be?" she shouted.

"Yes, but only if it's important," Raffi joked from the background.

"Yeah, hello there! What happened to your nose?" Walli asked him straight up.

"Let me tell you, the forest is full of dangers." Raffi's head turned to Katrina.

"Huh? And what happened to your hair?"

"Walli! Don't ask him so many shameless questions!" Katrina's face had flushed.

"Oh, I see."

"There is nothing to see."

"I need to go, too." Raffi interrupted the increasingly hostile banter. He got up and shouldered his bag. The blood around his nose had crusted up.

"I have my last semester exam tomorrow morning. This will be another long night." Raffi strolled towards his car. Katrina followed him out. Raffi threw his bag on the passenger seat and jumped behind the wheel.

"Well, want to go swimming again next week?" Raffi asked, leaning out of his car window. "Now that the criminal case has been closed and my innocence has been proven?"

Unsure of herself, Katrina looked over her shoulder to the cabin doorstep, where Walli stood gawking at them. Her little sister nodded emphatically.

"Perhaps," Katrina laughed. "You know exactly where to find me by now."

"Finally, that took a while," Walli sighed with playful indignation.

"Do you want a ride home, you two?" Raffi asked them. "Katrina?"

"Oh, no! We will be all right. We both have our bicycles here."

"Then hurry up! It will be dark soon."

"Don't worry! I have a light on my bike," Katrina joked.

"Well, then! See you soon!"

Raffi got the car started and rolled off. After a few meters he reversed and backed up to where Katrina stood. Once again, he stuck his head out the window.

"I forgot. I had wanted to ask you earlier. What poster have you got up above the door?"

"Oh, that?" Katrina felt embarrassed. "Just a gag, a hex sign. Obviously, I don't need that anymore." And she stretched up to pull the tacks out of all four corners and retrieved the cardboard with Luise's dara knot on it.

"So, you do believe in magic after all," Raffi joked and stepped on the gas. Noisily, he rumbled over pot holes and gnarly roots down to the main road.

Katrina waved after him with Luise's drawing in hand. Soon the motor sound was barely audible and faded out altogether.

The bells in the village chimed the Angelus. "Beautiful," Katrina whispered to herself. No longer did the dreadful fear of sin vibrate in the very familiar bell sound. Katrina let out a deep sigh. A terrible day had taken such a fortunate turn. How nice that the church had "remained in the village" all this time, according to the old saying. Finally, she got an idea for the essay marathon. Perhaps there was a story to tell about those old bells. One of the old folks, perhaps Frau Bürkel, must have brought it up in the past. Frau Bürkel? Maybe her stories weren't so crazy after all.

"Hello! Will you stop staring holes in the air?" Walli complained. "Can I take something home for you on my bike?"

"No, that's all right," Katrina snapped back to reality. "Luise will help me get my things with her car. But could you please tell her not to come any more tonight. I would rather catch up on some sleep at home."

"Will do. I will leave now. So, when are you coming home?"

"Pretty soon. Just you go ahead. I still have to scrape a few things together."

"You always take so long for everything. Don't dilly-dally!"

"No, not today, I promise."

"For real? Mmmhm! I better lay the key out for you in case you get in late. As grandfather always says, children must come be home before the wolves are let out."

"Will you go now! And don't let the bad wolves catch you!"

"And how come they won't bite you?"

"Younger children taste better to them. In my case, they will lose a few teeth, for sure. Just go now!"

"All right, then! Bye, now!"

"Yeah, yeah."

Weber Jakob and Messner Pauli set their backpacks with the precious votive tablets down on the living room table at Pauli's house.

"So, it's official, we will hang the pictures up again first thing tomorrow morning," Pauli determined. "Perhaps we should have the blacksmith make a lattice for the portal?"

"Yes, that's right!" Jakob turned to leave.

"Wait a minute, Weber, I think I know now who might have broken into the chapel," Pauli blurted out.

Weber raised his eyebrows in surprise.

Pauli dug for the bear claw in his pants pocket. "What does this tell you?" He dangled the pendant in front of grandfather's eyes.

"You wouldn't suspect Katrina of all people! Don't you dare!" Weber grumbled with indignation.

"No, for heaven's sake! You totally understand me wrong. But this here is something very special."

"I see. But what does this have to do with the church robbery?"

"Does it not remind you of anything at all?" Pauli dangled the bear claw faster. Weber grabbed it to look at it in his palm.

"Hunting trophy, claws, stag's teeth. You better ask a hunter. They like to wear such things on their hats."

"Nothing else?"

"No. What you are getting at?" Weber sounded strained. It had been a tiring day.

"Claw is correct. Precisely, a bear claw. It will lead me to the truth," Pauli proclaimed, beaming all over his face. He grabbed the pendant back from his partner in crime.

"What do you mean? The truth? How?"

Pauli hesitated. Apparently, he could not reach the same wave length with the ever so practicable Weber Jakob. So, he decided to drop the topic in a strange way.

"It's a pendulum, see!"

"What nonsense! Do you think a dowsing rod can catch criminals!"

"Oh, don't underestimate those things, Weber! I have often found water, even iron parts, with it!"

"But saints? What a bunch of crap!"

"All right, you will see it, too, one day!"

Weber stared at Pauli long and intensely. But Pauli had already put on his best poker face.

"So, you think you know who'd done it?" Weber asked Pauli sternly.

"But I won't say a thing, as long as I am not dead sure." Pauli had a high-pitched tone of ambiguity in his voice.

And that was the end of that conversation.

21

Lovelorn

The Celts were everywhere recognized as an especially fearless breed—and it was the savvy and wisdom of the druids, which had liberated them from fear. Fear, in and of itself, is the greatest burden of the soul. And who liberates himself thereof, releases unfathomed powers.

—Carla Ludwig, *Das Horoskop der Druiden (The Horoscope of the Druids), 8*

Friday, July 5, evening

In a hurry, Katrina piled her loose leaves together next to her typewriter. She grabbed a cardboard box to gather up her few possessions. Bread, marmalade, cheese, eggs and other food items; dish towels, magazines, toiletries—she threw all her utensils together. The sum of it was very manageable. Everything fit comfortably in the box. She stuffed her clothes into the duffel bag, just like she had done on the day she escaped into the forest. Clean up the table, stack the school books, sort the papers, collect the color pencils . . . she grabbed around a little too fast—ca-chonk, the cup flew off the table. All her pencils scattered over the floor into all corners like a bunch of greased Mikado sticks.

"Grrrh! Was that necessary?"

She got on her knees, scurried on all fours across the floor, and crawled into the dustiest nook under the table. How could one live without a color as important as carmine red? She padded around under the corner bench. What was that? She pulled it from between the crease of two floor boards.

Her lucky clover! It glinted in front of her eyes. She was now wide awake. How in the world had it gotten in here? She had been looking for it so long with Luise. And only Luise had been aware of her missing charm. And there hadn't been anybody else in the forest cabin, right? Loiterers? Possible, while she was in school, but not probable. She would have noticed. Of course, even Raffi had figured out how to get in. And what about the suspicious Cola bottles? She felt a cold shiver chasing down her back.

But here it was, the four-leaf clover, her lucky charm. It dangled brightly on its thin silver chain. The joy about her find made her cheeks glow. So much luck, all in one day! Especially since this was the last evening, or perhaps last hour, in the cabin. What a lucky coincidence! Even more so since Pauli had swiped her bear claw. Her cheeks were on fire with excitement. She pushed all doubts aside and feverishly, with trembling fingers, put the necklace on.

"So, I've got you back!"

She clasped the pendant, Mike's love token, and could feel her heartbeat reverberating in it. Her heart galloped. She was awake like she had not been in a long time. On the day that she was vindicated, she had also recaptured her lucky clover. Was that a sign? Perhaps she had judged Mike completely wrong? Hadn't he made her a confidante of his lapis lazuli ring, which he had robbed off his princess, a wonderful piece of jewelry. It had shone like bright gold, although Mike had said that it was actually made from bronze. She recalled the image of the winding twines, twisted together like two serpents in an embrace of love, with a dark blue stone in the middle, like a deep water. It must have been a great love.

The lapis lazuli granted her the power and possibility to escape the power of her fate.

What a beautiful, blue stone! There had to be an ancient Romeo and Juliet story behind it, by gosh! And this sudden idea struck her like lightning. The ring was 2000 years old and yet so artistically crafted. Could there have been a secret love covenant—just like the lucky clover had been for her? Yet— "He's done her in," old Frau Bürkel had fulminated at her. What should she make of all this? A Bürkel prophesy did not fit into Katrina's happy world at the moment.

"Well, let's see, what comes to mind," she mumbled to herself and quickly pulled a piece of paper out of her neat stack. The backside was still unused. There was no more turning back now. The story had to come out. For nothing in the world did she want to miss the kiss of the muse and forget her high-flying thoughts before she would arrive at her house on bike. She fed the Adler a sheet of paper and typed up an ancient romance story.

Who rides so late through night and wind? It's the princess on her freedom stallion.

Father had gone to market at the garrison and mother slept in bed with the girls. Mara was wide awake. Her Falcon stood ready by the stables in nervous anticipation. White was a loud color in the night. But, hussa, the faithful Falcon sprang right ahead, directed by the skillful pressure of her thighs. They flew in a wild chase through the moonlight. Her long hair waved with the stallion's mane in unison, up and down, with every pounding of the hooves. She let the joy flow freely from her heart.

The Falcon knew its way. Their destination was the hamlet, the three huts at the edge of the riverside forest. When the houses came into view, she silently glided off the horse's back and led her steed in the nightshade of the forest closer to the cluster of dwellings. A faint trail of smoke still rose from the forge. They didn't have much time. At sunrise, Arno was expected to toil at the smith shop again.

Now she called into the dark with the voice of an owl. She waited. Arno was in no way a muscle man like his father, but his body was tough and well-defined. He had an even, pleasing face and kept it free from a beard, as it was the fashion among the garrison soldiers. He was widely known for his smithing talent but scorned by his old man. His father only valued the iron force of true Damascus steel, what else, and not the toy things, good-for-nothings, which the lad crafted in his intricate way.

"Womanish crap," his father often scolded. The reputation of Arno's artistic skills had traveled thus far that even the Roman officers sought the wonder-smith's services to craft for them especially ornate window grates. Often the deals didn't come to pass because Arno's father had much more practical things for him to do, like horse shoes, wagon shafts, oxen yokes, carpenter tools, and nails of all sorts. The creation of delicate and filigree bell flowers should be left up to nature, the father judged. Such activity, at best, was a pure waste of time and material to him.

It wasn't her first rendezvous with Arno in the night. But today it should be a decisive meeting for the two lovers. "What nature joins together, man must not separate," the druids always said. The two lovers had no other power than to let nature take over.

Soon, Arno answered the owl's call and caught up with Mara by the oak tree. Wordlessly he followed her on his bare feet. Hidden by the shade of the dense, young pine growth, she tied up the Falcon, took Arno by the hand, and ran with him to the glade. They dropped down in the soft cushion of moss. Tomorrow would be the shortest night of the year. Today it still lasted a few minutes longer. Time wasn't on their side. They had to make the most of it.

They sat there for a while, speechless, and gazed at the silver sheen that the moon cast on the swamp grass. There, on the bed of moss under the oak tree, the two lovers consummated their union with unspoken consent. The elders were against it, but nothing could restrain the passion arising from the depths of two bonded souls. Still entranced from the primal force that had overcome them, the lovers rested on their bed of moss. The constellation of stars had shifted since their first rendezvous in the spring. In the last couple of months, the Great Bear had ascended from his low position right over the blue spruce tree tops up to the middle of the sky, where the heavens would open up soon.

Arno sat up and reached for his pants. He fished something out of his pocket. It was a small bundle, wrapped in leather scraps. He handed it to his girl. She opened it carefully. In it was a sophisticated ring with a blue stone in the middle.

"Just for you. The color of your eyes and hair."

She was speechless. But something glinted in her eye. She put the ring on her finger and held it against the light of the moon. It fit perfectly and the stone shone like fresh river water. How marvelous this ring was! But she would have to conceal it from her folks.

Out of nowhere, an acorn plunged into her lap. At this midsummer night time, it was much too early for an acorn. Arno as well didn't have an explanation for it.

"Come on! Let's plant us a life," she said to him. She got up, laughing, and ran to the middle of the clearing. Arno followed her to a subtle, mossy incline in the middle. With a stick, she dug a small hole, dropped the acorn in it, and carefully covered up the spot again. In a short while, day would break. Their rendezvous was short.

Who is riding so late through night and wind? It is the mother with her . . . And out there, by the clearing, still stands the mighty oak tree, a thousand years or older.

Ooh, and she already knew the end to this tragic story. Sad, very sad. *Romeo and Juliet* was by definition a tragedy. And so was Mara and Arno's story. But the advantage about it was that the sad, sad ending had already been written. Smart move? Why not. She just had to put the donkey on the tail. And the tail of the tale was that nobody gets happy, not even nature.

Katrina stretched her arms and legs. Then she cracked her folded fingers, a sound that annoyed the hell out of her mother. She had gotten tired from hitting the keys like a mad woman. Carried away late into the night. Her last evening in the forest cabin should have been an early one and the story short. Yet the words kept flying from her fingers, as if dictated, and perhaps she could convince Schiller with her extra effort of a better grade. And yet she wasn't finished. She stopped short of the terrible end. Perhaps she should include the old fart, the Centurio, too.

Again, she stretched her arms up and yawned big this time. It didn't make sense to go home just now, when her extra credit was so close to being finished. She had yet another story to tackle for the essay marathon. Those bells in the village.

"I need a break," she sighed and threw herself on the hard cot, which she had well gotten used to over the last week. Just a little nap. Walli had promised to put the key out for her.

The stuffy cabin air lulled her into a restless slumber. With each breath of air, the pressure on her chest increased, like sacks of flour being stacked on her chest, but she could not force herself to wake up.

Something was burning, it blinded her eyes, stung, but her lids would not lift. He, someone, was chasing after her. She ran through long tunnels, burning houses, rubble fields, but he came always closer. He, the danger. She knew him, but could not produce his name. Sweat poured as the raging flames pulled closer. She climbed higher and higher up the steep mountain. At the top, a white stallion nervously scuttled back and forth, neighing, calling out for her. But gravel and rocks made her feet slide back with each step. The pressure on her chest increased, the light burned through her eyelids, it got brighter. Danger always got closer to her. Wake up, wake up, or he will get you!

Katrina bolted from the cot. Her t-shirt stuck to her back, soaking wet. She was trembling. How real could a dream be? It was as light as day. Was she still dreaming? Had she overslept?

But it wasn't day yet. It was the middle of the night. It was deathly quiet, no creaking, no murmur, not even a trickle of spruce needles could be heard. The light came from the table. Someone was sitting there? Who? Katrina froze in fright. It was a blurry, unreal figure, frazzled at the outlines because of the abundance of glowing, harsh light, yet a human countenance. A specter, a ghost was reading her papers? Katrina squinted her eyes together, but the human-figured light remained seated at the table.

Don't look at it directly, just don't look at it.

She cowered in the remotest corner of her cot, pressed herself against the wooden wall, and ogled the scene from the corner of her eyes, to avoid staring at the glowing light. She blinked, blinked again, in vain. The stark flicker continued as if real. Gradually, her terror settled down to a level of pure marvel. She caught herself gawking at the apparition in awe. Slowly, the ball of fear in her stomach dissolve and disseminated through her extremities to be discharged like a burst of electrical current through her fingertips and toes into the insulating berth.

Genuine kindness and warmth streamed from her core. She felt at ease with the strange light. A pleasant feeling of comfort and recognition rippled all over her. All fear had vanished, as if naturally so. The shining figure now turned its face towards her. Katrina closed her eyes. She still saw the figure with her inner eye. It was a woman. She smiled at her with love and encouragement, as if to say that she was pleased with the written pages. This internal eye contact lasted for the eternity of a second.

"Grandmother?" Katrina whispered and opened her eyes. All was quiet. The light was gone, and so was the figure. It was dark. Or, was there a faint afterglow by the chair?

The next moment something chafed by the window shutter. Katrina, still caught in her dream of the blazing light figure, like in a trance, ignored the sounds. There, the shutter burst open with a thunderous bang. Someone tumbled to the floor. The specter raised its massive size. Even though the night concealed him almost entirely, Katrina knew. Beni stood in front of her cot, all six foot and 300 pounds of him. It could only be him, the way he smelled and spread his vibes. She felt her stomach revolt.

What the fuck!

The massive shadow didn't speak, only stood there like a frozen statue. Katrina pressed her back into the harsh wooden boards behind her cot. She snuggled into the wall so desperately that the wooden textures melded with her body. But she could not as easily vanish into thin air as the many heroes in her stories.

Fourteen, fifteen, sixteen . . . She should have rather been praying, but for an Our Father there probably was not enough time. Or was there?

Twenty-one, twenty-two . . . How fast the safety distance diminishes when driving a car.

Beni just stood there without a stir. Like a statue. But for how much longer? Only his labored breath was clearly audible.

"Hey, you! I have paper for you."

That didn't sound like Beni. The intruder had purred these words in direction of her cot with a honey covered baritone voice.

The breaking of the silence, was Katrina's command to grab the torch light and shine it on his face. Blinded by the beam, he looked utterly puzzled.

"Paper? How did you get that idea! Get out of my cabin! Buzz off! Right now!" She screamed at him with unbridled fury.

"Aren't you a stinky, doll! Don't you need something to write on? Look, here, this nice paper . . ."

"Are you nuts! You can't just break in here!"

"And, see, chocolates! I brought them for you, too . . ." He made a step forward.

Katrina hadn't even registered his words. "Get lost, or else
. . ."

Ten seconds of silence.

"Not that again," Beni sounded grouchy. "You with your
'or else.' Can't you think of anything better?"

"Ouuuut!"

"Will you just stop hollering! You'll wake up all the foxes
in the forest!"

Immediately, reality set in. There she was, all alone, in the
night, in the forest, with her worst foe. No help far and wide.

"Fuck off! Now, I said!" she hissed in her most malicious
tone and took a swipe at him with the torch light. But he
deflected the hit like a pro.

After this intermezzo, Beni still stood frozen on the same
spot, not sure about which next step to take. The torch light kept
him at bay, like the lion tamer's whip transfixes a large cat. Had
he run out of words? Talking had never been his strength, much
less the romanticism of courtship. He was all flushed red and
his nostrils trembled. Obviously, he was thinking long and hard
about his approach. She had to prevent that at all cost.

"What's up, will you leave now?" Katrina repeated.

"Here, your favorite pralines . . ."

"Favorite pra-what? How would you know?"

Katrina shone the light on Beni's hand. Lindt, small
desserts. That was just her brand.

"Irmi told me. You sometimes get them at the store."

"This witch! But I don't need any pralines from you!"

Silence. Beni still hadn't moved an inch. Katrina again felt
the skin on her back rooting in the grain of the planks behind
her. Escape route cut off. Dead silence.

"You, Katrina! Don't you know, I fall for you!"

She couldn't believe her ears. He had scratched the bottom
of the barrel. Was she still caught up in a nightmare? Her

stomach rumbled. How could she extricate herself from this quandary? Beni threatening her with love? This Goliath wasn't going to go away so soon.

"I have a crush on you! Had it for a long time!"

This could only get worse, but he wasn't finished yet.

"Already since the May Dance."

'Dance, what dance?' Memories flickered through Katrina's mind. She had unfortunately given in to one of Luise's misguided adventures. May Dance, what a disaster! Both soured as wall flowers and had eventually ended up at the Disco Tower.

"You were the only rose among all the ditsy . . . thistles."

Beni took a small step in her direction. He stretched out both his hands, one with the box of pralines, the other with the ream of paper. Katrina gagged.

"There, for you! Take it!"

What now, what now?

She hesitated for a moment, then she resolutely grabbed both paper and pralines from Beni's mighty paws.

"Thank you! That is so nice of you!"

How do I get to the door, the door, the door? What do I say? She searched for the most innocuous phrases of conversation, but nothing useful came to mind. She heard herself saying, "Do you want a Cola?"

"Jaaah!" Beni seemed surprised about her change of heart.

"Then sit down there at the table," she said with casual emphasis. She got up, fished her last Cola from the box, and put it on the table. She laid the opener besides the bottle.

"But you too!" he commanded and dropped his full weight on the bench. Katrina sat down on the chair across from him. Beni filled her glass.

"Your stories?" he asked with polite curiosity in his voice and shoved away the papers with his elbow to make room for the Cola. She nodded.

"You're a good writer!" A compliment? The last thing she would have expected from him. But she could have cared less about her literary pursuits at the moment.

Then he took a big gulp from the bottle.

Katrina shot up and dashed for the door.

"Waiiit a minute, lassie! You stay here! Don't leave me now!" And he lunged after her.

No escape remained, no window or door, not even from her own skin.

The bolt stuck by a millimeter. Katrina yanked the handle The door didn't open. Beni grabbed Katrina by the middle and swung her around in a circle. She twisted like a rag doll in his iron embrace.

"Don't you bite me now, lassie! Only kissing allowed!" Sarcasm swung in his voice. The true-type ruffian had returned. He tried to force a kiss on her.

Pearls of cold sweat formed on Katrina's forehead, from exertion and fear. She was hardly able to breathe in his devilish clutch.

"Let go of me! Right now! Or I will tell Mike!"

He listened up, stopped short. "Your sweetie, huh?"

This word sounded strange coming from Beni's mouth. Apparently, she had stopped him in his tracks. He released his grip, holding her away from himself at arm's length, to see her face better in the dusky glow of the torchlight coming from the table. He cocked his massive head.

"Mike? What do you want with him, ha? He already has his princess!"

Hell-e-lujah! That had hit her core like a Chinese gong. What the heck did he know about old Bürkel's freaky prophesy? 'And the princess, that was you,' she had said wagging her gnarly finger at her. Had she gossiped about that episode with other people as well, that crazy old woman? Katrina could well imagine it.

"Have you gone crazy!" Katrina screamed at Beni's face with droplets of spit flying. "What does Mike have to do with that skeleton? It is already 2000 years old!"

"Skeleton?" Beni broke into hysterical laughter. "Who is talking about a skeleton! Are you daft! Mike's princess is as lively as a kitten in the haystack! She dances like a dervish!" Another gurgling, demonic snort followed. "Ha, ha, the carnival princess of Feldkirchen!" Scornful laughter exploded at her.

The floor melted under Katrina's feet. She stared right into the abyss of Beni's gloating grimace. No time. A lot of work. So much for the stupid excuses Mike had given her. And everybody knew it? Or did Beni intentionally lie his head off?

"You better write him off, that Mike!" Beni triumphed. "He has for long had another gal. Everybody knows that."

'And that Mike has done her—you—in.' That was the story of the princess then. Not at all like Romeo and Juliet. In that epic the lovers died for each other. And die, she could have easily this moment, sunken into the floor, hadn't a bottomless rage gotten the better of her.

Beni continued his lecherous game. "Just be glad that you got away from this buffoon, this cockalorum. Take me instead! I have a crush on you. I have the hots so bad, I could explode, all for you, Katrina . . ." He stared at her in deep fascination, fixated on her obvious defeat, enthralled by her red lips and willful, untamed curls.

In his gleeful relish of an apparent victory over such a smart girl, Beni dropped all caution. Her resistance seemed to have waned. Limp she stood right before him, as he kept holding her by the shoulders. Beni almost got worried that he might have pushed her too far.

Whoopee! That jab hit his shin right on. Katrina tore open the door and ran away from her nightmare.

"Crissakes! Cruzi-turk! Just you wait . . .," Beni cursed after her. Limping, he also lunged out the door into the pitch-black forest.

"Just you wait! Fuckin' devil woman! Wait until I get you!" But Katrina didn't wait.

The wild chase through the forest night got lost in the bushes. Katrina could hear Beni barrel through the underwood. She knew this part of the wild like the back of her hand, but in this pitch dark she could not help but stumble helplessly over roots, and rocks, and bushes. If she could make it to the clearing, she could safely reach home on the farm road. Once on the open road, this hulk would not be able to catch up with her. She was unbeatable in long-distance running.

However, her struggle through the young trees' jungle, a dense pine thicket, held her up with tears and tangles. Crawl, duck, climb, tear. It seemed as if Beni ignored all branches and slashed his way through the forest like a snow plow. She could practically hear him steaming ever closer to her.

"You, broad! Just you wait! I will get you now!" he yelled into the darkness.

Katrina sidestepped and detoured him, but as hard as she tried, he stayed on her heels. He was like a car on the road, and Katrina the squirrel, zigzagging through the night, unawares that cars can't change their tracks. She panted. Her advantage got smaller. Her hair wildly pelted her face, hampering her orientation. She sweated profusely, large pearls of salty liquid dripping off her forehead. Her old, extra-large t-shirt kept getting caught in the brambles. She tore away from the underbrush, ignoring holes in the fabric, and stumbled. Blackberry thorns scratched her bare calves. Unfortunately, she had escaped in her house slippers, and not running shoes. Like poor Cinderella, she had to fish for her slipper in the dark, which cost her valuable seconds. It was dark, so damn dark. None of the faint outlines seemed familiar to her. Had she gotten lost?

Beni huffed closer, dangerously close. Katrina ran faster. Here the thicket was much too dense. Dang, the detour was too risky. She had no choice but to race on. She howled from fear and pain. A branch in her path tripped her. Her ankle twisted. Ouch! God-damn shit! Just get on, no matter, just don't turn around!

Now she lost speed and breath. The clearing must be near. Just keep on, run faster, teeth clenched, just run on.

She didn't hear them coming. The trees darted past her. In between them, splices and slivers of the moon flew by. Katrina gasped. She had never exerted herself this much before. Her limits were being tested. She lost speed, her body switched to reserves. Beni was still huffing after her.

Crash! She slammed flat on the ground with her face. Over, it was over! Now he would do with her what he wanted to. She lifted her chest up. Damn, her elbow stung like crazy. So, this was it. Running, no chance. Beni crunched closer. He could only be ten meters away now. As much as she wished, she could hardly melt into the ground. What now? She grabbed around the forest ground for a suitable branch. A twig? Only a measly twig!

She sat up, braced herself. The thin sickle of the moon had come through the clouds and dusted a faint silvery light on the forest. Who was standing there, hardly a stone's throw from her? The forest man? The ghost from last week? A fearsome sight to look at, with a blue sheen all over his shaggy fur clothing. Next to him another one, and another, and another.

Like Krampus during knocking night, with fur and horns, mummed with sack cloth, gaiters on their legs, bearded, roughneck faces painted blue, long, matted hair like red-tinted Spanish moss, swaying in the wind. A whole company of hobgoblins. Now approaching. They didn't make a sound. They melded like specters with the dark-black mottled background of the young trees' thicket. Had she inadvertently bumped her head? She must be fantasizing. But her twisted ankle and her stinging elbow made her feel the pain for real. Too late to pray for a wakeup call, only a miraculous lift off could help. She was encircled by either imaginary or real Rübezahls[xxv]. She fervently wished they would clear off. Squinting her eyes didn't make them go away.

To the contrary, they slowly stalked in her direction, as if they hadn't noticed her at all. Katrina crouched even lower into the ditch. All kinds of woodsy slivers and spikes from the ground pricked through her clothing in the most inconvenient places. She ducked down more. The forest demons soundlessly headed her way. "Good heavens, Lord . . ." she implored the Almighty, eaten by panic. Didn't a horse whinny just now? Now it snorted in her ear. The ghastly forest men had approached at an arm's length. If they didn't turn around, if they didn't stop, they would trample her any second. She crossed her arms over her head and pressed her face into the forest moss. She squeezed her eyes shut as hard as Loisl did when the ghost horse jumped over him and the witch howled in unison. And she feared for the worst.

Hardly a moment passed. Someone let out a dreadful howl. It was Beni. Katrina tore open her eyes. The clearing lay just ahead of her, she hadn't noticed it earlier. Over the treetops the first golden rays of sunlight filtered in. A skylark tweeted its morning song. The forest men had vanished without a trace. All quiet. Beni was nowhere around.

Katrina sat up, examined her elbow, patted dirt and burrs from her clothes. With each second the day got brighter. She scrambled to her feet. With relief she looked around herself. She knew exactly where she was standing—the witch's mound. She was surrounded by a circle of mushrooms. Champignons. Had the fairy ring protected her? Who were those forest spirits? Perhaps she should have waited to remove the hex sign from her door jamb. And she would have been spared the apparition of the ghostly ragamuffins. But, of course, that spell would have been useless against a lovelorn Beni. On the other hand, the ghost army had averted the strike of a crazed ruffian, as it had turned out. How was that possible? Was the Krampus company on her side? It almost seemed so. Yet all explanations missed their point after a night such as this. Perhaps there was no explanation.

And grandmother, dearest, had she come to warn me from the other world? Warn me of Beni? She was bewildered. What else, who else could it have been? That shining aura of a person or something else? At the overpowering memory of this peaceful light at her writing table, a great warmth streamed from her core outward. It released a profound feeling of happiness in her. It reached right into her finger tips.

Katrina was exhausted. She carefully stepped out of the fairy circle. Got to get home fast. Soon the five o'clock bells would ring for the farmers to begin their stable chores.

The bells! The horrors of the night were gone. And the next story was waiting to be told.

Exactly. Katrina knew that story like the back of her hand. She had always paid attention to the old wives and curmudgeons' tales and sometimes even Frau Bürkel's ramblings. The story was right there in front of her eyes.

Today, the Song of the Bell sounded quite different in the village.

336

22

Strike Out

Now with full power of the rope
Rock the Bell from vault with care,
That she in the realm of ringing
Rises in the Heavens' air.
Pull ye, pull ye, heave!
She does move, does wave.
Joy she bring this solemn city,
Peace be the first chime she's ringing

—*Friedrich Schiller, Song of the Bell*

Saturday, July 6

Back to the hen house. The story of the bell just had to be
written, before it all evaporated like the sounds of the Angelus.
And if only scribbled with pencil on the back of old posters.

> Each time when Alfons, the most conscientious custodian
> ever, rang the bells for mass, the dissonant clanking in
> honor of his Lord God irritated the heck out of him. Of
> the former four beautiful bells only the smaller two had

remained up in the belfry, St. Michael and the tiny funeral bell. The larger two had already been transported to Hamburg's war factory last year. Not even the pastor's rage could have prevented the bells' removal, especially since he had already been booked for treason for spreading the truth from the pulpit. But now good old St. Michael, the veteran's bell, which his father had donated on his safe return from the trenches of Verdun, was up for grabs and soon to be melted into cannon balls. "What a sin," farmer Huber's wife had secretly whispered to him, as she was watering the flowers on the family grave. That's what most in the village thought. Only, you couldn't say a thing.

Alfons was eaten by pain about losing the bells, even more so because his father had sold off his best farm lot to fulfill his promise. His father had told him often with pride about the hoisting of their new bells. The mighty Trinity, he said, was so heavy that the village team had to stretch the pull rope all the way through the guesthouse corridor to get it up. But gone was now the Holy Trinity, and soon St. Michael would be too. How could one speak of "war morals" if bells were forged to commit deadly assaults in form of shrapnel? Bloody hell! For such a damn butchery his father's blessed bell was for sure too holy!

Angelus now. It sounded choppy, clanky, out of tune with only two bells left. But even these meager sounds should be silenced for good tomorrow? He stopped ringing the bells and stood there like a salt pillar listening to the waning sounds. A ray of sunlight stole through the leaded glass window high up in the sacristy. It hit a pile of ropes in the corner. Alfons stared at the corpus delicti. The

pulley from Sägmüller's sawmill was ready to perform Satan's work. Teifi! They were serious! Alfons didn't know how long he was standing there, but the light had moved on. A twinkle rushed over Alfons' wrinkled face.
Suddenly, he had an idea. The details, however, were still quite obscure to him.

Thus, in the night, he put the harness on Fritz, his white half-blood gelding. He was a good horse and easy to work with. Fritz was the smartest horse in the village. Even the most envious neighbors had to admit to that. Alfons only had to click his tongue or wave his hand, and Fritz trotted or pulled in the indicated direction. This was good, because Alfons could not afford any noise. Luckily, his hay wagon already had the modern rubber wheels, not the old, noisy, cumbersome, iron-clad spoked wheels.

Old Fritz seemed to be fully aware of the seriousness of his task and tiptoed like on cat's paws across the cemetery gravel. It was a partially cloudy half-moon night. Next to the sacristy, Alfons jumped from the wagon, unhitched Fritz, and led him by the halter to the massive Linden tree in front of the cemetery enclosure.

"Now you stay here, Fritz, until I call you," Alfons whispered his horse in the ear and gave him a friendly stroke over the head. The horse nodded, as if it had understood every word. Alfons scampered into the sacristy.

"Gee whizz! Holy crap! This junk is heavy!" He was barely able to drag the monster pulley up the spindly steps.

At midlevel on the bell tower, Alfons stopped to catch his breath. The pulley alone weighed half a centner, add to that the rope. By now he was sweating profusely and doubting his own sanity. The bell? Old Mike weighed five centners at least. Was he mad? Should he better stop now before anyone noticed? He was in good shape from his daily farm work, but he was of small build, not really a Samson or Hercules. Now the bell clonked the full hour. And Alfons remembered exactly what he had come here for. He was already halfway.

This was not only a physical test for Alfons but also the ultimate challenge for his mental capacity. Having arrived at the bell cage, he swung the rope over the empty yoke of the Trinity bell and attached the carbine in the cannons of Michel's crown. His practical smarts had also told him to bring an old potato sack to wrap around the clapper to keep the bell quiet. Then he loosened, as far as possible, the screws in the steel brace, which kept the bell attached to its yoke. Now he was ready to remove the grid from the tower window. As he dropped the rope down, it landed on the wagon with a loud racket. Alfons cringed. He waited. But everything stayed calm, no lights came on.

He scampered down the rickety stairs, picked up the rope, wrapped it around the Linden tree, and attached it to Fritz' harness. Then he moved Fritz back a bit and straightened the rope taut.

"Keep tight, Fritz, always keep tight," he conjured his horse. The horse snorted in agreement.

Quick, back up into the belfry. "Now we will see, oh, dear!"

Alfons glanced down at Fritz from his high up position. His horse stood there like a monument. Then he completely removed the screws from the metal braces on the yoke. This effort took the last out of him. With a violent, cracking jolt the bell plunged into the pulley rope, almost smiting out the plank floor of the bell cage. It came to stop a few centimeters above it. Alfons could have been squished or fallen through a bottomless tower to his death. But Fritz proved his quick wittedness, braced his full weight against the sudden force, and held the bell in position. If there ever was a taut rope, an acrobat could have had a circus number on this one.

Alfons wiped the sweat from his brow. "Thank God in heaven," he whispered.

Now the bell hung at the pulley, but how would he get it out the tower window? Was St. Michael's skirt too big for the opening? No going back now. He attached a second rope to the bell crown and also dropped that rope out the window. Then he rushed down to the church yard again. He slung the lighter rope around the gnarly cypress tree at 90 degrees from the church tower and his horse power. The end of the rope he wound around his own waist.

Never before had Alfons heard anything about triangulation, but he had hoped that in time the correct idea would come to him. He fervently prayed that he was strong enough to pull the bell through the opening with the smaller rope, while Fritz had to release step by step the pulley rope.

Alfons clicked his tongue. Fritz walked a step forward. Alfons tightened up his rope by an arm's length. He clicked again. Fritz made a step. Alfons pulled. Step by step they repeated the process.

"Halleljuah! It's coming out the window!"

Very slowly the large bell sauntered downwards in small pushes, until it came to rest on the hay wagon. The heavy weight pressed the vehicle's wheels deep into the gravel. Alfons covered up his tracks as best he could, hitched Fritz to the wagon, and carefully directed him on the backroad out of the village towards the lake. There he backed up his valuable load flush against the floodgate. He was about to take the harness off of Fritz and plunge the bell and wagon into the lake.

For Christ-sakes, whoa, halt! Was it a fox, a dog, or a cat, Fritz got spooked and nudged the wagon backwards. The top-heavy load, the massive weight of the bell, tipped the scale and pulled wagon and horse into the water. Amidst a roaring splash the vehicle sank into the lake and the struggling horse with it.

Alfons, terrorized, could only watch the disaster. Fritz paddled and thrashed about in mortal fear, but the freight and wagon pulled him down. Without a thought that he couldn't swim at all, Alfons jumped right after. The mechanics and buckles of the harness he sure could handle blindly. But he was dealing with a horse in despair of drowning.

Somehow, gasping for air and swallowing plenty of water, Alfons got a hold of the right leather straps and buckles.

After a terrifying minute, in which Alfons squashed his hand at the wagon shaft, Fritz, with a loud snap, tore free from the remaining gear. With powerful strokes, the horse struggled to the reed grass-lined shore.

Alfons, scrambling and paddling for dear life as well, hoisted himself out of the lake by the floodgate. He bent over and coughed up a bunch of water. He shivered like a rat struck by lightning. Finally, he caught up with his trembling horse in the meadow.

"I promise you, Fritz, we won't do that again so soon!" he whispered in his ear while stroking his head. "That was crazy!" The horse nodded and snorted.

Meanwhile, the wooden wagon with its rubber tires floated in the middle of the moonstruck lake. The bell had sunk to the muddy bottom.

The next morning no bells were ringing, but there was a wild commotion in the village. The block warden had initiated interrogations about the disappearance of St. Michael's bell.

"Maybe the angels in heaven have snatched it up," old Frau Huber teased Wastl, the block warden. "You know, just like on Easter, when the bells fly away to the holy city of Rome."

Contemptuously, the block warden goose-stepped off. He hadn't expected any sense from an old farm wife. And nobody else had any information on the vanished bell either.

When Alfons was asked what happened to his hand, he said that a log had fallen on it when he was lumberjacking. Farmer Huber marveled the most. He helped Alfons pull his hay wagon out of the lake. But he didn't dare to ask him anything, because Alfons often engaged in the strangest deals. Otherwise, he was quite all right, this Alfons.

On the same day as the Americans marched into the village, the pastor received an anonymous tip. The St. Michaels bell rests at the bottom of the lake, it said.

Accordingly, they fished it out again. Many had suspected Alfons. But he didn't admit to anything.

He never wanted to be a hero.

Right on time and almost simultaneously, Katrina, pedaling her bike, met up with the two old detectives, who arrived on Pauli's motorcycle. Grandfather Weber and Pauli carried the pictures in their backpacks. They looked at each other.

"Shucks, how on earth is this possible?" Pauli gaped. The chapel door was widely ajar when the three arrived. Pauli cautiously pushed the door fully open. He was the first to venture inside. Katrina, still dizzy from her sleepless night, felt her heart compress and then give a jolt. Would these conundrums ever stop?

There was yet another surprise.

Pauli's squinty eyes became as large as marbles. How was it possible? There, the other missing pictures were already hanging on their rusty nails again, admittedly not in the right locations, but returned without a doubt.

"A miracle has happened," Pauli murmured.

"Not quite." Luise stepped into the light from under the shadows of the gallery. "Can you see? I brought them back."

"You, Luise? Why did you have the pictures?" Pauli gasped. "Did you steal them?"

Katrina wondered the same.

"Nonsense, Pauli! These pictures are not my style."

"But where did you get these paintings?" Grandfather Weber could not conceal his anger.

"And how, in God's name, did you get in here, Luise?" Pauli sputtered without waiting for an answer. He had obviously lost his composure.

"Here!" Luise handed Pauli the rusty key.

"Young lady!" Pauli snatched the key from her and waved it in front of Luise's eyes. "Where did you get this key? I thought I had the only one? The other one got lost, as far as I know."

"Lost no more. This one was in Katrina's tin can." Luise nestled the rubber band from her pony tail in order.

"What! Katrina!" Pauli swiveled around. He jabbed at the air with the key. "Katrina, you had the key all this time and didn't tell anyone?"

"Shut up, Pauli! Leave Katrina out of it. She probably had no idea," old Weber interrupted. "That key in the cabin that was mine, all right! I was custodian once too. Did you forget that?"

"I see, how reckless of you!" There was a not-so-subtle hint of irony in Pauli's voice.

"Katrina, believe me! I had no clue that this key was in there or what door . . ." Luise was seriously sorry.

"But the pictures? Where did you get them from?" Katrina's eyebrows flared. She didn't know what to make of this situation.

"That would interest me too, young lady!" Pauli had serious wrinkles on his forehead.

"All right," Luise whispered, staring at her feet. "If you promise to keep the police out of it, I can explain it to you . . ."

She was stopped right there. An eclipse shoved across the entrance. The light went out in the chapel. Beni.

"What can you explain?" Beni barked at Luise. He grabbed her by the arm. "Will you finally admit that you stole the votives, you, you . . . painted schickse that the cat dragged in!"

He noticed Katrina and glared at her sideways. "Aha, Frau Weber! You up already? You look like a ghost. Have you been sleeping with the mushrooms last night?"

Katrina's stomach churned.

Beni showed a prickly stubble beard and dark rings under his eyes. His jacket, covered with burs and dirt all over, was torn and tattered. Had he turned into a hobgoblin himself? Katrina, took cover behind her grandfather, whose face visibly darkened. His moustache vibrated at top alert. He was screening the chapel for a handy weapon. Pauli raised his fists into boxing stance.

That's when Luise snapped.

"Let go of me, shithead! We have nothing to admit!" She boxed Beni in the face. Beni's head jolted sideways. He looked stunned. A furious Medusa glared at him. She lunged out for a second strike. Beni caught her fist just before it hit.

Instantly, Beni's face, stung with surprise, transformed into a gloating grimace. "Hold on, young lady! Why go ballistic, my friend, grab an HB cigarette instead,[xxvi] ha, ha!" And he locked both of Luise's wrists in his iron grip.

"Stop that, asshole!" Louise screamed, trying to bite him in the arm. Beni deflected.

"Let go of Luise, right now, or else . . ."

"Not that again! What 'else'? Don't make me laugh, Weber floosy!" Beni grimaced at her.

Katrina's resolve returned. She wanted to scratch Beni's eyes out, but her grandfather pulled her back to safety.

"Let go of this girl, you houndling!" Pauli's battle cry came out shrill. He flung himself on Beni's back. But Beni shook the small man off like a bothersome fly.

"With you I will have a word later," Beni scoffed at Pauli sideways. He turned his attention again on Luise, who was squirming in his vise-like grip. Her face had lost all color.

"Cough it up, schickse, spill it!" He shook her with all his strength. Luise's head was bobbing like a ragdoll's.

"Confess! You stole the pictures! You gypsy slut! My great-grandfather, may he rest in peace, painted them. Just the idea of you touching them . . . I could barf all over!"

"Yes, you already look like vomit," Luise hissed at him.

Beni spit on the chapel's tile floor.

"You dirty bastard!" Grandfather Weber stepped up. "Look at you! How dare you defile our sanctuary like that? Have you lost all decency? What's left in you, shameless prick, of the pious votive painters? Your ancestors would be ashamed. Let go of Luise, pack your pecker, and run home to Mama. Or else I will tell Regina another story about you!"

Beni startled. No one knew his mother's rash temper better than him.

"Are you nuts! Let Louise go!" Out of nowhere, Daniel pounced on Beni. Like mad, he pulled and jabbed at Benis arms to free Luise.

"Haven't I told you to stay in the car! Sister or not, she snagged the votive paintings. You stay out of it! Let her fess up to it!" Beni, red-eyed, stared Daniel down.

"Stop, I have had enough of this!" Daniel's hair whipped around his face, as he shook his mane. His dense eyebrows hooded his flashing eyes. He got Beni's attention. "Let Louise go! Now! Or I will spill the rat poop!"

That hit home. Beni released his grip. Luise bolted and huddled behind old Weber. Like a wounded toro in the bull fight arena, Beni swayed numbly on his spot for five seconds, struck by the well-aimed discharge of words.

"No, you won't! I'd rather kill you right now!"

Beni charged at Daniel. Along the way he grabbed the tall, wrought-iron candle holder for the eternal flame. Daniel tore the procession cross off the wall to intercept the blows. Hitting, swinging, stabbing, an explosive fight broke out. Beni missed Daniel's head by a hair's breadth several times. In this raging collision, the quaint pews flew about like bowling pins in an alley.

"Jesus, Mary, and Joseph," Pauli sputtered. In lieu of a better idea, he dashed towards the tower and pulled the bell rope. He rang the bell as hard and loud as he could, as desperately as the stallion in fear of starvation before him. Old Weber dragged the girls into the farthest, safest corner.

Wild strikes and hits and misses echoed through the nave. Daniel tripped backwards over a bench. He crashed to the floor, lying on his back like a forlorn bug.

"Now I've got you, vermin!" Beni screamed with a killer's glee and wound up for a full-circle swing like at the Volkfest's high striker game[xxvii]. Daniel rolled away from the hit with lightning speed.

Beni struck out—and shattered the chapel floor. The floor tiles crashed from the impact, shards flew in all directions—and gone was Benedikt.

The underworld had swallowed him with thunder.

Soon everything was as quiet as a funeral. Timid sun rays sought their passage through the dense cloud of dust. Daniel whimpered.

"So now he did it! For heaven's sake, don't just stand around like stupid pillars! Do something! Help!" Pauli yelled filled with horror. And he added, all tattered and confused, "He just went straight to hell."

Or not quite as far.

Carefully, Pauli crawled on his stomach closer to the rim of the gaping hole. Weber and the girls scooted cautiously after him. They could not believe their eyes. Beni had knocked a giant hole into the tile floor. The candle holder went through and Beni plunged right after. Below the chapel was a basement or a cave of some sort.

From the rim of the cave opening sounded the laughter

of a hyena. A trembling filled the stinking air, it grew into a roar, the first rocks ripped. The gruesome horror converted the Roman knight

"Benedikt!" Pauli yelled into the hole. "Benedikt, can you hear us? Answer! Are you alright?"

For a few moments all was silent. Then a groan could be heard, chased by a curse. "Crucifix, I can't get up!" Beni whined from below.

"Serves you right," Pauli lectured down into the cloud of dust. He was relieved. And to his companions at the top he said, "He is still alive."

"Yes, unfortunately. What now, Pauli?" Katrina was shocked and relieved about the fateful turn of events.

"Our firemen will know what to do. They should be here soon. I thought I heard their siren." And quite pleased with himself, he yelled into the abyss, "Just you wait! Now you have time to repent your sins, right so!"

"Luise, you must tell us, where did you get the pictures from?" Katrina's grandfather demanded in a strict tone.

"Say nothing, Luise, not a blip!" Daniel clumsily raised himself on his legs. He was still huffing from the exertion and was tending to his scrapes and bruises. A small trickle of blood seeped from his burst lip. "Leave her alone, Herr Weber! Luise has nothing to do with it!"

"But perhaps you?" Pauli quipped cynically. He pulled the bear claw from his pants pocket. "Do you recognize this?" he warily asked Daniel.

"Why?" He crinkled his nose in contempt.

"This is a bear claw." Pauli swung the pendant right in front of Daniel's eyes. "Where do you think it came from . . ."

"No idea."

". . . that same coffee service, which you swiped from me two years ago, and which I later retrieved from the peddler."

"Bullshit! Prove it!"

"Nothing easier than that. Look, Katrina told me that she had this bear claw from Luise, who found it at your place. Only the person who snatched my coffee service, would have known about its existence. And, am I right, you have never really been to America?" He dangled the bear claw pendant faster.

Daniel stared right through it.

"And who swipes once, does it again", Pauli concluded.

"Let it go, Daniel! Just tell them the whole story," his sister pleaded. Her worry was audible.

"Yes, you two better tell us the truth," Pauli demanded. "Especially, because I have even more evidence." He jumped right into a plea argument like a prosecutor. "When this Aschenbrenner Luki told us yesterday about a 'fine lady' who dropped the paintings on him, I suddenly got as sharp as a knife. The same happened with my Prussian coffee service. There was also an extremely fine lady hawking away my heirlooms. Don't you go gallivanting around in women's clothes at times?"

"So what! I play Saucy Flossy in a cabaret show!"

"Maybe it's not just theater in your case . . ." Pauli grinned a wry smile.

"Will you shut up, old goat beard!" Daniel screamed so loud that Pauli jumped back a bit. He could feel the spray of saliva anyway. "This is none of your beeswax."

"Daniel, it's time to give up," Luise sighed. "It wasn't hard to put the key in the tin and the paintings together. I found them behind the canvasses in our atelier. Please, Pauli, Herr Weber, can we leave the police out of this? We brought all the pictures back."

"And what about our saints then?" Grandfather Weber inquired.

"The Anno Dazumal has them. They pay better . . ." Daniel sounded crushed.

"Not anymore. We were told yesterday that a collector beat us to it." Pauli glanced at grandfather Weber. The old man shook his head.

"Will you dingbats already get me out of here!" A pained voice rose from the hole. Pauli nonchalantly waved off the request.

"Yes, we will help you out, all right!" Old Weber shouted down into Beni's crypt. The fire siren flared up in the distance.

"Why in the world would you do such a crooked thing, Daniel?" Pauli shook his head.

"I just needed money."

"Oh, yeah! Money? We all need that! What for?"

"For the car."

"Ditto! I have often wondered how you can afford such an expensive chaise," Pauli prodded on.

"Well, I had a loan."

"Who would give a miserly student like you a credit?"

"Beni."

"Now look at that! What a nice guy! How does he have so much money that he can just throw it out the window?"

"Keep your mouth shut, you pansy!" Beni yelped from the bottom of the pit. "You bastard! You stole the votives! I will strangle you. Just you wait! Will you dumbheads get me out of here now!"

Loud moaning followed. "Zefix, that hurts!"

The five at the top looked at one another.

"Never mind that guy," Luise murmured. "He is built like an ox. He can take a hit."

"You've got nerves!" Pauli said.

"Oh, he doesn't feel much."

"Why is that?"

"Because he is totally hammered." Daniel interjected.

"And you?" Pauli asked.

"Mostly sober. I have gone back to Bacardi."

"Then it was you who left the Cola cans in the cabin?" Katrina said. Finally, the penny dropped.

Daniel nodded. "Anyone can get in there."

"Dang it! Snoopy dog! What a chance in a million that you of all things found this chapel key!" Pauli was still processing the turn of events.

"Yes, but I put it right back!"

"Ha, ha! Very funny!" Pauli put his hands on his hips and rested his case. Yet he still wasn't done with his analysis. He fished for the pendant in his pockets.

"Look here, girls!" He turned the pendant so that they could see the underside. Very minutely and intricately there was a feather engraved on it. "See this feather? It's one of a kind. It sounds strange, but believe me, I once got this bear claw from an Indian."

"But there are no Indians around here." Luise wondered.

"No, not usually!" Pauli giggled. "But during the war, there was one. Joe had taken off from a forced labor camp in 1945. A huge guy. He was all hungered out and covered with scabs. I brought him food and I let him into the chapel. His braids were this long," Pauli indicated the length down by his hip. "And he knew all kinds of stuff about sheep, even though he didn't speak German," Pauli added with admiration and glowing eyes.

"So, what happened with the Indian?" Luise asked.

"Joe was gone from one day to the next," Pauli said. "I could have ended up in a concentration camp myself. The block warden, Wastl, was a really bad snitch. He took away the key from me. Oh, that Wastl, was a full-throttle idiot. He would have also melted that tiny bell up there in the tower, hadn't the war come to an end. My father, the Lord have mercy on him, was no less! Fortunately, neither of them got a whiff of Joe.

Except for your grandfather and Alfons, who saved our bell. Everyone needs their allies at times, right?" He winked at grandfather Weber.

And then he turned to Luise, "No offense, Luise! You've got your head screwed on right, but your late grandfather, Wastl, was a real scumbag."

"Yep, Pauli! But I am not responsible for the bullshit that my ancestors pooped. I can only try not to make the same mistakes."

"You may say that again, young lady! But maybe your brother hasn't learned anything."

Daniel had hunkered down like a small pile of misery on an upside-down kneeling bench. "How can you make the same mistake twice! Church robbery, a felony . . ."

"Pauli, you don't know Beni . . ." Daniel whimpered.

Katrina flinched. She knew what he meant.

"So, tell that to the police, Daniel." Pauli was at his best.

"No police, please, Pauli," Luise implored him.

Pauli wasn't listening. He grinned all over his stubbly face. "Very nice! Now at least I have my bear claw back, if that is all right with you, Katrina?"

Katrina nodded. She instinctively clasped her lucky clover. How exposed she suddenly felt. Apparently, Daniel and Beni had loitered around in the cabin before she moved in there. That's how her lucky charm had ended up in the corner under her bench. Clearly, Daniel had taken advantage of her insobriety and tried to rush her passion with the help of drugs. She stared at Daniel's arm with the dragon tattoo showing under the torn sleeve. Yes, that was surely him, the dude from the St. John's night ritual.

The siren was coming closer. Pauli had lost steam. Grandfather Weber hadn't gotten quite to the bottom of things.

He stepped up to the pile of misery and put his hand on Daniel's shoulder.

"Daniel! Have you paid Beni back already?"

"Most of it." Daniel was close to sobbing.

"Where does Beni get so much money from?"

Silence.

"Certainly not from his chinchilla mice." Luise had spoken loud and clearly.

"What then?" Pauli listened up.

Luise made the same gesture that Pauli used when he took a snuff.

"What? Snuff? Glacier Pinch[xxviii]?" Pauli asked, confused.

"Are you dense, or what?" Luise seemed irritated. She waggled invisible cobwebs out of the air with her arms in frustration. "Coke."

"Cola?" Pauli raised his eyebrows.

"KO-KA-IIIIN," she screamed.

"Shut uuup!" The dark hole screamed back.

"Drugs?" Pauli whispered horrified. "What? Drugs in our village? I can't believe that. Where did he get them from?"

"Well, you better ask him down there." Luise stated factually. "He is the one who deals them."

Katrina paled even more. And icy bleakness spread from her stomach to all other body parts. No, she would have never guessed what kind of adventure she had embarked on during that jinxed starry night. The "love pearls"? Scales fell from her eyes. No wonder that Beni had behaved like Frankenstein's monster, boozed up and wasted as he was.

"Do you really believe that from selling mice fur you can afford a Golden Eagle jeep?" Luise sarcastically landed one more well-aimed blow on Pauli.

"But what shall we do with these two rotten scoundrels now?" Pauli asked.

All was quiet.

"Leave that to me!" Old Weber had spoken.

"All right! So, what's your plan?" Pauli grumbled. "And where have our saints disappeared to?"

No answer.

The horn from the fire truck was blaring up the dirt road to the chapel.

"They are here!"

23

Eternal Truths

In Bavaria, one town name is reminiscent of this Celtic custom: the earlier mentioned Rosshaupten[xxix] near Füssen/Allgäu, where a Viereckschanze[xxx] and rows of burials are traceable. In the oldest legend of St. Magnus, this town is named *caput equi* (horse head).

—*Rudolf Reiser, Die Kelten in Bayern und Österreich, 206*

And a second later

As one command the firemen, Girgl, Huber, Gabelsberger and son Mike, and half a dozen others stormed into the chapel. Katrina exchanged a brief glance with Mike, but the general devastation pulled his attention in a different direction. The men guffawed at the mess with the hole in the middle. After they had assessed the situation, they purposefully went to work with pulley and ropes. Girgl was lowered into the abyss first, and then the stretcher followed. Soon enough the badly battered Benedict was lifted into daylight on a make-shift gurney. They set him down on the tile floor. He appeared to have several broken bones, but he was still cursing very lively. Then the helpers pulled the badly bent candle holder up from the hole. They were waiting for Girgl to give them a sign to pull him up, too.

"What's going on down there, Girgl? Don't you want to come up?" Gabelsberger shouted into the sink hole.

"I found something strange," it resounded from below. "You can pull me up now!"

Girgl floated up from the dark with a horse's skull in his arm. "There is a lot more trash like this down there."

The stallion's head, she saw it clearly in her mind's eye mounted on the stake. The lifeless mane was waving proudly and ghostly around it in its death.

Katrina plopped down into a pew.

"What is going on around here?" Walli shouted snapping for breath. She had jogged all the way from the village after the firemen, of whom her father was the captain.

"Papa, what have you got there?"

Then Walli screened the chapel and her eyes fell on Beni, who was writhing from pain on the stretcher. She saw the gaping hole in the floor and was dumbstruck, for a change.

"You best take this rotten fella to the hospital," old Weber directed the volunteer firemen.

"What happened, grandfather?" Walli squawked. "Did you push him? Who pushed him down the hole?"

The men were too busy to answer a pesky fly. Katrina was entranced. Luise huddled with Daniel in a corner. Nobody took note of Walli.

With joint force, the men readied themselves to haul the now deathly pale Beni on the wobbly stretcher to the fire engine. He was still under shock and couldn't feel most of the pain.

"Daniel, it was Daniel! He took the pictures!" Beni moaned from the swaying gurney. "See how he mangled me! Lock him up, that hound!"

"Oh, tell that to the police!" Pauli grinned. Mischief was in his eyes. Girgl, on purpose, jolted his end of the stretcher handle. Beni whimpered from pain, as if stabbed with a knife.

"You better believe it! But I will deny everything else!" Beni groaned raising up his head. His face was distorted from the pain and effort.

"What will you deny, you shithead?" Katrina had followed the firemen outside. She stomped alongside the gurney.

"You, you better shut up, or else . . ." Beni whined.

"Or else what? Or else I will tell the police another story, right? And I do have witnesses, is that clear?" She looked towards Pauli. He nodded his affirmation.

"What story, what is she talking about, grandfather?" Walli pulled on the old man's sleeve. He didn't care to look.

"Not that, too!" Beni slumped down on the gurney, as if all the hot air had puffed out of him. "Look! I can't move, fucking shit! That hurts! Daniel almost killed me! I will report him to the police for this brutal assault!" he howled.

"No, you won't!" old Weber growled down on him. "You had it coming. You have knocked out heaven's floor unto yourself."

After this strict verdict, he turned to Gabelsberger senior, who was the taillight to this odd paramedical procession, and said, "I would say, you check out his chinchilla stables as well. You might even find our saints again."

With this insinuation the old man had played high stakes poker, but his gut feeling acquired from years of tracking game in the forest rarely faulted him. They would find some dirt, not only mouse poop, on him. That much was certain.

"Don't you dare, houndlings!" Beni screamed, enraged but powerless. He was by now even more tightly buckled in. "You all know perfectly well that I haven't stolen anything!" he hedged with a noticeable tint of terror in his voice. "I just bought our saints back from the hawkers."

"Sure! Tell that to your grandmother," old Weber murmured.

"Right, you wanted them for yourself," Pauli guessed.

"Just let the police look at his stable," Luise interjected. "Those chinchilla mice alone don't buy such an expensive jeep."

"What's going on?" Walli pouted. "What's in his stables?"

"Lots of white mice. They make a lot of dirt," Luise whispered in her ear.

"Then he better muck it out!"

Benedict continued grumbling all the way until the doors of the fire engine had fallen shut behind him. Huber had made sure that Beni was strapped according to protocol for the journey, before he sat down behind the wheel. Then the fire truck took off with siren and blue lights, down the bumpy dirt road tracks. They transported their cursing freight to the county hospital. The remaining crew traipsed back to the chapel.

"I hope that you have good cause for your suspicion, Weber," Gabelsberger addressed the old man. "Actually, I am hoping you're wrong, but apparently you know more than I do. Good that you are speaking up, finally." And he reached out for a handshake. "If what you're saying is true, we'll get the saints back too."

"Yes, you will see!" Pauli assured him. "The policeman's description of our 'Bavarian art collector' fit Beni to a tee." Pauli had fished his theory out of thin air, which surprised himself. A white lie was justified in an emergency like this.

But Walli had gotten curious. "Which policeman?"

"Well, the one from yesterday, when we picked up our votives again," Pauli explained.

"Then you think Beni has stolen our pictures *and* the saints?" Walli asked.

"Perhaps, not quite exactly, but it's all possible," Pauli oracled. "He sure must be to blame for something."

Walli kept twisting an unruly strand of her hair around her finger. In her confusion, she started chewing on it and spit it out again. Nothing made much sense to her at this point. Neither did Gabelsberger comprehend.

"Are you absolutely sure, you want me to send the police over to search the Moar farm? This is not child's play anymore." Gabelsberger scrutinized Weber like a judge in a criminal case.

"We have good reasons."

"But you won't tell me?"

"Trust us. Just take a look!" Pauli locked eyes with Weber Jakob. He nodded.

"I already heard about your detective talent, Pauli," Gabelsberger joked. "But what's going on with these other two over there?" he prodded. "They look quite shaken up. What do they have to do with all this?"

"Daniel and Luise? Yep, that Daniel is a real hound . . ." Pauli quipped.

"Without them we wouldn't have gotten those pictures back again," Weber grunted.

"Well done, I must say!" Gabelsberger praised them.

"It wasn't easy but well worth it." Pauli was giddy from the excitement. "Gabelsberger, church warden, do you still have the phone number for the county office? You must call them first thing in the morning so that they take a look at this." Pauli took a deep pride in all matters regarding the treasures of his village. Maybe another archaeological find would make just as many waves in the newspaper. And he liked this kind of attention.

Gabelsberger gave the horse's skull on the pew a final fleeting glance. Since the Celtic princess had been excavated from his Stube, he also felt much in charge of this great discovery. He adjusted his hat and bid his farewell.

Katrina was even more entranced by the bleached horse's skull. So, there was something to those old stories. Today she had the proof, the Celts were proverbially among us, "unter uns"[xxxi] as the Adler typewriter had dictated her. Pallidly, the horse's skull gleamed from the walnut-brown, patinated church pew. The Celtic stallion? Luise may have been point on with her pagan worship. There was the proof: "her" chapel had been built on top of a heathen cult. Another indicator was the altar block, which had been cut from a rock called "tuff." It carried the blazing sun on it, which was a powerful symbol of life in Celtic as well as Christian mythology, where it stood for the savior, Jesus Christ. Her fantasy attacks, therefore, hadn't come by chance.

Katrina hadn't been able to exchange one word with Mike, because like all helpers he had his hands full making order in the chapel. As his father waved at him to go, Mike turned on his heels and followed him.

Girgl, as well, didn't want to miss his ride, because he had left his stable work unfinished. On the point of leaving, he turned around to Katrina. Speaking visibly cost him some effort.

"Katrina, I am sorry, but I got so mad at you. I couldn't help myself. No offense," Girgl said. Katrina had never before seen her father this shaken. Apologies were not his thing. Girgl wiped the dust from his eyelids with his ragged sleeve. Then he picked up the remaining coils of ropes and headed to the door. "Wait for me! I am coming!"

On the doorstep he turned around once more. "But don't you forget to lock this place up. You've got the key." And then he ducked out.

"Even two," Pauli murmured. Now the two old ones were alone again with the three girls and Daniel.

"And what now?" Pauli asked as he frowned at Daniel. "Shouldn't we have better handed this one over to the police?" Luise seemed a degree paler today, and Daniel sat there like a pile of misery.

"Folks, we promised Luise to keep the police out of it. She returned the pictures," old Weber decided.

"I don't understand a thing grandfather," Walli yelped. "Luise has stolen the pictures? Not Beni? Your story always keeps changing. I can't believe . . ."

"Will you shut up, twit!" Daniel barked at her. "Who has asked you anything?"

"No, you shut up, . . . rogue!" Pauli swore. "You should be booked! If I only think about my beautiful coffee service . . ." He lost his train of thought and took a deep breath. He blinked several times. Then he remembered Walli's question.

"Walli, don't you worry about Luise. We figured it all out. Katrina will tell you the rest. But I am still so darn mad. I want to lock that sad hooligan up myself."

Daniel squinted at Pauli in terror.

"I know something better." Old Weber straightened his hat. "Let him work off his sins. He's got talent, that boy. We'll make him polish up the picture frames around here."

"Good idea! Or refresh the gold leaf! He's got a whole workshop at home for jobs like these," Pauli agreed. A fresh glint stole back into his eyes.

"Right so! Someone needs to start taking care of this chapel." Weber let his eyes wander across the jumbled mess and the crooked pictures on the wall.

"And first thing tomorrow morning, we will send the blacksmith up here to take measure for window grates." Pauli winked at Weber. "And Daniel can help us with that, too."

Luise seemed relieved about this Solomonic verdict.

Daniel nodded his drooping head. "I promise you, Herr Weber, I won't do nothing like that again!" His voice sounded meek and beaten.

"Don't promise me, promise it to yourself!" With that, all had been said. Weber pointed Daniel to the door.

Daniel and Luise turned to leave. Before walking out, Luise addressed Katrina. She was looking very serious. "Believe me, Katrina, I really had no idea until yesterday about all this shlimazel here." Then she pulled her brother by the sleeve outside into the sunlight.

"All right then, so let's get these votives right and hang them up again. Nothing in here is in order any more. Look, this droving accident can't be from World War II, that must have happened in the 19th century. That belongs for sure on the other wall." Like a busy bee Pauli buzzed back and forth in the chapel, avoiding the gaping hole in the middle, and directing Katrina and Walli, until all pictures had found their trusted, rusted nails. Then they pushed the pews into the farthest corner to make room for the repair works and the scientists from the state conservation office. Grandfather Weber watched their every move from his supervisor post by the door.

"Very nice," Pauli said, complacently looking around. "I like it much better now. I guess our job is done. Let's go home, then."

"May I ride with you, Pauli?" Walli begged. Pauli looked at Weber Jacob. He nodded and said, "I don't mind walking on foot. Just take Walli with you." And in the blink of an eye Walli stormed outside.

"Just look at that girl! How cheeky!" Pauli blustered half in earnest and scampered after her. "Soon enough this child will take off with my own motorcycle." Walli already sat in the sidecar honking at him. Pauli jumped on his seat and revved up the motor. Suddenly, he paused.

"Now I almost forgot to lock up," he shouted over his bike's droning noise. He readied himself to jump off.

"You better go now!" Weber called out to him. "You need to be at mass on time. I can take care of this. You can rely on me!"

"Yeah? Really?" Pauli chuckled and tossed him the key. "People still say to this day that you were a better custodian than I. If they only knew that you lost that key for seven years. God speed, bye-bye now!" And instantly the unusual vehicle rattled away. Walli hooted and waved back at grandfather as much as the bumpy trail allowed it.

As her grandfather was about to lock up the door, Katrina pulled him at the sleeve towards the votive painting next to the large tablet of the miraculous protection from the French raiders. "Look, grandfather! Oma painted this one."

"Yes, I know this marterl well" He pulled out the small, yellowed notebook from his inner coat pocket. "In here, Kathl has written down all her thoughts, way before my time. If I only had listened to her more often."

The old man leafed through the notebook, until he arrived at the place where the page was missing. "She had seen the future coming," he murmured in piety as if reciting a mystery from the rosary. "Look at this, you already were in her book as well, not only Martl."

Grandfather handed Katrina the missing page, which he had retrieved from his drawer from under the biscuit box. It was the passage about the valiant warrior woman in a knight's suit, who swung an unusually dangerous weapon, the sharp lance-pen in her hand.

> "Then she directed her long spear, the tip of it looking like an ink pen, at me and said: "Only you can help me. You know me well, I am . . .

And now the missing page:

> . . . Katharina with the sharp pen. All hypocrites will tremble at my words,"

Katrina read in a quiet voice. Then the entries continued with threshing and rosary praying and pig slaughtering.

The two sat in their pew in silence. What else could be said? Only the tears rolled, they both knew it, but neither looked at the other.

"Katrina," grandfather whispered after a while, "you are just like your grandmother, just as smart and insightful as her."

"I am so ashamed of myself about what I have done with her diary."

"But it has brought out the truth. Kathl, God bless her soul, would not have let you find her diary if she minded. I know her so much better now. And if you want to go study later at the university," grandfather grabbed his backpack, "for that case I have put something aside. I can help you out, even if it doesn't suit Girgl. He can't do anything about it, as long as you know what you want." That was the longest speech the old man had made in years.

"Bless your heart, grandfather, but time will tell what I need." This minute, Katrina couldn't even foresee the end of the day, much less the end of school. Instead, she reached into her pants pocket. "Look, I also have brought something for you." She handed him the red matchbox toy car.

"Where did you get this?"

"In the forest cabin." And then she smirked. "I didn't know that you were still playing with toy cars at your age."

"Not I, but Martl did. It was his favorite toy car. Thank you for bringing it back to me, Katrina!" Her grandfather for the first time showed a true smile on his face since the time when he had made his clock go fifteen minutes fast. "But now we really should go home," he urged.

Both were lost in their own thoughts as they trotted down the hill and along the farm road. Katrina was pushing her bicycle absentmindedly beside her. Grandfather shuffled on her left. When they passed by the Moar farm estate, two police cars were parked in the courtyard. The explanation came biking towards them in the shape of Walli.

"They already found the saints," Walli panted out of breath. "And the drugs too. I guess Beni will have to sit for a while after they patch him up again. This dipshit still carried that powder in his pants pockets when he was admitted to the hospital."

"Cruzi-turk! Is that so?" Grandfather glanced irritated at the cavalcade of vehicles in the Moar driveway. "What wickedness! I hadn't expected that, bastard!"

"Why not? You yourself have sicked the cops on him and you wanted to search his chinchilla stables yourself," Katrina reminded him, a little confused.

"Well, sure," Weber grumbled, "but only because of the saints. Because I thought that he wanted to swipe our antiquities for himself. But drugs, like Luise was talking, I hadn't believed that at all."

"You are a real fox then! Nobody called your bluff, and it all turned out true," Walli jubilated. "Do you want to teach me Schafkopf[xxxii] some time?"

Her grandfather strictly waved her off. He had no sense for humor in that matter. "A good while in the slammer serves him just right. The way he maligned Katrina, this rapscallion! He should be hung up by the large toe and be flogged until he's blue. Never mind he is a descendant, and what a rotten one, of the most pious holy icon painters!"

This degree of passion Katrina would have never expected from her old, glum grandfather. She didn't dare imagine what else he would be capable of, had he known the full scope of her encounters with Beni.

"But why did you let Daniel get away?" she asked cautiously.

"Well, his sister did the right thing and brought the pictures back. That Daniel, poor bugger, is punished badly enough. If you don't know whether you're a stud or broad, a spiffy car can't help you there either. You will see, birds like him can't survive here in the country. He will fly off to the city soon."

The girls looked at each other in utter surprise. Then, like at command, they broke into roaring laughter. Their grandfather was amazingly up to date for his age, even when he didn't let on.

"Shameless girls! What are you laughing about!" Weber thundered, feigning outrage. "It's about time that you get going, run home! On your bikes you are much faster than I!"

As ordered, they rode their bicycles ahead of their grandfather through the village towards home. At the curve by the guesthouse, where the bus stop was, a familiar figure strolled towards them. Katrina stopped in her tracks, but Walli veered away and kept going on her path. She had recognized the situation.

"Hey, there, Mike! We just got Saint Sebastian and Saint Nepomuk back," Walli shouted craning her head at Mike while pedaling past him. "Beni had them in his stables."

"So, I already heard, Walli," Mike shouted after her. And gone she was.

Katrina stood there holding the bike, unsure what to do. Mike walked straight up to her.

"Do you have time?" he asked.

Katrina nodded.

"Let's go!"

Katrina stuck her bike in the rack by the bus stop. The two walked at a fast pace together, in silence, out the village and towards the river valley. They had almost reached the riverside forest, when Mike suddenly halted. He turned to Katrina and looked her in the eye. Apparently, Mike was straining to find the right words. His eyebrows tensed and his pupils pulsed.

"Katrina, you must believe me. That calamity at the solstice fire, I had nothing to do with it. Beni played a dirty joke on me." And then he said, "Here!" He handed her a small manila envelope, the content of which she could only guess too well. "I didn't mean to embarrass you, by all means."

She quickly stuffed the packet with her bra inside her bag, no comment. What was she going to say? He had certainly not come forth with any consolation. She didn't care about the rectification of a disgrace. Did he not have the courage to speak the truth? That another girl was more important to him?

Mike silently picked up his walk again. Katrina trotted alongside him. Finally, he stopped once more, and so she had to stay too.

"Katrina, I don't think that you should keep waiting on me. You will want to study at the university, and that you should! Perhaps you will be a doctor or a teacher, what do I know about that. I am only a carpenter. And we also have a farm at home. For that no one needs to go to college. And it takes too long anyway. You don't want to brush your talent under the table! You will get ahead better in school without me."

Here it was, the truth. Everything was all different once more.

Something inside Katrina felt frighteningly broken, as if shards of glass jiggled in her abdomen. Broken love, could it be? Now she knew what she had been waiting for. The decision. He had taken it off her hands. She took a deep breath and tried to smile.

"I understand," she heard herself say. They slowly walked in silence along the dirt road.

"I am so glad that the votive paintings came back," Mike said after a while to bring up a different topic. "That was a remarkable accomplishment by you and the old guys."

"And the saints we recovered too," Katrina sheepishly threw in to make conversation. "And perhaps a noble steed as well, a surprise for your princess," Katrina tried a crummy joke about the newest archaeological finds.

That horse head image reminded her of something else. "Did you get any more results about the excavation in your house? Have you found any more jewelry?"

"Not I, but the investigators. There were a couple of fibulas, some rivets like for a belt, three coins, and a few ceramic jugs. The State Conservation Office took it all to the labs in Munich to prepare it for a later exhibit."

"Too bad about that . . ."

"Why, it might be the safest way."

"Do you still have the ring at least? May I see it again? It's an awesome piece."

"The ring? It's gone."

"Gone? What do you mean? Did you give it . . ."

"Let me show you. Here, see!"

He pulled the matchbox from his pocket. Slowly, he pushed it open. Inside lay a few brown morsels intermixed with some dark-blue splinters. The ancient piece of jewelry should have been stabilized by experts. Now it had crumbled and was destroyed. And yet it still hadn't missed its bewitching impact on at least one person.

The power and possibility to escape her fate . . .

It all wasn't as obvious as it seemed.

A car honked behind the two. It was Raffi. He slowly pulled up beside them, leaning out the car window.

"I have been looking all over for you, Katrina! What are you doing out here? Going for walks on this important day?"

Katrina didn't answer.

"And why so dreary you two? Come on, hop in! Let's hang up the pictures in the chapel!"

"Sorry, you missed it all! You should have gotten up a little sooner," Mike said.

"For crying out loud, how could you amateurs even sort out these artistic treasures without me," Raffi joked. "After all, I have studied that subject matter."

"No worries, nobody knows those old stories better than us," Mike retorted.

"Do you mean all without science?

"You bet! We don't need photos. We have our treasures memorized."

Now Katrina recognized the slick prankster hidden in her just lost heartthrob. That sense of humor was what had attracted her to Mike in the first place.

"Can't believe I missed it! Too bad! But hop in anyways. Whereto?"

"No, I am good," Mike replied. "I am heading out to fish. But maybe Katrina wants a ride home. She can tell you a few things about the underworld around here and the finds we make."

Katrina got in the car without speaking a word, Raffi stepped so abruptly on the gas that the gravel sprayed from under his wheels. They left a trail of dust behind them.

Raffi sensed the thick air inside the car. He tried to start a conversation.

"As a matter of fact, do you know why the May poles are painted white and blue?" Raffi posed his quiz question to a dumbfounded Katrina.

"Duh, the Bavarian state colors."

"Wrong! I had expected better from you!"

"Huh?"

"Because, as you know, a long, long time ago, there were these landing posts for the very fast flier angels. But one fine day these air wights, after painting the heavens blue, had forgotten to wash their hands . . ."

"You, silly . . ." Katrina shoved his shoulder so that the steering wheel tottered.

"Are you nuts? Watch out!" He set the car straight again. "But to finish my story . . . these air wights, with their little blue paws, they smeared the sky paint all over their landing post. And so, when they trundled down on them, they made blue streaks all around, like in a candy stick spiral. And that's why the May poles are ribboned white-blue."

Katrina burst into laughter, against her will, but she laughed.

"And when you look at them sideways, the twirls look like rhombuses," Raffi continued.

"Ugh, you scientists know nothing! Did you mean to say rhombi? Those come from the dragon scales," she spluttered and turned on the cassette player ultra-loud.

Smoke on the Water came on.

"Where are we going now, since the pictures are up already?" Raffi asked.

"Into the forest, obviously."

"What for?"

"Picking mushrooms?"

"All right, then. I will find you only the very biggest ones."

"Toadstools perhaps?"

"Yes, psychedelics, please!"

And at home, Girgl nailed the third horseshoe from the Great Migration of the Germanic Peoples up on the stable doors.

The E N D

Exhibit at the Bad Tölz Heimatmuseum.

Afterword

Celtic Stallion Origin

OR: That Bavarian Seventies Show

I grew up in a Grimm's fairy tale on a small German farm, with a grandmother, a grandfather, hard-working parents, three siblings, about fifteen cows, rosaries and church duties, and many goblins and mystical creatures. Stories lurked around every corner. Most sagas wafted around St. George's Hill, "Biahn" in local terms, especially the *Schimmelkirche*, or White Horse Chapel, on top of it. This tiny church still proudly beckons from its glacial moraine in the Isar river plateau, brightly visible from afar. It stands on a very special hill—an old Celtic sanctuary once voted the "most romantic spot in Germany" by *Stern Magazin*.

On this hill, called Biahn from "bieten" (= offering), a fiery dragon may occasionally cruise above the trees. Or a hound with glowing eyes comes looking for easy prey. There also lives a vicious witch ("drud" in Bavarian dialect, or "druid"). She scares little kids with her atrocious howls and drags them into her lair. And once in a blue moon, a mysterious white horse canters up the steep south side to the chapel dedicated to St.

George. No wonder, St. George the dragon (!) slayer rides a white stallion. Get it? But, no, our ghost horse here is not a holy steed. There is a story (or two) about it. The stallion, a not so friendly ghost, often scared the heck out of the journeymen who were walking past White Horse Chapel on their returns from rafting trips. Drove some insane!

So, there are stories galore! Luckily, the bad old witch might have been burnt for good at the stake. Out in the eastern fields, not too far from the Weiher Creek, a farmer once plowed across a barely noticeable elevation. He hit a field of charcoal. That's where the witches were burnt, we think. No wonder they called it witch mound! This and much more I gleaned from a school teacher's essay called "About the Field Names." (To be honest, the coal could have also come from charcoal making.)

In grade school we all learned about White Horse Chapel's Celtic roots. Several large foundation boulders on its backside seem to prove that. One rock has a channel carved in it. That is how the blood was caught. What blood? Animal blood for sure, such as from horse sacrifice, but who knows, maybe the blood of fair maidens too. The Celts were not squeamish about death. Fearless, they were the ultimate danger to the Roman Empire. Dead or alive was just as well to them. The Romans dreaded "the ferocious blue devils" for their savage rituals such as head hunting. What scant little documentation we have about the Celts, comes from Roman scribes and a few archaeological relics.

In my childhood, my village walked a pilgrimage to White Horse Chapel twice a year. Along the way to St. George's sanctuary, the rosary was prayed for good weather and other blessings. And what is or was inside the church? Lots of little miracles, attributed to St. Mary of the Sorrows and to St. George, or one of the Fourteen Holy Helpers depicted on an imposing wooden panel. The walls used to be decked with small votives, primitive paintings in honor of prayers fulfilled. Each one told the story of a hardship or miracle. In the seventies, most of the votive paintings were stolen never to be retrieved. That's in contrast to the two saints that temporarily disappeared in the 1920ies but were later recovered in a private search through Munich's antique stores. The mural of the excruciating martyrdom of St. George, however, could not be "stolen" and was restored. It still wraps around the upper half of the inside wall. Gaze at the pictures and wonder . . . My grandfather for a long time was the caretaker of this little shrine. He always swept the bat poop, cobwebs, and other debris out the door before a service. And that little church, blessed by the amazing grace, still stands bright and proud on its forested hill. Wait a minute, there is a story about the bulb on its tower too! It had to do with a miraculous salvation during the French occupation.

Yes, that's where it all happened. That's where 17-year-old Katrina scampers through her nighttime adventures in the 70ies. She is inquisitive. Katrina wonders about many strange things that had gathered in her 200-year-old farm house attic. Among so many pious implements, she finds a folder with saintly watercolor paintings done by her grandmother in her youth. And a diary filled with hot stories on top. To a curious teenager like her all this was so mysterious.

Let's jump ahead 30 years. Sensation struck the village in 2000. A burial site dated around the year zero was found during a home renovation: a young Celtic maiden had been laid to stately rest near the village creek. Many generations had moved in and out of the farmhouse built atop her grave. A big bell chimed in my head! So, the old stories from fourth grade must be true! I read and read and read. What if the Celtic maiden would come alive again? Those fearsome old Celts were pretty much like us Bavarian village people: strong, proud, hard-working, wary of strangers, grand with celebrations and stingy with words. Buttoned up. Feisty. Rather hit first and explain later—in one word, tribal. One of them, the Celtic princess, was unearthed and publicly laid to rest again in a diorama at the Heimatmuseum Bad Tölz, my school town.

Meanwhile the Celtic stallion started riding through the night again. How exciting! But people didn't pay attention to him anymore. Only the pure of heart could still see him.

From 2000 on, the village idyll went downhill. The Internet came in strong. Large-scale agriculture took hold. There was no more living to be eked out on a small farm. If there were 35 active dairy farmers in my childhood, only five farm operations are left now. On one farm, cows are now getting milked by a robot. Cash crop king corn, for methane gas/electricity, conquered the fields, depleting the scant humus layer. And construction boomed. Cranes loomed over the farmhouses in 2016 and dirt piles crapped up the front yards.

Now it's the year 2024 onward. And it's too late. So here we come to the worst part: business complexes were built on both sides of the village's access road practically overnight. Seen from Google Earth, the village looks like it has a hydrocephalus on a naturally grown village outline. Gone are the strawberry fields and pick-your-own-flowers operations. We can't see the forest from the farm house window any more.

What happened? The heir to a major farm estate, a rich grocery merchandiser, traded a big chunk of farm land cheaply to the municipality in exchange for a hypermarket building permit. And build he did, as did the developers, and the out-of-town entrepreneurs capitalized on it as well. The municipality promoted the project to build tax potential, the companies bought cheap land to write off their debt, and the concrete won't grow any more grass for the next 2000 years. Such is capitalism!

Land is priceless. Now it's gone. The Celtic stallion would turn over in its grave if it weren't already a ghost.

Add insult to injury, an archaeological study was required on the doomed land according to Bavarian state law. The dirt was bulldozed, the Ice Age gravel soon lay bare. On it, a patchwork of brown squares, morsels that had been pillars, showed the pattern of what once were foundations for houses. My ancestral village lay bare-naked like the skeleton of the Celtic maiden in the museum. Now her village, an ancient landmark (*Bodendenkmal*), was to be covered with concrete. The archaeologists didn't find any treasures, only a few shards and bones and metal morsels. They should have left the old village sleep.

So, I wandered, aimlessly and desperate, over the gravel field, from one archaeological hole to the next, looking for I don't know what. I heard those ancestors speak to me, tease me, "Huh, you think we're stupid and leave our best pots behind?" Forget about it! Time had crunched, whatever there could have been, into tiniest morsels. The plough would have done the rest. Nothing? However, as one old saying goes, "What you have been looking for, will find you when you look no more." My scavenger hunt took me by surprise: I chanced upon a horse's tooth and a nail from a horseshoe, plus a few shards that looked significant to me.

Proof enough: the white horse ghost, the Celtic stallion, is still out there!

I had found my relics, the nail, the tooth, and the shards, on those gravel mounds ten years after I had written my book, *Der Keltenschimmel* (Celtic Stallion). In it, among other things a Celtic maiden courts her lover, a pauper nail smith. He walks barefoot. She rides a white stallion, her favorite horse. Their story ends in tragedy. These images hit me out of the blue. Or otherworld?

But what can I tell you? I am not the author, just the narrator.

Katrina wrote down the truth and took a hit for it. The misty past of White Horse Chapel was a main channel for her inspiration. Soon the witch hunt was on. On her quest, Katrina got help steering through the troubled waters from the spirits of the past.

Just reach out.

Just listen.

That's what's left of the Celtic Village—archaeological finds.

Inspiration

Der Maibaum. Web Page Gästehaus Winkler, Tegernsee. https://www.winkler-kreuth.de/maibaum.html. Accessed 26 February 2023.

Dietrich, Josef. *Von den Flurnamen der Gemeinde Ascholding.* Manuscript, 1927/28.

Filser, Karl. *Flößerei auf Bayerns Flüssen.* Zur Geschichte eines alten Handwerks. Hefte zur Bayerischen Geschichte und Kultur, Band 11. München: Haus der Bayerischen Geschichte, 1991.

Groth-Schmachtenberger, Erika, und Erica Schwarz. *Die Isar vom Karwendel bis zur Donau.* Freilassing: Pannonia Verlag, 1970.

Kapfhammer, Günther. *Brauchtum in den Alpenländern.* München: Verlag Georg D. W. Callwey, 1977.

Ludwig, Carla. *Das Horoskop der Druiden. Was Bäume über uns verraten.* Niedernhausen: Falken-Verlag, 1999.

Melf, Elisabeth. *Harten Adventwochen folgte ein karges Fest.* Münchner Merkur. Without date.

Nöhbauer, Hans F. *Die Bajuwaren. Die legendäre Herkunft und der fabelhafte Weg eines deutschen Stammes aus der Urzeit in die Gegenwart.* Bern und München: Scherz Verlag, 1976.

Pferdeopfer, Reiterkrieger. Fahren und Reiten durch die Jahrtausende. Archäologie in Krefeld. www.archaeologie-krefeld.de/news/PferdeAusstellung/Pferde.htm. Accessed 26 February 2023.

Reiser, Rudolf. *Die Kelten in Bayern und Österreich.* Rosenheim: Rosenheimer Verlag, 1984.

Schinzel-Penth, Gisela. *Sagen und Legenden von Wolfratshausen und Umgebung.* Frieding-Andechs: Ambro Lacus Buch- und Bildverlag, 1992.

Theopold, Wilhelm. *Votivmalerei und Medizin.* München: Verlag Karl Thiemig, 1978.

Wagner, Andreas. *Todesmarsch. Die Räumung und Teilräumung der Konzentrationslager Dachau, Kaufering und Mühldorf Ende April 1945.* Ingolstadt: Panther Verlag, 1995.

The hen house after a spring blizzard.

About the Author

AnnElise Makin, born in Munich, lives in Mesa, Arizona. She is the owner of the Imakinations Agency and the BookProShop publishing service. She has earned two MA degrees from the University of Texas (Anthropology/Photojournalism) and enjoys multicultural encounters. Over her long and varied career, she has been a newspaper journalist, a textbook editor, and a school counselor. Books have been her passion ever since she learned to read. She has authored three books and co-published several other titles. All publications are available on Amazon.

Additional Titles

Der Keltenschimmel. (German)

1974. Seventeen-year-old Katrina lives in an ancient Bavarian village full with ghosts of the past. The white stallion ghost is only one of them. Her grandfather might as well be a ghost, too. He doesn't talk any more. Both make irritating clatter noises, Katrina on her type writer, the old man on his dengel (peening) bench. Katrina must produce stories for her teacher's Essay Marathon, but they all flounder as flights of fantasy. But after she plagiarizes her deceased grandmother's diary, she wins a newspaper story competition and all hell breaks loose. That's only the beginning of her troubles.

Available on Amazon

Random Accident in Sector Noah 135/56
OR: The Last Book on Earth

Written by AnnElise Makin
Illustrated by Priyanka Makin

In the very distant future, when humans have everything under control, except for the weather, earthquakes, and random accidents, little Sandy discovers a book. She is shaken by it. Her celestial friend Bob helps her understand the pictures. Sandy sees the garden and wants it. But how? Bob has a few items left in his toolbox to come up with a roof top garden. Except he has only one color left, green. But then there is a random accident. Oooh!

Available on Amazon

The Bandana Book
Stories of True Grit and Heart

STORIES BY:

ANNELISE MAKIN
BETH DOTSON
B. MERMELSTEIN
DAN BALDWIN
EDDA BUCHNER
E. SHERWOOD
EMILY TOADVINE
HARV. STANBROUGH
KATE EARLEY
K. HUNTS-IN-WINTER
NOEL ALVAREZ
RENATE MOUSSEUX
TUULA SUMPTER

. . . AND OTHERS

The Bandana Book is a collection of stories about the amazing versatility and purpose of the universal, indestructible bandana. Any old sample of this snuff-snot, rag-tag survival equipment comes loaded with stories about fate, resilience, and family pride. Garnish some of these blurbs with a good dose of humor, you get a bowl of hilarious stories from all walks of life. Our storytellers collected a bunch of delicious tales that run a gamut from spicy calamities to outright hilarious yarns.

Now available on Amazon.

Endnotes

[i] "Bub" is Bube, boy, a diminutive term; "Moar" is a traditional Bavarian reverence (title, assignation), which comes from Latin "maior domus." The English word "mayor" comes from the same root. In the Bavarian context, the "Moar" was usually the richest farmer with the most cows who lived right next to the church, who had the say in the village.

[ii] Über den Wolken muss die Freiheit wohl grenzenlos sein. Alle Ängste, alle Sorgen, sagt man, bleiben darunter verborgen und dann, was uns alles groß und wichtig erscheint ist nun nichtig und klein. Reinhard Mey

[iii] Volksfest = country fair and carnival with rides and beer tent.

[iv] Ancient custom in Bavaria on December 5, the night before St. Nikolaus, where young men dress up as hideous devils in homemade costumes of cow horns, sheep pelts and burlap sacks, and walk house to house to scare people and ask for treats (Schnaps, cookies, etc.). This is a remnant of pagan rituals to honor the spirits of nature, reminisce about the ancestors, and wish for good fortunes for all.

[v] Bavarian custom of knocking on neighbors' doors for treats and shared fun during the winter season on designated days, similar to trick-or-treat.

[vi] A votive memorial for little Martin

[vii] *Tatort (Crime Scene Investigation)* is a German television crime show, which started on 29 November 1970 and is still running.

[viii] Ross verrecken, großer Schrecken. Weiber sterben, kein Verderben.

[ix] December 21, shortest night of the year, winter solstice, and day of patron saint Thomas.

[x] Siegfried is the main hero in the German Nibelung saga, who slays the dragon.

[xi] The typical Bavarian parlor with a corner bench, table, china cabinet, and, frequently, a tiled stove. This was the special place to receive visitors. For every-day meals, families gathered at the kitchen table.

[xii] The movie is *Rebel Without a Cause*, which was translated as the said Bible quote.

[xiii] "Tatzelwurm" in German.

[xiv] Striezl are traditional frybread "logs" made from yeast dough and quark, a type of cottage cheese.

[xv] His generation of farmers used to "eat" Ersatz coffee, not drink it from cups. They cut pieces of bread into the coffee and ladled it all out with a spoon.

[xvi] [Just like the summer solstice], The Feast of Juul, Yule Tide, had always been observed during winter solstice. The word derives from Germanic jol or wheel, the moment when one cycle ends, and a new cycle begins—life continues. Based on this image peoples in the Alpine regions of Europe still roll large burning wheels down the mountainside as both a celebration of fire, warmth and light, and a symbol of a new beginning. In other parts of Europe fires would be lit during that night to symbolize the warmth and light of the returning sun and a Yule log was gathered and burnt in the hearth as tribute to the Norse god Thor. From: Robert A. Selig, "Pagan Winter Solstice," German Life, No. 6, 2020, p. 18.

[xvii] "So ein Tag so wunderschön wie heute, so ein Tag, der dürfte nie vergehn."

[xviii] "Margaret mit dem Wurm, Barbara mit dem Turm, Katharina mit dem Radl, das sind die heiligen drei Madl."

[xix] In Germany, the three Thursdays before Christmas are known as *Klöpfelnächte* or *Knocking Nights*. A long time ago in the Bavarian region of Germany, people believed evil spirits and witches went about causing mischief on Thursday nights during Advent. Children dressed in devil costumes and walked through the streets banging lids, clanging cowbells, rattling tin cans, and making noise in general. Sometimes a small gift was thrown through an open window, anonymously. Children knocked on doors, recited poems, and received treats in return. There are some parts of Germany that still carry on this tradition. (web-holidays.com)

[xx] Waldeslu-hu-hust, oh wie einsam schlägt die Brust. Ihr lieben Vögelein stimmt in die Lieder ein und singt aus voller Brust die Waldeslust.

[xxi] Pun on Walküre (Valkyrie). "Wald" means forest.

[xxii] Standartenführer = Colonel of the SS (Schutzstaffel)

[xxiii] "Drahtesel" in German.

[xxiv] Fluchen wie ein Besenbinder.

[xxv] Rübezahl, a giant German mountain spirit.

[xxvi] "Halt, mein Freund, wer wird denn gleich in die Luft gehen! Greife lieber zur HB [cigarette]." Advertising slogan for German cigarettes.

[xxvii] Hau den Lukas

[xxviii] Gletscherprise

---

^{xxix} Ross = horse; das Haupt = head

^{xxx} Quadrangular Celtic enclosure

^{xxxi} Unter uns = below/under us, literally; which means "among us"

^{xxxii} Schafkopf, sheep's head, is a card game, odds are similar to poker.

View from St. George's Hill towards the Alpine range.